THE
GAMES
GODS PLAY

ABIGAIL OWEN

THE GAMES GODS PLAY

Entangled Publishing, LLC
644 Shrewsbury Commons Ave., STE 181
Shrewsbury, PA 17361
rights@entangledpublishing.com

Red Tower Books is an imprint of Entangled Publishing, LLC.

Visit our website at www.entangledpublishing.com.

Edited by Liz Pelletier
Cover art and design by Bree Archer and
LJ Anderson, Mayhem Cover Creations
Endpaper illustration by Kateryna Vitkovskaya
Interior map illustration by Elizabeth Turner Stokes
Stock art by Victor Torres/Shutterstock, LongQuattro/Gettyimages, Pit3d/
Depositphoto, Ricky Saputra/Gettyimages, T Studio/Shutterstock, duncan1890/
Gettyimages, NORIMA/Gettyimages, atakan/Gettyimages, Paratek/Shutterstock,
Mitya Korolkov/Shutterstock, ekosuwandono/Shutterstock
Interior design by Britt Marczak

Hardcover ISBN 978-1-64937-641-1
Deluxe Edition ISBN 978-1-64937-656-5
Ebook ISBN 978-1-64937-658-9

Printed in the United States of America
First Edition September 2024

10 9 8 7 6 5 4 3 2

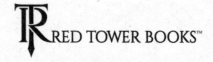

RED TOWER BOOKS™

MORE FROM ABIGAIL OWEN

DOMINIONS

The Liar's Crown
The Stolen Throne
The Shadows Rule All

INFERNO RISING

The Rogue King
The Blood King
The Warrior King
The Cursed King

FIRE'S EDGE

The Mate
The Boss
The Rookie
The Enforcer
The Protector
The Traitor

BRIMSTONE INC.

The Demigod Complex
Shift Out of Luck
A Ghost of a Chance
Bait N' Witch
Try As I Smite
Hit by the Cupid Stick
An Accident Waiting to Dragon

To Robbie—

my husband, my rock, my Jeopardy! *partner,*

my swoon-worthy hero, my star—

just one lifetime with you isn't enough.

In *The Games Gods Play*, the Greek gods walk among us—and they are as unspeakably beautiful as they are deadly. As such, this story features elements that might not be suitable for all readers, including blood, gore, violence (human, god, and monster alike), perilous situations, hospitalization, illness, injury, vomiting, abuse, bullying, theft, isolation, death, grief, use of alcohol, common phobias (including heights, burning, drowning, bugs, and darkness), graphic language, and sexual activity on the page. Readers who may be sensitive to these elements, please take note, and prepare to enter the Crucible...

PART 1

THE CRUCIBLE

The gods love to toy with us mere mortals.
And every hundred years…we let them.

PREFACE

Fuck the gods.

I got so close. So damned close to finally reaching my goal, finally seeing my curse broken, and maybe, just maybe, finally feeling the love of the one man I long for.

As I go limp on the blood-soaked ground, all I can think is, *What if.*

What if I hadn't tried to tear down Zeus' temple?

What if I hadn't met Hades?

What if I hadn't tried to reach for more than this world was willing to offer me...?

A tear squeezes from the corner of my eye. Then Zeus' feet come into view directly in front of me. Probably to finish the job.

Honestly, I'd rather go fast than sit here and bleed anyway.

"Bring it, asshole."

1

A REALLY BAD IDEA

A sizzling zap of electricity snaps directly over Zeus' temple, and I flinch while the crowd *ooh*s and *ahh*s. People from all walks of life, cultures, and pantheons live in San Francisco, but there's no denying this is Zeus' patron city.

I don't need to spare the shrine a glance to know what it looks like — pristine white stone with classic, fluted columns aglow in purplish-white flashes and sparks cast by the never-ending arcs of lightning captured above the roof.

I shake my head. He is *very* proud of the lightning thing — this being the only god-powered city in the world. Although if Zeus is in a pissy mood…well, it tends to affect the lights. I can only imagine how much time those who enjoy uninterrupted power must spend on their knees in that temple.

I'd rather live in the dark.

"We shouldn't be here," I mutter under my breath as I tick a checkbox on my tablet, then glance around the bustling crowd to try to spot one of our pickpockets moving in and out of the unsuspecting masses.

My only job tonight is to observe, which is really all I'm ever asked to do. Observe and record. But of all the piss-poor schemes my boss, Felix, has come up with over the years, this one ranks right up there with attempting to capture a pegasus to sell on the black market. That put our den on Poseidon's shit list for years. Yes, den. The name isn't exactly creative, but we're thieves, not poets.

I mentally shrug. At least Felix isn't hells-bent on trying to steal Hades' pomegranate seeds again. Rumor has it Hades isn't as forgiving as Poseidon.

Besides, it's not like pledges have a choice in what jobs we do.

We were offered as collateral to work off a debt of some sort by our parents, and most thieves look forward to every job we get. *Any* job is one step closer to clearing the books. Not me, though. I have no debt anymore. I was so young when my family surrendered me to the Order, I don't even remember my own birth name. But I'm twenty-three now, so that was a while ago and not something I like to dwell on.

A strobe of light illuminates the low clouds overhead a heartbeat before a loud crack sets car alarms blaring and babies crying.

This time I really jump but manage to force my gaze to remain straight ahead.

"Scared of a little lightning, Lyra?" Chance, a master thief to my left, chides. He's acting as the drop point for all the lifts tonight but takes his attention off his job long enough to toss me a condescending smile. Asshole.

One of the older thieves in our den, he should have paid off his debt by now but hasn't—and the fact I'm our den's clerk and know exactly how much he still has to go pisses him off. It also makes me his favorite target.

But the best way to deal with his brand of dickhead is to ignore him.

So instead, I focus on the unsuspecting, sycophantic multitudes as more and more crush together at the base of the temple, filling the winding street that circles up the mountain to it. They're all here to get the best view of the opening ceremonies of the Crucible at midnight. The opportunity was too good for Felix to pass up—perfect for a rash of pickpocketing. Stealing so close to a sacred building is a big risk, but our boss reasoned away hazarding the gods' wrath by saying this is both a test for the newest crop of pledges and a chance to rake in one last score before the ceremonies begin.

He is going to get someone killed. Or worse…

Which I guess is why Felix has a lowly clerk, in particular *me*, up here babysitting tonight. Given the added danger, he needed someone to keep an eye on things who would, and I quote, *avoid letting anyone anger the gods at all costs*, end quote.

And he's right. I wouldn't wish the gods' ire on my worst enemy. Even Chance.

As my old mentor, Felix knows that. In fact, he's the *only* one who knows exactly why.

A small throng of revelers wearing Zeus-themed sweatshirts rushes past me to get higher up the hillside, and a few shoulder check me to the left, then right as they muscle their way through the crowd. I deftly use the opportunity to shuffle several feet away from Chance. He really is my least-favorite person. I'll still keep an eye on him in case he gets in danger of upsetting a god, but I can do that from a distance just as easily.

When I glance back at him, I let out a sigh. He's no longer sneering at me and has turned his attention to his job again.

A young pledge with soft brown curls weaves her way up to Chance and brushes against the sleeve of his overcoat, tossing out a quick "excuse me" before scooting by him. Even though it's summer, it's chilly enough that no one looks twice at the master thief's clothing choice, which is good. He needs lots of pockets.

I didn't even see the drop, and I was looking closely for it. I'd always hoped one day to become a thief myself, but sadly, I lack one important skill—subtlety.

Without a backward glance, the pledge melts into the crowd, no one around us the wiser. Chance slips his hand into a pocket, then frowns. It takes fishing in two more pockets before he discovers the loot. Which means even he didn't feel the handover.

The new pledge is good. Then again, her mentor is the best of us.

For a second, I indulge in picturing what it would be like to be out there with her as one of the thieves, rather than back here watching it happen. But that's not my lot in life. I've made my peace with it. At least I've made it this far without starving, ending up in the gutters, getting myself murdered...or worse.

I do all right.

I even have my own stash of coin tucked away in a place where no one will ever find it. Cold cash, not some numbers on a screen. One day, I might just give up this life, and I'll have the means to do it.

You'll be even more alone, though, a tiny, doubt-laden voice whispers inside me.

I shift on my feet. *Yeah, well...maybe I'll get a cat. Or, no. A dog.*

No one can be lonely with a dog, right?

I glance toward the iconic Golden Gate Bridge, with its brilliant white Corinthian columns, matching the temple and supported by massive suspension lines. At midnight, they'll close the road to traffic and allow the people piling in to cover it. The bridge stretches from the Minos Headlands where the temple sits across the mouth of the bay to the dazzling city on the other side. The twinkling lights beckon while the bay itself is black as night, the darkness broken only by the lights of ships floating by.

Out of the corner of my eye, I see one of the younger pledges home in on an elderly couple. They're walking hand in hand, obviously in love, and I can't help the tightening in my chest. The woman is struggling to keep up, walking with a cane, and the gentleman shuffles his feet beside her, making each step take twice as long so he matches her pace. She looks up and smiles at him for the gesture, and I know the last thing they need to ruin their night is to realize light fingers have taken a wallet or watch.

Before the young thief gets too close, I whistle a signal all pledges know means to stop.

So much for just being here to observe and record. Hopefully Felix doesn't find out and punish me for overstepping.

She pauses, looks around, and then her face lights up a little and she waves an eager hand. Not at me. At someone behind me.

"Hey, Boone!" the pledge calls. She must think he's the one who whistled.

I force myself to not immediately turn and look.

Boone's is the one face I search for every day, but that's *my* business. After making a note on the tablet to talk to the girl about not drawing attention while on a job, I let myself peer around and see him off to the left.

Boone Runar.

Master thief. Every person's fantasy and every parent's nightmare.

And there's nothing I can do to stop my heart from clumsily tripping over itself at the sight of him. Especially when he grins at the apprentice, kneeling down to her level and saying something that makes her laugh before they both turn serious. He's probably reminding her about drawing attention.

I lower my tablet and take the opportunity to enjoy the view.

Well over six feet of muscle, brute strength, and a fuck-with-me-and-find-out air thanks to, again, the muscles and the recent addition of a scruffy brown beard a shade darker than his hair. Then there's the way he dresses like a biker. Lots of jeans and leather. The vibes he gives off aren't a lie, either. He can handle himself.

To look at him, you'd think he'd be a total dick twenty-four seven. Many of the master thieves, like Chance, are. It's a defense mechanism. Survival tactic. But not Boone. It's the way he is with the apprentices, a patient guide, that I like the most.

After a second, he sends the apprentice on her way. When he rises to his feet, he searches the area, and my stomach tightens in anticipation. Not that he's looking for me. No doubt he's either trying to find his own apprentice—the first girl who already made her drop—or one of the other master thieves.

Despite the fact that he looks right in my direction, Boone's gaze sweeps over where I am. Twice.

Then he leaves.

I blow out a long, slow breath and watch as he makes his way back through the crowds until I can't see him and wish, for the billionth time, my mother's water hadn't broken in Zeus' temple the day I was born.

The day I was cursed.

2

IT ONLY GETS WORSE

"Holy shit…" Chance barks a laugh right in my ear.

I jump because I had no idea he'd moved closer again, let alone—Hades take the man—right next to me.

"I see it now," he says in a sly aside. "Lyra Keres, are you in love with Boone?"

His words drop between me and the rest of the pledges nearby like little bombs.

Each one exploding in my chest. Direct hits.

You'd think I'd be immune by now. But can anyone ever "get over" wanting to be loved—but being cursed to never be loved in return? If the pain ricocheting in my chest is any indication, the answer to that is a resounding no.

Ripples of smothered gasps and murmurs loud enough to be heard above the constant noise in this sea of people surge through the pledges, and at least two glance in our direction with wide, curious eyes.

Don't give him the satisfaction of a reaction.

Unbearably aware of our audience, I stare at the tablet in my hands, humiliation crawling over me like ants.

Damn him.

Escape would be nice, but I can't just run. Weakness will always be exploited.

Pulling my pride around me like a familiar, tattered cloak, I cock a hip and offer him my most sugary smile. "You have your entire life to be an asshole, Chance. Why not take a night off?"

A few snickers sound from the pledges, or maybe it's from the total strangers surrounding us, and a vein pulses in his neck. Everything about

Chance is pointed—from his nose, to the angled cut of his eyebrows, to his cheekbones, to his knees and elbows. Usually his voice matches. Even when he's in a good mood, his speech is sharp and clipped.

It's when he goes smooth and sweet, and his pale blue eyes in his paler face get swallowed by his pupils, that you have to watch out. Like now.

"Do you think he's noticed?" His words have an edge to them that makes the hairs on the back of my neck stand up. "No wonder you always find a way to give him the best assignments."

"You should be farther into the crowd," I say, my jaw tight. I'm standing off to one side, slightly up the incline of the mountain, and step a foot to the left as though to get a better view.

Of course, he ignores my attempt at putting some distance between us and steps closer again. "Don't worry," he says. "I'll be sure to tell him the next time I see him. Who knows? Maybe he'll throw you a pity fuck."

It takes a lot not to curl over as I absorb that hit.

Oh gods. I'm starting to tremble. Screw it. I'm not sticking around for this. I mutter, "You're an ass, Chance."

Tucking my tablet against my chest like body armor, I walk away, knowing that, as the drop man, he can't follow.

"Nah, I don't think you could ever be anyone's pity fuck," he calls after me. "Someone would have to actually care about you enough for that to happen."

Every single part of me freezes and then goes blazing hot. Chance might as well have taken out the bow he's so proficient with and sent an arrow straight through my heart. Clean kill in one shot.

And he said that so loud. No one within a wide radius could have missed it.

I breathe through my nose, chin held high with fake confidence. Without glancing back, I throw Chance the middle finger over my shoulder and force my legs to function and carry me away.

He won't be the only one meting out punishment for this exchange later. I just broke one of the Order's cardinal rules. Never abandon the job when any thieves are still in play. Felix will be *pissed*.

But I don't care.

Head down, I keep walking, away from them, away from the crowds, and up the mountainside into a copse of decorative trees that surrounds the temple, where it's blessedly empty and quiet. The second I know I can't be seen anymore, all the starchy pride that got me here disappears, and I sag against a tree, ignoring the knot that digs into my back.

No one comes to check on me.

Because Chance was right about one thing. I don't have any friends. At least not any who would truly give a shit if I didn't make it back tonight.

Worse, Boone is going to hear about this. Which means I'll have to face him every single day, knowing that he *knows*. Worse, knowing that he could never feel the same.

Underworld take me now. I'd even prefer a corner of Tartarus.

I swipe away the moisture that manages to escape my stranglehold and glare at the tears on my hand, a few rolling past a thick scar on my wrist. I promised myself a long time ago, after I nearly died from a ruined street scam that ended with my wrist sliced open and not a single person checking on me in the hospital, that my *issue* was *not* worth my tears. And yet, here I am…

"That's it," I mutter.

Something's got to give.

Whipping my head around, I glare at the temple sparking above the branches. Fuck Chance. Fuck this curse. And definitely fuck Zeus.

I stick my tablet in my jacket pocket and shove off the tree, the burn of anger heaping coals onto my hurt and humiliation but also filling me with a new sense of driving purpose.

One way or another, I'm putting an end to this damn curse…and I'm already in the perfect place to do it.

Time to have it out with a god.

3

THE LAST MISTAKE I'LL EVER MAKE

Raw emotions bubble inside me like a poisonous potion in a witch's cauldron.

I haven't entirely decided what I'm going to do when I get to the temple. I'm either going to beg that egotistical fucking god Zeus to remove his punishment or I'm going to do something worse.

One way or the other, my problem will be solved.

And, unlike earlier, now I don't give a shit that midnight is the start of the Crucible and all the "rules" that come with the cryptic festival.

We mortals know only how the festival begins, how it ends, and how *we* celebrate in between. They begin with each of the major Olympian gods and goddesses choosing a mortal champion during the rites at the start. The festivities end when some of the mortals selected return. Some don't. The ones who do make it back don't remember a thing, or maybe they're too scared to talk about it. And the ones who don't, well, their families are showered in blessings, so it's supposedly an honor to be chosen either way.

Regardless, mortals have been throwing this festival every hundred years since what feels like the dawn of time, everyone hoping they'll be chosen by their favored god. What can I say? Humans are foolish.

Zeus is probably in his heavenly city on Mount Olympus, busy preparing for the start of the Selection Ceremony, but I'm having it out with him right now.

It can't wait. I just need to get his attention is all. Luckily, everyone knows the one thing Zeus is most attached to in our world—his fucking temple.

Adrenaline pumps in my veins as I hurry through the trees. The temple is already cordoned off, but at least I've got enough thief training to be able to get around the barriers with no one noticing.

I skirt past a row of perfectly manicured bushes and approach the place from the back, where I'm less likely to be seen. The arcs of lightning overhead fill the air this close to the temple with charged electricity, masking the sounds of my footsteps as the hairs on my arms stand on end like toy soldiers.

I should take that as a warning.

I don't.

I keep going.

Staring at the pristine columns surrounding the walled-off inner temple rooms in the center, I try to formulate a plan. Praying and begging first would be the smart move. But now that I'm standing here, alone in the dark, with my hands clenching and unclenching at my sides, every unbearable, excruciating millisecond of misery caused by Zeus' curse flashes through my head.

I'm shaking so hard with a vile concoction of anger and heartache and mortification that I rock on my feet. But the worst part of all is that, maybe for the first time ever, I admit to myself how fucking *lonely* I am.

I've never known what it's like to whisper secrets to a friend, or hold someone's hand, or have someone to just sit with me when I'm feeling low. We wouldn't even have to talk.

And I just…

In a haze, almost as if I'm watching myself from the outside, I search the ground around me and grab a rock. Cocking my arm back, I go to hurl it at the nearest column.

Only, a hand clamps around my wrist mid-throw, and I'm jerked back against a broad chest. Strong arms encircle me. "I don't think so," a deep voice says in my ear.

I forget every self-defense technique drilled into me and instead thrash against my captor's hold. "Let me go!"

"I'm not going to hurt you," he says, and for some reason, I believe him. Doesn't mean I don't want to be free, though. I have shit to deal with.

"I said"—I grit out each word—"Let. Me. Go."

His grip tightens. "Not if you're going to hurl rocks at the temple. I don't feel like dealing with Zeus tonight."

"Well, *I* do!" I kick out, trying to twist away.

"He's an asshole, I get it. Trust me," my captor mutters in a low voice. "But if I thought throwing a tantrum would change that, I'd have brought that temple down with my bare hands years ago."

It's not just the words—something in his tone makes me still in his arms, almost as though the two of us are sharing the same emotion. The same anger. The feeling steals my breath, and I find myself leaning back, reveling in the moment. As if, for the first time in my life, I don't feel utterly alone.

Is this what it's like to connect with someone?

Crickets chirp in the distance, their slow cadence in sync with his even breaths. In sync with mine now, too, I realize.

"If I let you go, do you promise not to attack a defenseless building again?" he asks softly.

"No," I admit, and I feel a sigh rumble in his chest. So I add, "That fuckhead doesn't deserve *any* prayers."

"Careful." His voice wobbles. Is he laughing?

"Why?" I ask, a surprising grin spreading across my lips when only a few seconds ago, I was ready to throw down with a god. "You worried someone might want to hit me with a bolt of lightning while I'm in your arms?"

"Talk like that could win a few hearts." His voice is soft, his breath rustling the hair at my ear.

I go stiff against him, my chin falling to my chest.

"Highly unlikely," I mutter at the ground. "Zeus made sure no one can *ever* love me."

A gaping hole of silence greets my bitterness. My interfering do-gooder drops his arms and takes a step back, probably worried curses are contagious. I immediately miss his warmth and shove my hands in my pockets.

"I…" He trails off as if considering his words. "Find that hard to believe."

I'm so desperate to escape this whole scene, the change in his tone doesn't entirely penetrate as I round on him. "Listen, I'm fine now. You can move on…"

The rest of my words wither on my lips.

If I went dead still earlier, I might as well have looked Medusa in the eyes now. The only thing about me that moves is the blood pumping through me so hard and fast, my ears thrum. My mind races to make sense of what my eyes are telling me.

Oh no. This can't be happening.

Suddenly, it's as if all the emotions that drove me here like a banshee with a bone to pick blow themselves out, leaving me empty.

I finally felt a smidgeon of connection with someone, and it's… I mean…

I *did* come up here to have it out with a god. Just not *this* one.

Even in the dark, only illuminated by constant strobes of lightning, I can see the perfection of his sculpted face—with its hard jaw, a high brow, dark eyes, and lips almost too pretty for his otherwise harsh features—as a clue of *what* he is. Only the gods and goddesses boast that kind of beauty. But it's the pale lock that curls up off his forehead into the blackness of the rest of his hair that gives him away.

Every mortal knows the story of how his brother tried to kill him once by taking an axe to his head while he slept, but only succeeded in leaving a scar that changed his hair in that one spot. Unmistakable. Not to mention unforgettable—and extremely unfortunate for me.

Tangling with *this* god is so much worse than my original plan.

Run. The instinct finally punches through me, urging me to make my legs move. But there's no point. Besides, the instinct to freeze in place is stronger.

"I'm afraid one of us shouldn't be here," I quip, my mouth *always* filling in for my brain when I'm nervous.

Not helping, Lyra.

I'm also not entirely wrong. What is *he* doing at this particular temple?

He says nothing, standing with his arms crossed, taking me in the same way I did him, only with a tension that fills the air with more electricity than Zeus' lightning.

I know what he sees—a slip of a woman with short raven hair, a smallish face, pointed chin, and catlike eyes. My one vanity. They are deep green with a darker outer ring and gold at the center, fringed by long, black lashes. Maybe if I bat them at him? Except beguiling is not in my list of skills, so I nix that thought.

He's still staring.

There's an intensity to him that sets me more on edge with every passing second, every part of me prickling.

Silence fills the gaps between us for so long that I reconsider running as an option.

"Do you know who I am?" he finally asks. His deep voice would be smooth except for the harsh growl at the bottom of it. Like a silky, still lake broken by ripples from something under the surface.

Is he serious with that question, though? *Everyone* knows who he is. "Should I?"

Holy hells, stop popping off, Lyra.

The god's eyes narrow slightly at my flippant response. Face assuming a hard cast, he takes two slow, long strides directly into my space. "Do you *know* who I am?"

Everything inside me shrivels like my body already knows I'm dead anyway and is just getting a head start. Fear has a taste I'm more than familiar with—metallic in the mouth, like blood. Or maybe I just bit my tongue.

The gods have punished mortals for much less than what I've done and said so far tonight.

My entire body quivers. *Merciful gods.*

"Hades." I swallow. "You are Hades."

The god of death and King of the Underworld himself.

And he does not look happy.

4

BEAUTIFUL, TEASING DEATH

Hades' barely-there smile turns condescending. "Was that so hard?"
It's too...deliberate. Like he's decided to play this a different way.
Only that makes no sense.

But gods don't have to make sense, I guess.

Drawing the notice of any of them is a bad idea. They are capricious beings who might curse you rather than bless you depending on their mood and the way the breeze is blowing. Especially this one.

"Now, let's talk about what you think you were doing," Hades says.

I frown, confused. "I thought you already—"

"And with the Crucible starting tonight, even," he continues in a disappointed voice, as if I hadn't spoken.

I sigh. "Do you want an apology before you smite me or something?"

"Most would fall to their knees before me. Beg for my mercy."

He's toying with me now. I'm a mouse. He's a cat. And I'm his dinner.

I swallow hard, trying to force my heart back down my throat. "I'm pretty sure I'm dead either way." Of course I am. Let's not heap even more humiliation on my early end. "Would kneeling help?"

His silvery eyes—not dark like I thought at first, but like mercury—swirl with cold amusement. Did I say something funny?

"Is that why you're here?" I ask. "The Crucible?"

Hades has *never* participated, and Zeus is hardly his favorite sibling, so why *is* he at this temple, really?

"I have my own reasons for being here tonight."

In other words, *Don't ask gods questions, reckless mortal.*

"Why did you stop me?" I glance at the temple, ignoring his tone entirely.

Instead of answering, Hades taps his thumb against his chin. "The question is, what do I do with you now?"

Is he enjoying my predicament? I've never thought much about the god of death—I'm a little busy with surviving mortality first—but I'm starting to really not like him. If Boone acted more like this, I'd have gotten over him ages ago. "I assume you're going to send me to the Underworld."

Seriously, stop talking, Lyra.

Hades hums. "I can do worse than that."

Just like with Chance, backing down now isn't an option. "Oh?" I tip my head, pretending like I don't already know. "I do hear you are creative with your punishments."

"I'm flattered." He gives a tiny, mocking bow. "I could make you roll a rock up a hill and never make it to the top, only to start back over every single day for the rest of eternity."

That already happened to Sisyphus ages ago. "I'm pretty sure Zeus came up with that."

His lips flatten. "Were you there?"

I shrug. "Either way, it sounds like a vacation. Peaceful, undisturbed labor. When do I start?"

My mouth is going to get me permanently dead.

I'm waiting to end up in the Underworld any second, or maybe for Hades' famous bident to appear in his hand for him to skewer me with.

Instead, he shakes his head. "I'm not going to kill you. Yet."

Really? Do I trust him?

He must see the wariness in my eyes, because a muscle tightens in his jaw like he's irritated I would doubt his word. "Relax, my star."

I hesitate at the endearment. It clearly means nothing to him. When he doesn't immediately talk, I manage not to as well, and instead I take in more details about the god standing before me.

He's not exactly what I expected. I mean, beyond the obvious dark-and-brooding thing.

It's his clothes. He's wearing worn boots and jeans, for Elysium's sake. The jeans sit low on his narrow hips and are paired with a sky-blue button-down shirt rolled up at the sleeves to reveal forearms a deeper tan than I would expect from someone who lives in the Underworld. Who knew forearms could be sexy?

Over the shirt, he wears vintage leather suspenders that I suspect meet in the back at the top of his shoulder blades, side holster–style. The metal rings on the suspenders look like they have a purpose that he's not using them for right now. Are they for weapons? Or does he have a bad back?

"Do I pass inspection?" he drawls.

I jerk my gaze back up to his face. "You look different than I thought."

Both eyebrows twitch up. "And what did you expect? All-black clothing? Perhaps a full leather getup?"

Heat flares up my neck. Something like that, actually. "Don't forget the horns. And maybe a tail."

"That's a different god of death." He makes an exasperated sound, then mutters something about abhorring expectations.

Meeting those expectations, I think he means. Strange that I have something in common with a god. I may be cursed, but damned if I'm going to let it dictate who I am.

"Your home in the Underworld is Erebus," I say pointedly.

"And?"

"It's called… Wait for it." I hold up a hand. "The Land of *Shadows*."

Someone should duct tape my mouth shut.

Hades slips his hands in his pockets, casually relaxed in a leashed-predator sort of way. "I always thought that naming was unoriginal. It's the Underworld. Of course there are shadows."

This conversation seems to be going off the rails a bit. "I guess." And then, because my brain can't help itself, I actually consider what he said. "I mean, technically, you're not the god of shadows or even the goddess of night." Now I'm on a roll. "And if the fire-and-brimstone thing is true, then it seems like it would be quite well lit down there."

His eyes glint at me like sharpened knives.

I can't tell if he's offended or surprised by my running commentary.

Unfortunately for both of us, I have a good imagination—and a lot of opinions. "You have a perception issue, if you think about it."

"*I* have a perception issue," he repeats.

"Yes, you do. If they can't see for themselves, mortals will believe what they are told. I was always told that Hades is shrouded in darkness, smells of fire, and is covered in tattoos that can come alive at his will."

His gaze trails down my body with such slow deliberation, it sends the heat from earlier crawling farther up my neck and into my cheeks. "And yet you're the one dressed in black and with tattoos, my star," he points out.

I follow his gaze to my black fitted shirt paired with jeans—so it's not *all* black. One sleeve has ridden up slightly to expose the pale skin of my wrist where the black ink tattoo peeks out. Two stars. A third star is on my other wrist, and when I put my arms together, they form Orion's Belt.

One of the few things I remember before being taken in by the Order is watching Orion move across the sky outside my bedroom window. The constellation is an unchanging, ever-fixed mark in the night.

Is that why he called me his star twice now? I tug the sleeve down.

"So…" He comes out of his casual leaning to step closer. Close enough that I can breathe him in, which is when I learn that the god of death smells like the darkest, most sinful, bitter chocolate.

"What's your name?" he asks.

I definitely do *not* want a god knowing my name. "Felix Argos."

Hades doesn't call me on the lie. Just watches me, gaze assessing like he's debating something. A creative new punishment for me, probably.

"So…" I mimic his earlier phrasing and glance to the side of the temple and the way down the mountain. Escape is so close. Just out of reach, like the open door of a birdcage with a cat sitting outside. "What happens now?"

"What did you mean about being cursed?"

Ugh. I don't want to talk about *that*. I hedge instead. "You don't know?"

"Tell me like I don't."

"What if I don't want to?"

He lifts a single eyebrow, and I get the message. Trying not to clench my teeth, I refuse to think about how Hades is only the second person I've ever shared this with.

After taking a deep breath, I say in a rush, "Twenty-three years ago, when I was still in my mother's womb, she and my father came here to make an offering and pray for blessings on the birth. Her water broke, and your brother apparently took offense at her defiling his sacred sanctuary. As punishment, he cursed her baby—me, as it happens—that no one would ever love me. There. End of story."

His gaze turns colder, so calculating that I take a step back.

"He made you unlovable?" he asks as though he isn't quite sure he believes me.

I give a jerking nod.

That curse is why my parents gave me up. They said it was the debt, but I know otherwise. It landed me in the Order of Thieves at three years old. It's why I have no ride-or-die friends. It's why Boone…

Up until tonight, I've tried to convince myself that things could have been worse. I mean, I could have ended up as kraken fodder or with snakes for hair and stone statues as my friends.

But it led me to this moment. Facing a different god. A worse god.

One who obviously finds my curse interesting. Why? Because Zeus gave it to me? The current King of the Gods is a dick. That's one thing Hades also agrees with me on. The question is, what is he going to do with me now?

Hades waves a hand at me, the action almost languid. "You may go."

I may—

Wait… What?

5

NEVER ASK A GOD WHY

"I can...go? Really—"

Hades lifts his eyebrows slowly. "You wish to argue?"

"No." Never look a gift horse in the mouth...or a gift getaway in the escape hatch.

"This way," he says.

He heads toward a path that takes us a different way down the mountain. I guess I'm supposed to follow? Hades prowls when he walks. I focus on his boots, because staring at his back—those leather straps do meet between his shoulder blades—or his perfectly formed ass, for that matter, just isn't an option.

I hold my breath, every inch of me prickling with uncomfortable awareness that only grows as I keep up with him. It's the whole "raw power of the gods" thing. That's the only reason for the prickles, I tell myself.

I'm not sure I believe me.

We walk in silence until a sidewalk paralleling the main street comes into view. Along with crowds. I stop walking. He stops, too, glancing back. "Problem?"

"Um..." I stare past him, and he follows my gaze. Three more feet and everyone will be able to see us together. See *me*...with the god of freaking death.

"Don't worry about them," he says as though reading my mind. "Only you can see who I truly am. Everyone else just sees a regular mortal man."

Right. Awesome. Except the pledges still hanging around this place might see me with a strange man and ask questions. Can I get out of this?

"Come on."

I guess I can't.

We emerge onto the teeming sidewalk, and I pause. Should I say goodbye before we part...or something?

I offer him a small salute. "I appreciate you not smiting me."

I think I'm home free as I turn to walk away, but he spins me toward him by the shoulders, grip firm. Suddenly, I'm staring up into eyes of swirling, molten metal, but burning. The way coal burns black.

"Be more careful with your words, my star," he says in a voice that isn't as smooth as before—it's more like raw silk now. "You never know when the gods might take up the gauntlet you just threw down... And any other day, I probably would have."

Every single particle of me is strung so taut I might snap at any second, adrenaline so hot in my veins that my skin tightens. But that's the problem. In this moment, I feel more...*alive*. As if every second I have left is precious because those seconds are numbered.

"Smiting is a quick death," I whisper. "There are worse things."

His eyes flare as he searches my expression, and I hold my breath, anticipating the flash of pain before the nothingness of death. That's how I imagine it.

It doesn't come.

Instead, his expression alters. The change is subtle enough, slow enough, that at first, I'm not even sure I'm seeing it, but the burn of warning turns...softer. A different kind of heat.

Hades lifts a hand to draw a fingertip from my temple to my jaw, the touch a mere whisper against my skin, leaving a trail of heady sensation in its wake. He stares at me, and I stare at him, and I know I should look away. Of the two of us, I'm the mortal, so *I* should be the one to break, to give in, to acknowledge defeat.

I can't. I won't.

"You're right, my star," he murmurs. His gaze trails lower to linger on my lips. "There are worse things."

Then his gaze goes from fire to ice in a blink. He straightens abruptly, spins me around, and gives me a little push into the crowd, like he's releasing an undersized fish back into the ocean.

Somehow, even though the rest of me has gone offline, my feet manage to walk me away. I'm thirty feet away before he calls after me.

"Stay out of trouble, Lyra Keres."

I come to a dead stop but don't turn. That is *not* the name I gave him.

I'd love to know how he knows mine or why he bothered to ask, since he clearly already did, but self-preservation has finally kicked in, even if a bit late, and escape is literally right around the bend.

So, I lift a hand in a wave of acknowledgment…and keep walking, counting my steps like they might be my last.

6

THE CHOSEN FEW

Being required to attend the opening rites of the Crucible is worse than a trip down the River Styx.

Felix is losing his shit. I know he is because every time I catch a glimpse of him through the crush of people, he's gnashing his teeth together and looking around wildly. Nice of him to make an appearance, finally. At least I've managed to rejoin the others on the city side of the bridge without catching his eye.

A minor miracle, actually.

I haven't been spotted by Boone or Chance, either. I have a plan to keep it that way. As soon as things here really get started, I'm sneaking back to the den. Not just to avoid various confrontations, but also to process everything that I've been through tonight. Especially a certain god.

Felix swings his gaze in my direction, and I duck, trying to make myself as small as possible. Maybe he doesn't know I abandoned my duties earlier, but this isn't the time to find out. When he turns back without seeing me, I let out a silent breath of relief, then can't help but smile a little to myself. Frustration really doesn't sit well on his craggy features.

Not that I can blame him. This is a thief's paradise. All these pockets so very ripe for the picking, and all his pledges have had their hands tied, since it's now a little past midnight and the festival has officially begun.

The gathered people are smooshed together in milling multitudes. It feels like every living soul within a thousand miles of San Francisco— even those who don't worship this set of gods—is here.

That makes sense if I think about it.

Most mortals have a vested interest in who is crowned ruler of the Olympian gods next for several reasons—a favorite or most hated or feared god or goddess, or a certain god as a patron, like me. And some are more directly impacted. I'm guessing many farmers favor Demeter to win, to bless their crops and harvests. Soldiers would favor Ares. Scholars and teachers want Athena. And so on.

Even mortals who worship other gods are interested because of the spectacle of it all. Or maybe they dislike a god with similar or competing powers to their own. Or maybe, most simply, they just don't want to offend said gods.

No matter which way you look at it, the world is watching with interest.

And despite that, every single valuable is safe now.

No wonder my old mentor looks harried. Not a single whistle sounds. At least not the kind our pledges make when they coordinate around a potential mark.

And this will last the entire month.

I shift back and forth on my feet, staring at Zeus' temple across the way as it does nothing beyond the usual lightning display.

Up in that temple, the gods' mortal acolytes burn offerings, whisper prayers, and perform whatever rites they deem necessary. Since this only happens once every hundred years, I'd place bets that they're just making it up as they go.

Not that we can see any of it from here. No cameras are allowed to record inside the temple—another edict from the gods. But it means I'm stuck with millions of others staring at the white-columned building atop the mountain on the other side of the bridge like it might suddenly turn into a dragon and breathe fire.

So far, all that's happened is a single puff of white smoke that trailed upward into the sky, probably from a sacrifice.

People have filled the street along the bay all the way to the fringes of the city itself, and those of us standing at the very back have been channeled in between buildings. That's where I am.

The other pledges are gathered in little groups, debating if Hermes will pick a thief or not. It's happened before. After the initial round of smirks and glances aimed in my direction, they've gone back to ignoring me, which is good for my escape plan.

Several people around me stare at their phones, watching various forms of "live coverage" of even more people around the globe standing in streets in other cities, staring at various temples of these gods. I catch snatches of commentary here and there, not that they have much new to report yet.

"Legends hold that the gods and goddesses got so sick of Zeus as their king, they fought among themselves to be the one to topple him, resulting in the Anaxian Wars," a news anchor is saying on a device near me. "It got so ugly that they wrecked wonders, knocking the Colossus of Rhodes off his feet and turning hundreds of warriors to terracotta."

I snort a laugh. That pissed off a whole different set of gods, apparently.

The newscaster is still talking. "They destroyed cities like Atlantis and Pompeii and eventually demolished their home of Olympus, which has since been rebuilt."

Everyone knows this story. After that, the gods formed a pact that they would never directly fight one another again, and the Crucible was created—where they just let us mortals duke it out on their behalves, apparently.

A gasp rips through the masses around me. "Zeus," someone calls out. "Zeus is choosing."

"Where?" a few others ask loudly.

After that, voices rise in a mottled swell of sound. I inch closer to a man to my left who is watching his phone with avid interest.

Sure enough, at a simple temple I don't recognize located somewhere else in the world, a massive bolt of lightning shears out of a clear blue sky and strikes the temple with a clap of thunder so loud it appears to shake the very ground. Then a deep voice booms out—maybe from inside the building where he is, because I don't see the god anywhere. "I am Zeus—first King of the Gods, god of the skies, thunder and lightning, god of weather, law and order, kingship, destiny and fate."

I roll my eyes. Destiny and fate are the same thing. Aren't they? Pompous jackass.

And it should be King of the *Olympian* Gods, by the way. But all the gods of my pantheon are egotistical enough to want to lay claim to the whole thing. So, King of the Gods it is.

"On this, the first day of the Crucible, I shall select first." The god pauses, almost like he's waiting for applause or something. Given we're all unsure about exactly how this works and what it means, and I'm guessing the crowds surrounding the temple where he is are now having a hard time hearing around the ringing in their ears from the thunder, they all remain silent and watchful.

"I choose…"

7

STAY OUT OF MY WAY

It's like the hush crawls out of the video and hangs over the people here, too, as we collectively wait and watch, breathless with curiosity, no one daring to so much as cough. Who will he pick?

Another bolt of lightning flashes down, this time striking outside the temple, at the top of the steps between the two pillars of the main entrance. The noise makes several people scream. Out of nowhere, a man appears where the lightning struck, visibly disoriented.

Zeus' voice booms again. "Samuel Sebina."

I stare at the phone. Zeus' chosen mortal has to be even taller and more muscled than Boone, with ebony skin and short black hair. He seems too stunned to do more than look around. As fast as he appeared, he's gone. Who knows where?

Another cry goes up. "Hera!" someone shouts. "Hera is choosing."

Heads remain bowed over phones as people watch.

"I am Hera, goddess of marriage, women, and the stars of the heavens." From a nearby phone, I catch a sultry voice you might think belonged to Aphrodite emanating from one of her own temples somewhere else in the world. "I choose…"

I don't hear the rest because to my right, Chance is pushing his way in my direction. Trepidation floods my body in an itchy wave. More embarrassment, retribution, or calling Felix's attention to the fact I left my post earlier—all are strong possibilities of what happens if he finds me. Time to get out of here.

I scoot sideways into a narrow alley between buildings. When I glance back, Chance is craning his neck. Yeah. He's definitely looking for me. It takes a few evasive maneuvers, but I finally round the corner and nearly collide with a broad male chest.

"Whoa, whoa, whoa!" Boone exclaims in an overly jovial voice. "Slow down, Lyra-Loo—" He cuts off the nickname he gave me as kids so abruptly it's jarring.

Oh gods. He knows. About Chance. About my crush. Everything.

Not that I'm surprised.

"You were humming again," he points out with a grin. "I thought Felix trained that out of you."

I put a hand over my mouth like I can pull those sounds back inside. Humming was a habit as a young pledge. I hadn't even noticed I was doing it. It's been a while since my training days, though, so I guess it's back.

"Sorry," I mutter and inch around him.

He moves, blocking the way. "Where are you going in such a rush?"

I'm pretty sure, in the history of our entire acquaintance, he's never cared enough to ask me that. I shuffle back and force myself to look him in the eyes. Deep-brown eyes. I always liked his eyes.

And I could just bawl. Years of waiting for him to pay more attention to me, and he chooses today. The one time I don't want it. I glance back but don't see Chance. Yet.

"Nowhere," I say.

I step. Boone steps, blocking me again.

"Excuse me." I step again.

He blocks again.

"What?" I snap.

He blinks at me, probably because I never snap at him. Then a mottled flush creeps up his face, and he runs a hand around the back of his neck.

Oh...no. He doesn't want to actually talk about it, does he? I'd really, really, *really* rather not. Especially not here or now.

An odd light enters his eyes, and he opens his mouth only to close it again. Sure enough. "Lyra—"

A loud murmur rises from the crowds in the streets on either end of the alley.

"I don't want to miss this." I manage to dodge around him, catching him on the hop for once.

"Wait." He grabs my arm and swings me back around, reminding me of another man who did that to me tonight. I'm beginning to feel a bit like a rag doll, and about to say as much, but Boone is close enough I can smell the scent of the generic soap the den supplies in the bathrooms. I still for a moment, then shake my head. I have *got* to get out of here before Chance catches up and makes this all worse. I look pointedly at his hand.

He follows my gaze, then lets go abruptly. "Listen. I... Fuck... I'm sorry. Chance is an ass. If I'd been there, I would have done something about it."

This is just getting worse by the second. I don't need him feeling sorry for me. And that's what this is.

"It's fine, Boone," I say. "I handled it."

"I heard." He grimaces again. "You're sure—"

"Yeah. Not a big deal. It's not your problem anyway." This time when I go around him, he doesn't stop me.

I get far enough that I think he's actually going to let me go, but instead he's suddenly beside me, not stopping me but walking with me. "You're not trying to watch." A statement, not a question. His voice is rife with curiosity now. "So, where are you going?"

I shoot him a sideways look. "I don't need your pity friendship, Boone. I'm fine. Really."

"This isn't pity." He offers a lopsided smile tinged with remorse.

I wish I didn't know better. It's not his fault.

"I thought we were cool," he says.

Right. Normally, I'd shoot some chipper sarcasm his way. I just don't have it in me. So I try a different tack and tell him the truth. "I'm going back to the den."

"You're going back now?" Doubt laces his voice as he looks over at the crowd we're leaving behind. "What about the festival? The gods are choosing."

"I'll see the highlight reel later." As long as Zeus isn't king again, I really don't care about the results. Hermes would be nice for the Order, though.

I gesture back toward the temple. "Felix won't like both of us missing this. The upper bosses said we all had to be present to honor Hermes."

He turns serious. "Chance isn't easy to hide from for long. I'll walk you back."

I should have known he'd figure it out. "Don't you want to watch?"

That cocky grin gets me every time. He holds up a cell phone. "Got that covered. The view from where we were sucked anyway."

Sticking to me like a burr, Boone keeps one eye on me and one on the phone, reporting the gods' selections as we make our way through near-empty city streets. The way we go, the fastest way, takes us past Atlas Tower.

Lifestyles of the uber wealthy and questionably powerful. Despite all the riches the condos in that skyscraper contain, it's off-limits to all pledges. The inhabitants have enough time, money, and spite to make sure intruders meet grisly ends if they get caught. Also, everyone knows Hades owns the penthouse.

The hairs on the back of my neck stand up as I wonder if he's there.

Why am I thinking about him right now? He's the least of my worries. I *live* with an asshole named Chance, and as much as I'm ducking him tonight, I know it's only a matter of time before he takes a wrecking ball to my life.

I toss another quick glance at Boone and let out a long sigh. As awful as it was before, I'm certain having a *secret* crush on a guy will feel infinitely less painful than one your nemesis can taunt you with.

When we get to a chain-link fence blocking off the entrance to tunnels that lead under the city streets, Boone unlocks the gate, locking it again behind us. Just inside the tunnel entrance, hidden behind stacks of garbage, we pull out rubber boots. It's the pledges' jobs to make sure the various entry points to our underground den stay stocked with these and flashlights.

I straighten from putting on a pair when Boone says, "Looks like another is about to go. I think it's Artemis."

I wrinkle my nose. If they stay true to pecking order, they've already selected the first ten mortals. That went fast. After Artemis, only one god will be left who still needs to select. I sigh again. I thought I'd get more time before everyone returned.

I grab a flashlight and start walking down into the graffiti-covered cement passageway.

Boone holds the phone out as we keep going so we can both see.

With no flourish or fanfare, one of Artemis' famous golden arrows shoots out of nowhere to jam into the ground on the screen, and a mortal appears in a poof of smoke.

There's a stir among the crowd, and Boone murmurs, "Well, would you look at that. Artemis picked a man."

"Huh," I say and keep sloshing through ankle-deep water, tossing only a quick glance at the screen to see a leanly athletic guy with light-beige skin and dark hair blink back at the camera.

Historically, the goddess favors women exclusively.

Boone just shrugs without breaking stride.

With practiced ease, we reach our destination—a solid-looking wall covered in a heroic depiction of Hermes, with his helm tucked under one arm and the Talaria, his winged sandals, on his feet. Graffiti, of course, to blend in with all the other art down here.

I pause to swing my flashlight both ways, checking that we weren't followed but only catching the glow of a rat's eyes before I douse the light. Boone switches off the phone, too. In the pitch-black darkness, I press my palm to the cement wall, feeling for the crypticodes I know are there—small, hidden, raised bumps, a system of letters that are imperceptible to the mortal eye, but we thieves know how to find them and can read them by touch. A way to leave directions for one another—which buildings to avoid, where there are holes in surveillance camera coverage, and so forth.

I don't bother to read this one, since I know what it says. But at the end of the letters is the button, also hidden from sight, that I depress, triggering a thick cement door to swing open on a gust of breeze. We swiftly step inside before it closes just as fast. Every year or two, a new pledge doesn't move quick enough, and it's a bloody mess—one that is my lot to clean up—and a true shame.

As soon as the door seals shut behind us, the secret, god-made chambers that make up our den are immediately illuminated by lanterns blazing with a blue fire that never dies. Fire, it is said, that Hermes gifted the Order to light our dens all over the world.

Boone turns the phone back on.

"You get a signal down here?" I ask.

"I stole Felix's wifi password." He sets it on the floor as we both stop to take off the boots.

When I'm done, I put mine and the flashlight on the shelves available for all the pledges to use as we come and go. Boone's still struggling with his, and I study his downbent head. He didn't have to help me play keep-away with Chance.

He glances at the phone. "Looks like Hermes made his choice."

I swallow before asking, "A thief?"

Boone squints at the screen, then shakes his head. "Zai Aridam?"

I pause at that. "Where have I heard that name before?"

He flips the phone around to show me, and sure enough, that name is scrolling across the image, and it finally clicks why it's familiar. In the last Crucible, a hundred years ago, a man named Mathias Aridam was Zeus' pick. He never returned. Actually, not a single mortal returned from that one. But their families were all blessed beyond measure.

Aridam. That family took their blessing and moved away from anyone who knew them. This can't be a coincidence, can it?

"That's all of them," Boone says. "I hope they each return home at the end."

He's likely in the minority there, as we were still enjoying the result of so many blessings bestowed when no one returned from the last Crucible. I don't say that out loud.

"Ready?" Boone gets to his feet.

I take a deep breath. "Sure. Why not?"

My stomach sinks when it looks like he's about to answer my absolutely rhetorical question, but a shock of screams bursts from the phone's speakers and we both glance down.

"What the—" We stare at the screen.

"Merciful hells," I mutter.

Zeus' temple now has a massive, billowing column of red flame out front, pouring black smoke into the skies. Only one god would use that as an entrance.

Hades.

I bet he *was* scoping out the temple earlier just for this. Of course that would be my luck. The one time I've gone anywhere near that forsaken place in all my life, I run into him.

"What is *he* up to now?" I mutter, ignoring the questioning glance Boone shoots me.

"Greetings, living mortals." Hades' voice doesn't boom. It flows. My stomach clenches in stark recognition of that distinctive fathomless slide of a voice.

"As you all know, I have lost a dear one recently—my lovely

Persephone."

I squeeze my eyes shut at that.

Persephone. His darkly, obsessively beloved queen—Persephone. His *dead* queen.

I shiver.

"In her honor…I, too, shall choose a champion," he announces.

Holy shit. Hades doesn't participate in the Crucible. Technically, he's not even part of the major Olympians. Here in the Overworld, rumor has it that because he's already King of the Underworld, the others in this pantheon don't want to give him even more power, so he's not allowed to become King of the Gods in Olympus as well.

A heave of murmurs rips through the crowds around the temple loud enough that the live feed picks it up.

And the mortal he picks. To be chosen by the god of death…yikes. I don't care exactly what it is the gods have those people doing as champions—but *that* particular mortal is going to be so screwed.

Hades offers the crowds a slow smile. "And I shall choose…"

Suddenly, thick black smoke swirls around my feet, filling the chamber, and an immediate, knowing dread tries to tear a hole in my stomach. I jerk my head up to stare at Boone, who stares back with dawning horror widening his eyes. "Lyra?"

Oh my gods. "You've got to be—"

The smoke envelops me completely, and my vision goes black. Only for a second. It's like I slow blinked, and when it comes back, I am not in the den, watching all this happen on a tiny screen.

Instead, I'm standing at the entrance to the Temple of Zeus in a dissipating cloud of black smoke that smells of fire and brimstone, with Hades by my side.

With the worst timing ever, that bastard pulled me here mid-sentence, and my mouth finishes what I was in the middle of saying. "—shitting me."

The two words drop into the stunned silence that has taken over the temple and all of San Francisco. Probably the entire fucking world.

Hades smiles directly at me—cunning and supremely satisfied, as if I couldn't have thrilled him more with those crass words. Then he wraps his hand around mine, lifting both, and faces the crowds. "Lyra Keres!"

PART 2

DEATH'S VIRTUE

This offending soul would like to thank Death for the honor…
but decline.

8

FORTUNE'S FOOLS

I'm dead. I'm dead. I am so very, very dead.

"Don't do this," I whisper, ducking my head and hoping no one can read my lips or hear me as I essentially beg Hades to let me go. We're still standing in front of the masses, waiting for I don't know what.

"It's done." There's no give. No pity.

He's finally getting around to punishing me for earlier. That's what this has to be. I have the worst luck with petty gods and this damned temple.

"Smile, my star," Hades commands, soft but still compelling. "All the world is getting a good look at you before I take you away."

In a disorienting flash followed by an immediate thunderclap that sends my ears ringing, someone else is standing with us.

Zeus.

Current power-hungry King of the Gods. I like to think of him as a narcissistic toddler.

Like Hades, this god is impossible to mistake, with pale curls that look like they've been shocked white forming a halo over his forehead, which strangely doesn't make his fair skin look washed out. He doesn't even look thirty...and Hades looks even younger, despite being the older of the two. I guess it's true what they say about good genes and exercise. Zeus, though, is too pretty for my taste, although it is said his skin bears the scars of the Anaxian Wars. Something about Hephaestus and a volcano.

He's dressed in an impeccable three-piece suit, though it is all white with a green tie that looks like he's oozing algae from the neck.

Arrogant eyes so blue they almost hurt to gaze upon rake Hades from head to toe.

If I wasn't so busy trying not to lose my shit over my own situation, I might've been amused by the comical mix of frustration and fury contorting Zeus' otherwise angelic features. Turns out beauty, even godlike beauty, turns ugly with nasty thoughts.

The crowds trailing down the mountain, across the bridge, and into the city erupt at his appearance.

"The Crucible is of no interest to you, brother," Zeus says with a smile, his voice booming across the headlands as he turns to play to his audience.

"And yet we both know you can't stop me," Hades muses casually for only us to hear. Then, in a voice that also rolls across the hillside, he says, "My *brother* wouldn't be afraid of a little competition, would he?"

The responding cheers bring a scowl to Zeus' angelic face, and electricity sparks over his head in tiny, popping bursts of light.

I lean in Hades' direction. "Are you actively trying to get electrocuted?"

He's watching Zeus, and I'm not sure if the sneer on his lips is for his brother or me. "I didn't know you cared."

For me, I guess. I give an inelegant snort. "I don't. But I'm in striking range of where you stand, and I, unlike you, happen to be mortal."

He still doesn't look at me. "That instinct to save yourself first is going to serve you well."

What in the Underworld is that supposed to mean? I might be cursed to never be loved, but that doesn't mean I don't care about others. In fact, in a lot of ways, it makes me care too much, putting everyone else's happiness before my own. But that's not my biggest problem right now...

I open my mouth to tell him that if he thinks I'm going to participate in this farce of the gods' one-upmanship, or whatever is going on here, he's mistaken.

But before I can reply, before even Zeus can, Hades says above the roar of the crowd, "Let the games begin!"

Then there's a flash of lightning the exact moment I do that blinking-disappearing thing again, this time without the smoke effects. The blinking thing lasts a little longer this time, and I swear I feel a steadying touch at the small of my back.

When my vision blinks back in, Hades and I are no longer standing before the temple in San Francisco at night. We're on a wide, semicircular platform that protrudes from a mountainside and appears to hover over a sheer drop into clouds with the sun shining above.

We're alone, but probably not for long.

I need to talk my way out of this. Fast. I look around for any ideas and freeze. All thoughts of escape move to the back burner as I gape at a sight mortals have only dreamed of witnessing.

Olympus—the home of the gods.

Built among and on top of towering mountain spires, the pristine white buildings seem to be part of the very rocks themselves. Of easily identifiable ancient Grecian origin, they show perfect symmetry and, of course, the distinctive tall columns from various eras.

I can't see any signs or lingering scars from the Anaxian Wars.

"Stop staring," Hades says.

"I've never seen anything like it," I breathe, forgetting for a microsecond who I'm with.

"It's not *that* impressive."

I shoot him a sidelong glance. He is the only god who doesn't make a home here. Ever. "You sound bitter. Sour grapes?"

Is it possible for silvery eyes to turn pitch-black? He smiles in the way a shark does, showing you the teeth he's about to eat you with. "Not at all." He looks away, gaze skating over the vista before us. "I've seen better. Trust me."

Better than this? I'm not sure that's possible. "I'll believe it when I see it."

"I can make that happen."

Was that a threat?

I pretend I didn't hear him, looking up and up and up to the single massive temple sitting atop the tallest peak. Just below that, three faces are carved into the mountain side by side. Zeus, Poseidon, and Hades—the three brothers who defeated and imprisoned the Titans who ruled the world before them. From each of the open carved mouths pours a waterfall.

The water pouring from Zeus' mouth is an almost iridescent white that turns into misty clouds that swirl their way down to the mountain below, shrouding Olympus from the eyes of the Overworld. The waters from Poseidon are turquoise, like pictures I've seen of the Caribbean

Sea, so clear that even from here I can make out details of the rock face beneath.

And the one from Hades is…

I lean over. "Does your waterfall feed the River Styx?"

"Yes."

"The water is black." I can tell by the way his lips twist that I don't have to point out what I'm getting at.

"It's not black in the Underworld."

"Really? What color is it? Please tell me it's pink."

He bends closer, intent on me. "You'll find out soon enough if you're not careful."

I hide my wince by looking away.

Hades' waterfall doesn't fall far, turning into a river that seems to disappear into the bowels of the mountain, but Poseidon's river winds its way along the surface, splitting to follow each peak. It flows under beautiful, curved bridges, feeding the lush greenery that covers the mountains, and disappears in places to come out of carved statues farther down.

And everything here sort of…glows. I'm surprised I don't hear heavenly choirs. Olympus is overwhelmingly perfect. I suddenly feel small. Insignificant.

I shouldn't be here.

I am the last person who should be here. There must be a way out of this.

"I'm…" I'm what? Sorry? Terrified? Suffer from wrong-place-wrong-time syndrome?

Before I can pick the right words, Hades blocks my view and says, "We don't have long. I need you to listen."

9

TAUNTING GODS

I swallow what I was going to say next, fear snaking up my spine. "O—kay." I draw the word out, my eyes darting around for whomever is apparently coming for us.

One eyebrow lifts, probably at my immediate agreement, but Hades doesn't comment. "What I've gotten us involved in is…important."

Choosing a new ruler of the gods? I would say so, but I don't get the impression that's what he means. "Important how?"

He shakes his head. "The less you know, the better. The only information you need right now is that until the end of the Crucible…"

I blink at him. "Until the end… What?"

He searches my gaze for a beat. "You are mine."

My throat tightens in immediate reaction even as my foolish stomach decides to flutter. I've never been anyone's. And, despite recent events, I have feelings for Boone. There should be no fluttering.

"We need to present a united front if you want to win. Understand?"

I shake my head. "I don't understand anything. Why the united front?"

"You'll find that out in a moment. But before the others get here, I'll make you a deal… Win and I'll remove your curse."

He might as well have slapped me. I jerk back so fast I stumble, and he grabs my hand to keep me upright. He can do that? I can lose my curse?

I'm still processing this when the rest of the deities and their chosen champions arrive without so much as a whisper of sound. One second, we're alone. The next, we're not.

And they're all staring at our hands.

Instead of dropping his hold, Hades steps closer to me and turns so we both face the new arrivals. I get the impression that he's looking each and every one of the other gods and goddesses directly in the eyes, his own like chips of ice.

Is he daring them to stop him? To protest? To speak up?

They don't.

Not even Zeus, despite the glaring and crackling. Then again, Hades threw down a gauntlet to his brother in front of the entire world.

Hera stands closest to us. Elegantly regal, Zeus' long-suffering spouse is dressed in intricately decorated, layered golden armor over a lavender undergown. A swift look around tells me all the gods and goddesses are in armor now, Zeus included.

Meanwhile, the mortal standing beside Hera appears to be the youngest one here. Sixteen at most, with a chiseled chin stuck out at an arrogant angle that I think might be covering fear. He's dressed in a deep-purple suit with an impressive overcoat that has tails that sweep the ground. Gold laurel leaves nestle in his dark, silky hair.

I glance around, and sure enough, all the mortals are decked out in fancy clothes in colors matching their gods—green, purple, turquoise, and burgundy.

What color did I get?

I drop my gaze, and irritation rises then falls in a way that is all too familiar. While everyone else is clothed in splendor, I'm still in my jeans and T-shirt. Marked as separate, yet again.

"Hey." I gesture to myself and then at the others.

Hades looks me over with blank, uncaring eyes. "You're fine."

Someone nearby snaps their fingers, and I'm instantly wearing a black, spangled wisp of a dress made of a sheer material that leaves little to the imagination.

"Really?" I grumble under my breath. "Never mind, then."

Hades' brows slash down. "Aphrodite." Her name might as well be a curse on his lips.

The goddess of love and beauty offers an unperturbed smile, clearly missing the undertone of ire in Hades' voice. Her armor isn't cutesy hearts like I halfway expected—it's rose gold and curved into couples and groups of all genders doing...all kinds of things.

Beside her stands a very tall, blond mortal wearing a satiny wine-colored gown with a slit up to her hip showing off the best pair of legs I've ever seen, and even she isn't *this*...exposed.

Hades points an accusing finger in my direction.

"What?" Aphrodite bats long-lashed, innocent eyes. "You weren't listening, so I thought I'd help. So much better, don't you think?" Then she tips her head. "Where is your armor?"

Hades slips his hands into his pockets, a seemingly casual move that up close looks more like leashing a tiger. "I only wear armor if I'm going to fight."

Beyond Aphrodite, I think Dionysus winces, but the goddess merely arches her eyebrows. "How boring."

That's when what Hades is wearing finally sinks in. No more jeans and boots. I run my gaze from the top of his shiny black hair with its one curling, stark-white lock down to the high-collared, formal black velvet jacket, embroidered subtly in black thread with a single butterfly on his collar and stars along the cuffs and bottom hem, and then farther down to—I almost laugh—polished black shoes. "Now *this* is what I pictured. I mean, except for the tail."

He shrugs a nonchalant shoulder. "Sometimes one must play to the crowd. The Overworld is ruled by a mob mentality, is it not?"

He's not wrong. "The immortal world, too?"

"Definitely."

"Remember what I said about your perception problem?" I glance around. "Maybe you have one up here, too."

While Hades' lips remain smiling, his eyes narrow at me. He waves a hand, and the noise of the waterfalls and, well, the sound of everything but his voice disappears. "Are you trying to manage me?"

My ribs tighten around my lungs. "Are you manageable?"

"No." He snaps his fingers.

The only indication that anything has changed is a rustle of material. I glance down to discover that I'm wearing a formal pantsuit paired with a sheer cropped jacket and silver-strapped stilettos. The material is soft and silky against my skin and luxurious in a way that makes me want to run my hands over it. The long sleeves and high collar of the jacket give the outfit an almost innocent air. Stars are embroidered in silver, two on one collar and one on the other, reminding me of my tattoos.

It's simple and not nearly as fancy as the others'.

THE GAMES GODS PLAY

The little girl in me who used to marvel at the beautiful clothes the pledges would swipe from wealthy marks wants to look in a mirror and see the entire effect. To feel pretty just for the fun of it for once.

Hades has turned so still I'm not sure he's even breathing. I lift my head to find his gaze on me. On me. As if he's taking in every inch.

I blow out a quiet breath and say the first distracting thing that comes into my head. "Next time you snap your fingers, maybe send me home instead."

"That's not going to happen."

I'm not giving up. "It isn't too late to back out of this."

"No, Lyra."

My chin juts out. "Then don't expect me to cooperate."

He goes a different kind of still, caging me with his gaze. "You *will* obey me in all things, Lyra Keres." A command, not a question, and with absolute certainty of my submission.

A small flower of curiosity blooms. What *would* it be like to just... obey him?

Heavens help me.

Containing my reaction behind a mask of indifference is like trying to stop my heart from beating.

After years with the Order, I know how to operate under someone's thumb. But this is different. I've been the only one keeping me safe and making decisions for myself, despite the Order's involvement, since I was three years old. Who knew the simple idea of submission to a powerful being like Hades would be so...enticing?

And it shouldn't be.

Maybe I'm broken.

"I'm a better partner than I am a puppet," I insist.

In a move I don't even see him make, he steps into me, his shoulders blocking my view of all the others. He doesn't speak as he studies me with silver eyes gone diamond sharp as if he's trying to figure out where my soft, squishy, vulnerable parts are. Then he leans forward just slightly, and I know he means these words for me and me alone. "I don't do partners."

Am I a puddle on the ground yet? I clear my throat. "That sounds... inefficient."

I was going to say *lonely*, but I have a feeling he'd know I'm talking about myself, too.

-44-

His lips quirk almost imperceptibly, but then he turns serious. "Things will go better for you...if you heed me."

Why do I feel like there's a deeper meaning to his words? A warning, but one meant to help me. I don't picture Hades as the helpful type. Is this about the games-and-winning thing again?

With a *whoosh*, the sound of the waterfalls returns.

"What are you doing, brother?" Poseidon calls out from across the platform. "Your poor mortal looks scared half to death."

Hades doesn't move, doesn't look toward his brother. Instead, he lifts a single eyebrow at me. "Is that what you are, my star? Scared?"

10

ROCK. HARD PLACE. AND ME.

Something in Hades' expression and voice is different from a second ago. Or maybe I'm reading him wrong. It's difficult to tell, but I'm pretty sure he's now putting on a mask for the others. Playing a part for them. I don't like it.

Meanwhile, he and Poseidon are still waiting on me to respond.

What's the safest answer here? Hades has only given me hints about what's going on, but my gut is telling me that if the other deities see weakness in me or division between us, they'll pounce. Growing up as a loner in the Order taught me that the hard way.

I clear my throat and raise my voice. "He was just...laying down some ground rules."

Hades' slow, pleased smile teases parts of me I didn't know I could feel. He leans closer, lips brushing my ear, breath sending shivers cascading through me. "That's my girl."

I hate that infantilizing shit...and yet my body hasn't gotten the message. I'm going to pretend he didn't just push a whole lot more buttons I didn't know I had until right this second. "I'm not your anything," I whisper back.

He doesn't seem to notice as he finally pulls away, smile completely gone as he turns to face Poseidon, who's watching us with eyes sharp and curious.

"You selected an interesting champion, brother." The ocean god looks me up and down. "And a thief of all things, by the looks of her."

Asshat. My eyes narrow before I can stop myself. "Secure the services of a lot of thieves, do you?" I ask him.

Poseidon's eyes darken half a second before he raises his arm to backhand me. With a speed that renders him nearly invisible, Hades shifts between us. He says nothing, doesn't touch him, but his brother goes ashen. After a moment, Poseidon snarls and stalks away.

I'm left blinking. Hades protected me.

Me.

Logic tells me it's because he needs me to win their stupid contest, but I can't help how I feel like I can breathe a tiny bit easier.

Just for a moment.

Anyone close by also seems to drift farther away, maybe because tension now rolls off Hades like steam off a geyser.

In a nervous move, I tentatively raise a hand to my hair, which is still short, but I can tell it's curled on top and maybe styled into some sort of twisting effect with… I pause. Then drop my hand abruptly. "Is this a tiara?"

I glance at the other mortals. Each and every one of them is wearing a headpiece that matches their clothing, but they're all in the style of the ancient Greek laurel diadems. What I'm wearing definitely doesn't feel like leaves.

Almost like my nerves calmed Hades, the tension eases from him. The change is subtle, but from up close, I can see it.

"I thought women loved tiaras?" Now he couldn't sound more bored.

"The point is to *not* stand out."

"Why?"

He can't be that unaware. "Are the histories right that you've never chosen a champion during the Crucible?"

"Yes."

"Then that already makes me different." *And not in a good way.* I don't say that bit. I don't have a death wish.

That logic doesn't so much as make a dent with him. "Then there's no reason to blend in. Is there?"

I grit my teeth, giving a little growl of frustration.

Hades lowers his voice, and the timbre changes, sounding more genuine. "You'd stand out even if I dressed you in rags and covered you in mud."

Only because I'm *his* chosen mortal, he means. There's no need for my belly to turn squishy.

"Try not to make it worse, at least," I mutter back, smoothing my hands down my pants.

He chuckles. Not in a mean or calculating way—he's honestly amused. A shock wave of horror shudders through me, because it's loud enough the others hear, and I feel every single eye that wasn't already trained on us turn in our direction.

I really hate this sensation.

"Stars are *my* symbol," Hera calls to Hades in a voice like the sweetest cream, smooth and lovely.

I search her face more closely. Something about the way she said that… I wonder if being Zeus' queen has made her feel like not much is hers in this world. I know what that feels like.

"And?" Even I wince at Hades' tone. He slides one hand in his pocket, and Hera eyes the move warily. "You may be the goddess of the stars," he says, "but everyone knows who commands the darkness."

Good grief. Does he have to antagonize *every* god and goddess right from the start?

If I make it home after this is all over, I'm switching to a different pantheon of gods.

I sigh. "You don't have to deliberately provoke them."

He says nothing to that.

The thing is…there's something in his attitude that I envy. He doesn't care. Not one shit is given if he's welcomed here, let alone accepted or loved.

As if he can't stand not being the center of attention and needs to take it back, Zeus claps his hands, and two rows of golden chairs appear to one side of the platform.

"Take your seats," the current King of the Gods says.

Hades immediately takes me by the hand—his warm, roughened skin is somehow grounding even while his grip is insistent—and escorts me as though I am royalty. He doesn't choose seats in the back row or off to the side. Nope. Hades places us front and center.

Zeus, who didn't get there quite fast enough with his mortal, glares again as he takes the seat to my left, even as Samuel—that was his name, right?—gives me a nod. Terrific. I'm sitting directly between two gods who seem to be locked in some kind of silent battle of wills. Best seat in the house, apparently. Or a good place to get myself killed before I even know what's happening.

"I am so fucked," I mutter, then pin a smile to my lips that feels as though it might crack my face.

Hades leans over but says loud enough for Zeus to hear, "Only if you would like to be."

Oh. My. Gods.

My spine goes as straight as if Zeus jammed an electric rod right down it, and I refuse to look at Hades. Or answer, for that matter. He doesn't mean it. I know he doesn't. He also doesn't know the kinds of unfortunate responses I've been having to him. That kind of nonsense is just to rile Zeus up, for whatever reason, and doesn't deserve an answer.

I can feel Hades watching me, probably with that taunting expression that I'm starting to resent.

"No?" he asks. "More's the pity."

Then he settles back in his seat, apparently happy to enjoy whatever new brand of torture is coming next.

"Zeles," Zeus calls out, "let us have the rules for the Crucible."

11

THERE'S ALWAYS A TWIST

The Crucible.

Now it really sinks in. I've been selected to win a *competition* that not everyone returns from—and I have no one left behind to even bestow blessings upon if I don't make it back. My heart starts to race, but I try to calm it by imagining the contest will be games, like chess or Twister. I can play chess. Maybe a footrace?

I lean toward Hades and whisper, "Like the Olympics?"

There is a world of difference between hurdles and something like pole-vaulting or even cage fighting. I'm trying not to let myself even consider anything close to monsters.

Hades points at the Daemones circling above us.

Zeles spreads his black wings wide, and with a downbeat, the Daemon twists in the air to land facing us. The man is clearly not a smiler. His warm brown skin is on full display as he isn't wearing a shirt, showing off an impressive, chiseled torso. Maybe it's hard to fashion shirts around the wings?

Horribly conscious of Hades at my side and the others all around, I force myself to focus as the other three Daemones line up behind Zeles.

"Welcome, champions," Zeles says. Still no smile. "Congratulations. You have the honor of being selected to compete in the Crucible, representing the god or goddess who chose you."

A competition that not all the mortals return from isn't mentioned, as though that fact is meaningless to the gods. This is going to be way worse than I imagined.

"Not only do you represent your patron god or goddess, but you compete in their stead. This is how we choose our next ruler. This is how we ensure the Anaxian Wars never happen again." By using mortals as chess pieces the gods get to move around on a board only they can see. Which makes me what?

A pawn.

I close my eyes. That's exactly what I am. A pawn in the gods' petty games, and a throne is at stake.

Zeles raises his arms like he's blessing us. "May your time in the splendor of Olympus encourage you to play your hardest for your gods and goddesses and, in the end, give you a piece of beauty to carry with you into the Overworld, or into the Underworld, should you falter."

Ummm... Was that supposed to be inspiring and uplifting? I glance around at the other champions in my eyeline, who are all staring at Zeles with blank expressions. Or maybe they're so rattled they're in shock, too? He pretty much confirmed death is a strong possibility in this. Right?

"Before we establish the Labors and the rules," the Daemon continues, "let's introduce everyone now that we are all gathered together."

He said Labors.

As in Heraclean? Not good.

I'd rather hear more about the games-and-rules stuff, but at least now I'll get names and know who goes with which god or goddess. More information is never useless.

One by one, the thirteen deities introduce their champions by name and home origin and a tiny bit of background. I catalog everything I can about each one. We are truly an assorted group of people from all over the world, with varying genders, ages, statuses, skills, and walks of life. And with not a single trait that we all seem to have in common among us. Not obvious ones I can see, at least.

Zeles moves closer to us, his great wings brushing the floor with a whisper of sound. "There is a prize for the mortal who helps win their patron the crown," he announces.

One of the champions seated behind me murmurs with interest. Others shift in their chairs. The Daemon waves his hand, and a group of people descend the stairs, appearing from around the bend that follows the mountain's curve. They assemble at the foot between curling balustrades.

"Let me introduce you to Mathias Aridam and his family."

"Holy shit," I mutter, shock popping the words out of my mouth.

THE GAMES GODS PLAY

The man looks as young as I assume he did the day he won—no older than about his mid-forties. Thanks to the gods' providence, I assume. The rest of his family haven't seemed to age, either. Not that I knew them before, but there were pictures. Rumors were his whole family had been so despondent at his death, they moved away, and clearly the rumors were right. They just missed that the family moved to Olympus.

Zeles speaks again. "As the winner of the previous Crucible, Mathias got to request any boon from the gods. At his request, he has lived here in Olympus for the past hundred years with his family. In that time, his homeland in the Overworld has been blessed by the gods and goddesses in abundance and peace. Zai, as his son, now has a chance to continue his father's legacy."

I'm not the only one who turns to stare at Zai, who's seated in the back row beside Hermes. His light-brown skin is sallow underneath, his dark eyes sunken as if he hasn't slept a full night in his life, and he's too thin for his frame. He looks like he wants to disappear into his chair.

Meanwhile, Zai's family barely acknowledges him, shifting their gazes his way only briefly. Stunned gazes, if I read them right.

"A child of a previous winner has never been selected before." Zeles waves the Aridams away, and after Mathias shoots his son an oddly pointed look, they disappear up the stairs.

"*That* is what you have a chance to win here," Zeles says. "The throne for your patron, a hundred years of immortality for you and your family in Olympus with everything you want or need provided for, and blessings upon blessings heaped upon the lands and people of your home."

What about the losers? I know previous champions returned home, but some didn't. Are they punished? The gods are not exactly known for their forgiving natures.

"Now, for the rules of the Labors..." Zeles backs up in line with his siblings. All four Daemones stiffen, going into an almost trancelike state. They speak in eerie unison, as if they're reading from a script. "The gods and goddesses of Olympus will be divided into four groups by virtue— Strength, Courage, Mind, and Heart—the virtue each favors most."

So...with Hades as my patron, what virtue am I?

"Each god and goddess has already devised a contest in which the champions will compete. The champion who wins the most of the twelve Labors wins the Crucible."

Not a fight to the death, at least. Win or don't win. I can handle that. I'm already starting to think about allies. Not to win, just survive.

Samuel would be top of my list, with his size and strength, along with Rima Patel, Apollo's pick. Her navy, floor-length dress flatters her slim build and highlights her wide, brown eyes. She's a neurosurgeon, which could be helpful if not all the Labors are physical. Jackie Murphy, Aphrodite's champion, is another possibility. At least six feet tall and late twenties, I'd guess, she apparently grew up on a rural property in Australia, evidenced by enviable muscles and deeply tanned skin that's clearly seen sunlight every day.

Not that teaming up with anyone is likely. Not for me, at least. I now carry a double whammy of my curse along with being Hades' champion.

Pretty sure they're all going to steer clear of me. That or be gunning for me. I can practically feel the crosshairs on my back.

Still, worth a try.

"Or…" The Daemones interrupt my thoughts in stereo monotone. "If champions should die in the course of the Crucible and it happens that only one remains alive at the end, that champion wins by default."

A pebble of dread drops into my stomach, rolling down a whole pile of dread already in there. They basically just said we are allowed to kill each other to win by default.

Allies and adversaries just took on a whole new meaning.

"What in the bowels of Tartarus have you gotten me into?" I whisper-hiss at Hades.

He doesn't answer.

Smite me now, I want to say. It would be faster and probably less painful.

"Champions may bring with them into each challenge any mortal tools, excluding modern weapons, that they can carry along with the boons they might earn throughout the Crucible. From this point forward, the patrons may coach their champions and encourage them, but they may in no other way help or interfere with any champions, theirs or others."

It's telling that they had to write that into the rules.

"And we, the Daemones, shall stand as judges and rule keepers of the Labors, with final determination of the winner."

Suddenly, the Daemones all blink out of whatever trance that was, and Zeles says, "There is one change to the rules this century. Due to Hades joining the Crucible and the effects on humanity should the god of death be crowned king, we have elected to allow humanity to receive their dead and be aware of each event's winner."

The people around me gasp, mortals and gods alike. I briefly wonder if anyone would care if my body was returned to the Order.

"Now, champions," Zeles continues, "you can choose not to play, and your patron god or goddess will select another in your place."

I turn sharply to Hades, mouth open, ready to opt out. "I—"

He shakes his head, then tells me in a lowered voice, "The last person who tried to pass on playing in the Crucible...Ares selected that man's daughter instead."

There's no one truly close to me he could choose, but even so, I close my mouth on a slow, silent sigh. Message received. Everyone knows that saying no to a deity never ends well for mortals.

No one else declines the "honor."

"Excellent," Zeles says. "Any questions?"

Where do I even start?

But the other champions shake their heads, so I don't speak up. It's probably smarter to wait and ask Hades when we're alone anyway.

"Without further ado, I open this century's Crucible," Zeles declares. "Champions, prepare for your first Labor. It starts now."

12

I NEVER WAS ANY GOOD AT TESTS

I sit ramrod straight in my chair. Now? No time to digest this? Or get ready? Mentally prepare? Just…go play and hope you don't die.

They aren't kidding around.

Zeles folds his wings tighter against his body. "This first Labor is more of a challenge to get you started. It is not one of the twelve in which you will compete against one another… And this is the only Labor in the Crucible in which every single one of you has the chance to win."

He lets that sink in a second.

I'm still stuck on the fact that we're starting immediately.

"And you *want* to win this one," he says. "Those of you who play well will earn *two* gifts from your patron—one relic and one skill or attribute—both of which you can use to assist you through the rest of the Crucible."

Zeles claps, and the space around the tables of decadent food is instantly filled with a thousand glittering artifacts of all shapes, sizes, and types, placed and piled all around the platform, even up on the wide balcony rails. It's so cluttered that it looks like an antique shop vomited.

"Champions…hidden somewhere on this platform is a token, an item that you and you alone must find. A different one for each of you." Zeles looks us over. "When you find it, you will be taken farther into Olympus…" He waves up the sweeping staircase. "Along with your patron. When you reach your god or goddess, you win the challenge, and they will bestow upon you their two gifts."

It can't be that easy. Can it?

"If you do not reach your patron inside Olympus within the hour…" The Daemon points to a sundial on the floor at our feet. "Then you forfeit your gifts."

Ah. There's the catch. Not getting magical gifts when the others do would be a serious deficit to start with. That sits with me about as comfortably as sitting here between gods.

I glance at Hades, who I find watching me—studying me, more like. Trying to figure out if I'm smart enough for this little test? Only, he's not allowed to help me now, is he? And, news flash, I haven't trained or been tested by the Order in years—and didn't do well when I was. I'm not sure how my skills as an office clerk are going to help much, either.

My shoulders sink. He picked the wrong damn champion.

Hades' hand reaches for mine, lifting it up and placing it to rest on the arm of his chair, our fingers intertwined for all to see. So I know this is another little show for the others.

It's working. To my right, I can see the open-mouthed shock on Dionysus' face.

Hades' silky voice curls around me, seeping into my muscles and tightening them like rachets with every word. "Don't worry, my star. I'll keep you safe, and this test is cryptic, but there will be signs to help you along the way."

"Enough of that," Zeus snaps at Hades.

Even Zeles looks a little thrown, his wings twitching. Given where my hand is perched, I don't blame him. None of the other gods or goddesses are screwing around with their champions this way. Then again, I think that's the point.

Hades chuckles darkly but holds up his other hand in a gesture of supposed surrender. "I won't say more."

Zeles' lips thin, but he moves on. "Champions, your time starts... now."

The other champions surge from their chairs, several running to the riches piled haphazardly before us.

Yanking my hand free, I hop up with more haste than grace and stumble a little—enough that Artemis, seated near us, sneers. Her intelligent, hazel eyes remind me of the hawk she hunts with. She's built like a huntress—lean and strong yet light—and the way she moves her head, scanning everything, only adds to the impression. Her armor is what I'd have expected, all moons and bows and arrows over a green gown that complements her mahogany skin.

Green for the virtue of…Strength, maybe? Or Heart? I can't remember, and I could see Artemis valuing either one.

I purposefully give her a goofy grin and a shrug, and she turns away, obviously considering me both clumsy and naive. Not a bad thing. Given where and how I grew up, I learned early that a little misinformation can only benefit me. Boone *still* thinks I'm afraid of the dark.

Speaking of, what in the world is he thinking right now? Watching me disappear from the den only to show up at the temple with Hades had to be a shock.

Hades, still relaxed in his chair, waves toward the tables and piles. "Run and play, my star."

Does he really think this is fun for me?

I bite my tongue to keep from asking that out loud.

"Look at that glare." Aphrodite *tsk*s. "Better watch out, Hades. I might steal her from you. I would love to be glared at like that. So much… passion." She breathes the last word so it's practically a moan.

Heat surges up my neck and into my cheeks.

The long, black hair curling down her back sways with every move of her hips, her light-brown eyes never leaving mine as she comes closer. She looks about my age, maybe a year older—but her eyes tell a different story. "I could put all that passion to better use," she murmurs in a seductive purr of a voice. "Don't you wish to—"

"Addie!" Hades snaps, out of his chair.

Addie?

Immediately, everything about her demeanor changes, the softness of her features hardening. Hells, the softness about all of her hardens until a warrior stands in her place, staring daggers at Hades. "You're such a sourpuss. No fun at all." Then she winks at me and walks away.

Hades shakes his head. "Watch out for her. If she says the words 'don't you wish to,' clap your hands over your ears, because if she gets to the rest, you'll be compelled to do whatever it is she asks then and there"—his gaze cuts from her to me—"no matter if it's something you want to do or not. Fuck an enemy. Betray a friend. She can even make your body obey her against your will. Your reactions, your movements… sensations."

The last thing I want to talk about with Hades is sensations. "I won't listen when she says those words. Got it."

A slight tilt to one side of his mouth is his only response.

"I thought you would all disappear until we find you with our artifacts?" I ask, flicking a glance toward Zeus, who hasn't stopped glaring at Hades since he took my hand.

Zeles answers. "They will disappear when the item is found or be instructed to leave in the final few minutes."

In other words, they want to watch us squirm.

"Better find it quick, then." Hades walks away to stand at the base of the stairs, as far away as he can get from the rest of the gods and goddesses, who have all moved to the tables of food and drink.

I join the other champions among the tables, debating the best plan for success.

A gong goes off, and Dionysus' champion gasps. Her dark-brown hair is arranged in an intricate braid, and she's wearing a pantsuit made from wine-colored velour embroidered with grapevines that match her patron's armor. Meike Besser, I think her name was. She has a rather large, hawkish nose with intelligent brown eyes beneath thick brown bangs. She shoots me a rosy-cheeked smile, then ignores the piles of antiques and wanders over to the food tables.

"Fifty-five minutes remaining," Zeles calls out.

Is he going to count down every five minutes for us? That won't be nerve-racking at all.

Meike, meanwhile, picks up a bite-size morsel from the table of decadent treats, studies it, then takes a tentative bite. She immediately chokes, her breath expelling in a harsh *whoosh* and dust flying from her tongue. She picks up a cup and drinks only to splutter and spit that out as well, the red stain on the white marble floor not wine...but blood.

We won't find our tokens among the food, apparently. It is also not for the mortals.

As Meike straightens, I notice that some of her long, dark bangs are stained red. Seriously, the gods are assholes.

Focus, Lyra.

Thanks to learning that tidbit from Meike, a plan starts to form. I take my time, strolling and looking about, but I don't touch anything yet, keeping an eye on the other champions and searching for patterns in the items. Not that I'm seeing any.

Another gong. "Fifty minutes."

"I'm curious…" Hades' voice sounds from right beside me, and I jump. I'm not used to people getting close. His habit of popping up wherever he wants, even when he was just standing all the way across the platform, is going to take some getting used to.

"I don't have time to talk," I say.

"I know, but you don't seem to be trying very hard. At least the others have picked a few things up. Don't you want to earn your gifts?"

"I'm starting out slow."

"I can see that. Why?"

I shrug. "Just learning what not to do first. Seems prudent in dealing with a game devised by a bunch of bored gods."

"Interesting. Have you learned anything so far?"

"Yeah. Don't eat the food."

13

FOLLOWING THE CLUES

A shout pulls my gaze to the right in time to see a stone statue of a cherub turn into a gargoyle and snap at Isabel Rojas Hernáiz, Poseidon's champion, dressed in a gorgeous heather-colored gown. She pushes one of the other champions back, then immediately yells at the gargoyle in rapid-fire Spanish.

I tilt my chin in Isabel's direction. "And don't touch the statues," I add.

She even chucks a gold cup at the thing, which bounces off its stone forehead with a *tink*. The growling gargoyle unfurls a pair of wings that make a grinding noise as it flies away. I grin at the string of profanities still coming from Isabel. Didn't Poseidon say she was a beauty queen before her current job in tech?

"That's right," Isabel calls after it as she picks up whatever was near the gargoyle that she wanted.

I mentally add her to my list of possible people to team up with.

"I have a token to find," I say to Hades. "Stay out of trouble."

His low chuckle follows me and lodges under my skin like a splinter I can't see.

Followed shortly after by yet another gong and time check.

That sound is really starting to jangle my nerves.

While time slips away, I continue looking for patterns in the items while surreptitiously watching the other champions. But by the time two more gongs go off and Zeles calls out, "Thirty-five minutes," I'm starting to rethink my plan. It's not getting me anywhere. The others must be wrestling with similar doubts, because their movements all turn a little more rushed, faces more pinched.

I pause on Zai, giving him a closer look.

He has picked up a delicate glass bauble, I can't tell of what exactly, and is trying to surreptitiously study the underside more closely. Long enough that I start to wonder what he sees. He coughs when he sets it down. Then he moves on to the next item and does the same, looking at the underside, though he puts that one down quicker.

My heart beats a little faster. Maybe patience paid off. Is he onto something?

Starting well away from Zai to keep from drawing attention to him, one at a time, I pick up different items—a scepter, a chalice, an orb. All priceless. Felix would fall over in a dead faint if he saw these riches.

I mix looking at the bottoms with other actions as I gradually make my way to the trinket he stared at first.

I set down an orb and sigh, glancing around, which is when Hermes steps into my line of sight, his winged feet and iconic helm the fanciest parts of his ensemble. Other than a gold cape that flares behind him when he walks, his armor holds no further adornments, no symbols. I've always liked my patron god.

I get the feeling that he doesn't like me, though. Shrewd eyes in a narrow, arresting face are trained on me as he weaves through the antiquities, stopping only when he's close enough that I can hear his lowered voice. "I know who you are—one of my Order's pledges."

Not now, I'm thinking. *Talk to me later when I'm not under the gun.*

I bow before him like I never have with Hades—or any of the others so far, for that matter. "I have always honored you as our patron god, Hermes. I hope—"

He jerks a hand up, and I stop, mouth hanging open until I remember to close it.

"I am not your patron during the Crucible."

Unsure, I rise slowly from my bow. "Of course—"

"Stop talking," he snarls.

I snap my mouth shut so quickly, I bite the inside of my cheek, but I refuse to wince.

He stares at me hard like I hold the secrets of the world. "Why you?" he mutters to himself. "You're nothing."

Ouch. But I guess I'm not the only one asking.

Meanwhile, the clock is running, and he's wasting too many ticks.

Be warned," he says. "Watch your back."

"Are you threatening me?" I ask, glancing in the direction of the four Daemones watching every soul on this platform very closely.

"That would be against the rules." Something in the way he looks when he says that—everything about him, his eyes, his jaw, his shoulders, rigid—keeps me from relaxing. "Then again," he muses, "the rules will no longer apply after the Crucible is over."

So this *is* a threat.

I'm not hazardously brave enough to call him on it, so instead I lean to the left slightly to peek around him, right at Hades. I don't say a word, but I guess Hermes gets the hint when he turns his head to see where I'm looking.

Does he really want to tangle with that particular god? Even after the Crucible? Not that Hades will give me a second thought when this is done, but Hermes can't be sure of that. "I get the impression that Hades is very possessive of anything he considers to be his, and he seems to be one to hold a grudge." I look at Hermes. "Am I wrong?"

Without another word, Hermes stalks away.

Fantastic. The Crucible has hardly started, and I'm already public enemy number one.

The gong goes off again, stringing my nerves tighter. "Thirty minutes," Zeles announces.

I look around at how many items are here. Thirty minutes isn't going to be enough to check them all, and I still haven't made it to the thing Zai saw to even know what I'm looking for. I move faster now, making my way across the platform to where he was, still trying to hide what I'm doing. I can practically hear the sundial ticking down the seconds like a clock with cogs. It's not until one of the other champions shoots me a sidelong glance that I realize I'm humming. Again.

I clear my throat and pick up a slender baton, only to jump when it suddenly turns into a hissing snake in my grasp. It winds its way up my arm. Another trick of the gods, I see. Am I supposed to scream? Run away and hide? They're amateurs at pranks compared to pledges.

"Not so fast, little fella." Reaching up, I grasp it gently by the head and peel it away before it can loop around my neck. I look at it. "I don't have time for a distraction right now."

"Oh, give him here," an impatient female voice says. Demeter's golden armor sets off beige skin and wheat-colored hair. Even her eyes seem to spark with gold. I give her the snake, which winds around her wrist and snuggles into her like a beloved pet.

But she's focused on me. "Why would Hades pick you?"

Everyone's number one question, it seems. "You should ask him."

I turn away but pause when she says, "He probably just wants to fuck you."

Wow. I open my mouth but stop myself just in time. What if this isn't her being a bitch? What if this is a mother jealous on her daughter's behalf? Persephone's death must still hurt her terribly. "My condolences," I say, "on the loss of your—"

Demeter's expression turns poisonous, and it leaks into her voice. "Don't dare speak of her, mortal." A nearby urn of beautiful lavender-colored hydrangeas withers, turning black at the edges.

I glance toward Hades. His expression is stony. No help from that area. I say nothing, and Demeter, chest heaving with the emotions she's unable to control—a mother visibly heartbroken—walks away.

Great. I am going to be even more popular here than I am in the den. I can already tell. At least they mostly ignored me there. And at this rate, I'll be competing with no gifts to help me and twelve gods, and their champions, all rooting for my demise.

Forcing my head back in the game, I finally get to the small glass flower shaped like a rose Zai stared at earlier and fight to control my expression as elation flutters through my chest. A symbol is etched into the bottom of the glass. A bow and arrow. This is the token meant for Artemis' champion.

I set it down quietly and keep going like nothing happened.

At least now I know what I'm looking for—the one with Hades' symbol.

Gong. "Twenty-five minutes," Zeles calls.

Forget hiding what I'm doing. I rush now.

Suddenly, Hermes disappears. I mean *poof*, no longer there. So does Zai a second later, and a little bell rings.

"I guess he found his token," Ares' champion comments in a distinct Canadian accent. Between the Shirley Temple pin curls on her head and—I squint to make it out—"babygirl" necklace at her throat, Neve Bouchard looks nothing like I expected from her patron god. I know better than to let my guard down around her.

The rest of the champions turn even more frantic at the proof that our tokens can be found. I pause and take in the tightness of their faces, the fumbling of their fingers, the worry pinching their eyes.

We are, all of us, just trying to survive this.

And damned if there's anything I can't stand more than an unlevel playing field. I've been living with exactly that my entire life, thanks to Zeus.

I glance at Hades, who is now propping up the stone wall far from the rest of us as he watches me. When I catch his eye, he frowns.

What I'm about to do is really going to piss him off.

Gong. "Twenty minutes."

Damn it.

I'm doing it anyway.

14

NO GOOD DEED

With zero hesitation, I walk back to the glass rose and pick it up, waving it in the air. "Which of you is Artemis' champion again?"

A man about my age looks up from a pile across the platform. I recognize him from Boone's phone screen, though he's more put-together now. He has the classic, clean-cut looks I only see on TV shows and movies and is dressed in a dark-green suit embroidered to match the moons and arrows decorating his patróness's armor. When our gazes meet, he walks toward me, saying, "That's me. Why?"

Only his lips and the sound don't quite match up.

Which is when it strikes me that Hermes, who among other things is the god of languages, must be translating so that we can understand each other. But he didn't do that for Spanish. Except I speak Spanish. Languages are one of the things thieves are taught from the start and one of the areas in which I excel. Still, that translation is a handy little trick.

I hold up the rose so he can see the goddess's symbol etched in the bottom, and his jaw drops. "Why would you help me—"

"Just take it." The second I place it in his hand, Artemis disappears and her champion follows.

"Hey!" Dionysus, his cherubic face sort of purpling, a lock of his golden hair falling over his forehead, waves at the Daemones like they should intervene. "She can't do that."

Zeles glances at me, then shrugs. "It is not against the rules for the champions to help one another."

Excellent. I take a deep breath and raise my voice. "Look for your god's or goddess's symbol on the bottom of an item."

There is a frenzied dash to check all the things around us. I really should have waited to give away the trick until after I found mine. I turn to do the same and collide with Hades' glare. He smolders at me, and I mean that in the truest sense of the word. I'm surprised flames aren't rising off his head. I shrug, and he looks to the heavens as if other gods might have an idea of how to deal with me.

Another champion disappears with their patron. Then another. And another gong clangs.

"Where is it?" I'm whispering to myself now, picking up and setting down item after item after—

"Lyra Keres."

I look up to come face-to-face with Ares, and I feel the blood drain from my cheeks. The god of war, with his deep-auburn hair, pallid skin, and shocking dark eye, looks battle ready in fearsome armor of black gold with a vulture across the breastplate, its wings outspread, mimicking the black metal wings that stretch out behind him. His helm also looks like wings and covers half his face, including the eye he lost during the Anaxian Wars. A wound given to him by Athena, or so the legends say.

In his hand, he holds a tiny bowl of obsidian glass. He tips it so that I can see the bident and scepter etched on the bottom. I hold out a shaking hand to receive it.

"In case you feel like being helpful to everyone again," he says in a voice that could make a mountain tremble in its wake, "remember this."

He hurls the bowl to the ground.

"No!" I shout and lunge for it.

But I miss, splaying out on the marble floor, hitting hard enough to knock the wind out of me as my token shatters into a thousand pieces.

"No, no, no, no…" I reach out in desperation to touch one of the glass shards, hoping it will be enough, but I don't disappear. I'm still crumpled at Ares' feet, and the realization of what I've just done to myself feels as if he took the spear strapped to his back and impaled me with it.

Before anyone can so much as move, a horrendous sound—one I imagine a grouchy dragon would make when awakened from slumber… actually, four of them—has me clapping my hands over my ears. I'm not the only one, either. The remaining champions do the same.

The Daemones, in a whirlwind of feathers and fury, grab Ares by the arms and fly him away.

"No!" Neve shouts.

The woman's red-gold hair is styled in pigtailed ringlets. Her green dress with a short, ruffly skirt that flounces every step she takes reminds me of a baby doll as she stalks toward me. "You dumb bitch!"

I scramble back. Only something behind me has her pulling up sharply. Her face loses color so fast, it looks like a vampire sucked her dry, her blue eyes and freckles standing out in stark relief.

"Ares interfered, and that *is* against the rules," Hades says from where he still stands across the platform.

He levers away from the wall to walk toward us. And that's when I see it. The way the champions hurriedly scatter away as he walks among them...and so do the gods and goddesses, though not as blatantly. As if he trails death in his very wake and they shouldn't get too close.

Is it always like that wherever he goes?

I shakily push to my feet by the time he gets to me.

He's still staring Neve down when he reaches us and tells her, "It was a mild infraction, and he'll get a commensurate punishment. It won't affect you. Get on with finding your token."

If daggers were glares, the one Ares' champion shoots me would've lodged in my heart. I cross her off my list of potential allies.

Before Hades can lay into me, I grab his arm. I don't know why. Maybe to give myself something solid to hold on to. His muscles tense under my touch, but that hardly penetrates the panic starting to set in as my own consequences hit me.

"I—I won't be able to—" I won't get my gifts now. I'll be the only champion going into the Crucible without magical aids.

If I thought I was in trouble before...

Hades shakes off my hand, and my heart sinks. He's done with me already, prepared to abandon me, and I curl over a bit on myself. But he takes me by the shoulders, face close to mine, and meets my eyes directly. "There is *never* only one way to win any Labor that is part of the Crucible."

My mind can't keep up with his words, and I frown. "What?"

He gives my shoulders a slight squeeze. "There's more than one way. Find it."

I didn't even find the first way. Zai did. All I did was pay attention.

I glance around at the champions all wildly searching now. Where do I even start?

He sighs. "Try to remember what I told you about this game at the beginning."

"That's enough." Zeus is the one to growl the words. "You're getting awfully close to interfering yourself, brother."

A muscle at the corner of Hades' lip twitches, but he lets me go and suddenly offers a smile so filled with charm that for a second even I am a little dazzled, like I can't quite catch my breath. Turns out the god of death has dimples.

"Of course," he says.

He walks away and leaves me here trying to remember what in Tartarus he said before.

Something about... Oh heavens, what was it about?

Get your shit together, Lyra.

Usually, the voice in my head is my own. But every so often, Felix pops in there, or memories of him when he mentored me.

I pick up and discard another dozen items in rapid succession, and when none zap me away, my shoulders sink. I hug a bright-green bowl against my chest as my eyes dart from item to item. I need a plan. There's not enough time left to pick through it all—nor is it likely any item remains that will transport me to the end.

I take a deep breath. Panic will get me nowhere. I need to think. What the hells had Hades said exactly? *This test is cryptic, but there will be signs.*

He meant something by that? Something more than just being an unhelpful ass?

Think, Lyra. What could he have been saying?

I single out the important words. Test. Cryptic. Signs.

My fingers are gripping the bowl so tightly, a rough edge rubs against my palm. I go to set it back down, but something niggles at me. Why would a god *ever* allow a blemish on one of their artifacts?

I run my fingers along the rough edge again and realize it *wasn't* a mistake... There are tiny, raised bumps just along one edge. *Crypticode!*

I don't dare glance in Hades' direction as I run my fingers against the lip of the smooth marble bowl.

Please let me be right.

"What in Olympus' name is she doing?" I think that's Athena's voice. I don't turn to see.

Closing my eyes, I feel along the system of bumps, which are formed into dots and dashes a lot like Morse code. That little bell keeps going off as more champions find their tokens.

But I stay focused, reading the code on the bowl. *Directions.*

The rules said if you *reach* your god or goddess, you win the gifts. And presumably the token was one way to reach them at the finish line, so to speak. But the rules didn't say you couldn't find a way to your patron *yourself.*

I quickly set the bowl down and pick up another object, feeling around until I find the same pattern of small bumps. Every item in here must have the same directions on it—directions that make the hope wither in my chest like the hydrangeas after Demeter got upset.

I look up the path that is almost entirely stairs that wind and climb the mountainside into the heart of Olympus, and my hopeful heart drops back to the soles of my feet to be trampled.

Fuck me.

The gong resounds. "Five minutes. Gods and goddesses, leave to wait for your champions at the appointed location."

I'll never make it in time.

Out of nowhere, Hades appears at my side. "Go."

I lift my chin and take a deep breath. I haven't spent all my life tooling around the steep hills of San Francisco for nothing.

I grab his arm for balance while I strip the fancy heels from my feet. Then I throw them to the ground and take off running up the stairs.

15

YOU BETTER WORK, BITCH

The stairs are steep and winding...and marble. Slick marble. In no time, my lungs and legs are burning hard, my breath so loud that I sound like the little engine that could struggling to chug up the mountain, and I keep slipping, too, which slows me down more.

Up ahead, a burst of movement catches my eye, but I'm busy watching the stairs to keep from tripping, so I don't see what. I round the corner and have to leap back as a massive head rushes me with sharp-tooth-filled jaws. A trumpeting roar of challenge ricochets off the mountains all around as a hydra rises up, blocking the stairs, its seven heads writhing and snapping at one another, three of them focused on me.

I can practically feel Apollo's chariot moving the sun through the sky faster. The time I have left to get to the top is ticking down. I can't fight a monster even if I had a weapon on me, which I don't.

The hydra stares at me, and I stare at it.

A silver butterfly flits behind one of the heads, and I gasp. The monster sways and snaps its jaws as it blocks my path, but it doesn't attack. I watch the butterfly flutter in circles behind the giant beast. Wait. No. I watch the butterfly...*through* the beast.

Is this an illusion? Like the food or the gargoyle?

What am I supposed to do? I'm out of time.

Heart hammering, I take a deep breath, lower my gaze to my feet, and *go*. I sprint right at the hydra and yelp when yellowing, jagged teeth surround me as I plow into what should be its open maw. But the second I make contact, it disappears in a wisp of smoke and the stairs are clear.

I stagger and catch my breath. I have no doubt Hades sent me the butterfly. I might just kiss that damn god of death when I get to him.

At that thought, I miss a step and almost go down but manage to keep my feet under me. I have to run through two more monster illusions on my way up—a cyclops and a griffin—but now I know to just barrel on through. They don't slow me a bit.

By now, I'm losing steam. I can't drag oxygen into my lungs fast enough. My legs feel like they're filled with thousands of little weighted balls as I clomp up the stairs on feet I can no longer feel.

I slow.

And slow.

And slow.

Until I am using the rail to drag myself up. Boone would do this better. Hells, any pledge but me.

I have to be close, don't I?

I wince. I can see the top now, at least, but my body won't get me there. Not in time.

"You call that trying?"

For a second, I think I've hallucinated Felix up ahead of me, until I force myself to focus and realize that Hades is standing at the top of the stairs. Is that far enough inside Olympus to count for this? If I get to him, do I win?

"I know you can do better than this, Lyra."

Asshole. This god put me here, and now he's going to taunt me? Hot anger churns in my chest and flares all the way to my toes, feeding a needed burst of adrenaline that zings through my muscles and clears my mind for a moment.

I force myself to move. To move faster than my body wants me to. To move faster than I should. And I pay for it. Every single nerve is screaming as if lit on fire. My vision starts to close in, darkness trying to consume the edges and narrowing my sight to a tunnel. But I fix that remaining pinpoint of sight on Hades and don't stop.

I don't even pause when a gong sounds and my heart drops. But it wasn't like my heart wasn't getting me up these stairs anyway. I've got nothing left in me but *sheer will.*

"Move!" he bellows. Like it matters to him if I make it.

And the gong goes off again. These must be ticking off seconds now, marking the end of my time. Taking the steps two at once, I run in rhythm with the chimes.

"Five," he yells.

He's counting down.

Shit.

"Four."

Keep going. I pump my sandbags for legs and pray I don't miss a step. If I slip now, it's all over.

"Three."

Almost there.

"Two."

It's going to be close.

I'm still a body length of steps away from him. I don't have a choice… I leap and fly through the air, and for the briefest moment I think I might actually get to the top safely, until gravity yanks me down and I belly flop on the stairs with a shock of pain splintering out from too many parts of me—all the parts that hit sharp corners.

And with the final toll, my hand lands on the well-polished black leather toe of Hades' shoe.

Did I make it? The ringing of the bell is still fading away, and I'm still on the stairs. Did I make—

A sucking feeling, like the time I got caught in a tide in the ocean, drags me away. And suddenly I'm lying not on stairs but on a flat, smooth, blessedly cold floor. I manage to push to my hands and knees, but I'm too exhausted to lift my head, and my vision is still fuzzy. My breath rasps harshly in and out, in and out, as if I'm still running the race.

A fire-and-flame rumble of a voice reaches me from far away. "I knew you had it in you."

I lift my head, smile at Hades…then vomit all over his fancy shoes.

16

WHY DO THESE THINGS HAPPEN TO ME?

If there's anything that should earn me punishment from a god, it's emptying the remains of my meager dinner all over his shoes. Which is why I flinch when he reaches down. Except he brushes my hair out of my face and holds it back while I catch my breath.

"You didn't like your shoes anyway," I grumble between gasps, then scoot away from his strangely comforting touch, and also away from the puddle, because gross.

"I'll give you this, Lyra Keres. You are unpredictable."

It would be really nice to take a moment to unravel that, but my stomach heaves again. This time, I manage to keep it in. Unfortunately, I'm a sympathetic vomiter. If I see it, hear it, or smell it, I make more of it.

"Here." A snap sounds above my head, and the vomit disappears. Not only that, but his hand comes into view holding a cup of ice water so cold the glass is already sweating.

If anyone is unexpected, I'd say it's him.

I take it and gratefully gulp the cool liquid down between quick breaths, sucking air into my still-starved lungs. I focus on that, on getting a handle on my bodily functions, until I can breathe enough to talk.

That's when I finally look up at him. "Thanks."

I hope he knows that I'm not just thanking him for being decent just now, but for the butterfly, and the crypticode, and making me mad enough to keep pushing, which I'm pretty sure is him breaking the interference rules and just not getting caught, unlike Ares. So I'm not going to say any of that out loud.

Hades crouches in front of me, hands loose, gaze searching. "I'm not someone you thank, Lyra. I'm someone you fear."

Like everyone scattering away from him every time he walks close? Does he really believe that? Or is he playing into a reputation that I'm starting to question just a little bit? If he's truly evil or unfeeling, he wouldn't have given me water. "Consider me shaking in my boots."

His lips hitch. "You're not wearing any shoes right now."

"I never would have made it with heels on." Images of snapped ankles and concussions dance through my head, and I give a delicate shudder.

"And the rest of your outfit?" he asks.

I glance down. I'm now only wearing the pantsuit—I ripped the beautiful jacket off somewhere along the way up. "It was getting in my way."

"I see…"

I take another swig of water.

"So…do you wish to receive your gifts or not? You certainly earned them."

Oh my gods. The entire reason I nearly killed myself getting up here in the first place. He holds out a hand, and after only a brief hesitation, I take it and let him help me to my feet. Which is when I finally bother to look around.

The room isn't what I'd expect. Not Grecian but instead maybe Victorian? The walls are red silk brocade with intricate black wainscoting at the base. Red velvet curtains hang over the door and windows. All the furniture—a table and chairs and a chaise longue—is black wood and red velvet. And the ceiling… A dragon carved of black wood curls around the base of the chandelier.

"Where exactly are we?"

"Still in Olympus." His voice has gone dry as dust in a drought. "This is a room in my house."

Really? "I thought you never stayed in Olympus."

"I don't."

I raise my eyebrows, still looking around. "I see. So they just, what… hold a place for you?"

"Something like that."

"You didn't choose the decor." I'm not asking.

His eyes squint ever so slightly. "This is all Addie's doing. Her tastes tend to be a bit over-the-top." Only now there's a subtle layer in his voice that sounds almost like affection. For Aphrodite? The goddess he warned me about.

I wrinkle my nose. "I guess she didn't get the memo about you abhorring expectations."

Hades chokes on a sound that might be a laugh. "I don't think I ever told her that." He looks away. "Besides, I don't spend time here, and it made her happy to do it."

My chest warms, but I push down all soft sentiment immediately. The last thing I want to do is think of Hades as anything more than what he is—the god of death who callously dragged me into this mess.

I shouldn't be thinking he can be sweet.

"Now." He straightens his shoulders. "Lyra Keres, I confer upon you two gifts to aid you in the Crucible."

"So formal. Can't we just do this quickly and be done?"

He considers me. "I could just not give you *any* gifts."

I give him a flat look. "You know, a gift isn't a gift if you have to earn it. We should call them prizes."

He sighs, expression descending to boredom. "Do you want your *gifts* or not?"

17

TO THE DUBIOUS VICTOR...

If I'm not careful, I'll have run up those stairs and vomited on his shoes for nothing. So I pin a sweet smile on my lips. "Of course I want my prizes."

"I thought so." Now he's back to being an ass. "The first gift chooses you."

"Are all the others doing this in their individual houses?"

Irritation at my interruption crosses his features, then fades. "Yes. If we don't know what gifts the others have given, it makes things more—"

"Challenging. I get it." I roll my eyes. "You gods truly do like to have your fun."

His gaze turns derisive, and his perfect lips curl. "Don't include me with them. I had nothing to do with the Anaxian Wars and nothing to do with their Crucible, either."

Which means his entering *this* time is deliberate and not just to punish me. Curiosity kicks in so hard, the rest of the room fades, my focus narrowing on him and him alone. "Then why now?"

Hades' face tightens, just for a heartbeat, before he smooths it back. But I caught it. He slipped, telling me that.

"Let's just say I have a different game to win."

I blink back at him. "And I'm your pawn?"

After a second, he shrugs, the action so uncaring, so callously casual.

I blow out a long breath, trying very hard not to lose my cool and knee the god of death in the balls. The more I'm around him, the more I forget who and what he is. That's a dangerous thing to forget. "How about we get on with the prizes?"

"Watch it," he warns, and I think maybe the fires in the braziers in the corners curl toward me a little. "You amuse me...for now."

In other words, I'm not reaping consequences as long as I *keep* amusing him.

I'm too tired to deal with this, so I do what I do with Felix when he throws his weight around. Lowering my gaze timidly like a dutiful little mortal, I clasp my hands in front of me and wait.

A heavy sigh reaches me.

"You're a menace," Hades mutters, then takes off his suit jacket. He rolls up his sleeves like he could only stand being confined by those clothes for so long.

I glance away. *Forearms aren't sexy. They are just body parts.*

"Here." He takes my right hand in his, clasping them palm to palm, then closes his eyes and whispers a few words I don't catch. Almost immediately, he jerks his gaze down to our hands.

No, not to our hands. To his arm.

As if he'd roused sleeping spirits, lines appear in the wake of his touch, and I stare as tattoos that weren't there a second ago materialize on his skin. Not tattoos, though—not black lines of ink. These are colorful and glittering, and each set of simple lines forms a different animal—a blue owl, a green panther, a purple fox, a red tarantula, and...a tiny, adorable silver butterfly.

As if they are alive, they move across his skin, the tarantula greeting the butterfly with what seems like a little wave of one of its legs, the owl flapping its wings at the snarling panther. I can't look away, fascination holding me in thrall.

The owl in particular looks at Hades in question. Asking permission, I think?

"It's okay. Go to your new mistress and help her," Hades commands.

The tarantula, closest to our clasped hands, is the first to move, scuttling across his skin and onto mine, and I gasp at the sensation of tiny bubbles as it finds a new home on my wrist. Then the fox slinks forward, its tail the last thing to disappear around Hades' palm before it sits on my arm and wraps that tail around its paws, cocking its head in curiosity. The other animals follow, picking their places on my skin and blinking up at me.

All except the butterfly.

"You too," he says. But she stays in place, wings slowly flapping.

"Looks like I'm not the only one who doesn't listen to you," I whisper. His gaze snaps up to my face, but I don't meet it.

"It's fine," I tell the loyal little creature. "You can stay with him."

"You promised to obey me, Lyra."

I raise my eyebrows, then offer my most pleasant smile. "Did I?" I never really agreed.

Hades releases my hand, the warmth from his rough palm against mine seeps away…and the absence feels like a loss.

Get a grip.

"You're lucky," he says finally. "They haven't left my arm for someone else since my mother gave them to me."

His mother? The Titaness Rhea? A being he and his brothers fought and caged in Tartarus with all the other Titans. These are from *her*? I stare at them.

"Draw your finger from your elbow to your wrist," Hades tells me.

When I do, the animals disappear, closing their eyes and lying down as they sink into my skin and fade away.

"Wow," I whisper.

"Now, when you awaken them, they will listen to you."

I raise my gaze to his. "To do what?"

"Whatever you need. They can bring you items. Or you can send them to find information—scout out the best route, overhear conversations, spy on other champions." His lips tilt. "Maybe on the gods, if you're careful."

Sounds like a good way to land myself another curse.

"You don't have to send them all at the same time," he says. "Just like the animals they represent, each has different talents you can use."

I look back down at my skin, which is now blank as if they were never there. As if they're not sleeping under the surface.

Hades clears his throat. "You are also allowed a gift from me personally…"

He pauses.

Long enough that it hits me. The god of death is…hesitating.

His gaze drops lower. "I offer you a kiss."

By now I should stop being shocked, especially by Hades, but the impact of that word reverberates like a tuning fork striking metal. It shivers through me all the way to my core, where a new sensation stirs. An uneasy sensation.

A *haunting* sensation.

I've never been kissed. I shouldn't want it. Should I? Or is this just curiosity?

He steps into me, forcing me to tip my head up. "This kiss will mark you as mine."

In the less than twenty-four hours I've known him, I've felt a thousand different emotions when it comes to this god—fear, hate, irritation, envy, frustration, grudging gratefulness. Most of those feelings run along the lines of anger, the burn of it rising and falling with each passing event.

I didn't deserve this. Any of it.

So no one is more surprised than me when the word "mine," uttered in that silky voice with his mercurial gaze intent on my face, stirs in my belly a quivering, like his precious butterflies are all trapped inside me.

No. Definitely no. Horrifyingly no. A very hard no. I am not getting fluttery over any god or goddess, but especially not this one.

With a tiny step backward, I frown at him. "What kind of gift is that?"

He looks right back at me. "This mark will give you safe passage through the Underworld so that you may return to the Overworld and not get trapped down there."

"Oh."

I don't move back when he takes another step closer. That's a gift worth receiving, even if it involves a kiss.

Hades takes one more step, and his unique bitter-chocolate scent wraps around me. He uses a gentle finger under my chin to tilt my face up to his, then leans down slowly. Only instead of a brotherly kiss somewhere neutral, his lips hover over mine, almost touching.

His breath is warm against my flesh before I realize what he's doing, and I make a tiny sound in my throat.

Immediately, he freezes, gaze lifting to meet mine, though he doesn't move away. "Problem?"

"Can't you just kiss my forehead or cheek?" Gods, I sound like a petrified virgin. Which I am, but no need to *sound* like it.

After a second, he slowly shakes his head. "It doesn't work that way. Do you want a different gift?"

No. This is a gift no one should knock back. Worse, I shouldn't want to kiss him, but that curiosity thing has me firmly in its clawed grip. It's not like I'm risking my heart.

It's just a kiss, Lyra.

Decision made, I close my eyes and tilt my face toward his like a sunflower following Apollo. "Go ahead."

He doesn't move for so long that I almost open my eyes again, but then his lips touch mine.

Softly at first, but that's not the surprising part. It's that he doesn't simply kiss me and then be done with it. Instead he brushes, then brushes again before pressing his lips to mine more firmly. He only lightly touches my chin with his fingers and my lips with his, but his warmth seeps into me...everywhere.

His lips gently part mine, shaping, teasing, becoming more demanding, and I don't pull away. I'm too caught up in the *everything* of it. My head spins, and I don't know which way is up, down, or sideways. I open under his touch and lean into him, and he doesn't hesitate, the kiss taking on a heat and a life of its own as he plunders and owns and takes even as he gives.

And I don't want to stop.

Because the god of death's kisses are...delicious.

A craving stirs for more as his chocolate scent swirls around me, blending with the taste of him.

He makes a sound deep in his throat, then his kisses change again, turning hungry, hot, and menacing, like the predator I know he is, but it's too late for me. Too late in so many ways. I'm lost in my response to him. Matching him kiss for kiss in heat and heady, intoxicating peril. Exposed and undeniably vulnerable and yet powerful in my own right because he groans.

Hades *groans*.

With no other warning, his power releases through that touch. It snaps through me in a wildfire of sensation, searing every single tiny nerve, every inch, spreading outward from my lips. His magic consumes me like a blaze as it sinks into and under my skin to lie there in wait like his tattoos.

Marking me as his.

An involuntary tremble takes hold of me. In its wake—as the blaze cools and the magic settles—comes the cold snap of reality, of where we are, of the only reason he's kissing me. And I go as still as a corpse under his touch. Hades must sense the change in me, because, though he still holds my chin with his thumb and forefinger, I feel him pull back slightly.

I blink my eyes open to stare wordlessly up at him, holding my breath—because what could I possibly say in this moment?

"I wondered…" he whispers, more to himself than me. Those silver eyes spark almost like they're touched with starlight, and for the wildest second, I think maybe he's as shaken as I am.

But then he offers me a knowing smirk.

Damned if I'm going to stand here and awkwardly avert my gaze like a girl who just had her first kiss. Instead, I scowl and say the first thing that comes to mind. "Of course the god of death kisses like a demon."

18

BACK WHERE I WAS

A new chime of bells has me looking away, breaking Hades' gaze and his hold on my chin.

All he says is, "That bell is the signal to rejoin the others."

After unrolling his sleeves and putting his jacket back on, Hades turns and, in a formal gesture I've only ever seen in movies set in bygone eras, offers me his elbow.

That's it? Kiss me until I'm hazy and hot, and then back to business?

I frown, and he nods at his proffered elbow. As soon as I place my hand on his sleeve, we disappear, only to reappear on the platform, which is now clear of both the food and all the items.

The other gods are waiting. And glaring again.

Zeus snorts. "For the first time in over two millennia of the Crucible, all the champions have received their gifts."

He shoots me a look. Is it my imagination, or did lightning spark in his eyes?

I don't realize I'm curling my fingers into Hades' arm until he puts his other hand over mine. I force my muscles to relax.

"What happened to her shoes?" Hera asks, looking me up and down.

"Her shoes?" Aphrodite's chuckle alone is like audible sin. "What happened to her top?" Then she *tsk*s. "Sleeping with champions isn't prohibited, of course, but already, Hades? That was fast."

Her teasing reminds me so much of Boone. Experience tells me that instead of spluttering, blushing, and denying, it's better to say nothing and look bored. Which I do.

Hades trails a finger lightly over my knuckles in a seductive touch. "It won't be *here*, and it won't be hurried." He looks at both of his brothers.

"And I won't have to transform into an animal to convince her."

Oh. My. Gods.

Heat creeps up my neck. Couldn't he have just not said anything, either? How hard would that have been?

An odd crackling electricity fills the air, soft but there, and I think Zeus might be about to lose his shit. Until Hera slips her hand into his. "Let it go," she urges softly. "You know he lives to taunt you."

After a second, Zeus' shoulders relax. Then he steps forward so that all eyes turn to him. He's back in charge. "You will live here in Olympus with your patron when not playing in one of the Labors."

More than one of the other champions winces or pales or gulps. I, however, am nearing full-on panic. *Live*…with Hades. With *Hades*.

Zeus is oblivious to our reactions. "We hope you will enjoy your time here in Olympus. Your first official Labor begins tomorrow."

Can't wait.

Before I accidentally slip and say that out loud, my vision blinks out once more. Like when we came to Olympus, the journey is completed in darkness with no sense of sound or feeling beyond the arm under my hand, and no pressure or movement, either.

When my vision returns in an abrupt *swish*, it's to find myself in… Wait. Where am I? I scan the sunken living area of a massive apartment. Is this…where I think it is? The view out the floor-to-ceiling windows confirms it—I'm somewhere in San Francisco.

"Is this your penthouse?"

"Yes." His breath ruffles my hair.

"I thought the champions have to live on Olympus until the Crucible ends."

"And you are. We're only visiting, and this is still my territory. There's a difference."

I'm beginning to sense that Hades likes to see just how far rules will bend for him.

I step away, focusing on the room rather than him.

None of the decoration is Grecian—not even a hint of it. I guess I should expect that from Hades. The wealthy in this city are usually blessed by Zeus because they pander to his colossal ego, which includes leaning into all things ancient Greece. Instead, the room boasts a mix of items of various cultures and time periods scattered among the chromes and black leathers of modern furniture.

And not a single photograph or personal item. I know cameras are a more recent invention and this guy is *old*, but still, no painted family portraits or mementos of any kind.

"Tell me more about your curse," he says.

I back up a bit. "I assumed you knew or could see...I don't know...a mark or something."

"No."

"Zeus didn't tell you?"

"There's not a chat room for the gods where we share our daily cursings."

I frown. "You curse mortals on a daily basis?"

"No. And since he didn't say anything today..." Hades crosses his arms. "I'm guessing he forgot."

So easy for them to ruin someone's entire life and not even bother to remember. "I already figured that."

Though nothing alters in his demeanor, I get the impression Hades is...satisfied, maybe? Smug? About what, I'm not sure.

"So the curse is you can't be loved?"

I nod. "It means no one will want to work with me to get through the Labors. Not in a mean way. Just in a vague, they-keep-their-distance kind of way. No one really forms an attachment to me or cares if I live or die, I guess. And with the Labors in particular, there's the added incentive of you."

He shoots me a flat look.

"You could send me back—"

"It's too late. When the Daemones asked if anyone wanted to decline, that was your last chance. The Crucible is a binding magical contract between the gods who enter, confirming they will finish, and, after the champions agree to participate, they're included in that contract."

"Is that the immortal version of 'read the fine fucking print'?" My voice rises to a squeak, and I clear my throat. "That really needed to be explained better."

"It wouldn't have made a difference. You were my only choice."

He leaves me standing in the middle of the sunken living room as he walks to the foyer. He points down the hall. "Your room is that way. Third door on the right. There is an en suite bathroom." Then he stalks away, shutting the door at the end of the hallway behind him.

I stand in the foyer, staring after him, a little more than dazed. Then I tip my head back, only to blink at the ceiling, which could have been painted by Michelangelo himself—a frieze depicting the Underworld and all its levels.

Where I'm going to end up sooner rather than later if I'm not careful.

"I don't need the reminder," I mutter to the universe in general. "I already know I'm fucked."

19

LOOPHOLES

I don't know what I was expecting, but the room Hades pointed me toward is distinctly feminine, mostly in creams set against antique wood furniture with pops of lavender in the form of blankets and artwork. Through the wide-open door to the bathroom, I spy a massive claw-foot tub and actually sigh out loud.

The Order's den only has a few communal bathrooms shared by all of us with single-stall showers so narrow, I bump my elbows against the walls when I wash my hair or shave my legs, and they regularly have no hot water.

This is luxury. My reward for surviving a shitty day.

I toss the tiara on the bed, strip off the clothes that were never mine to begin with, and within minutes, I'm soaking in beautiful bliss. Heaven.

My muscles, already turning sore from my sprint up the stairs in Olympus, release in the hot water like they are sighing, too. Under the bubbles scented with jasmine and vanilla, I trace the bruises cropping up in interesting purple stripes from my belly flop on those stairs.

"I'm lucky I didn't break something." I drop my head back against the rim of the tub.

Being banged up isn't a whole lot better. The first official Labor is tomorrow, and I'm going in damaged while the other champions are in perfect health. Terrific.

What did I ever do to the Fates, anyway?

Eventually, the water cools, and I force myself to get out of the tub. I pause in the doorway at the sight of lavender pajamas—modest, with long pants and a short-sleeve shirt and even a bralette and underwear— folded and waiting neatly on the bed. The other clothes are gone, but the tiara is still there.

I shake my head. "Hades is a good host. Who knew?"

It isn't until I'm dressed and pulling back the covers that I finally take a good look at the tiara as I pick it up to move it off the bed. I go marble statue–still, staring at the thing.

"It can't be…"

Black gold, it is designed to look like butterfly wings spreading from a black jeweled center. The wings are dotted with black diamonds and pearls. And that's what I'm staring at.

Because the black pearls with their hint of pink are familiar. Too familiar.

I count, then count again.

That's what I was afraid of. There are exactly six.

I execute an about-face a soldier would admire and march out of my bedroom and through the penthouse. I stop in the middle of the living room, not sure where to go. The sound of a blender, of all things, whirs from off to my left, and I follow it to find Hades in the kitchen. His hair is damp from a shower, that errant pale lock curling on his forehead instead of brushed back. He's changed into jeans and a faded blue T-shirt that's seen better days that reads, "Sure, you can pet my dog."

If I wasn't still thrown by the tiara, I'd laugh because his dog is Cerberus, the three-headed hellhound who notoriously doesn't like anyone.

Also, Hades is barefoot.

I mean, so am I, but he's a god. I have never, in my entire life, pictured gods or goddesses barefoot. In a kitchen, no less.

He glances up. "Smoothie?"

What alternate dimension have I fallen into? I shake my head.

"Help yourself to any food in the fridge, then." He waves a hand.

Just like we're regular people. Sharing a space like it's no big deal. But it is. It's a big deal to me. I'm not entirely sure how to handle this Hades, who is suddenly all solicitous courtesy, which feels wrong coming from him, like wearing clothes that are a size too small. "Don't do that."

He frowns. "Do what?"

"The polite-charm thing."

"It's how I put others at ease," he says.

The god of death tries to put others at ease? There's a disturbing thought. "Are you sure that actually works?"

"I was until now," he mutters.

We're getting off topic. I jerk my hand up to show him the tiara. "Tell me these pearls aren't what I think they are."

He glances at the tiara, then goes back to making his smoothie. "They are."

"Why would you—" I stop, then start again. "What possible reason could you—"

"They might help you." He says this as casually as if he's listing off the foods in the fridge.

I lower the tiara to my side. "You already gave me my two gifts. You're not allowed to give more."

"I gave you the tiara before the Daemones said I could no longer help you, and it's not a gift. It's clothing."

That's a flimsy loophole if I've ever heard one, and thieves are good at loopholes.

I frown. "So the pearls can help me?"

"Yes."

"How?"

"If I don't tell you, then it's definitely not a gift. Just a mystery you figured out on your own."

I stare at him, something finally sinking in with me that should have much sooner. "You know *all* the loopholes. Don't you?"

His eyes crinkle at the corners, though his lips don't lift. "I decline to answer on the grounds that my words might incriminate me." Then he turns the blender on, filling the kitchen with noise.

In other words, he does.

I drop onto a stool at the large island, across from where he's standing. "But...these are Persephone's," I point out the second the blender stops.

He doesn't react to her name like I semi-expect—get all scowly, broody, *don't say her name or else*, and so forth. Instead, he shrugs. "They can't help her now."

Help her? Legend says he used them to trap her in the Underworld with him, not *help* her. Right? A thousand questions circle in my head like dogs chasing their tails. But I don't utter a single one. For once. It's none of my business.

"They are yours now," he says.

Mine. My pearls that do something that used to help Persephone.

What did the stories say about hers? I mean, to start with, they were pomegranate seeds. "Do I eat them?"

His eyebrows lift slowly in…is that *reluctantly impressed* from the god of death? "I can't tell you," he says.

So, yes, I eat them.

"I thought only four were left."

He shakes his head. "Mortals always get details wrong."

No surprise there.

I try to think. "Persephone's pomegranate seeds kept her in the Underworld." I'm talking to myself now, turning the tiara this way and that. "Or…maybe they took her there? And I'm protected in the Underworld." That has to be it?

I glance directly into silver-bright eyes studying me in a manner that makes me want to look away. He's too intense. Too…him.

"Am I close?" I ask.

"You're definitely quick, but you'll have to wait and find out."

I battle back the warmth of a blush. "Why do I need protection?"

He shrugs. "You seem to gravitate toward danger." His pause hangs in the air.

Jackass.

But I know I'm close, at least. A way to escape a Labor? Or to protect myself when we're in Olympus. Does it matter? Twelve Labors, though, and only six seeds. I'd better save these puppies for near-death experiences.

He finishes making his smoothie and carries it into the living room, where he turns on the TV. "Here," he says. "You should study your competitors."

I follow him and realize he's turned on the news coverage of the opening ceremonies. Already the mortal newscasters are discussing and showing clips of the worldwide festivities, the gods, and, of course, their champions, whose stats they are starting to list as they question who we are and why we were chosen.

My face flashes up on the screen—an image of me with a mulish scowl standing at Hades' side in the temple.

"They haven't found anything on you yet beyond your pledge name," he says, sounding satisfied.

They won't. My existence was erased when the Order took me in, and

THE GAMES GODS PLAY

they are very good at what they do.

"Lyra Keres is a mystery," the commentator says, "but I think the bigger mystery is why Hades has joined this Crucible."

I'm staring at the screen, and the words just sort of fall out. "Why me?"

He turns the sound down. "I picked you because when we met, despite being afraid, you didn't back down or cower, even from a god." He rests his head back against the couch cushion as if he's suddenly weary. "Especially from the god of death."

I've seen the way others cower and avoid him. Even the gods, whose fear-filled gazes glaze with a curious kind of desire. I know what he must feel. Not the being-feared part, but being isolated even in a crowd.

Still, did he seriously pick me because he thought I might actually have a chance? Not to punish me, but because he liked my...what? Sass?

A sharp laugh bursts from me. There's probably an edge of agitation to it, but I don't really care. "Felix always said my big mouth would get me in big trouble someday."

"Felix?" he asks.

"My boss in the Order."

"I see." His gaze settles on me in a way that makes me want to shift my weight on my feet.

I'm not entirely sure I believe him about his reason for picking me as his champion, but it's something, I guess. But the fact that he wanted someone who wouldn't back down from gods is concerning.

"You're sure you can remove my curse if I win?" I ask.

He nods.

I think about that. I've never let myself picture a future without it. If I'm honest, I've never let myself picture a future beyond my next meal, really. Not because I worried I'd die at any moment—our lives in the Order weren't that precarious. There just wasn't any reason to dwell on what could never be.

I settle onto the other end of the couch and tuck my feet under my legs. "What kind of games?"

"What?"

"The games I am oh so honored to play on your behalf. What are we talking about here? I'm guessing a rousing round of Tiddlywinks is unlikely."

ABIGAIL OWEN

"Each contest is planned well in advance, lodged with the Daemones, and can't be changed after the Labors start. And the nature of each isn't revealed until that god or goddess's turn."

Why did that feel like a cagey answer? "What about in the past? What were those like?"

He doesn't answer right away, like he's considering how much to tell me. "They vary."

Vague. "Give me broad strokes, then."

"I admit I haven't paid close attention in the past."

What? "Then why..." Forget it. He's already answered that equally vaguely. "I'm a planner. I'll do better if I know what to expect."

"They will likely be themed around the god or goddess's virtue and their particular powers."

Which reminds me... "What virtue will I be associated with?"

Hades cocks one brow at me. "Do you find me virtuous, then?"

Okay, I *guess* that answers that question.

"What else?" I ask.

He thinks for a minute. "Some will be things like solving puzzles."

Hmmm...puzzles...depends on the kind, but okay.

"I've seen some that are like solving a mystery or rescuing an innocent in peril."

Cool. Cool. Cool. So far, not so bad.

"A few obstacle courses."

I wasn't the best at that during training, but I wasn't the worst, either.

"And some will be like the labors," he tacks on.

So I was right about that? "Like fighting hydras and holding up the world for Atlas. Catching a giant boar. *Those* kinds of labors?" My voice rises as I talk. I'm doing a lot of that today.

He shrugs.

"Gods don't die," I point out, anger creeping into my voice, "and demigods are hard to kill."

"What's your point?"

The anger bubbles hotter, spiking my blood. "Mortals can't respawn or use another life or just restart the damned game." I pick up a pillow off the couch and hurl it at him.

It hits him right in the face before dropping to the floor. He stares at it like he's never seen a pillow before, then slowly lifts his gaze to mine.

I'm expecting smoldering fury, but he only looks confounded.

It's probably been never since anyone pitched a pillow at Hades. "You're an ass, just like the rest of them."

His eyebrows lift, and then his expression and voice soften ever so slightly. "You'll be fine, Lyra. I will stay by your side through it all."

He's not allowed to interfere, which means I'll be guaranteed an audience at my death. Splendid.

"You're unbelievable." I snarl the words.

His smile turns teasing. "You finally noticed?"

Oh. My. Gods. I'm going to kill him if I don't leave now.

Taking my tiara with me, I cross the living room in the direction of my bedroom, muttering every colorful expletive I learned in the Order along the way.

I'm halfway there when I hear a sinfully amused chuckle. Of course Hades could laugh in the face of certain death. Too bad it's *my* looming demise he finds so humorous.

20

WHAT ARE YOU DOING HERE?

Pledges are taught to sleep with one eye open.

Not literally. But we do sleep lightly—one of the first and longest lessons, which takes years of being interrupted and surprised at all hours until we develop reflexes that alert us to every possible threat. As for me, I also guard all incoming loot, since I don't have a roommate and there's extra space, so it's a habit I had no choice but to continue to practice.

Not that I'm getting much rest, given what happens tomorrow, but when I suddenly wake in the dead of night, I don't question it.

Something's wrong.

I don't open my eyes. I don't want whoever is in this room with me to know I'm wise to them. Pretending to roll over in my sleep, my back to the door, I wait, every sense tuned to the slightest change.

I really wish I had a weapon on me.

My tension reaches screaming pitch, and that's when a hand clamps down on my mouth. I immediately start thrashing, but an arm squeezes around me and twists me so I'm face-to-face with them.

Which is when I recognize a certain thin, white scar at the corner of his mouth. I jerk my gaze up to find Boone Runar staring back at me with dark eyes.

"Damn it, Lyra," he whispers. "Calm down or you'll wake him."

"Damn it yourself, Boone," I whisper back as I push to sitting. "You scared me. What are you doing here?"

He stares at me from where he's now crouched beside my bed. "Me?" He shakes his head. "What about you? Hades, Lyra? Seriously? The god has a three-headed demon dog as a damned *pet*."

"Really? Because I thought he was the god of sweetness and light," I grumble.

Boone glares. "What, exactly, did you get yourself into?"

"A fuck-ton of trouble. How did you know I was here?"

"The lights are on in Hades' only Overworld home," he says dryly. "The entire world knows." And Boone's a master thief for a reason, even in a building that's off-limits. For very good reason, it turns out.

"Fine." Having this argument with him while I'm sitting up in bed in silky PJs is ridiculous. "Regardless, you shouldn't be here. Why are you, anyway?"

He sobers at that. "To help, if I can."

I rear back as disbelief ricochets through me. Twelve years, we've known each other—ever since he came to our den when I was eleven. Counting earlier today, this is the second time he's wanted to help me. Ever.

He has no idea what I'll be doing. How's he going to help?

Boone drops onto the other side of the bed and whisper-groans. "Oh, wow. This is amazing."

The mattresses in the den aren't exactly comfy. "Functional" is a kind word for what they are.

He thumps a duffel bag on the bed, not between us but in front of him. Then he proceeds to open it and pull out various items. The first few are clothes.

"You touched my things?" The hairs on the back of my neck prickle. "How'd you get into my room?"

"Felix," he says.

Swallowing my questions, I watch as he keeps pulling my clothes out of the bag. He probably emptied my drawers. I can't decide if I'm more embarrassed that he dug through my stuff or about to float away on a happy cloud. Because he's here. For me.

My logical brain takes over, tamping down on the giddiness. At least I don't have to rely on the gods' dubious sense of appropriate fashion.

Next, he pulls out...

"A tactical vest?"

"I didn't know what you'd be doing. I brought anything I could think of." He shrugs. "I figured you could at least wear this, even under your clothes if you have to, and stash a weapon or two in it for self-defense."

My eyes sting, and I blink rapidly as I tentatively take it from his grasp. "Um…okay."

"I've already prepped it with some things."

I raise my eyebrows at him, then start rummaging through the zippered pockets and pouches to find tools common to our trade are tucked neatly away—wire twine, wire cutters, bolt cutters, a small screwdriver with several interchangeable heads, and even a small torch for cutting metal.

The thing is, I don't know what I'm facing, either, but given the little Hades described, a thief's tools might come in handy. They certainly can't hurt.

I get to the last pocket, a deep, vinyl-lined one on the back, but this time I drop what I pull out to the bed on a gasp. I stare at the gleaming gold-and-silver weapon lying there.

My relic.

21

THIS IS REAL

Every pledge who graduates to master thief magically receives a relic. We believe the gifts are from Hermes for use in our trade. It is the only thing of significant value that we never have to steal or surrender to pad the Order's pockets.

However, as a clerk, I didn't technically graduate. There was no ceremony. No relic should have come to me.

But this axe showed up on my bed one day.

Silver with golden markings, it has a gold handle, the end wrapped in turquoise leather. A circle with a symbol of Zeus' head stamped on it divides the larger blade from a smaller one on the backside that's shaped more like a tip of a spear.

I assumed one of the other pledges was playing a mean trick, trying to get me caught with a relic that wasn't mine, but every time I returned it to the coffers, it magically returned to me. No one—I mean absolutely no one—knows I have it.

"What is that?" I try to play naive. The relic looks like an ordinary handle to a weapon or tool, if only the handle remained, and I turn it this way and that as though trying to figure out what it is.

Boone rolls his eyes. "I've known about this for the past few years," he says.

And never turned me in to Felix? I eye him sideways. "How?"

"I saw you practicing in the weapons range one night when I was late returning from a score gone sideways," he says.

Oh.

Well...

Blast and brimstone.

I swallow.

Boone isn't done, though.

Next, he pulls out a lockpicking kit. Not one of the cheap, larger, unwieldier ones the Order provides, though. This is Boone's personal kit that he paid for himself, having to work off his own family's debts for longer to buy it. It's smaller. I'll be able to slip it into the biggest pocket on the back of my tactical vest.

But... I shake my head. This is worth a lot to him. "I can't."

"You can," he insists. "I'll just use one of the Order's until you get back."

I stare at him. "I might not come back."

His lips go crooked, but he doesn't say anything before he digs back into the duffel bag. "And then there's these."

He holds out a drawstring leather pouch that rattles a little, something inside clacking. Curiosity always was a failing of mine. When I don't immediately reach for it, he bounces it on his palm. "Come on, Lyra-Loo-Hoo. You know you want to."

I pluck it from his grasp, then pour what's inside into my hand and stare.

Teeth?

"Um..." I look at Boone. "Gross?"

"My relic," he says, as if that's not a big deal.

I almost drop them right there, and they clatter in my hand a bit. "Hells, Boone. You can't give these to me."

"They're *my* relic. I can do what I want with them." He shrugs. "They haven't been useful to me as a thief anyway, so..."

I still don't want to take them. "What are they?"

"Dragon teeth."

The teeth are stark white, tan at the roots, and they come in so many different shapes, all of which remind me of ancient weapons. Single long, curved swords. Tiny, straight daggers. Three-pronged caltrops. And hammer-like molars made to crush instead of rend. "They're so..."

"Impressive?"

"Small."

I glance up to find his shoulders silently shaking. "They've been enchanted to be carried more easily, but they will still work fine. You plant them in the ground—any ground—and within minutes they will grow into bone soldiers that cannot be killed and who will obey your commands. Use them wisely."

"What, exactly, do you think I'll be doing?" I ask cautiously. It's almost like he has an idea, but I'm well aware that's not possible.

"Who knows?" he says. "If you use them, great. If not, I'll take them when you get back."

He has no idea that of all the things he brought me tonight, if I'm going against monsters at some point, these teeth might come in the handiest. Even so, I can't take his relic. "These...have to be worth a small fortune. Even if you don't use them, you could sell them and finish paying off your debts ten times over, probably."

He shrugs. "I received my Deed of Fulfillment two years ago."

I go still, staring at him with wide eyes. Two years? "So you want to stay in the Order?" I ask slowly. "Become a boss?"

"I have reasons for hanging around."

I don't ask. He doesn't say.

"Still...these could set you up when you go legit." I hold them out. "You shouldn't give them to me. Everything else is more than enough."

He lets me pour them into his palm, then takes the leather pouch and drops them in with little clicks of bone on bone...and holds the pouch out to me.

I have no clue what to do with this Boone. Yes, he's always been nice to me, but in an oblivious, we-work-together sort of way, layered with the flirty way he is with everyone. Maybe even in a pity sort of way. But self-sacrificing friendship? No.

For the second time in two nights, tears mist my eyes, and I blink at the sting.

"If you don't take them, I'll just throw them away," he says.

Knowing him, he means it, too. I huff. "Stubborn to the bitter end."

Boone winks. "Says the pot."

I grumble some more, but I snatch the bag from his hand. "How long will they last?"

"Until whatever you need them for is over. One use only."

"Got it." I set the pouch on the bedside table and look at him expectantly.

Only instead of leaving or whatever else he thinks he needs to do, he remains still as an awkward silence fills the room.

"You were always fascinated by dragons," I say to break the silence. "Always reading about them. I guess now I know why."

He glances away, and I realize that we aren't close enough for me to know that. I'm giving myself away a bit, except he already knows about my feelings from Chance.

Boone gets up off the bed, and I'm not sure why, but I get up, too, and walk him to the door of the bedroom.

"I'll check if it's all clear," I tell him.

It feels like the world flipped upside down and started spinning backward—him in my room, the risk he took to help me tonight.

I reach for the doorknob, but he gets there first, stopping me. "Something else?" I ask.

He searches my gaze, but differently now, like he's trying to find a secret in my eyes. He hitches his chin as if he's silently laughing to himself. Or maybe *at* himself, because his expression is solemn.

"You've always thought I hated you. That we all did," he says.

"I…" Someone put me out of my misery. "Not hated…exactly."

"I know I'm right. Don't bother denying it."

I slowly close my mouth, and he nods, again to himself. He turns the knob and sticks his head into the hall, taking a good look, then pulls back inside. "For the record, we didn't hate you."

I twist my lips around the tears clogging my throat and around the words that would tell him why I already know that. The thing I figured out a long time ago about my curse is that it doesn't make people hate me, it just makes them…not *choose* me.

But not after the Crucible. Not if I win.

And it hits me for the first time that maybe with the curse lifted I have a shot with Boone. It's strange that I didn't think of it before. Then again, I was dealing with some shit.

"See you in a month," he says and offers me that signature cocky pirate grin before slipping away.

I close the door and lean against it, my head dropping back with a soft *thump*.

"Fuck," I mutter.

Boone coming here cleared the fog of denial I've existed in since the moment Hades called my name. Or maybe it's the fact that he was concerned enough to bring me all these things that finally has me thinking straighter.

Either way, the truth I've been avoiding until right this second is now crystal clear, flashing in neon lights in front of my face. Inescapable.

There's no way I can get out of playing in the Crucible.

I'm really going to have to do this.

And now I have a stake in the game.

22

THERE IS NOTHING NORMAL ABOUT THIS

I feel more than see Hades walk into the kitchen the next morning, and I know he's staring based on the way the back of my neck prickles. A long, drawn-out study. Just as my stomach starts to clench, he speaks. "What, exactly, are you wearing?"

It turns out Hades' voice is growly in the mornings, and a little bit grumpy. And the fact that the terror-inducing god is not a morning person is…kind of cute. There's no stopping the shiver that whispers over my skin. I chalk that up to the fact that I barely slept last night, and now exhaustion is dragging at me like extra gravity.

I glance down at myself, then go back to the eggs I'm scrambling. "The uniform I was provided."

The two-piece athletic set of movable, breathable material showed up in my room at the butt-crack of dawn. Simple pants and a long-sleeve shirt with a mock collar—sports clothes. I'm trying very, very hard to pretend it's for comfort and not for running for my life.

Hades' name is stamped across the front in yellow block lettering, looking cheaply made and a little bit like a prison-issued jumpsuit. It is gray, like an ugly gray that makes my skin look sallow. Gray is also *not* one of the four colors that went with the virtues we're supposed to be divided into.

"Is mine this color because you have no virtue?" The question pops out before I can filter for a god's ego. I realized late last night he'd never really answered my earlier question.

"Was that supposed to be funny?"

A little bit. I shrug.

I can hear his confident steps before he comes into my field of view, standing next to me at the counter in a pair of low-slung jeans and a light-blue T-shirt. "I value something different than the others."

Having a curious nature really sucks sometimes. "What?"

"Survival."

Oh.

Something else we have in common, only a different kind of surprise has my eyebrows winging up. "You're a god. Immortal. Survival seems built in."

"Surviving isn't just not dying." His voice roughens.

If anyone can relate to that, it's me. "You're right. It's not."

"Anyway…" he continues and waves at my clothing. "Not this." His voice takes on a smoother edge that I'm starting to identify as irritation.

I'm not sure why *he's* annoyed about what I'm wearing. I'm the one wearing it. Sure, it's not the height of athleisurewear, but so what? "Do I need to look good to try to not die?"

"Last night, you were all about blending in. I promise this won't blend in." He crosses his arms. "It's also a deliberate affront to me. Making my champion look *less than*."

"'Less than'?" I snort. "Again…I'll be in a contest that might require running and hopefully not screaming." Seriously, who gives a shit? "These are fine. Actually, I appreciate that the style didn't run along the lines of the insulting, absurd image I find most people love to indulge about women in sports or fighting."

"I'm going to regret asking." He settles a hip against the countertop. "What insulting, absurd image?"

Oh. I scoff. "I don't know if gods watch movies… I mean, you have a TV and watch the news, so it stands to reason—"

"The point?"

"Right. Well, any 'top' that is just a flimsy bra I could spill out of is beyond impractical, unless I'm using my breasts as a distraction." There might be a choking sound beside me as I expertly flip the eggs. "And good gods, corsets seem great for the figure and posture but shit to move around in, let alone fight in. Talk about restrictive." I roll my eyes and turn off the burner with a flick of my fingers. Most fantasies about women, in my opinion, are dumb as fuck. "Forget leather, which holds in all the sweat. And knee-high boots are hot and all, but try jumping off a rooftop in three-inch heels and see what happens."

"I think I'll pass," Hades says. There's a long pause, then he adds, "I wouldn't mind seeing you in the boots, though."

I sigh. How disappointing that he's like all the rest of them. "Don't you dare."

"I'll make sure to keep your requirements in mind." He snaps his fingers, and like yesterday, I'm instantly wearing new clothes.

I glance down, then move my pan off the burner so I can take a closer look.

The outfit is still sporty but of superfine quality. Black now—the color of the public-facing god of death, apparently—and the material seems patterned in black-on-black to look like…flames, maybe? The pattern covers all of the shirt beneath a vest but only a simple stripe up the fronts of the legs.

"Are my clothes now fancier than the other champions'?"

"I hope so."

I almost smile. He definitely likes sticking it to the other gods, and despite probably earning more black marks next to my name, that's something I fully support. "Playing to the crowds again?"

"Exactly."

I pause, twisting my neck to peer closer at the vest. It's the tactical vest Boone brought me last night, which Hades kept as part of the outfit—I'm sure of that—except now there's a butterfly embroidered on the chest in a rose-gold thread.

But there's more.

My hands are covered in fingerless gloves with smaller rose-gold butterflies on the back. The gloves tuck into gauntlets covering my forearms that are a supple, movable leather and yet protective. My feet are encased in boots that protect my shins, but I can tell I'll be able to run and even climb in them easily.

Wow. He actually listened.

"Why butterflies?"

I don't look directly at him, but I still catch the way he shrugs. "I like them."

Me too. I don't say that out loud, though. No need to bond over bugs.

Deliberately, I pull my shoulders back. I'm also not going to thank him. The reason I'm wearing this is because I'm his champion. I won't thank him for any of it.

I scrape half the eggs onto a plate and take them and a cup of tea to the kitchen island to grab a stool there.

"I left some for you," I tell him, then frown. "Do immortals even need to eat?"

"Yes, but only for..."

He pauses long enough that I glance up, meeting his glittering gaze directly for the first time this morning. Something I've been avoiding until now. "For?"

"Pleasure."

Good grief, the slide of that word on his tongue. The wicked, teasing light in his eyes is too much to handle this early in the day. Not to mention I've been doing everything I can to not think about his *gift* since it happened.

Only now, *all* I can think about is that kiss. About the way his tongue felt brushing against mine. And if the swirling in his eyes is any indication, he's thinking about the exact same thing.

23

BREAKFAST OF CHAMPIONS

"Must be nice," I offer, then go back to keeping my head down and eating my breakfast.

A minute later, he sits next to me at the island, his own plate piled high. "How do you know how to cook?" he asks.

"In the den, we take turns manning the kitchen and eat buffet style. First come, first served." During very specific hours, and then all the food is locked away. You snooze, you starve.

"Even the bosses cook?"

"You're quite chatty this morning," I grouse.

"It's worth getting to know my champion's skills, strengths, and weaknesses, don't you think?"

I'd honestly rather he not. "The bosses are pledges who paid off their debts and earned the right not to do anything they don't want to."

"I see. Do you plan to earn that privilege?"

My stomach twists, my palms suddenly sweaty. I really don't want to explain that I've already paid off my debt—I just have nowhere else to go. I stare at the eggs on my fork and hope he doesn't catch the slight tremble in my voice. "I enjoy cooking."

An awkward silence settles between us as I try my damnedest to ignore him. Until he hooks a foot in my stool and tugs me around to face him, his legs bracketing my knees, and he's close enough that instead of breakfast I smell...him. Bitter dark chocolate.

I've always had a thing for chocolate.

Hades doesn't speak, just stares.

I stare back, fork miraculously still piled with my bite of eggs suspended in the air. With a glare, I stuff the bite in my mouth and rebelliously chew, then swallow. "Is there a reason for making me gaze adoringly upon your magnificence while I eat?"

Horrible choice of words. I wait for some sort of comment about how adoring him was bound to happen sooner or later, or how nice it is that I finally recognize his magnificence.

It's a good thing I finished that bite of eggs, though, because I definitely would have choked on it when he says, "I may take you up on that veiled challenge to make you do exactly that."

Could he? I mean with his powers, not just the raw-magnetism thing he has going? "You don't fool me." I brave it out. "You're not Aphrodite."

After another tension-pulsing pause, his lips quirk. "Thank the Titans for that much, at least."

I let out a silent breath and immediately suck it right back in as he continues to keep me here, only now his gaze changes, turns more intense, his eyes a pure, radiant silver in the sunlight. "And to answer your earlier question…maybe I enjoy gazing at *you*, my star."

Holy hellhounds. This is more than a poor mortal should have to deal with. I keep forgetting who and what he is—I really should just keep my mouth shut and my head down around this god.

But if I lower my gaze now, he wins. So instead, I crook an eyebrow. "I mean, I know I'm cute and all, but falling for me is probably a bad idea."

Not that he could. This might be the first time I've forgotten that. Even for a second.

"We don't want things to get awkward," I add, tone nonchalant.

He smiles—a real one—and the impact is like a strike to the chest. Those hidden dimples appear as a laugh escapes him.

I swallow for a different reason this time.

With a shake of his head, he turns me back to the island. "At least now you're looking at me instead of avoiding eye contact."

Leave it alone. Let him have the last word.

"You look terrible, by the way," he remarks.

There goes any truth to gazing at me for the fun of it.

"I know. I didn't sleep well." Between Boone, Hades, and the first event looming over my head like a guillotine's blade, sleep was a long shot anyway. I run a weary hand over my face. "You should see the bruises under my clothes."

His immediate frown reminds me of Zeus' thunderclouds. "Show me." A command.

Maybe he'll feel bad if he sees and take pity on me. I lean back, unzip my tactical vest, and pull up my fitted shirt. Even I wince at the sight of the black-and-blue line across the bottom of my ribs.

"Fuck." Hades growls the word, and I blink at him.

Then he grabs a cell phone out of a pocket in his jeans—gods have cell phones?—and types rapidly. Almost as soon as he sets his phone down, a man appears in the kitchen with us.

He's an older gentleman, with wrinkles around his brown eyes and graying hair at the temples and in his beard.

Hades is in full autocratic mode, tossing around the orders. "Asclepius, she needs repair."

Like I'm a broken computer or something, but at least I know who this is now.

Asclepius. That explains the aging. Gods don't age, but according to some versions of the story, Asclepius started as a mortal man who was punished by Zeus for the crime of restoring the dead to life. Afterward, he was welcomed into Olympus as the god of healing.

Asclepius takes one look at my bruising, then holds a hand over me. His beige skin glows blackish blue now, like the color of my bruising, and a lovely warmth spreads outward in my chest. I gasp as the nagging ache of each wound disappears, and before my eyes, the purplish mark on my stomach fades. The glow from Asclepius' hand changes color to match, until all that's left is healthy tissue. I poke at a spot with my finger and smile. Not a single twinge of pain.

"That's a neat trick." I look up at Asclepius. "Thank you."

His eyes crinkle with an answering smile. "No more belly flops on the stairs, young lady."

"You knew about that?"

Crooked teeth flash at me. "All the gods, demigods, and other immortal creatures keep track of the Crucible. The winner *tends* to affect us."

I should have guessed.

"We watched the entire night with interest." He slides a look between Hades and me.

Terrific. I'm like a reality show celebrity for the immortal world. Just what I always wanted.

Asclepius gives Hades a stern look that I picture a grandpa making. "You should have called me sooner."

I straighten. Someone who dares to talk back to Hades? Not just that...he's reprimanding Hades. "Oh, I like you."

Hades' mouth thins. "She didn't tell me."

Asclepius snorts. "You should have known. You were right there when she hit those stairs."

Before Hades can answer, Asclepius pats my shoulder. "I won't be able to do this after the first Labor starts, my dear. Any magical healing is reserved only for the winner of each and the champions who share the victor's virtue."

Great. The Labors might require healing. And I'm the only one in the Survival virtue, which means if I don't win, I don't get healed. Just one more check mark in the "against Lyra" column.

I should stop keeping that list. It's depressing.

"Best of luck. Play well." Then Asclepius is gone as fast as he appeared.

Hades is still in thundercloud mode, so I roll my shirt back down, zip up my vest—it's much more comfortable now—and turn my stool back to the island so I can finally finish my food, which is probably cold at this point.

"Next time, tell me," he says.

"Fine."

We both fall into silence, but he feels far too broody at my side, and it's making the muscles in my shoulders coil. "Do you know what today's challenge is?" I ask.

Hades shakes his head. "Only the god or goddess who devises the Labor knows. They aren't even supposed to tell their own champion, though I'm guessing most find a way around that."

I pause mid-chew, then finish the bite. I'm never going to get these eggs into me at this rate. "Will you be devising a Labor?"

"No. I've been informed it's too late. I would have had to square it with the Daemones a year ago."

Terrific. I will be unprepared for every single Labor, while at least one champion will likely have a leg up in each. I chew that over along with more breakfast.

I'm a little lost in my own head, which is probably why Hades' question is like a bolt from the blue.

"Who was the man in your room last night?"

24

CAUGHT OFF GUARD

I splutter and choke on inhaled egg, gulping down tea to try to help. When I can finally breathe, I carefully put my fork down. "You didn't hurt Boone, did you?"

"No. He left here unharmed and unaware of my notice."

Well, thank the gods for that. But I can't get a good read on Hades, whose expression is as neutral as it gets.

"He's your lover?" he asks, sounding bored.

I'd laugh if he wasn't poking at a sore spot that will probably never heal. "Obviously not," I say carefully instead.

It turns out gods *can* feel guilty. Just a tad, the expression gone as fast as it came, but I caught it.

"He's one of the master thieves in my den. Not even a friend." I pause, because after last night, I'm not certain that's true.

"Then why was he here?"

A very good question. I wish I knew. "To bring me my things. He was helping me avoid someone when you selected me — and watched me disappear."

"Your not-friend was helping you avoid *who*?"

"It's a long story."

"And you don't want to tell me." What is going on with his voice now? I thought I was starting to get a grasp on his tones and their meanings. A glance shows his face is still neutral enough. Even so, he sounds off.

"Not really. No." I get up and go to the sink to wash my plate and the pan.

"Are you in love with him?"

I set the pan down in the sink with a bit of a clatter and face him. "You really cut right to the heart of things, don't you?"

He cocks his head, looking mildly interested. "Are you?"

Hells, I *really* don't want to talk about this. "It doesn't matter." I turn back to the sink.

There's a telling pause behind me. "It's good if you're not. The less worry you leave behind, the better you'll do in the Crucible."

Which brings me back to reality with a *thump*, and I hadn't even realized I'd left it. His voice wasn't tight because he cared about what was going on with me or how my life might be affected. All Hades cares about is his end goal, whatever that may be, and I'm just a stepping stone to get there.

Something I'd be smart to remember.

There's a tiny *ding* behind me.

"Fuck." His muttered curse is soft and urgent.

A second later, he reaches a hand around me and turns off the water before he spins me to face him, his silver eyes muted and serious. "I thought I'd have more time to prepare you. The first Labor is about to start."

My heart tries to make an escape up my throat, clearly ready to leave the rest of my cursed body behind. I swallow it back down. "How do you know?"

He holds up a phone with a group text. The gods have a group text. Seriously? "My brother just told me," he says.

Poseidon's name swims on the screen for a second. It takes that long for my brain to engage. "Poseidon. So…water? Ocean?"

Hades nods.

Maybe I should have worn something waterproof. "What's his virtue again?"

"Courage."

Courage? "So probably not checkers," I mutter under my breath. Then, louder, "Monsters?"

"I don't know. In the last Crucible, he made the champions face each of their greatest fears all at the same time." He's not joking or teasing now, and the fact that he's not makes me more nervous.

He must see that, because he offers a reassuring smile—one I'm pretty sure he hasn't used in a millennium because it's so stiff, no dimples in sight, and that makes me even *more* nervous. Hades is trying to reassure me. This is bad.

"You have everything you need?" he asks.

Pearls. Dragon teeth. Boone's lockpicking kit. My relic. A few other tools. Those are all stowed away in my vest. I carry Hades' two gifts—the tattoos and his kiss—as part of me, within me.

I nod.

"Good. Don't take unnecessary risks. Let the other champions do that."

Now? Now is when he decides to give me advice?

"Watch your back. The instinct to survive is wired into us all, but especially mortals, since, like you said, you have no reset. It makes all living creatures ruthless, no matter their personality or behavior otherwise."

"That, I already knew," I mutter.

His fingers dig into my arms. "Use your gifts but only if you must. It's better if you can get the other champions to use theirs and save yours."

I nod again. For some reason, the instructions he's rattling off are settling me. Maybe because it reminds me of my training years, when Felix would throw instructions at me so fast I could hardly keep up. This feels…familiar.

I focus on his words, on his voice.

"Nothing is ever what it looks like when gods are involved," he says. "Question everything."

"No shit."

His lips crook even though his eyes remain serious. "And if you need me, all you have to do is get to me."

I frown. "Will you be there? You can't interfere. Rules."

His expression takes on an arrogant cast. "I'm the god of death, and death doesn't know any rules."

I give a shaky laugh. "Finally, something positive about having you as my patron."

Olympus save me. I can't believe I just said that. My eyes go wide, and I guess he reads my thoughts, because he slides one hand up to cup the back of my neck, drawing me close, his face right in mine. "Focus, Lyra," he says.

Right. Focus. I nod. Then nod again. "Okay."

"I didn't say call me. I said *get to* me. There's a difference. Do you understand?"

Another riddle to solve. Great.

Frustration passes over his features. "I can't say more than that."

"I'll figure it out." Eventually. Maybe.

My body starts to feel a little funny, like it's lighter and sort of bubbly, especially my feet. I glance down to find them fading from sight, nimble leather boots and all, and the sensation creeps higher up my legs.

"I hope the water is warm at least," I murmur. I don't know why I say it.

"Look at me," Hades commands.

And I do. I look right into molten gray eyes swirling with emotions I can't possibly decipher right now.

He squeezes my shoulder. "No matter what, Lyra, remember one thing."

One thing? He just told me like ten. "What?"

"I picked you for a reason. You can do this."

The god of death picked me. Chose me. Has faith in *me*. Despite my curse.

The sensation is up to my chin now, and Hades starts to fade from sight as I disappear. His voice follows me into the nothingness.

"You can do this, Lyra…because you're *mine*."

PART 3

LET THE GAMES BEGIN

Quitters never win, and winners never quit.
But survivors change the game.

25

POSEIDON'S LABOR

*M*ine.

Hades' last word chases me all the way across the world, which comes back into focus the same way it went out, with that bubbling sensation but growing heavier as it works its way back down my body.

Until the chill of water jolts through my nerves right as a wave rolls over my head.

It ebbs, and I come up spluttering, because damn, of course the water is cold as fuck.

I go to wipe the salt water out of my stinging eyes only to jerk against restraints. Through fuzzy vision, I look up to find I'm tied by the wrists, my arms overhead. The rope is attached to the top of a thick wooden post. I use my shoulder to try to wipe the water off my face, then blink and blink until I can see more clearly.

Water and rocks.

A cave?

I'm in the middle of what looks like a large cavern, wide open to the ocean on one end, allowing sunlight to spill inside. The cavern is made of the strangest formations I've ever seen. The rock before me is brown and shaped in rectangular columns—rows and layers of perfect vertical columns up to where the roof curves overhead. Up there, what looks like the bottoms of the columns poke out, and they could have been dipped in gold paint the way they glitter. The beautiful greenish water swells in and out, forcing me to lift my head or get a face full.

A shiver racks through me as my muscles try to generate warmth. It's August, so I guess this is the warmest it gets here, and living on the Pacific Ocean, I'm already used to chilly water. But most people wear wetsuits to swim in water this cold. I'm still in my champion clothes, which cling to me but don't provide warmth.

"Hey!" A male voice rings out. "Where in the Overworld are we?"

"A cave in the ocean, dumbass," a snappy female voice answers in Spanish. "Do you really need to know more?"

"What kind of fucked-up Labor is this supposed to be?" someone else yells.

What exactly were they expecting from the gods? Charades?

A flare of black wings through the small patch of visible sky tells me the Daemones are here. So where is Poseidon? Or do we just get started on our own and figure it out?

I strain against the ropes to lean out and look to my right and left.

The other champions are here, all dangling from their own posts in a straight line, each spaced about twelve feet apart. Some are just waking up. A few are thrashing about, starting to panic. To my right, easily identifiable by her red hair and green outfit, is Neve, who is not panicking but looking around like me. She catches my eye and shoots me a glare. Of course they'd stick me next to the one champion I've already pissed off.

To my left, in the direction of the cave opening, I recognize the only shaved head among the group—maybe the sexiest shaved head I've ever seen. He is Dex Soto, Athena's champion, dressed in turquoise like the others of the Mind virtue. If my memory is right, he's from an island somewhere in the Caribbean.

A cry comes from farther down the line past Dex, and I lean out as much as I can, my shoulders protesting the stretch at this angle.

My heart trips at the sight of the ocean beyond the cave bubbling up like a geyser erupting from underneath, churning and frothing, until Poseidon bursts through, lifting his trident to the sky. Behind him, two dolphins launch into the air, doing flips before diving back into the water.

Is he kidding with this right now? Does he really think any of us care about a grand entrance when we're tied to posts in freezing water?

But, of course, the display isn't for us. It's for the immortals watching these proceedings so avidly. Seems like Poseidon might be as much of a showman as Zeus.

Riding a wave that swells around him, he slides into the cave to float directly before me on a spinning column of water that lifts him higher. I must be positioned in the center of the group.

He is clearly in his element, no longer wearing armor but shirtless, showing off his sable skin and impressive physique…and also not hiding anything with skintight pants that look like metallic blue fish scales that shimmer in the water. He has tattoos over his chest and arms and what I'm pretty sure are gills at the sides of his ribs. And his dark-blue hair, when wet, turns black, matching his trim beard.

"Welcome to Fingal's Cave!" He says this like we're here on vacation.

"We're in Scotland?" Neve's question has the god smiling.

"Yes, young mortal. Staffa Island is one of two magical sites that sit directly across the sea from each other. They are at opposite ends of a bridge built by the Irish giant Fionn mac Cumhaill to enable his passage to Scotland to battle his gigantic Scottish rival, Fingal. The Celtic gods have been kind enough to loan it to me for this Labor."

Neve doesn't say anymore, and I'm left wondering. I don't know that set of gods like I do my own. Is Fingal's Cave a good or a bad thing?

"For your first Labor, your bindings…" Poseidon waves at us. "Are *not* your only problem. There will be a bigger challenge."

His smile turns enigmatically self-satisfied. "There is no time limit. The winner will be the one who finds a solution to the bigger challenge first."

He looks down the line of us as we all swish back and forth on our poles, pulled by the ebb and flow of the swells, hung out on lines like bait.

The water is semi-clear, but I can't see too far down. What's in here? I run through all the ocean creatures the ancient Greek gods like to use. A selkie? Sirens? A hydra seems like overkill and too big for this cave.

At least my shivering is starting to ease as I adjust to the water.

Poseidon continues. "This Labor will test not only your courage but your wits, and even an ability to work with those who would see you fail. All skills a leader would need."

Why would being a leader be anything the Crucible needed to prove? The mortal winner won't be leading anything. Their god or goddess will.

Poseidon's smile is damn near gleeful, though I can't tell if he's bloodthirsty or just incredibly proud of what he has in store for us today. It's the first Labor, so does that make it the hardest? Or will they get progressively more difficult?

"Oh…" He chuckles. That dickhead actually chuckles. "You've probably already noticed the temperature of the water. It's summer, so it won't kill you right away, but it will start to affect you the longer you're in it. I suggest you hurry."

Fuck me.

The Crucible truly is just a game to the gods. *We* aren't real to them or worth worrying over. This isn't life and death to them, just a little sport.

Damned if I'm going to let them kill me for sport. The other champions, either, if I can help it, even the ones who hate me already. None of us asked for this.

"Best of luck to you all." He turns his head to look at his champion, who must be tied up farther into the cave. "But especially to you, Isabel."

Then he dives back into the water, sending another wave cresting over my head. At least this time I see it coming and can brace myself. By the time I wipe my salty face on my shoulders again, he's gone.

There's a beat of silence as we all absorb the fact that he's just going to leave us here to figure it out.

"We're going to drown," one of the men I can't see cries out. "The water is getting higher."

That sets off several others, their high-voiced, rapid-fire chatter bouncing off the cave walls.

My heart tap-dances on the inside of my ribs, but even a pledge who ends up a lowly clerk learns a thing or two during training. Working through fear is one of those. So I close my eyes and think.

One thing is certain…something worse is coming, and we're not going to be able to face it tied to posts.

26

FIGURE IT OUT

"The tide isn't coming in." Neve is telling this to herself, but I manage to catch the words. Her Canadian accent sounds thicker—maybe because of the danger. "It's going out."

I open my eyes to pay attention to the water. She's right. It's lower than when we first got here. Which means I need to work faster to get free. Right now, the water is holding some of my weight.

Tied up like this, I can't reach anything in my vest, so using one of my tools to cut the ropes isn't a possibility.

Movement to my left catches my eye, and I find Dex has managed to flip around and is climbing up his pole.

Damn, he figured that out fast. But I should also take his lead. My wrists may be bound, but my feet are not. I use the movement of the water to swing sideways and probably look like exactly what I am—a worm on a hook trying to wriggle off.

It takes me several tries, but eventually, I manage to hook one leg around the post, my rope twisting with me. I wait for the water to flow back out, then wrap my other leg around. The rough-barked wood posts clearly haven't been in the water long because they aren't slimy.

Leaning back, I wrap my hands around the rope, which is thin, but my gloves help with the grip. Using the rope and my thighs around the post, I start to climb. I'm able to use the lift of the swells when they roll by to help boost me for the first few scoots, but soon I'm above the waterline, a soggy, heavy mess, dragging my own waterlogged weight up the pole as my muscles scream.

Fuck. This was easier in my head than in reality.

"Look at them!" someone yells nearby.

Them? Out of the corner of my eye, I see Neve shimmying up her pole, only *way* better than me, and nearing the top. On my other side, Dex is already there. I'm not surprised about Neve, who strikes me as the independent, fuck-the-world type. Dex, either, really, who is tall but lean in the way wolves are in the winter, giving them a meaner edge.

"How did you do that?" someone else calls.

"Turn around and use your legs and the rope," I shout back and slip a little from the effort.

Then I keep going, focused entirely on what I'm doing. One hand over the other, scoot the legs, try not to slip.

"Oh my gods," Neve snarls off to my left. "Quit with the fucking humming."

The noise cuts off in my throat. I seriously need to get that little habit back under control. When I finally make it all the way, I can't figure out how to heft myself up to sit on the flat top. And I'm running out of strength quickly.

I force myself to focus. My wrists are still bound. Now that I have slack to look at the knots, I know I can't undo them with my teeth. I need my relic to get free, but it's in a zippered pocket at the small of my back.

I won't be able to reach around.

I lose my grip and slide down the pole a few feet but manage to catch myself.

Think, damn it.

On either side of me, Neve and Dex, who I guess don't have knives, are struggling to get on top of their poles. Dex has managed to pull himself up enough to lay over it on his stomach. Neve is breathing hard, her brows puckered in a ferocious scowl. A few others are making their way up now, too.

My relic is the answer. I know it. But how do I—

I grunt as an idea hits me between the eyes. I'm taking a big fucking risk and have one shot at this if I'm lucky, but it's the only option I can see.

Holding myself up with my shaking thighs, I lift my bound hands over my head and start tugging my vest up. My shirt drags up with it. More than once, my legs slip and I have to pause and get a grip. Finally, it pulls free with a tug.

I'd love to take a breather, but my legs are jelly and I'm slipping more. Working as fast as I can, I manage to unzip the pocket at my back and pull out my relic. First, I cut the rope that secures my wrist bindings to the post. My legs give, and I tumble back into the water, dropping my vest. Still clutching my weapon, I helplessly watch the vest sink until it's snagged on a small rock outcropping, maybe six feet down.

Shit, shit, shit.

When I come up for air, I let my quivering body float as I awkwardly hack through the bindings around my wrists as fast as I can without cutting myself. The rope isn't thick, so I'm quickly freed. My body quakes from the cold. I need to get out of the water before I can't—we all do. I duck back underwater and swim down to my vest, slipping it back on with jerky motions as I kick back up to the surface.

"Stop climbing!" I yell to the others. "I'll come to you and cut you free."

"Don't believe her," Neve snarls. "She'll just gut us with that axe."

"She already helped us once," Meike yells back, her bangs plastered to her forehead by the spray of the sea. "We *all* have our gifts because of her."

Something falls into the water from a pole closer to the cave entrance. I look just in time to see Kim Dae-hyeon —Artemis' first male champion in…maybe ever— swear as a bulging backpack sinks under the water.

That sucks. Hopefully he can get to it.

Kicking to stay afloat over another swell, I shout at Dex, "It's up to you. Come down to the water if you want my help."

Dex is climbing down. It'll take him a second, so I swim past Neve's pole to Trinica Cain, Hephaestus' champion…one of the Courage virtues. She's the only other champion from the United States, from somewhere in the South, I think.

Her dark waves hang over her face, and discerning eyes stare back at me from between the strands. "Are you going to gut me like she said?"

I like Trinica already. No-nonsense and practical. "No. But I have to climb your pole to get to your hands, so we'll have to touch. Don't bite me or something, yeah?"

She nods.

I try to avoid pulling or leveraging myself on her, which would hurt her hands and wrists more, and manage to get up the pole high enough to cut her down. She falls in with a splash and comes up coughing and wild-eyed. "I need my hands!"

I drop back into the water and cut her wrists free as fast as I can, and she wraps herself around the pole.

"Get to the wall." I point.

She nods, and I move from pole to pole, skipping Apollo's champion—Rima Patel, world-class neurosurgeon turned fish bait—who's already freed herself. Next, I get to Zai, who managed to sit on top of his pole, at least, although by the shaky looks of him, that took all he had physically. He waves me off. "I'm safe up here for now. Get the others."

By the time I reach Isabel, it's more difficult because the water is still receding. Too fast. This isn't a normal tide.

Isabel mutters through chattering teeth in a litany of angry Spanish about the cold water, sadistic gods, and why the fuck is she here anyway. She and I really need to be friends. As soon as she's free, she flips her long, blond hair out of her face and twists it up into a knot on top of her head while treading water. "Do you have anything else that cuts?"

I hesitate a beat, and she sees it. "It'll go faster with two of us," she points out.

She's right. "I have this." I pull the wire cutters out of a different pocket and hand them to her.

We both swim as fast as we can to the other champions, past where I'd been tied up. I can see already that Samuel Sebina, champion of Zeus, must have broken his rope by strength alone. He's helping Meike on Dex's other side. Meanwhile, Dex has climbed back down, but it's obvious that with the lower water level, his arms and wrists are hurting now.

"Hurry," he groans at me.

"Hold on."

I hear him grunt. "Like I have a choice."

Because there's more strain on the rope with his weight, it snaps like a twig after the first saw. I follow him into the water and free his wrists. In a blur of movement, he grabs the axe from my hand.

27

THE WARNING STONES

B efore I can react, Dex slashes at me, but a swell of water pushes him out of range before the blade makes contact.

Heart hammering, I swim backward, putting more distance between us. "Dick move."

"Sorry, but I'm here to win."

Mental note to stay away from Dex from now on. "I'm here to *not die*," I tell him. "Victory is all yours."

"Yeah, right." He waves my relic in the air. "Thanks for this, though."

With strong strokes, he swims away from me toward the opening of the cave. What? Does he plan to swim all the way from wherever this island is to the shore?

His funeral—

The pearls. I have four of the six tucked into a pocket of my vest. *I could get away if I wanted.* Hades would come get me in the Underworld, if that's where I end up.

No. Dire needs only.

"There are words!" Trinica points across the way from where she's climbed up onto a ledge.

Sure enough, the sinking water has revealed words in English carved deeply into the cave walls. At first, they barely show over the waterline, but it goes down fast enough to make them out. And as soon as I read them, a kick of dread plows into my gut.

IF YOU SEE THESE WORDS, THEN WEEP.

Not good. Very not good.

A glance tells me most of the others are free now. Isabel is assisting

Aphrodite's champion down her post, but Zai is still up on top of his own. And I can't cut him free.

"Isabel!" I call out. "Dex took my axe. Help Zai when you're done."

Her head comes up from what she's doing, and then she waves an acknowledgment, so I start cutting a swift path through the water away from the carved warning in the rocks, back toward Trinica and several others now up on the ledge.

I'm almost to the wall when Neve's eyes go wide as she stares over my head toward the carving. Trinica must see the same thing, because her mouth forms the words *Oh shit* before she's waving and yelling at all of us. "Get out of the water! Get out of the water!"

If I've learned anything in this life, it is to not hesitate when someone yells at you to run. So I swim hard, heart pounding like it wants to break through my rib cage as I cut through the water, feeling like I'm not going fast enough as my muscles cramp from the cold. Any second, I expect something to catch me by the feet and drag me under.

Every time I lift my head to breathe and make sure I'm swimming the shortest path to the ledge where the other champions wait, I can see their faces grow slacker and paler with fear and shock. I hit the rocks and try to climb up, but unlike the wood posts, the surface is slick.

"Come on. Come on. Come on." I'm muttering to myself as I crab walk my hands, trying to find a spot, any spot, to pull up, when suddenly a large hand appears before me. Randomly, my brain gloms onto the detail of long, tapered fingers before he grabs me by the wrist.

I look straight up into midnight eyes crinkled in a smile.

"I've got you," Samuel says in a deep voice—his English is accented, but I can't make out from where—then hauls me out of the water one-handed as if I'm a very wet feather.

I'm congratulating myself in relief as my feet touch down, only to have Samuel yell, "Watch out!"

He tackles me to the ground, wrapping me in strong arms and taking the brunt of the impact against the rocks as we both go down.

That doesn't help absorb the horror that hits me at the sight of the thing sliding back into the water, inches away from where we were just standing.

28

THE GODS LOVE MONSTERS

I pull my feet away from the edge. "Where in Hades' name did that thing come from?"

"There seem to be eggs under the words on the rocks." Samuel lets go of me, and we both get to our feet.

Sure enough, I look over just in time to see a black-and-red pod the size of my fist, half in, half out of the water, stuck to the cave wall like a barnacle beneath the carved letters. A wave swells, then recedes, and a monster erupts from an egg. Small. Much smaller than what just attacked us.

Nearby, the bigger version of the nightmare creature breaches the surface before diving back under, so I get a better look. It is black with red edges and shaped a little bit like a seahorse but the size of a small pony, except all its undulating parts are made up of leafy-looking appendages, like strongly colored kelp. Instead of a sweet little horse's face, there's a long, narrow, snapping snout with jagged teeth that fit together in a way that I imagine would rend flesh from bone. A crocodile sea dragon?

The ripple in the water tells me the thing is headed straight for Isabel, who is still trying to climb up to Zai.

I open my mouth to warn her, but Samuel beats me to it. "Isabel, watch your back!" he booms.

She turns just as the sea monster rears up and lunges at her with those snapping teeth. She slashes with the wire cutters I gave her, and the creature whimpers and drops back into the water. But it doesn't leave. It swims around the pole as Isabel frantically climbs to join Zai near the top. They are treed prey.

There's a sick popping as another little sea monster thing breaks free from its egg and drops into the water. Now there are three of them. Worse, as the water dips lower, I can see the silhouettes of at least nine more eggs under the surface.

What...one for each of us? What's making them hatch?

Over the roar of the ocean waves and the calls and cries of the champions, I catch a strange squelching sound nearby. There's water dripping behind us. But the drops aren't coming from the ceiling—they're materializing in midair, a few feet above the ledge floor.

Goose bumps creep over my flesh. Where's that coming from?

Samuel swings out a hand like he's swiping at the air, but there's a *thud* a heartbeat before Dex appears out of nowhere, a metal helm falling to the ground beside him with a *clank*. Samuel grabs Dex by the wrist and yanks my axe right out of his grip. Without looking at me, he hands the relic to me as he shoves Dex back a few feet. "Couldn't swim out of here, I guess?"

"There's an invisible wall," Dex says. "It won't let us out."

The sneer on Samuel's face says it all. He considers Dex to be a bit of a coward. I don't. He's just trying to survive like the rest of us.

"If I had the chance to escape, I would, too," I say.

I get distinct looks from both men—one resentful and the other speculative.

At the very least, now we know one of Dex's gifts—the Helm of Darkness, which can render him invisible. The question is, did Samuel also use a gift to be able to see him?

"Somebody *do* something," Isabel yells.

The sea monster leaps, thrashing its long tail to propel itself higher into the air, snapping at her feet as she and Zai both huddle at the top of his pole.

I'm the one with the weapon, so I guess that means me. "I'll try to get them," I tell the people near me, though I'm not sure if anyone cares. Other champions are scattered across the ledge, which runs all the way around the cave. "Somebody figure out what's going on with those eggs and how to stop them."

Over uneven rocks, I sprint the length of the cave, waves crashing into my thighs and stumbling me back every few feet as I circle around to the end closest to Isabel and Zai. There's no way I'm going to outswim those beasts. But at least they can't come up onto the ledge—

"Get back!" someone yells.

The largest of the monsters surges almost all the way out of the water and onto the rocks, just missing Jackie and Amir, Aphrodite and Hera's champions, respectively. With a hiss, the creature slips backward into the water again. Damn. The other large one is still circling Isabel and Zai, which means these things are hatching and growing *fast*. And as soon as they get a little bigger, they can reach us up here, too. We're not safe for much longer.

We need to find a way to kill them. Would my axe even work? How would I get close enough, and where would I hack at a monster like this to stop it?

"Fuck me," I mutter. Because I have an idea, but it sucks to have to use it so soon.

Samuel makes his way to where I'm standing, which is a good thing. I'm going to need him if my plan will work.

"Get ready to pull me out fast," I tell him. He's saved me once already, so I'm going to trust him. I move to the very edge of the rocks, crouching with my knees to my chest.

"What are you doing?" Isabel yells.

If I can, I'm going to slide into the water without those things noticing. "I have a gift that can help us, but I need dirt!"

"Dirt?" she squeaks.

Farther down the ledge, Trinica flaps her arms to catch my attention. "I can see them from here," she calls. "Go on my count."

So instead of looking down, I look at Trinica as she studies the water, expression intent. She's old enough to be my parent, with a cool head under pressure to show for it. She holds up a hand, head swiveling as she tracks the three creatures. "Go!"

I slide in as gently and soundlessly as I can without a splash, then duck underneath and swim for the bottom fast. I feel along the rock wall, pressure pressing in on my ears painfully, but I keep going until—thank the gods—I hit a patch of sand. Unzipping the compartment where I stored them, I pull out a few of Boone's dragon teeth.

I think I hear Hades' voice in my head shouting, *Faster, Lyra.*

I shove three teeth into the sand and bury them, then swim up, gasping for air when I hit the surface. No time to figure out if I'm hallucinating. That will have to come later.

"When you see bones, jump into the water and swim for Samuel, and he'll pull you out," I yell up at Zai and Isabel.

"Bones? There's something wrong with her," Zai says to Isabel.

"You can tell her after we all get out of this alive," Isabel snaps. "Get back on the rocks," she yells at me.

Keeping my head out of the water so I can hear any shouted warnings, I get moving. Any second now, my bone soldiers should sprout. Any second now.

I'm reaching for Samuel's hand when Meike yells, "Behind you!"

I don't know if she's yelling at me or the others, but all it takes is a look over my shoulder to find out. A black-and-red kelp-leafed ridge protrudes from the water, winding back and forth like a serpent, swimming straight at me.

Spinning away from Samuel, I drop under the water, ignoring the stinging of my eyes as I search, weapon ready. I am not going to be eaten today, damn it. Not in my first Labor.

The monster zeroes in on me, cutting through the water wicked fast. I desperately search for its weak point, a place to cleave its slender body with all those leaflike appendages. If I do this wrong, I'm just going to piss it off.

With my luck...

As it shoots forward, jaws wide, I lunge to the side and see a different way. In a snap decision, instead of chopping at the monster, I wrap my arms around its slender, slick body, riding it like a bucking bronco.

The thing goes wild in my grasp, thrashing and flipping. It tries to leap out of the water, and I get one breath of air as I breach the surface. When the monster and I come back down, instead of trying to get out of my grasp, it turns on me, not to bite me but to wrap its kelpy body around me like a constrictor, so fast that it almost pins my arms, but I manage to get one out.

The thing is crushing me as it drags me deeper into the water, squeezing tighter and tighter and tighter. If it doesn't drown me first, it's going to pulverize me. I stab and stab at the trunk of its body, but it's not working. I'm not hitting anything vital enough to stop it.

Out of nowhere, a white blade slices through the water, coming straight down into the top of the monster's head. Immediately, it goes limp.

29

DRAGON TEETH

I stare at a skeleton soldier, shield and sword and everything, all made of bleached-white bone, but instead of legs, it has a tail like a mermaid. Adapted for the environment it was born into? That's a bonus.

By the time I manage to wriggle out of the sea monster's coils, made extra difficult by all its leafy parts, my lungs are near to bursting. I shove off the rocks to try to get up to the surface as quickly as possible. My body screams, desperate for a breath, but I haven't reached the surface. I can't. I suck in salt water just as Samuel grabs my hand and drags me out.

I land on my stomach, coughing and spluttering. It takes way too long to rid my body of the water in my lungs. Every inhale is so painful I expect to start coughing blood.

"What are those?" someone at the other end shouts. I know exactly what they're looking at. Three of them. That's how many dragon teeth I used.

"Kill the sea monsters!" I order the soldiers made of bones.

The water erupts in a battle of creature against creature as we all watch in horror. "Isabel, Zai, swim!" Samuel yells.

They both jump off the post and make it to us, where Samuel hauls them out one at a time. Isabel lands on the rocks beside me.

"You're bleeding," I sit up for a closer look at her leg. Two rows of jagged cuts seeping blood line her calf. The sea monster must've gotten a bite in while she was on the post.

Isabel whips her shirt over her head, leaving her in a sports bra, and ties it around the wound.

"Zai thinks you risk too much," she says to me, "and I'm inclined to agree." Then she looks up and grins. "But I like risk takers."

I want to grin back, but I'm too busy having a moment.

"We got it!"

One of the male champions is standing on the rocks above the carved words of warning along with Rima and Amir. Diego, I think his name is. Older, maybe in his forties, he's not short but not tall and of a wiry build, with floppy, silvering hair and a genuine smile that lights him up like a beacon. He's Demeter's champion, and his tracksuit is burgundy in color, which means Heart is his virtue, not Mind. Interesting.

I can't get a read on Rima, but Amir's arrogance seems to have been stripped away as he grins in almost boyish pride as the Heart champion claps him on the shoulder. The two men have stripped off their soaking-wet shirts and pants and have draped them over the remaining unhatched eggs, covering them completely. Amir's underclothes cling to his lanky, still-growing form, and Hera's kid champion looks far too small for this fight. I can tell by the way Diego situates himself between the teenager and the once-deadly waters that he sees it, too. So paternal, I note, and wonder not for the first time about the families my fellow champions left behind.

"They must hatch when they hit air," Zai says next to me. Clinically. As if this is a very interesting scientific fact he's just discovered.

About that time, the water goes suddenly quiet. Only the natural roll of the ocean disturbs the surface as we all stare down into the depths. "Are they dead?" Meike asks.

"Gods, I hope so," Jackie mutters.

With a clatter and a splash, one of my skeletons rises out of the water, supporting itself with its bony tail. It salutes me and then immediately falls apart, bones scattering and sinking to the bottom of the cave, no doubt with the two other skeletons.

"They're all gone." I collapse on the rocks and roll to my back, staring at the geometric shapes above my head. I grin on a rush of pure relief. "One Labor down."

A laugh escapes me. I hear a few others make similar sounds, somewhere between relief, shock, and lingering terror—reality setting in.

We made it through one. With no one killed.

Beside me, Isabel suddenly screams, a sound that is a rending shriek of such agony I'm surprised she doesn't bring the whole cave down on top of us. I jackknife up to see her frantically unwinding the bloody shirt from her leg.

Only instead of gashes where the teeth sank in, there are…holes. Holes in her leg turned black as ash and growing deeper and wider as we watch with revulsion, spreading like they are eating her alive.

"Help her!" someone yells.

Isabel writhes and screams, holding on to the top of her leg like she could make it stop, but the bite is consuming her flesh so fast, creeping up to her knee now. I whip a thin coiled rope out of one of my vest pockets and tie it around her thigh like a tourniquet to stop the burning, or whatever this is, from going higher, but the charred flesh passes the tie-off like it's not even there.

Isabel arches off the rock, her terrible screeches echoing around the cave, and I think maybe my insides are bleeding with her, as if every scream is claws tearing at me. I've never heard a sound so awful. I scoot closer, taking her hand in mine. It's all I can do.

She looks at me, and it's not just agony in her eyes or fear…but knowledge. She *knows* she's going to die and there's nothing anyone can do to help her.

"I'm here." What else can I say?

Then Isabel takes one long breath that is both a scream and a groan before her eyes roll back in her head and she passes out, no doubt from the pain. But her body is still in trauma, her chest rising and falling fast, her limbs twitching as she tries to fight it. By now, the charring is up to her waist. All we can do is watch, helpless and paralyzed, as it consumes the rest of her until, with a death rattle from coal-black lips, she goes terribly still, no longer breathing.

No longer in pain.

She looks like bodies pulled out of house fires in movies—a corpse of flesh burned beyond all recognition. What the movies can't replicate is the putrid smell of it. I realize I'm still holding her hand and gently let go before rubbing her remains off on my clothes.

Samuel removes his shirt and covers as much of her as he can with it, then puts a hand on my shoulder, and I flinch at the touch. "She's gone."

It doesn't seem possible. She was just here. She was just—

"Congratulations!" Zeus' voice booms from the sky.

Zeus, not Poseidon. The ocean god is probably pissed at himself for devising a challenge that eliminated his own champion, and therefore himself, from the running. Good. I hope he chokes on failure.

"You have completed your first Labor, champions." The god's words echo around us. "Well done."

Not all of us, dickhead. I can't make myself look away from what's left of Isabel.

"And the winner of today's competition is…Demeter's champion, Diego Perez, who determined the cause of the hatching and stopped it."

The god pauses, probably giving us a chance to applaud or something. I feel sick.

"Diego—for your win today, you have earned a boon. The Ring of Gyges."

Vaguely, I'm aware of a spark of light in the cave, but I don't look over to see Diego accept the blood-prize.

Zeus' tone is benevolent. "This magical artifact grants its wearer the power of invisibility at will."

Much good invisibility did Dex.

"Go ahead, champion," Zeus says.

I finally glance up to see Diego standing above the words of warning carved into the rocks. A gold ring as thick as my thumb hovers in the air before him. He doesn't move but instead glances toward where Isabel lies, partially covered, beside me.

"Take it," Zeus encourages him. "It's yours."

30

WHEN HADES GETS ANGRY

The bubbling sensation that comes with fading away and fading back in at a new place takes me from where I'm sitting by Isabel's body in the cave to a black marble floor, still wet and miserable. Two booted feet appear in my line of sight. If feet can be angry, these are.

"What were you thinking, Lyra?" Hades growls at me. No, not growls...pops like firecrackers in the street at the New Year.

The last thing I need is to be yelled at after what I just went through. What's he mad about, anyway? I didn't win, but I didn't fucking die, either.

"Dragon teeth?" he thunders next.

Oh.

The mention of dragon teeth reminds me about hearing his voice in my head.

But I don't ask.

I don't say anything.

"Where did you get—" Hades cuts himself off. Then, if anything, his voice goes quieter. "The thief who brought you your things. He gave them to you."

I am not getting Boone in trouble for helping me.

"Did he give you the axe, too?"

I jerk my gaze up at that. "I—"

From out of nowhere, Hades manifests another axe—one that looks exactly like mine.

"It's a matched pair," he says. "Odin gifted them to the oldest son of Cronos after we imprisoned the Titans in Tartarus."

So *that's* the symbol on the handle—I thought it was Zeus, but it's

Odin. I bet Zeus loved being passed over for Hades, given that he was the King of the Gods at that point.

"About ten mortal years ago, I thought I lost one." He gives the axe I'm still gripping a pointed look. "I guess not."

My eyes go painfully wide. "It just showed up, and it wouldn't let me get rid of it," I say.

He slips his axe into one of the rings on the leather straps he's back to wearing. "I don't care why you have it. You used it in front of the gods."

"They'll think it's just a switchblade."

"I can assure you, they know *exactly* what it is," he snaps. "That makes two relics, and neither is the one from me. Damn it, Lyra. We were already pushing it with the pearls."

That was the last concern going through my head at the time. "There are no rules in the Crucible about bringing my own relics," I say quietly. "Just tell the Daemones where I got them."

The wrong thing to say, based on the way his silence now flays me.

"You think this is funny?" he murmurs eventually.

Anything but. "I didn't smile," I point out.

"Only two other champions used their gifts today. One did it to survive, and the other to *win* the Labor."

I frown. "Diego used his gift to win?"

"You've got to be kidding me," Hades snarls under his breath. "What do you think the glow was?"

Glow? What glow? "I missed that part. Too busy trying to not die."

"His gift is the Halo of Heroism. It gives him an edge in all four virtues—Mind, Heart, Courage, and Strength. It appeared over his head while he was working on the problem."

Well...shit. "That gift is going to make him undefeatable."

"What you *should* be asking"—he's back to thundering—"is why not a single other champion used their gifts when they could have."

He's right. He's right, but I can't deal with it.

I drop back to lay on the cool floor and fling an arm over my eyes. Vaguely, it's sunk in that we're in Hades' house in Olympus again. I just don't have the energy to care.

"Are you taking a fucking nap?" I feel him loom overhead.

I don't open my eyes. "Can you just...give me a minute?"

The ominous silence that settles in the room grows teeth and claws the longer I lay here. It finally penetrates the exhaustion, shock, and sorrow currently holding me in a state of numbness.

I blow out a soft breath. "How long has it been since anyone made you wait?"

"I. Don't. Wait." Each word is clipped at the end like he's biting off the sounds.

And I don't know what it is about him being a dick in this moment—maybe the arrogant selfishness of it, the "I'm an all-powerful god" of it—but a laugh bursts from me. An abrupt bark of sound that is as much of a surprise to me as it probably is to him and gets swallowed by the silence of his rising ire.

But now that I've broken the seal, I can't stop. Laughter pours out of me, violent and fraught. I manage to sit up, but I mean it. I can't stop.

It goes on long enough that Hades kneels down in front of me, frowning. "Lyra?"

Tears leaking down my cheeks, I shake my head, face and belly starting to ache from the traumatized hilarity that still has me in its clutches.

Frustration passes over his features, clamping his perfect lips tight until they're in a thin line. "Lyra, stop it."

Then Hades grabs me by the shoulders. The instant he touches me, the laughter stops, cutting off abruptly, and I stare at him.

And it all hits me.

I promised myself no crying. No crying, damn it. It takes everything I have to hold back the emotions. Almost like I have to force myself to be numb not to feel it. I know I'm staring at Hades, but I'm not really seeing him, focused inward. If I'd done anything like this in front of Felix, he would've told me to get my shit together or maybe even slapped me to shock me out of it.

I should get to my feet. Go change clothes and figure out my next steps. Not show this kind of weakness. Not to anyone.

Especially not Hades.

So when he silently sits down on the floor beside me, legs facing the other direction and right up against me, close enough to feel his warmth through my wet clothes, I don't know how to handle it. Not a shoulder to cry on, exactly, but silent support.

I could endure him yelling, leaving, blaming, even throwing things.

But it's like even an ounce of mortal fucking understanding, just the tiniest smidgeon, blows a hole through the emotional fortress I've built around myself over the years, and the tears just sort of escape. I bite my lip hard, trying to stop them.

And Hades does the worst possible thing—he softens.

He cups my face with one hand, his thumb skating gently over my lip where I drew blood. His eyes change from cutting steel to a swirl of mercury, and what I see in them is...understanding. "Don't do that."

I can't talk around the lump clogging my throat, so I just shake my head.

"You're going to be okay. I promise."

I can't remember the last time someone said anything remotely like that to me, and it hits me right in the feels. Then I shake my head because that's not it. It's not about me. Not at all. It shouldn't have happened. Isabel didn't deserve this. "I..." I have to swallow hard. "I held her hand while she..." I hardly knew her, but I just can't seem to let this go. "She was in so much pain."

So *much* pain.

"I know," he murmurs and wipes away the tears that escaped with the pad of his thumb. "I know."

I can't get the image of Isabel's face out of my head—the panic, the haunting certainty that she was going to die in her terrified eyes as she screamed and screamed. "I didn't let go. Not even...when—"

I can't say it. Not out loud. That will make it more real, make it worse, cement it in my mind.

"I saw," he says. The low rumble of his voice surrounds me, and something soothing about that sound finally seems to penetrate, and the tightness in my chest eases just a little.

I curl my hand around his wrist and give in, leaning into his touch, closing my eyes, listening to the steady in and out of his breathing, trying to time my own to the sound, to him. It helps.

Being with...him.

His comfort. His steadiness. His touch.

The god of death's touch.

What in the Overworld am I thinking?

My eyes blink open to find him watching me.

Hades puts a finger under my chin, making me look at him. "If I promise to take care of her in the Underworld—give her a lovely spot in Elysium—will that help?"

31

TO KNOW YOUR ENEMY

I stare into swirling gunmetal-gray eyes as, on the heels of realization of where we're sitting and how we're touching, awkwardness steals through me. It slowly stiffens each individual part of my body, working its way from my center out until I'm hyperaware of every place we touch. Of how I want to move even closer, press into him.

I'm twenty-three years old, and it's never been more obvious to me than now that I've never been held in the arms of a man. Ever. I need to extricate myself from this situation before I do something foolish. Like straddle his lap, lay my head on his shoulder, and ask him to just hold me.

"Lyra?" He wants an answer to his offer.

I'm not processing. The wiring in my brain has short-circuited, and oddly, the only random thing I can think about is... "Are you affected by my curse?"

He hesitates. And I have my answer. He can't feel anything real or lasting for me. No one can.

"I need you," he finally says.

I blink, trying not to let that make me feel anything and focus on the truth. "Right. You need me to win, and to do that you need me functioning."

I once found a small dog near the entrance to the den's tunnels. Pledges aren't allowed to have pets, so I carried him to the nearest animal shelter. The look he gave me when I left him there...that's what Hades reminds me of just for a second. A sort of lost kind of hurt.

It disappears under a mask of boredom in the next blink, so fast I question what I saw as he takes his hand away from my face.

"If it makes you feel better to believe that, go ahead," he says. "Do you want to take me up on my offer or not?"

To help Isabel.

Oh gods. Here I am thinking of straddling him when I should only be thinking of what happened. I'm so all over the place right now. Out of control.

"Yes." My next words come out on a harsh, accusatory whisper. "No one deserves to die that way."

He searches my eyes. "No."

"These Labors are fucked-up."

"I know."

"We're not disposable," I tell him, anger burning away the last of my despair. "Mortals. You gods toy with us like you think we are."

Hades lets loose a sigh almost as heavy as I feel. "The others do because for them, mortals come and go. Blips. If you think about the lifespan of a butterfly from a mortal's perspective, so short compared to yours…" He shrugs. "You think of it as a beautiful but doomed thing that is here, then gone too fast to get attached."

"But we don't delight in crushing that beautiful thing under our bootheel, either."

Hades doesn't defend himself or his fellow deities, and I lift my gaze to study his face, what's behind the look he's giving me. "You said the others do," I say slowly.

His brows twitch up. "So?"

"You don't think of mortals like that?"

"No."

"Why not?"

That expression, the lost one, returns. "Because they all come to me in the end." Those nine words are so laden with burden, I don't know how they don't crush him.

It hits me for the very first time that the King of the Underworld is exactly that. A *king*. The ruler of every soul ever to believe in the Greek gods and end up in his realm after they die. A ruler who must punish and reward the lives those souls lived. A ruler who must know the heartbreak of the people left behind in the mortal world when a loved one passes, because he'll see those souls, too, eventually.

"We're not butterflies to you," I whisper. "We're eternity."

His eyes flare briefly with something savage, but he doesn't speak.

My eyebrows draw together as I think through that, shaking my head. "But you forced me into the Crucible like you didn't give a flying—"

"I believed you were strong enough to survive the Crucible. There are other reasons, but I did think that." He winces. Hades actually winces. "I didn't realize you'd have such a soft heart under that tough shell, though. I'm sorry."

I stare at him.

"What?" he asks.

"You apologized." Astonishment rolls through me. "I didn't know gods could do that."

His mouth crooks to one side, flashing a hint of the dimple there. "Don't let it go to your head, my star."

"Right." The endearment makes a little part of me think maybe he must care a tiny bit to bother, if only in a vague, guilty way.

I'm not sure how to feel about that. It's easier to think of him as a callous, selfish, even malicious deity who is just playing his games at any expense. Particularly mine.

"You were really mad at me," I whisper. What pit of the Underworld did that come from?

Hades shakes his head. "I was…" He glances away. "Frustrated. When I'm truly mad, you'll know it."

I'd rather not. "You can really make Isabel's afterlife…nice?"

"Yes."

My chin wobbles annoyingly. "Thank you for that."

After only the briefest hesitation, he gives a single nod. Then he gets us both on our feet, setting me a little bit away from him. The discomfort of my sodden clothes finally penetrates, and I shiver, plucking at my shirt.

He glances down over me, and I try not to feel the prickles that follow in the wake of his gaze. Unaware of my struggle, Hades snaps his fingers. And now we're both in a dry change of clothes, and I might as well have showered, I'm so clean, though my short hair is also dry. I'm wearing jeans, like he is, along with my tactical vest over a tailored white button-down rolled up at the sleeves. Imagine the amount of time that handy trick would save every day.

"I was so looking forward to another soak in the tub," I grumble more to myself than to him.

Hades shrugs like he didn't think of that. "You'd have just wallowed and cried in there."

"No. That's not me at all." Although neither is the way I've been reacting since I showed up here. Embarrassment warms my cheeks.

Trying to look anywhere but at him, I glance around the room. The same one where he kissed me only yesterday, and suddenly that's all I can picture. All I can feel. His lips on mine.

Stop thinking about kissing the god of death, Lyra.

"Hey." His voice is soft again, compelling and yet harsh at the same time. "Don't do that. Don't tell yourself you can't cry."

I almost laugh. If only he knew what I was really telling myself just then. Thank the gods he doesn't.

"It's who I've been made to be." I look away again, running a hand through my hair. "So...what next?"

"First, you are to make yourself at home here."

I can't help myself. Cocking a hip, I say, "I guess I'd better kick you out, then. I hate having visitors."

Not even a snicker. "Are you done?"

I tilt my head. "You said I could be myself."

Ignoring that, he beckons me to follow, and I do.

We pass through the door into the rest of his Olympus home, which is all blacks and reds with embellishments of gold popping here and there. No photos here, either, I notice, just like his penthouse. Then again, I don't have any. Pledges aren't allowed to have pictures or videos of ourselves. No proof that we exist, should we get caught.

He takes me outside into a courtyard at the center of his home, one filled with flowering potted plants, fountains, and the hazy pink light of evening. He doesn't stop, walking through a gate that leads to a cobbled street overlooking the glory that is the home of the gods.

It's just as stunning a second time around. Maybe more so, because the skies are turning dark lavender that blends into brilliant orange where the sun is starting to dip, and the colors reflect off the whites of the buildings, which are lighting up from the insides.

I frown. "It was just morning."

Poseidon's contest started first thing.

"We're a long way from there, my star."

Right. It's a big world, and sometimes I need to be reminded of that fact.

THE GAMES GODS PLAY

"I have to go." Hades points at the gate to the street. "You don't pass this when I'm not here. Understand?"

"Um..." I do a double take. "What? Where are you going?"

He watches me from under his lashes. "I mean it, Lyra. The next Labor is tomorrow."

Tomorrow? The fuck it is. And he thinks he's just going to abandon me here tonight? "If it's tomorrow, sitting on my ass in your house is not what I need to be doing. I need allies—"

"You're not going to find any."

The words hit me right in the sternum.

And even though I try to hide my reaction, he sees anyway, his jaw going tight. But he doesn't take it back, either. "It's not safe here on your own."

Does he think I'm contemplating a leisurely stroll? "The gods can't touch me."

He takes a menacing step closer. "You think they won't push the boundaries of that rule? And what about the champions? They have no such limitations."

Which is why he should be doing this *with* me, damn it. "I have to."

"No."

I'm seriously considering hurling my axe at his face. "I can't just cower in here and hope I make it through the next Labor without being eaten alive."

He slashes a hand through the air. "Don't be stubborn about this, Lyra."

Stubborn? *That's* what he thinks this is?

Being dumped with the Order so young and carrying the curse I do, I had to grow up in a godsdamned hurry. I take care of myself, and always have, because no one else was going to. Even trying to throw a rock at Zeus' temple had purpose.

I cross my arms, glaring daggers at him. Instead of my axe, I hurl words. "Now that I've been through today, I know for a fact I won't survive all these Labors without at least one ally. I don't have time to sit around and wait on you to get back from... Where are you going? You didn't answer that yet."

The muscle in his jaw is clenching and unclenching now. "I have an Underworld to run."

"Delegate," I snap. "This is important."

"And souls like Isabel's aren't?"

I take a step back, hurt tumbling into my anger in a toxic mashup. "You know that's not what I meant."

Blowing out a sharp breath, he spikes a hand through his hair, rumpling it in the sexiest way, and I resent the fuck out of the fact that I notice at all. "Can you put it off?" I ask.

"Not this."

So much for being eternity to this god. I'm just another butterfly. Can't he see that going through another Labor alone is a one-way ticket to the Underworld? Or is he such a loner that it's not glaringly obvious to him? "I can't, either."

He eyes me sharply. "You're not going to let this go, are you?"

"Would you?"

"Fuck," he mutters. "Fine." Then he gets right in my face, his eyes glinting like sharpened knives. "You have that damned axe and one pearl in your hands at all times. I'll try to be fast."

This close, I can see lighter silver around his irises. "Fine." I echo his terse tone.

He hesitates, gaze dropping to my lips. Is he checking that his mark is still there to keep me safe if I have to use one of the pearls? The heat that sneaks through me turns to ice in an instant as he suddenly steps back.

…And then he's gone.

I stare at the empty space where he was just standing, not entirely believing my eyes.

He did it. He really left me.

Meanwhile, I now get to attempt the impossible with my lack of charm, my curse, and my tether to the god of death, whom no one wants to see become King of the Gods. Ever.

Why is this my life?

Knowing that I'm right, that the chance to find allies before tomorrow is too important to miss, I make myself push through the gate and out into the street.

My skin prickles in the cool breeze. Not the good kind. The kind that feels like eyes are following my every move.

32

THE STRONGEST POWER

I should have asked Hades where to start looking before he left.

I stare out over the peaks and valleys connected by the flowing rivers, with pristine buildings scattered among the lush landscaping, and try not to dwell on the fact I may not be here to enjoy the view ever again after tomorrow.

I sigh, pulling out a pearl and rolling it between my fingertips as I walk aimlessly.

Eventually I get to a crossroad and decide to turn right. Off the bat it becomes apparent Hades' home is one in a row of fourteen all lined up on the same side of the street, with views out both the front and back. Ten guesses as to who claim the other homes.

Each house—or mega-mansion, really—reflects the deity who lives there the same way their armor does, to the point of being almost one-dimensional. Poseidon's is all ocean, Zeus' lightning, Demeter's harvest, and so forth. Do they focus so much on what they are the god or goddess of that they don't think they can be anything else?

I'd rather not run across any of the major deities on my own, rules or no rules, so I hurry out of that grouping of buildings and around a small lake formed between the valleys of two mountains fed by Poseidon's brilliant blue waters. Up ahead and above me, buildings are spaced along the side of the terrain in a way that makes me think of a little mountain town, and that's where I'm headed.

Until, halfway across a larger field, I spot a pegasus in the distance.

Not just one but a *herd* of them, in all different colors, grazing peacefully in a field of tall grasses mixed with vibrant flowers everywhere.

It's not until I'm crossing a nearby bridge over a burbling stream that I stop. I lean against the rail of the bridge, staring at a rose-colored pegasus. Despite the lingering ache of what happened to Isabel, my heart settles as the mare lifts her head to look right back as though she were seeing into my soul. She's close to the road, and I can hear her feathers slide against one another when she ruffles her wings as she grazes.

The only warning I get that I'm not otherwise alone is the distinct pounding of running feet. That and the pegasus lifts her head again.

I whirl just in time to see Dex, murderous intent written in every line of his face, brown eyes narrowed to slits as he barrels toward me.

"You made me look like a coward," he hollers.

I grab my relic from the back of my tactical vest, sliding it free and taking the axe in two hands, lifting it over my head to throw.

Don't make me do this.

"Already?" At the sound of an amused female voice, we both freeze.

I lower my weapon to my side as Aphrodite approaches. She looks at Dex, and her smile is one sirens would envy. "Don't you wish—"

I drop my axe, and it clanks to the ground as I slap my hands over my ears, so I have no idea what she says to him next, but Dex suddenly relaxes, arms loose at his sides, then turns and walks away without a second glance at me.

I slowly lower my hands, staring at her.

And she smiles, eyes twinkling. "I'm guessing Hades warned you?"

"Yes."

She doesn't seem concerned as she watches Dex's retreating back. "I'm not a fan of bullies."

"Me neither," I say faintly as she closes the gap between us. "What'd you make him do?"

Her smile turns mysterious. "Nothing *too* naughty."

This is Aphrodite like I'm guessing very few people see her. She looks my age, wearing yoga pants and a sweatshirt, and her gorgeous dark hair is piled up on top of her head in a messy bun. No makeup, no adornments, just the raw beauty of the goddess—the kind of beauty that inspires poets and wars.

She reaches down, picks up my relic, and takes a long look at it. "Hades gave up one of his precious axes?"

"No," I say cautiously.

She arches an eyebrow in question as she holds it out to me. She must realize from my expression I don't plan to say more and asks instead, "Could you actually have hit Dex with it?"

I take the axe, flip it upside down, and shove it into the hidden pocket in my vest, the weight of the metal fitting comfortably against the small of my back. "Yes."

"*Would* you have?" she asks next.

Honestly, I don't know. But being honest with a goddess who is not my patron seems like a very bad idea. "Of course."

Aphrodite leans on the bridge railing, looking over to the rose-colored pegasus, who is still watching me while chewing on another bite of grass. "You did well today."

I glance down at my feet. That is not a compliment I want, not given what happened. "Tell that to Hades."

"Did my brother lay into you? He's all bark and..." She makes a face. The kind that if I made it, I'd look like a troll, but on her...jeez. "Well, his bite can be pretty bad, too, but he only uses it when he has to." She considers me. "A little like you and your axe."

I'm starting to realize that, too. "He was...fine."

Her gaze turns thoughtful. "That was a rough death."

"Yeah."

"I could make you feel better." She steps even closer, and her hand touches mine. Warmth flows through me, loosening my muscles and... "Don't you wish—"

I yank my hand away and clap my palms over my ears. "Thanks, but I'd rather work through it on my own." I'm probably talking too loudly now.

Aphrodite pouts, then mouths back, "Fine."

When I lower my hands, she says, "Hades is no fun, telling you about that. I was only going to take away the sadness. Just for a little bit. Replace it with pleasure."

If the tiny moment of warmth I experienced is any indication, I have a good idea what she means by *pleasure*. "Errr... It's sweet of you to offer."

In her own way, at least. And at least she's not trying to harm me right now. I glance around, realizing we're really all alone.

"But Hades told you not to let me," she guesses.

I can't help but chuckle. "A little bit that, but mostly...I earned the sadness. I'd rather feel it."

Which makes the goddess tilt her head to study me, and I try not to fidget under her direct, searching gaze. "Good for you, little mortal. Most of your kind would take the reprieve and not look back."

They probably would, and maybe I'm a fool not to.

She waves a hand down the path. "If you head this way, through the entertainment district to the other side, you'll find the temples where we go to listen to prayers. Maybe you'd like to honor your lost champion there."

My lost champion. As if this goddess has nothing to do with it. But, like Hades said, we're butterflies to them, and Aphrodite is being kind in this moment. I guess deities, like mortals, are complicated.

"But be careful." She glances at the weapon in my hand. "I hope you really do know how to use that."

In other words, watch my back. Got it.

"You're actually nice." The words pop out, and I mumble, "Sorry."

Aphrodite laughs. "Don't tell the others." She rolls her eyes. "It's hard enough to be taken seriously when love is up against powers like storm, war, knowledge, and death."

"Seems to me that love can calm storms, end wars, make fools of smart people, and bridge the gap between life and death. Doesn't that make it the most powerful?"

She stares at me with something like…appreciation. Warmth radiates from her in a way that makes me want to lean closer to bask in the glow a little more.

"For that, Lyra Keres, I will share with you a secret."

I blink at her.

"Two, actually, because I find I like you." She smiles—not the breathtaking kind, but self-deprecating, as if she can't quite believe she admitted that. "The first is that my Labor will be about the person you love most in this world."

Oh. My shoulders slump as my mind churns with a fear I didn't even realize I carried. I don't love *anyone.* Sure, there's Boone, but I'm not sure a crush—or admiration, for that matter—counts as love. There's no one else. Not really. Not Felix or my parents. I learned long ago it would be foolish to ever let anyone into my heart—a one-way trip to misery, given my curse.

I brush aside the memory of being wrapped in Hades' arms. That's not love, either.

What if I have no one? Oh, good gods. I'm going to show up to Aphrodite's Labor, and the whole immortal world will be watching. Hades will be watching. If there's *no one* there for me, *humiliating* won't even cover it.

Aphrodite's smile manages to be comforting and amused at the same time at the look of horror surely overtaking my face right now. She pats my shoulder awkwardly, then coughs and continues. "The second secret is more a...warning."

I wait.

"Hades is one of my favorites," she confides. The breeze picks up tendrils of hair that have escaped her bun, blowing them artistically around her face. "But he has a hidden agenda, playing in the Crucible. One I haven't quite figured out yet, but I *know* him. He doesn't do things without a specific reason."

I believed you were strong enough to survive the Crucible. There are other reasons, but I did think that. Hades' words rattle around in my head.

Other reasons.

"Are you warning me not to trust him?" I ask.

"I'm warning you that nothing is ever as it seems with my brother." Aphrodite shrugs like this is no big deal, but her gaze holds mine intently. "And when he wants something, he can be the most ruthless of us all."

33

ENEMIES & ALLIES

The swirling tornado of my thoughts sucks up Aphrodite's warning and won't let me be. I go over and over and over every word as I wander farther along the path.

I'm not really paying attention to my surroundings until I realize I'm in the center of buildings again, each lined up on either side of a cobbled street, looking like the ancient Greek version of idyllic Main Street USA or a European town square.

And I'm not the only person here by a long shot. The street is full of gods, demigods, nymphs, satyrs, and centaurs, all in modern clothing—at least for those who wear clothes. Most pay me no attention, though I get a second glance or two. Still, it feels safe enough, even with twilight darkening the skies.

This must be the entertainment district Aphrodite mentioned. I have never in my life thought of the gods and goddesses as needing entertainment. I've always figured that we mortals fulfilled that need for them. But turning around to take it all in, I can see several restaurants, an art gallery, a library, a spa, and even a dance club with bass thumping through the open front door.

I guess gods just want to have fun, too.

I get a lot of looks, but no one bothers me. I try not to let my guard down regardless. A burst of laughter spills into the street from up ahead, and I follow the sound to a building at the corner and read the sign above the entrance—BACCHUS' PLACE.

Dionysus uses his Roman name here?

Stop focusing on minutia, Lyra.

The more interesting fact is that the god of wine and revelry apparently runs a bar in Olympus.

"Makes sense," I murmur to myself. Not just because of who he is, either. There are enough stories of drunk gods and resulting babies that I'd venture to say Dionysus makes a killing with this particular establishment.

Maybe some of the champions will be here?

It's as good a place to check as any, so I head inside.

The place is...disappointing.

Like every mortal pub I've seen. I was expecting something as spectacular as the outside, but no such luck. A bar stretches along one entire wall—yes, of white marble, but still—wooden tables of various sizes are all around, and windows look out onto the street. Several TVs showing mortal sports and news and a K-drama hang above the bar. Those are, I guess, the biggest surprise. I didn't picture gods and goddesses lounging around with a beer and watching TV.

The place is packed. I don't recognize all the faces—there are so many gods to keep track of, and I'm not sure all of them in here are Grecian—but I do think I recognize Eirene, the goddess of peace, Hybris, the god of outrageous behavior, and Thrasos, the god of boldness. There's got to be a joke in there somewhere. A champion walks into a bar...

"Lyra?"

I pause. The bartender is looking right at me. "Um..." I glance around, but there's no one behind me. "How do you know my name?"

Dressed in the style of a goth, with deep-red streaks through her jet-black hair and black makeup around her eyes, she has a smile that's pitying in that "oh silly mortal" way. "After today, we all know you, sweetie."

Right. Hades' champion for the Crucible. All the gods are watching.

She adds, "Well done on your first Labor."

I guess I'll have to get used to being congratulated for surviving something that killed another person right in front of me. Not wanting to offend, I nod.

"I'm Lethe," she introduces herself. "Goddess of oblivion and forgetfulness. Looks like you could use some of that."

Frustration sparks at being so easy to read. "I'm fine. I'm looking for my fellow champions. Have you seen any of them?"

"Is Hades coming?" She glances over my shoulder.

Do I admit I'm alone?

I take too long answering, and her eyes narrow shrewdly. "In that case, you probably don't want to be in here."

"Turn that shit off!" a voice shouts from the back corner, slurring the words slightly.

A familiar voice I heard only this morning.

Warily, I turn and then lean to peek around a pillar. Sure enough, Poseidon is sitting at a table, still in his fish-scale pants with his blue hair tied up in a messy man-bun, visibly drunk as the proverbial skunk and sporting one hell of a black eye.

Shit. Lethe's right. I really shouldn't be here.

With a frown, I follow his gaze to one of the TVs, and my stomach tightens. I can't hear the broadcast, but I don't need to. The words splashed across the screen tell me exactly who the woman is. She's speaking at a podium of microphones, surrounded by what appear to be family, and my heart goes a little fetal.

The banner at the bottom of the screen reads— *Beauty queen Isabel Rojas Hernáiz's body returned by the gods. Partner of ten years, Estephany Roscio, speaks out against the Crucible and the Greek pantheon.*

The devastation that creases Isabel's partner's face, turning her eyes red and puffy from crying, is so raw, so brutally deep, I can hardly stand to look at her.

Lethe is pouring a drink for one of the other patrons but flicks a glance in the direction of the back corner. "Poseidon is in a mood. I'd steer clear if I were you."

"What happened to his face?"

"Artemis."

The bartender says this as if it explains everything.

A crash explodes through the room, and I about jump out of my skin. The initial violence is followed by a sudden hush punctuated with the sizzle of sparking. Poseidon's trident now sticks out of the screen that had been showing Isabel's family.

"Hey!" Lethe calls, moving down the bar to where she can see him better. "You going to replace that?"

"Does the little mortal really think I wanted to kill my own champion?" Poseidon barks at the shattered screen.

A nymph sitting beside him tries to calm him. "Of course she wouldn't think that. The mortals don't know what happened. The Daemones only returned the body and announced the winner of the Labor. They didn't explain *how* she died—or why." When that doesn't seem to work, she adds, "They're probably all blaming Hades anyway."

As everyone around her nods in agreement, I swallow the bile rising in my throat. Poseidon flops back against his seat with a *harrumph*, crossing his arms.

Lethe grimaces, then slides her focus from him to me. "You'd better get out of here before he notices you."

I'm already on that same page, my gaze darting between Poseidon and the door. But my breath catches as I realize the angry god's attention is turning—to me.

34

ZAI ARIDAM

In a blink, I slip out the door and back onto the street. I don't breathe easy until I leave the entertainment district behind entirely, heading west toward the temples.

Since Aphrodite offered the original suggestion, I decide to pray for Isabel in hers, so I aim toward the one that screams goddess of love thanks to the pink glow coming from inside it. Apparently, Hades isn't the only one who publicly leans into perception but privately is something quite different.

As I pass the temple dedicated to Hermes, though, movement inside catches my eye, and I pause. The boniness of Zai Aridam's shoulders is hard to mistake. His back is to me, and I can see the way his dark hair curls a little against the nape of his neck.

Hesitation stays my steps. Clearly, he is praying, and maybe, like me, he's struggling with what happened today. In which case, I should just give him privacy. But…

I need allies. It's the whole reason I'm risking my neck being out here.

Does this make me an opportunistic bitch? Probably. But I walk inside all the same.

Lit by oil lamps along the walls and between columns, the temple is a simple circular room with a shrine at the front—a beautifully carved, almost lifelike depiction of Hermes mid-flight, with his winged helm and winged sandals. He holds his staff in one hand like a weapon, and clouds spiral down from his feet. Serpents and wings adorn the domed roof, and two potted palm trees stand to either side of the shrine.

Zai is standing directly before the statue, head bowed. Freshly lit incense burns, rising in an undulating tail of smoke and filling the room with a layer of clove and cinnamon with lavender, lemon, and safflower blended in a scent so familiar to me, it's like coming home. After all, until now, I've prayed to this god more than any other.

"Do you come here to pray to the god of thieves?" Zai's question comes out of nowhere, since he hasn't so much as lifted his head. I didn't even realize he knew I was here.

"No. I was going to…" I hesitate, glancing around. Talking about praying to a different deity while in another's temple is probably a bad idea. "I saw you."

He lifts his head, turning slowly to look at me. "I see." He seems to study my face. I'm not sure what he thinks he'll find there. "So, you are here to kill me, then?"

I can't help the knee-jerk reaction that makes me hold a hand out toward him. "No!"

Confusion flickers in eyes the color of oak. "No?"

I shake my head. "No."

"Don't you blame me? For Isabel's death?" He holds himself completely still. "Or maybe you consider her death lucky. One less competitor."

I pull my shoulders back. "If that's how you see it, then we have no need to talk."

I spin around and am nearly to the entrance before his voice stops me. "That's not how I see it."

When I turn, he's sort of hunched over and his eyes are half closed, as if that little outburst was all the energy he had left and now he's having a hard time staying on his feet. Not for the first time, I wonder what's up with his health. Is he sick or something? He's spent the last hundred years in Olympus… Does their food not nourish mortals?

I consider leaving him alone to rest.

"What did you want to talk about?" he asks, opening his eyes fully.

I take a step forward. "It seems to me that you and I could—"

"Zai!" a voice shouts from somewhere outside. "Zai!"

Zai's eyes go wide with fear. "Hide," he hisses at me.

"What? I—"

"It's my father. If he sees you in here with me…" He shakes his head, but the implication of dire consequences for me is easy enough to pick up.

There aren't exactly a lot of places to disappear in here, but I squeeze myself between one of the columns and the wall and pray Mathias Aridam doesn't come to this side of the temple. Hopefully, the flickering of the lamplight doesn't give me away with a shadow on the wall.

I'm out of sight just as Mathias stomps into the room. "Here you are, boy. Wasting your precious energy on guilt for that woman still."

"She had a name, Father," Zai says. "Isabel."

I frown at the difference in Zai's voice from a second ago—it's gone flat, emotionless.

"A name that is not worth learning. She's already dead."

Wow. Heart of gold, this one.

Zai says nothing.

"You looked like a fool out there today." Mathias spits the words like a cobra. "Why Hermes didn't pick one of your brothers, I will never know. Either of them would have *won* that Labor, not looked like a drowning rat in need of rescuing. You reflect on *me*."

I picture the two young men who were with Mathias when the gods introduced us to the previous winner and his family. Tall, strapping men, so he's probably not wrong.

Still nothing from Zai.

"Allergies," Mathias scoffs next. "What a pathetic excuse for weakness."

So that's what Zai is dealing with? They must be bad to make him look so haggard.

"Everyone blames you." Mathias doesn't even pause for Zai to answer. "They are all saying you are the reason that woman died. What did you think you were doing?"

Felix might have been a callous father figure and boss, but—even with my curse—he would have never said words as vile as this to me.

Mathias Aridam is a nasty piece of work.

"*You* told me not to trust anyone," Zai says. The flatness is still there, almost like he's quoting facts from a schoolbook. "So I didn't let Lyra cut me loose."

"And she made you look even weaker than you are, showing you up like that."

Asshole.

Zai doesn't acknowledge what his father said. "*You* told me not to use the gifts Hermes gave me unless I absolutely had to. I didn't…even when I could have saved Isabel."

I put a hand over my mouth as my heart thuds painfully. Zai could have saved her today? He had to sit beside her, as close as I was, after she'd been injured helping him, and watch her die. No wonder he's in here praying.

"Don't you lay this at my feet—"

"*You* told me to let the other champions kill themselves dealing with any of the physical Labors. I listened." There's a small pause. "So far, listening to you seems to be the problem."

A clap of sound pops in the room. I know that sound. Flesh hitting flesh.

"You've always been an ungrateful whelp, but don't dare disrespect me, boy. I am a Crucible winner and your father."

Zai's voice is still as flat and cold as a sheet of ice. "A father who is looking down the barrel of being returned to the Overworld like a relic that no longer works. You *need* me to win to keep you here, living in the manner to which you've grown accustomed."

The crack of another hit comes swift and hard, followed by stomping feet that fade away, making it clear Mathias has left the temple.

A soft sigh reaches me. "You can come out now."

I scoot around the column to find Zai standing in the center of the room. The bright-red outline of a handprint stains his left cheek. Despite that, his hands are clasped behind him, his shoulders straight, head up, and gaze steady on mine.

"You were about to ask me to form an alliance with you." It's not a question—he's sure of what he knows. He also doesn't protest, doesn't point out the danger his severe allergies put him in, doesn't offer excuses or ask for anything.

"You have allergies? Well, Zeus cursed me to be unlovable a long time ago. You should know that up front."

He doesn't even pause before he nods.

I study him for a long moment. "You are clearly intelligent, and that little display with your father tells me you also have a backbone."

He says nothing, listening and watching without moving.

The problem is, I can practically hear Hades groaning when I tell him about Zai.

"If I help you with the physical parts of the Labors, can you help me with the intellectual parts?"

"Lyra Keres!" a voice yells. A drunken, slurred voice.

I flinch. Poseidon must've followed me after all. That or someone told him I came this way. Snitches.

"Lyra Keres," he bellows. "I'm coming for you!"

35

KISS ME GOODBYE

I don't have to tell Zai to get out of here. After all, it's entirely likely the ocean god would blame him, too. But Zai holds a finger to his lips as he points behind the altar.

A way out?

Right. He grew up here. He must know all of Olympus.

On silent feet, we escape into the night through a small door at the back of the temple. Except I guess stress triggers allergic asthma, because Zai immediately starts wheezing and coughing. With the efficient, quick movements of long habit, he takes an inhaler from his pocket, shakes it, and sucks. Twice.

I wince both times at the noise. I have no idea how well gods hear.

Zai points in one direction, then at me, before he runs off in the other direction—up the mountainside into the evergreen trees, every single step crunching loudly. No trees for me, then. I spin and make it to the corner of the building, checking carefully.

"Lyra Keres!" Poseidon bellows.

He sounds farther down, so I run between the temples of Hermes and Athena, toward the road, then pause there, hiding in the shadows. I don't immediately hear Poseidon running my direction, so I make my way to the other corner of Athena's temple and poke my head out. The sun has finally set, and I breathe a bit easier. I might be able to skirt back to Hades' home in the darkness without incident.

In a blur of hands and shadows, I'm grabbed from behind and held against a tall, barrel-chested body, one arm wrapped around my waist and a knife held to my neck. Not slicing yet but pressing enough that I suck in sharply, heart racing and mind going foggy with fear. Both of my arms are pinned. I can't do anything with the axe or the pearl.

"You," Poseidon says. "It's your fault my champion is dead."

Hells.

I hold still and say nothing. My mind is spinning with any way out of this. Anything I can do or say.

Think, Lyra.

There's got to be a way to stop him.

"You think you can win this?" he demands, breath hot on the side of my face, reeking of beer. "You can't. You think anyone will be a true ally?"

Oh gods. Did he overhear?

He barks a harsh laugh. "Even that pathetic whelp of Aridam's is going to turn on you. The other champions are already plotting to use you to get through the next Labor and then eliminate you. He's just reeling you in."

My spinning thoughts trip over that.

Is Poseidon telling the truth? Am I just being played? Past experience and a certain curse rear their ugly heads.

Focus. Get out of here alive. Worry about Zai later.

If I can just get to the pearl…

"Why in the name of Tartarus did my brother choose you?" In the dark, his eyes look black. "He must be hard up to get laid since Persephone died."

I gasp. "That's not—"

"I hope you enjoyed him, little mortal. Because I'm going to make that your last." Poseidon's grip suddenly tightens, the knife digging in a bit more. The slice of pain is enough to make me whimper. "Screw whatever the Daemones think they can do to me," he growls. "If I can't win, Hades sure as fuck won't."

My rapidly chugging heart drops into my stomach.

I point out in a low, wobbly voice, "Are you seriously threatening the god of *death's* champion?"

The blade lifts away just a teensy smidge. Questions make people do that unconsciously as they think. Apparently, gods, too.

In a blink, I slam my head backward and connect with the hard edges of Poseidon's nose and chin. He grunts in my ear, his arms falling away in shock, and I jab my elbow into his gut. Maybe because he's drunk, he falls over.

"I'm going to skewer you on my trident," he yells.

I shoot to my left even as I lift the pearl to my mouth.

Except when I spin around, I find myself running straight into Hades' strong arms, his features harsh in the night but more familiar to me in the dark. Maybe because of the way we met.

I haven't known him long, but I have never seen him so angry. Even earlier when he yelled at me.

That anger was big and loud and edged in frustration. Now he's so cold and contained, I shiver.

"Did he hurt you?" His voice is as gritty as soot.

Then his hands are all over my body. Not in a sexual way, but clinical as he checks every single part of me for injury. Even so, warmth seeps through each point of touch.

Then he brackets my face with his hands. "Are you harmed, Lyra?"

Warmth coalesces inside my belly, which is turning squishier by the second. I should not be squishy for the god of death, no matter how much it sounds like he cares. That's a terrible idea. "I'm fine."

He eases fractionally. Just for a moment, his heated gaze holds mine, and…there it is. That sensation again. He's standing before me, only touching my face, but his mouth might as well be on mine, tasting his fill.

Until his gaze drops to my neck and the sensation disappears in an instant as he goes stone still. I know he's seen the cut Poseidon's knife made. His eyes narrow, and that cold, leashed fury drops another ten degrees in temperature so that even my shivers have shivers.

Oh gods. This is what really mad looks like.

"She's bleeding," he says, the words clipped and short.

He's not talking to me. He's talking to Poseidon, who is still on the ground and swaying a little. The ocean god goes ashen with fear.

Hades walks over and squats down beside the other god.

He grabs the handle of the knife from Poseidon's limp hand and lifts the blade up, the sharp edge catching the light from the moon and glinting as he uses it to gesture toward me without breaking eye contact with his brother. "*She* is mine. And I protect what's mine."

He expertly flips the knife, blade angled down on Poseidon's thigh, and raises his hand in the air.

"Don't!" My voice is soft, but Hades stops immediately, his gaze cutting to mine. "Not for me," I add.

The god of death narrows his eyes in a way that makes a now-sweating Poseidon lean away, even though Hades is looking at me.

"Not for you?" he asks me silkily, his voice like sandpaper on fire by now. "Fine. For me, then. Because you are *mine*, and he dared to threaten you, let alone make you bleed."

That word again.

That possessive fucking word. I should protest. I should push back, lash out against it. Because I don't belong to anyone. Not even the Order. What I shouldn't do is react with something darkly sensuous that slides through my body, waking me up from the inside in glorious, gut-clenching, heat-pooling folly. And I definitely shouldn't *like* it.

I do. I like it. A lot.

No. No way. Wanting Hades will only ever end in sorrow.

"Exactly," I say. "I'm yours. You chose me, and I was about to take care of it my own damn way." Where the hells did those words come from? Calling myself his is the last thing I should be doing.

Something flares in Hades' eyes. Something dangerous. Something so seductively triumphant, my body quivers instinctively.

I have no idea what reaction I expected. Definitely not for him to slam the knife into the ground beside Poseidon's leg, making the god yelp.

"Go sleep it off, brother," he says in a voice gone all fire and brimstone, the skin tightening over his cheekbones. "You lost. Deal with it."

Hades disappears only to appear directly in front of me, wrap his arms around me, and disappear us both.

I know we're back in Hades' house in Olympus because of the red and black surrounding me, but I don't know which room because immediately his body pins me against a wall and his lips are on mine.

And…*oh gods.* I'm in trouble. Because I'm kissing him back.

This is different from the last time.

That kiss started out with a non-lust-related reason and turned into something else. This? This is already something else.

It takes the heat and quivering already running rampant through me and shifts them into a thousand sensations that turn my mind hazy and set the rest of me on fire. I've never been kissed, not before him, but I've dreamed of it. I never imagined anything like this, though. Like Hades wants to devour me. Like I *want* him to.

The god with razor-sharp control is chipping at the edges.

Because of me.

I didn't know I could feel like this.

Everything about me gathers in tighter and tighter, condensing, like the sensation has no outlet, and a whimper escapes my lips even as I'm kissing him back.

But at that one tiny sound, Hades goes abruptly, utterly still, then pulls away and drops his forehead against mine.

"Fuck," he mutters.

And I realize I was wrong. His diminishing control isn't about me—it's about his champion. I scared him tonight because he could have lost his place in the Crucible. If he's that afraid of losing, his reasons must be huge.

I take a deep breath to say something. Anything.

But he's already gone, leaving only a swirl of smoke where he stood pressed against me, the burn of sulfur sharp in my nostrils. I shiver as the heat from his touch fades, leaving behind only cold.

And regret.

36

HERMES' LABOR

I don't know how I could've possibly fallen asleep after everything, but I did. So hard that all my training abandons me and I have no idea anyone is in my room until Hades shakes me awake.

"The second Labor is about to start, Lyra."

I blink the sleep out of my eyes to blearily focus on his face hovering just above mine — on his lips. What would he do if I kissed him?

His eyes narrow. "Lyra?"

"What?" I shove my head into my pillow.

I should be alert instantly with a god in my room, but everything about me feels slow and groggy. And it's entirely Hades' fault. I tossed and turned all night, dreaming of his hand sliding along my —

"The next Labor, Lyra." He pulls the pillow out from under my head. "It's Hermes'. Get dressed fast — "

He flips my covers back — and swears.

The word clangs like a bell I'm standing too close to, or maybe it's the bubbling sensation that does it as Hades' gaze is fixed on my bare midriff. Either way, my brain boots up with a kick of adrenaline too late because I'm already fading away.

Without my vest.

"Fuck," Hades swears again.

I don't look away, centering on his swirling gray eyes as I go.

And all I can think is that I'm in my pajamas, without my clothes or tools…or shoes, for that matter. But also without the pearls or what's left of the dragon teeth, and especially without my relic.

All of that runs through my mind, along with the thought that Hades' eyes have specks of gold in the silver…sort of like mine.

"You can do this, my star." His voice follows me into the void. "I'll see you soon."

Not the most comforting words, coming from the King of the Underworld.

When I fade back whole again, it's on a yelp as I immediately tilt forward to gain my balance…over nothing. My arms windmill as I totter on a tiny rectangular ledge, but I breathe a sigh of relief when my ass hits a wall at my back.

I jerk upright, as straight as I can, and my fingers desperately search for a grip on the rockface behind me.

I stay like that for a solid minute, catching my balance and waiting for my stomach to stop twisting, my heart to stop pounding in my chest. I slowly exhale. That was close. Directly in front of me are mountaintops—and *clouds*.

Hermes. I should have guessed something high up. This god likes to fly.

Anger sparks in my gut, not burning away the fear but giving me the kick I need to do more than stand here trying not to fall. Looking down, I discover that the tiny ledge I'm on isn't part of the rock wall behind me. Instead, I'm standing on what looks like a block of cement, about a foot wide in all directions, jutting from the mountainside itself. Just enough room for my feet.

With my arms splayed behind me to hold on to the mountain, I look up and see stars—and the top of what appears to be some sort of glass cylinder surrounding me. I'm like a bug in a jar with the lid missing.

"You've got to be kidding me." My voice bounces off the glass walls that surround me on three sides—sides that are about two feet away and do *not* touch the platform I'm standing on.

My words are immediately drowned out by a whistling burst of wind that whirls at my feet from the emptiness around the edges of the platform and tangles the hems of my silky lavender pajama pants at my ankles. Goose bumps prickle as the chilly wind joins the cold seeping into my bare feet against the cement block, and they intensify at the thought that one step forward and I'll fall into the nothingness between the glass wall and the edge of my platform.

Just a sheer drop, if the echo of my voice was any indication, and death waiting patiently at the bottom.

I glance to my left and right and realize I'm not the only one in pajamas. Glass partitions separate me from the other champions balanced precariously on their own cement blocks, each of us about ten feet apart. That explains why I'm not hearing the others beyond muffled sounds. Zai is directly to my left, and I can't help remembering Poseidon's taunt when Zai's wide eyes meet mine.

I offer a hesitant smile, then look right and swallow. "Damn it all to Tartarus."

Hermes must really have it out for me.

Dex is to my right, his shaved head turned away as he tries to get someone else's attention. How is he already dressed in his uniform? Did he sleep in it? The bulk of his body blocks a smaller form, but I catch sight of Rima's face for a moment, her brown eyes wide and full lips pinched with fear.

Past those two, Artemis' champion, Kim Dae-hyeon, leans out so I can see his face—not dressed in green for Strength because he's in PJs like me and Zai. Okay, so we're not the only ones caught unaware. But why does Dae-hyeon seem at ease while the rest of us are visibly afraid?

Beyond, I catch a glimpse of Neve's red hair, and past her, the top of Jackie's head—the only blonde and also the tallest woman in our cohort. Her wider shoulders must be giving her trouble, because Jackie's moving too much. I want to yell at her to stay still, but she won't hear me. I can't see past her as the mountain curves away, but I'm sure the others are there.

Please don't let anyone have fallen off already.

The clouds just outside our glass barricades stir, and Hermes, along with the four Daemones—two to either side of him—lift gracefully into the night sky to hover before us. The wings of his sandals flutter in a blur like hummingbird wings. He's slighter than many of the other male gods, and keen intelligence looks out at us from black, almost catlike eyes under the black fringe of his hair. His pale skin glows as though the moon is his own personal spotlight.

"Welcome, champions, to your second Crucible Labor!"

Here we go.

"Today's Labor is about both smarts and strategy," Hermes announces. "You will need to be intentional in the way you play."

He smiles like a villain in a bad movie. "Your challenge is to solve a riddle."

My stomach twists like a Gordian knot. I am *terrible* at riddles. I did fine in school—yes, thieves go to school—but riddles? Just no.

"I will give you this puzzle to solve in a moment," Hermes says. "But first, the rules."

Of course there are rules.

Hermes unrolls before him, of all things, a scroll. "I have a list to get through. I will only say them once, so pay attention. Each of you will be allowed only three questions to solve this riddle correctly."

I glance at Zai, whose gaze is trained on Hermes hard, eyes squinted.

"You may have noticed that you are all starting out with a plank that is twelve inches long?" Hermes looks down the line of us. "Every time a champion asks one of their three questions, everyone else will lose an inch from their plank."

I swallow hard, rubbing my suddenly sweaty hands on my PJs. How much plank could I stand on if I have to? The taller champions with likely the biggest feet—Samuel, Dex, Jackie—are probably in the worst shape, but still, twelve inches is not a lot of space for anyone.

"When you ask one of your three questions," Hermes says, "six inches will be added to your plank."

Okay. I get it. The plank being shortened by others asking questions will be counteracted by us asking our own questions. A forcing function. But since we all start with twelve inches, we should still be okay. I hope.

"Once you ask your third question, you have five minutes to guess the answer. If you don't guess in time, your plank disappears. If you guess in time but guess wrong, you will lose the original inches that you are starting with and better hope the others don't ask all their questions."

Always a fucking catch.

"If you are the first to answer correctly, you win my Talaria to use for the duration of the Crucible and you fly off this mountain."

Those winged sandals, which could fly the wearer out of every Labor, are worth their weight in gold. I can already feel some of the champions changing their minds about trying for them.

"Once a winner is determined, the remaining surviving champions will then have to climb down."

In pajamas and no shoes?

Hermes can apparently be just as cruel as the other gods. "It is a treacherous descent, and it's possible not all will make it."

Why do I get the sudden feeling the riddle isn't the real Labor—it's surviving the descent down the mountain? And barefoot and in pajamas, I'm certain if I don't win this challenge...I'm not making it back alive.

37

WALK THE PLANK

Hermes waves a hand, and three women appear before us. They are
seated, cross-legged, on puffs of clouds, and it's immediately obvious
who they are because they haven't stopped what they are doing to be
here. Each is working diligently with thread and ruler and scissors, none
bothering to lift their head to look at us.

"The Fates," I whisper, distracted just the teensiest bit by a flare of
fascination.

Hermes hovers behind them. "You know these lovely ladies as the
Moirai." He motions to one of the women hunched over a spindle. A
cloud of gray hair frames her wrinkled, brown face. "Clotho spins the
thread of life."

He gestures to the next woman, who has silver hair braided and
twisted on top of her head. Something like a measuring stick sits in one
hand that's a deeper brown than her sister's. "Her sister Lachesis uses
her rod to measure the thread of life allotted to each mortal."

With a final sweeping motion, he points to the last woman, who's
biting her lip as she studies a length of thread with intense black eyes, her
gray hair cropped close against her scalp. "And their sister, Atropos, cuts
the thread and, in doing so, chooses the manner of each person's demise."

Atropos uses shears—actual scissors made of a shiny, silver metal—
to cut a thread right then.

A shiver races down my spine. That was it. Someone just died. Does
Hades know he got a new soul to rule? I can't help but wonder if the god
of death felt it happen, too.

"But now," Hermes continues, "they will represent something else
and answer each of your questions."

I have to say, while Hermes' Labor is fascinating, his presentation skills are not at Zeus' or Poseidon's level. There's no fanfare, no trumpets, no birds released or fireworks or anything like that. He just wants to get straight to seeing us suffer. I am reconsidering him as my favorite god.

"Now for the riddle…"

The wind blows a little harder, rattling the glass walls and reaching for me from below, and this time I'm sure I hear several whimpers from the other champions. Hermes needs to get on with it so we can get off this cold rock.

The god waits out the winds with a small, enigmatic smile that makes me suddenly wonder if that's Notus, the god of the south wind and bringer of summer storms. One of four Anemoi, the unseen ones—it's possible he's here to make this even harder.

"Of the three Fates," Hermes says, pulling my attention back to him and the riddle, "one Fate is True and will only speak truth. One Fate is False and will only speak lies. And one Fate is Random and may answer either way. They will not change in how they answer. Use your three questions—yes-or-no questions only—to figure out which all three represent."

He rises and falls slightly where he hovers. Is the wind playing with him now?

"Your time starts…now."

Hermes disappears, leaving the Fates before us, spinning, measuring, and cutting while they wait for our questions.

Immediately, a glow lights the night from around the bend. It has to be Diego, his Halo of Heroism manifesting to help him with the Mind element of this Labor. Courage, too, maybe. Crap.

Dex is looking to his right, gesturing to Rima. No, not just to Rima. He and Neve and Dae-hyeon seem to be arguing with Rima. Strength and Mind virtues allying? Great. Zai is Mind. Is he with them?

I can catch Dex's words here and there. Do I dare try to crouch lower, closer to the bottom of the glass, to listen better?

"—need to knock…off their…then…wait—"

Oh gods. My heart rate kicks up a notch.

I think they're debating all asking questions at once. Maybe several. That much could knock everyone who hasn't asked a question yet off the mountain to their death. Would they really kill eight people in one fell swoop? Would that give them enough questions remaining to figure out the answer? And only one of them can get it right in the end.

I can't see past Jackie, but so far, my own plank hasn't moved, so I know no one has asked a question.

Rima seems to be the reason that hasn't happened yet. I can't tell if she's disagreeing with the killing or if she wants to try to solve the riddle and needs to save her questions. Either way, I'm not sure the rest of us have much time.

I carefully turn to Zai, who is holding a large, leatherbound book with thick, parchment-like pages. Where did he get that? It's got to be one of his gifts from Hermes. He's flipping pages and mumbling to himself.

Trying to solve the problem. I should be, too.

Think, Lyra.

My plank suddenly slides smoothly and soundlessly back one inch, forcing me to scoot with it. I'm not the only one who wobbles, clinging to the mountain for dear life.

Then my plank moves again, and my heart pounds in my chest.

Glancing right, I find Dex, Neve, and Dae-hyeon climbing off their planks to hold precariously onto the mountainside. I'm not sure if they're planning to take us all out right now or if they're just taking themselves out of the equation for Rima.

Thieves are taught climbing skills—something I was never good at, but for a split second I consider doing the same. Except they might have to hold on for the rest of the hour, and it hasn't been very long yet. Their muscles will be jelly by the time they actually have to climb down.

But I can be more prepared than I am. Facing outward means if I lose enough plank, I tumble forward with nothing to grab except maybe a face-plant into the glass partition. But facing the mountain, I could try to grab on. Going up on my toes, I shuffle my feet in a careful circle and slowly pivot on my plank.

"Don't fall. Don't fall. Don't—" My plank moves just as I'm facing the mountain, and I sway, stomach pitching.

With one hand on the rock and the other flailing for balance, I recover.

Blast and brimstone, that could have been bad.

I take a single second to press my forehead to the rock and close my eyes, letting out a breath of relief.

"Olympus, if this is your mountain…" I whisper the words to one of the Ourea. Different mountains have their own gods, and I think we're still in Olympus, so it makes sense. "I pray that you give to us sanctuary from…" I almost say *death*, but a tiny part of me knows that would hurt Hades, to pray to be saved from him. I don't know if it's loyalty to him or something else that changes the words on my lips. "From peril."

Tucking my elbows into my body, I rest my palms against the mountain at shoulder height, searching for any holds close in that might work. I find a better grip with my right but am still searching with my left.

That's when my plank moves in again. Now my heels are right at the edge. Anyone with bigger feet has to be on their toes by now. The others had it right. Just get off the damned plank. I turn my head, pressing it against the rock, and gasp. Something around Dae-hyeon's neck is glowing blue. A necklace, maybe. His plank is farther out, too. He asked one of his questions.

I turn my head to find Zai is also standing on more plank than me, so he also asked a question. If *anyone* asks one more, I'm in trouble.

I need more plank. Quickly. My mind gloms on to the first thing I can think of. "Clotho?" I ask, not that I can see her. "Is my name Lyra Keres?"

"Yes." Her voice floats around inside my glass cage.

Immediately, my plank moves back out, and I adjust with it. As soon as I'm steady, the small breath of relief I take pinches off, because I immediately realize my mistake.

Sure, the question gained me six inches and extra time. There's probably a dirty joke in there somewhere. But Clotho's answer told me nothing. Or did it?

True would answer yes. And Random has a fifty-fifty chance of answering yes. But False would answer no, right? That must mean Clotho is either True or Random. A tiny thrill bubbles in my chest. I figured *something* out, at least. Maybe this riddle won't be as hard as I expect.

Just then, my plank scoots in again, and I panic. I have no idea what to ask next. And there's not enough time to think. Fuck.

I close my eyes and hold on and try to block everything else out. What would narrow it down? If I was in my tiny office in the den, working on a spreadsheet, trying to figure out which thief brought an item back, what questions would I ask?

Before I can think through a plan, my plank suddenly recedes again, and off to my left a scream rends the air. I whip my head around only to have to catch my balance as the horrible sound of a body scraping down rock comes from below me. It feels like they fall forever before there's an awful *thud*.

Then…silence.

38

RIDDLE ME THIS

After a long, pounding silence, my plank suddenly starts moving again. Fast.

Until I'm up on my tiptoes.

And because I'm looking his way, I know Zai is one of the askers because he has more to stand on. The furrow in his brow and the way he's still flipping pages in that odd book tell me he hasn't figured it out entirely.

Can I trust Zai? Poseidon's words rattle around in my head. But I am damn sure I can't solve this alone. If, like the others, we worked together... But how?

"Zai!" I call out.

I don't have enough room to kick at the glass. Hells. How do I communicate with him?

The memory of Hades' voice whispers through my mind.

The tattoos.

He said they could be used to find out information. Can they...talk?

I stare at my forearm, and an idea takes shape. Hades told me not to use his gifts unless I absolutely needed them, but teetering over this drop feels like a do-or-die moment.

I'm going to have to risk it and try to work with Zai.

It takes some maneuvering of my hands above my head to be able to trace a line up the inside from my wrist to my elbow.

Just like for Hades, in the wake of my touch, the glittering lines form on my skin. My owl, panther, fox, and tarantula all blink at me, each moving as they stir to life. Hades said to think through their skills to use them wisely, but this one seems pretty obvious. Well, assuming I'm right and the animals are capable of communicating with people.

"Hey, pal." I lightly tickle the owl, who flaps his wings. The sensation is like a rustling under my skin. "I need you to be a messenger to Zai."

The owl tilts his head, round eyes trained on my face.

"Tell Zai if he promises to fly me down if he wins, I'll tell him the question I already used and the answer." Then I describe what I've learned. "And tell him I have two left if he needs them."

My owl friend spreads his wings wide and leaps from my arm, becoming real and life-size as soon as he's away from me. A twitch of movement catches my eye, and I look up, then press my belly into the wall of the mountain, stomach churning. One of the Daemones is outside the glass of my cage, gaze intent on me...and my arm.

But she doesn't stop me or kill me or take me away screaming... so...I guess I'm okay?

The owl, not paying the Daemon any attention, swoops low under the glass, then back up into Zai's glass cage, and perches on the book in his hands.

I suck in hard as Zai startles, bobbling, but he doesn't fall.

The Daemon, in the meantime, backs away, but not by much. Awesome.

I can't hear the exchange, but my owl must tell him the message, because Zai looks at me, dark eyes lit up, then sort of blinks to himself with a frown before leaning a bit to look around me. Rima seems to be focused on trying to solve the riddle, and the other three are yelling and gesticulating at one another. Is he worrying about this apparent alliance? Or is he part of it?

Then he nods at me, says something to the owl, then listens.

And that's when I see it—the glint in his eyes matching the crook of his mouth.

Has he figured it out?

Zai talks to the owl some more. When the owl flies back to me, Zai closes his book with a snap I can almost hear, then waves a hand over it, which makes it disappear.

The owl swoops up to perch on my shoulder. He never opens his beak. Instead, I hear a voice in my head that isn't quite mortal, but instead a sort of low trill like hooting but in words. *"Ask this question..."* The owl hoos the question from Zai in my ear.

I squint at Zai.

He rolls his eyes and points, and I get it. Just ask.

I hang on to the mountain. "Lachesis. Paris is the capital of France if and only if you are true, yes or no?"

"Yes," the goddess says without hesitation.

My own plank moves out six inches. Someone yelps from my left, and I hope to Hades that the faint sound wasn't me killing them. I didn't hear a slide of rock or thudding body.

"Yes," I yell and nod my head for emphasis.

Zai nods, then faces the Fates. Suddenly, our planks start to slide back toward the mountain again. Not one inch, not two, but a lot. I have no choice now.

I'm hanging by both hands and one foot while I search for another toehold and pray that Zai didn't fall. I can't turn my head to see.

"Congratulations!" Hermes' voice booms from the sky. "The winner is my own champion, Zai Aridam!"

The god sounds so happy he could fly, but hopefully he's not, because Zai needs those winged sandals right now.

I whisper to myself, "Come on, Zai. Please hurry. Keep your promise and don't leave me here—"

"Right behind you."

His voice is so close and unexpected that I yelp and almost lose my grip. Felix would be hanging his head in disgust if he could see me now.

Two hands land on my waist, and I can feel the way Zai lightly bounces up and down in the air thanks to the wings on his feet. "Can the sandals hold us both?" I ask.

"Sure." He chuckles. A nice sound, surprisingly low and warm.

I won't be laughing until I'm safely off this mountain.

"Now," he says. "Let go with your right hand and try to wrap it around my neck." I manage that much, and his left arm moves around me more securely. "When I say so, jump and swing your legs over my right arm. Got it?"

"Got it."

"On three… One. Two. Three—"

Zai wheezes in my ear with the effort of lifting me, but I manage to wrap my arms around him like a baby sloth around its mama. When I'm against him this way, the frailty of his frame is even more obvious.

I'm safe.

Thank not the gods but Zai Aridam.

The relief that shoots through my veins might as well be a tidal wave, and the adrenaline makes me tremble.

"Zai, you have won the second Labor," Hermes is saying. "As for the rest of you..."

The others. "Oh my gods. Who fell?"

"Amir. He's moving, though."

So not dead? Yet. No way did the kid not injure something. I push at Zai's shoulder. "You should leave me and take him."

"I'll come back for him."

"But—"

"I'll be quick."

He seems determined. I frown. "The others—"

"All made it," Zai rushes to assure me.

I sigh on another *whoosh* of relief. "So far."

Hermes clears his throat as if we interrupted him. "The remaining champions may all start climbing down, and best of luck to you."

Zai floats us downward as soon as the glass that had been caging me in disappears. At a screech, I look up behind him, where my owl is flapping its wings to stay aloft. Clutching Zai tighter, I hold out my left arm, and the beautiful, brown-feathered creature with his horned face flies straight for me. He doesn't perch but sort of leaps right into my skin, growing smaller and turning into glittering blue lines. The tarantula waves its front legs at him, and the fox snuggles into him like one friend greeting another.

"That's a handy gift," Zai says.

In a very unexpected way. "Yeah."

"The Daemones don't seem too happy about it."

I glance over Zai's shoulder to where all four are lined up, wings flapping to hold them aloft. They're watching me with such intensity, my stomach clenches. Twice. Hades must have taught them how to glare. "I noticed."

"Be careful," he says.

I nod, then change the subject, not wanting to face the dread knotting in my stomach at gaining another enemy in the Daemones. So I ask instead, "How'd you figure it out, anyway? The book?"

"Not entirely. The book isn't the internet. It doesn't give direct answers but how to find the knowledge for yourself. Sharing your answers helped narrow things down."

He launches into a description of "if and only if" questions that is mind-numbing, but I think I follow. I'm happy to listen all the way to the ground, trying to keep up mostly to not start worrying over a new problem—facing Hades again.

With a new ally. I think.

After two Labors lost.

After that kiss.

39

CAN I REALLY TRUST THIS?

Zai lands us gently, like stepping off a stair, as if he's been flying with Hermes' sandals his entire life. But, despite starting to wheeze, he doesn't put me down right away.

"Thank you," I say again. "Hopefully I'll be able to pull more weight on the next one."

Zai's dark eyes—lighter up close, with golden brown streaks that shoot out from his pupils—remain serious. "You did great. I'm a Mind champion, and you're..."

I guess he realizes who he's saying this to, because a tinge of red sneaks up his neck.

"Exactly," I say dryly. "Nothing. I'm nothing."

He shakes his head. "Hades is a king as well as a god, and unlike Zeus, no one ever tries to take that title away from him. *He* is not nothing, so you are not nothing."

Zai is trying to be kind, so I don't snap his head off for basing my value on something I have no control over. "I guess we both fill gaps," I say instead.

"Exactly." He sets me down on my feet, although I sense the move is reluctant. Like he's not quite ready to let go of me. Then his gaze lowers, brows coming together. "Did Poseidon find you last night?"

Bloody hells. The cut on my neck. I shrug. "Yeah, but I handled it."

"How?" he asks, then reaches out to rub a soft thumb across the spot just below the cut on my neck. I swallow, suddenly aware I'm standing close to a good-looking man—and we're both in our pajamas.

"We should probably get dressed," I say, glancing over my shoulder at Hades' house. I'm surprised he's not out here already, upset I've lost another challenge.

When I turn back, Zai is turning a little red again. "Um—can we meet later today?" He coughs, rubbing his chest. "We should probably talk strategy and other possible allies."

I nod with enthusiasm. Dex and his unholy alliance almost killed us both. "Sure."

"We could meet at Hermes' house or maybe…here." His gaze shifts past me with a look of trepidation.

A choice between Hermes or Hades breathing over our shoulders? No thanks. "How about the bar in town? Or is that too public?"

Zai considers that, then shakes his head. "There are private rooms upstairs."

"That'll work. I'll meet you outside Hermes' gates, and we can walk together. Around noon? We can eat lunch there."

His gaze suddenly turns sharper with interest, and a wide smile overtakes his thin face. "Sure. See you then."

With no warning, he leans forward and wraps his arms around me in a hug that is…really nice. I stiffen but then relax into him, closing my eyes a little, trying to absorb this, because I'm guessing the next hug is years away. Zai's a good hugger, sweet and just enough squeeze without lingering.

His eyes crinkle with humor as he pulls back. "Not used to hugs?"

I laugh. "Not really a thing when you grow up in the Order of Thieves." I tilt my head. "I'm surprised you are used to them, though."

"My mom."

Ah. "I like her already."

"Me too." Then he gives me a little salute, which I take as my cue to leave first.

"You'd better get Amir."

Zai's eyes widen like he forgot, and he glances back toward the mountain. "Go ahead," he says.

He stays and watches as I let myself through the gates and the courtyard beyond. I'm still wondering if Hades is even here as I step into his house. I frown as I realize there are no locks at all on the doors. With gods and champions not happy with me? That seems…unwise.

"Hello?" I call out. My voice sort of echoes. Good grief, this place is a mausoleum.

No one answers.

I make my way to the second floor, headed to my bedroom, but as soon as I reach the top of the stairs, I spot Hades.

He's standing at the massive window that runs the length of the courtyard, from which he has a perfect view of the road where I was standing with Zai. It is incredibly unfair that his ass should look that good in jeans when the rest of him, held stiffly erect with his hands stuffed in his pockets, is so blatantly pissed off.

Again.

If he thinks I'm sticking around to be yelled at after yet another Labor I managed to survive, he can fuck right off.

I turn on my heel in the direction of my bedroom.

"Zai. Godsdamned. Aridam?" Hades pronounces each syllable distinctly, the words like cuts, and with the same tone an executioner would use to read a death sentence.

40

CONSEQUENCES

Walking away would only piss Hades off more, so I face him, arms crossed but with a deliberately sweet smile. "Didn't you just curse yourself?"

"What?" He's still glaring out the window with his back to me.

"'Godsdamned.' That's you that you're damning."

Hades turns slowly and pins me with a look that could skewer a wild bull. "*You* picked the runt of the litter for your ally. Not even a discussion with me first. With that unexpected and supremely inconvenient soft heart of yours, I *am* damned."

"Don't call him that." I eye him with deliberate patience. "And by that logic, *you* picked *me*, and so you damned yourself."

Hades' glare hones to dagger-sharp. "So I did."

"Glad we can agree on something. I'm taking a shower and a nap—"

Suddenly, Hades' demeanor shifts. Just slightly, in a way that's hard to pin down. He's still angry, but now it's smoother, like the difference between a charging bear and a coiled rattlesnake. "Starting a collection, are we?"

I sigh like I'm dealing with an irritating gnat. "What are you on about now?"

His eyes narrow, but I widen mine and give him my most guileless stare. If he's trying to make a point, I'm certainly not going to help him.

"First your thief-not-friend," he says. "Now one of the champions. Falling at your feet."

Falling at my feet? My laugh is edged in bitterness. He knows about my curse. "Are you being deliberately cruel because I didn't consult with you about Zai?"

If looks could skewer, I'd be bleeding. "It's possible the curse isn't what you think. They seem to like you well enough."

"They do not."

"You're willfully naive if you don't see it."

"And you're hallucinating if you do. One is only an ally. The other told me to my face that we're just friends. No one is falling at my feet. It is *not* possible, and you know it."

Actually, the person who comes closest to disproving my curse is Hades. With that kiss last night. Although lust and love are two very different things—which I saw all too often back home. I'd not really understood others' interest in one without the other, but as I stare at Hades' full bottom lip, I'm starting to get it. On paper, my crush on Boone isn't gone, but he's never spun me out of control like Hades. It's the difference between a cozy fire in a potbellied stove and burning down the entire house.

"Let's circle back to your *ally*," Hades says, thankfully oblivious to my thoughts.

The hard stare he levels on me would have most quaking in their boots. I just pinch the bridge of my nose. "What about Zai? We have an agreement."

If possible, Hades goes even harder, eyes like flint. "And you believed him?"

Now he's calling me gullible *and* careless. I raise my chin. "I do now." Mostly.

Hades gets even quieter. "You can't trust him." But his control breaks over the next three snarled words. "Damn it, Lyra."

I don't mind being yelled at, but sworn at? No. I raise one eyebrow, crossing my arms. "You want to rethink your tone?"

Hades stalks across the space between us, and I swear smoke is lifting off of him in black tendrils. "No, I don't want to rethink my fucking tone."

He doesn't stop coming, but despite the twisting nerves in my belly telling me I might have gone too far, I refuse to back up like a coward. I have to deliberately plant my feet to keep from running, though.

He jerks to a halt a mere foot from me, radiating a thousand nuances of frustration. "You will be the death of me, Lyra Keres."

"Why?" I ask. His lips flatten, and I raise my hands. "It's an honest question. Allying with Zai worked today. It *worked*."

"You got lucky."

I snort. "I picked the right ally, Hades. And growing up the way I did, I know what to look for. Thieves are, by nature and training, untrustworthy, backstabbing, and conniving. So just because I didn't run this decision by your committee of dictatorness doesn't mean I wasn't smart about it."

Hades stares at me, jaw working like he's trying to figure out how to deal with me. Which I'm guessing doesn't happen often to him. When he finally speaks, it's softer. "Lyra, I swear if you don't take this seriously—"

"If Zai hadn't figured out the answer in time, then I'd have climbed down." Hopefully without mishap. Which reminds me. "The others—"

"All made it safely down the worst part of the mountain. They're still walking the rest of the way. And the one champion who fell survived."

I blow out a breath of relief. "Amir."

"Can't be healed, since he's not a Mind virtue, but is being looked at."

I nod. "That's good—"

He grunts. "Your stubborn insistence on saving everyone around you—"

"Maybe not Dex," I mutter out the side of my mouth.

"What?"

What does he mean, what? Hasn't he been paying attention? "Dex Soto. Athena's champion. Took a swipe at me with my own relic. Tried to kill me on the road into town yesterday—"

"He did what?" His voice descends to something fiery.

I ignore the interruption. "He's on my Save Last list."

Hades stares at me with the kind of incredulity usually reserved for Felix and sometimes the other pledges. Only with them, it's...belittling. With Hades, it feels like I won a small point. "You're making lists now?" he asks slowly.

"I always make lists."

"Like who to save last? Not who not to save at all?"

I shrug.

"You should know that Athena's blessing gave Dex Soto foreknowledge," he says. "I suspected it in the last challenge when he started climbing so fast, but this time he was dressed and ready."

"So was Rima."

He shrugs. "Trust me. Dex is getting information on the Labors early. I'm not sure how early, though."

"Kim Dae-hyeon has a necklace that glowed when he asked the Fates a question," I add, since we're cataloging threats.

He nods, then says, "That's not your only problem. I think you're going to need to add some more names to your list."

My heart falters a little. "Why?"

"You didn't see those champions' faces when Zai flew you away. You made more enemies today than the ones you already had."

Well…hells. This is where my curse is going to start kicking in hard, then. "What was I supposed to do? Go it alone for every challenge?"

"You have me—"

A swirl of smoke like a tornado suddenly fills the room behind Hades, and when it dissipates, a massive black dog with three heads is standing in its place. Three heads filled with giant, razor-sharp teeth.

41

HADES' PET

I swallow back my scream when the dog doesn't immediately attack. And it's a good thing this place has high ceilings, because the beast is at least fifteen feet tall at the middle head. His coat is smooth and shiny and shows every ridge of his muscled body. He wears black spiked armor around his neck and shoulders, strapped under his chest, and more goes up each snout and over the crown of each head. All of his ears stand straight up, tall and pointed and alert.

"Oh my gods," I whisper, shuffling my feet to stand closer to Hades. "Is that—"

"Cerberus." Hades doesn't sound too happy. "What are you doing here, mutt?"

I elbow Hades. "Don't call him a mutt."

He delivers a glare that dares me to try that again. "He's *my* dog. I call him what I want."

Cerberus growls.

I freeze. "Is he going to eat me?"

"He's not growling at you," Hades grumbles through his teeth.

I give him a slow blink. "He's growling at *you*?" I can't contain my grin. "Can I pet him? He's amazing."

"No."

"Yes, pretty mortal. You may." A voice like a wise elder resounds in my head as though I'm standing in a cathedral, smooth like a river and so deep you'd never find the bottom.

Cerberus is talking to me. In my head. Seriously, best day ever.

"We love pettings from nice ladies," a similar but slightly different voice—a tad higher and more eager—says next. I immediately place that

voice with the head on the left, a giant tongue lolling out one side of his mouth like his head is hanging out a car window.

"Permission granted," says a third voice, gruffer and curter, his snout lifting into the air.

I stare at the dog. Three voices. Each head has its own personality. There should probably be questioning or hesitation on my part, but Hades is right here, so really, what could go wrong? I take a step toward Cerberus, who cocks all three heads at me.

"Lyra." Hades grabs me by my elbow. "I told you—"

"He said I could."

"He said—" His gaze cuts to Cerberus. "Traitor."

"Why is he a traitor?" I raise my brows.

"He only ever talks to me." Hades shifts on his feet before tacking on, "And Charon."

The ferryman who takes dead souls across the River Styx for coin. That little fact is a reality check. I might have been forgetting for a second there, while we were arguing, exactly who Hades is. King of the Underworld, with a monster for a pet and a reaper for his gatekeeper.

"Cerberus probably smells me on you," Hades says.

I frown. "*Smells* you?"

"My gift." His gaze drops to my mouth, and he might as well have brushed his thumb softly over the flesh there.

Oh. Right. That. I almost reach up and touch my tingling lips but manage to stop myself. Hades is watching.

"I'm talking to her because she likes me." I think the head to the right is speaking because it leans forward.

"She called me amazing. No one ever likes me except you." That's the tongue-lolling head.

The grumpy head says nothing—not the talker of the three, I guess.

"Yeah, well, her sense of self-preservation has clearly been tampered with," Hades says. "She's drawn to danger."

"Stop." I pretend to preen. "You'll make me blush."

I walk to Cerberus, who drops to his belly.

I mentally name his heads. Cer for the one in charge because he'd go by "sir," Ber for the grumpy one because he's cold, and Rus for goofy because it just sounds like him.

I reach up and scratch behind one ear on what I think is his goofy head on the left. "Oh my goodness, you are so soft!"

"What were you expecting? Leather scales?" Rus' tongue lolls out of his mouth on a doggy laugh, and his breath smells of sulfur.

I glance over at Hades, who is watching with resigned irritation, and I can't hold in a laugh. "Oh my gods."

"What now?" His words are dust dry.

"The resemblance is uncanny." I look back and forth between them, putting a hand to my chin and pretending to study them like works of art. "With that frowny face, you could apply to be one of Cerberus' heads. You're practically quadruplets."

"Very funny," Hades drawls.

Cer lays his head on his paws. *"Forget it. I'm much prettier."*

Hades' expression turns even more sour, and I laugh again. "True."

The god of death eyes his hellhound. "See who gets an extra cow for a bedtime snack tonight."

I make a face. "You eat cows for a bedtime snack?" I ask Cerberus.

"You don't?" That's all three.

"Are they dead when you—"

"What would be the fun in that?" Ber harrumphs.

I hold up a hand. "I don't want to know."

"Not to worry," Cer says. *"These are carnivorous cows and can fight back."*

I don't even know what to say to that. "Everyone has a thing, I guess."

Another woofy laugh blows more sulfur-scented breath all over me. *"Can we keep her?"* Rus asks Hades.

A small glow ignites in my chest. Is this how it feels to be wanted?

"Definitely not. I'd never know a day's peace again," Hades says. "Did you come here for a reason, mutt?"

Cerberus huffs—all three heads—then gracefully pushes to his feet to tower over me. I only come up to his shoulder. *"You are needed,"* the heads say in stereo.

I glance between them. Needed?

Hades' lips press tight. This isn't annoyance like a second ago, or even anger like when I came into the house. It's...

What is it?

It can't be guilt. I'm pretty sure gods don't feel guilt. Especially this one.

He slides a look to me that I can't interpret. "I'll be there soon," he says.

Cerberus nods, Rus gives me another nuzzle, and then the hellhound disappears the same way he arrived—in a cloud of smoke.

I shouldn't ask. It's none of my business.

I ask. "Not Isabel?"

"No."

"Then who—"

"You should dress."

It's obvious he doesn't want to tell me, but that only makes me want to find out more. "But it's important?"

"Yes." Curt and distant.

"All right..." I slowly turn on my heel.

"I won't be here when you come out."

I hesitate before I glance back. "I figured."

Zero reaction. "We should talk when I return, work out a better strategy moving forward."

"Don't worry," I tell him. "Zai and I are meeting for lunch and talking strategy. I've got it covered."

"The hells you are."

I don't bother to wait to hear his next words as I shut my bedroom door in the god of death's face.

PART 4

KEEP YOUR ENEMIES CLOSER

I've failed so many times,
not succeeding is now statistically impossible.

42

DID I ALREADY LOSE MY ALLY?

After bathing and dressing, I grab my tactical vest and slip it over my shoulders, then head out of my bedroom. I guess Hades must have left while I was in the shower. I try not to notice how the house feels quiet and lonely without his larger-than-life presence.

On my way to the stairs, I notice an open door that has always been closed when I've come by here, and my steps falter.

Quietly, I enter the narrow, windowless room—almost a closet, really. Painted entirely red, the room has only one thing in it. Well…lots of little things, but they all serve the bigger piece.

An altar.

Buttery sunlight pours in from a skylight overhead to fill the space with air and spotlight the altar itself. My heart constricts little by little, turning to a dull ache behind my ribs as I take in the details. I've seen altars to passed loved ones before, of course, but nothing like this.

It's colorful, with bouquets upon bouquets of narcissus flowers—mostly in cheerful yellows and bright whites but with pops of purples and oranges and reds as well. They surround a torch that rises from the center of the table made of black obsidian. A glittering skull forms the pedestal at the top of the torch for deep-red flames that cast sparks into the air.

Two pomegranate trees on either side bend to touch each other over the altar, like lovers embracing. Dark-green leaves are interspersed with the large red, ripe fruit with their distinct star-shaped tuft on the bottom.

Persephone.

This altar is for her.

She's been gone some time now. A hundred years at least. Though, I guess in the scheme of Hades' life, that's not long. But to have this here for the rare times he visits…he must still be in deep mourning.

Suddenly, I feel like I've intruded on something so private, so sacred, that I should never have laid eyes on it.

I bow to the altar, offering a silent apology to the deceased goddess of spring and Queen of the Underworld, then back out and quietly close the door behind me.

But the image and the knowledge of its existence feel like weights I've hung on my heart. It drags at me all the way to the gates of Hermes' house, where I'm supposed to meet Zai.

He's not here yet, though, so I wait, checking my watch. I'm right on time. He doesn't strike me as the type to be late. Should I go inside? Except if I bump into Hermes, I might make things worse for Zai.

I shift on my feet, trying to make up my mind. I even consider sending in one of my tattoos to get him. Then the gate opens, but it's not Zai. A satyr with mint-green fur on his lower goat half and purple hooves and horns emerges and offers me a note before returning inside without a word.

It's from Zai. A single sentence.

Meet me behind Hermes' temple. ~Z

Hades' concern is starting to ring true. This is not a good sign, if Zai feels the need to hide and send notes. He should be safe enough in Hermes' house, right?

I hurry down the road, looking over my shoulder frequently, like an escaped prisoner. I'm especially careful as I make my way through the Main Street area and only relax when I get to the temple.

But Zai isn't here, either.

I whistle the signal to come out before I remember he's not one of my fellow pledges and wouldn't recognize it. But there's a rustle to my right all the same, and a head pops up.

"Oh my gods, Zai." I manage to keep my voice down, but he waves at me to be quiet all the same, then glances around me past the tree.

"Did anyone follow you?" he whispers.

"I don't think so, but are you—"

"You're sure?"

I cock an eyebrow at him. "As much as I can be. What is going on?"

He takes another look around, wariness bracketing his dark eyes, then steps out from behind the bushes where he was hiding. The guy looks terrible.

"What in the Underworld happened to you?" I demand quietly.

He makes a face that I think is self-disgust, but it's hard to tell behind the swelling. "I have severe allergies to…well…Earth basically covers it."

"So you decided to hide in it?"

"I'll tell you when we get somewhere I might not die."

Dire. Fair enough. "So what do you want to do?"

"Get on my back. I have an idea."

My lips twist as I eye Zai up and down. Get on his back? In his current physical state, is he going to be able to hold me?

"I'll be fine." He sounds a bit short. "Just get on."

I shrug. He knows his own limits.

He grunts when I hop on and sort of stumbles a bit when he catches my full weight, but he doesn't go down. Then we're in the air, not just along the ground but gaining altitude quickly. Zai skirts mountains, staying just above the tops of the towering pine trees and against the rocks—so we're not seen, I'm guessing. The wind whips past us, tangling my hair as we go faster than before. He's getting even better with the sandals.

I don't know where we're headed until I realize we're well above everything, near the top of one of the mountains. That's when he rounds a bend and the massively impressive main temple of Olympus rises before us into the skies in brilliant, white-marbled glory.

Up close like this, the heads of Zeus, Poseidon, and Hades, with their multi-colored waterfalls, are even bigger than I thought. They're so intricately carved, it's like looking at a scowling Hades when he's all up in my space, as he's prone to get.

Is that where we're going? The temple?

Sure enough, Zai lands us on the path leading up to it. "No powers work on these temple grounds, including the gods' and goddesses'," he explains. Hermes' sandals disappear. Does he just think them away? "This is the only place in Olympus where violence is forbidden. Even if Dex and the others find us here, they can't hurt us."

I'm not so sure about *can't*, but it would take them a while to get up here anyway. So I use the opportunity to look up. And up. And up.

The temple itself is… Really, there are no words.

The Temple of Zeus in San Francisco, which is pretty impressive, is like a tiny candle flame beside a wildfire compared to this one. The roof is supported by at least a hundred tall, fluted Corinthian columns, two rows of them ringing the entire space. A pegasus, with its wings outstretched, rears up at the pinnacle of the triangular roof. Lion-head-shaped gutters guard the four corners, and statues of the Daemones loom on either side of the doorway into the inner temple itself.

All of it adds to the overwhelming sense of how small I am in the grand scheme of the world.

"Are we going inside?" I ask.

"We can't talk in there," Zai says. "The gods could hear us."

And we're discussing strategy, so I get it. I can't help the way my shoulders droop a tad, though.

Zai heads to a series of stairs that cut over the edge of the mountain and down to what looks like a viewing platform directly above the three waterfalls. Mist wafts up to cover us in a cool sheen, and the rush of the water is a muted roar all around us.

"Nobody will be able to overhear us here," Zai raises his voice to yell, then starts coughing.

He leads me to a bench with its back at the edge of the waterfall.

"What happened?" I ask, sitting down. "Why didn't you walk over with me?"

He grimaces. "Dex."

My eyes go wide. "Did he hurt you?"

Zai shakes his head but holds my gaze. "No. He did something worse."

43

ALLIANCES

I frantically search for injuries on Zai, but other than severe allergies, he seems unharmed. "What's worse than death?" I ask, then cringe a little at the question against Hades.

Zai drops his shoulders, staring at his foot as he kicks a pebble. "Dex fell climbing down the mountain and got pretty scraped up. But since I won, all the Mind champions are given healing, so he went to Asclepius first. Rima beat him back to the house." He sighs. "She warned me that Dex is blisteringly angry that not only did I decide not to ally with my fellow Mind champions, but I aligned with you of all people."

"You're worried Dex might hurt you, too, now." It's not said as a question.

"Oh no," Zai says. "Dex has always been in it for himself. But now, he got Rima to agree to kick me out of the house we share."

I frown. "You share a house?"

He gives me a confused look. "Of course. There's a house for each group of champions by virtue."

Ah. But none for me, because Hades.

It's a darn good thing I'm used to being an outsider, or I could develop a complex at this rate.

"I assumed you lived with Hermes." Holy crap. He lives with Dex? "You should have said so earlier."

And now I get it. He lost a potential found family when Dex kicked him out. I swallow the knot forming in the back of my throat. As someone who has only ever wanted to belong somewhere, wanted a family of her own, I totally get how this could feel worse than death for Zai.

I drop my gaze to my lap, fingers twisting together. "I'm sorry, Zai."

I look up at him. "If you want to not be allies—"

"Quit that." He says it gently. "Allying with you won me a pair of nifty shoes." He nudges my shoulder with his. "Besides, I took this likelihood into account when I made my choice."

My smile feels pinched. "Of course you did."

"I'll find a different place to stay. Maybe with Hermes." He shifts in his seat. "Although he's not thrilled, either."

Given Hades' reaction if I'd been kicked off the team, I can imagine. "You can stay with me."

Zai straightens so fast I'm surprised his spine doesn't crack. "With Hades? I don't think so."

"He won't hurt you." I have no idea what makes me so confident of that.

Zai is clearly not as sure. "He's the god of death, Lyra."

"And yet I remain un-smited," I point out.

"True." He doesn't look convinced. "But he needs *you* alive, not me."

Fair.

"What if he promises to keep you safe while in his house? How would that be?" I try not to wince at my own words after they're out. Talk about going against Hades' *don't agree to anything until you talk with me* edict.

"Maybe then," Zai says, still mired in doubt.

I nod, not pushing it. One problem solved. Sort of. Hades is going to *love* hearing about this when he gets home.

"Did you ask Rima why she is aligning with Dex? I mean, I know he's also Mind with the two of you, but still..."

I trail off at Zai's grimace. "She's not *with* him," he says slowly. "She's *against* you."

44

WHEN BAD THIEVES FORGET TO DO THEIR DAMN JOB

R ima is against me.

I'm determined to not let that work its way under my skin. I've had a lot of practice at not being bothered when others don't like me, or think I'm odd, or actively try to avoid me, or even just forget I exist. I can't say all that practice helps much.

It still hurts.

"Me?" I ask. "What did I ever do to Rima?" Pretending I don't have a curse and know exactly what's happening is how I've always handled things with the pledges. Zai is different. An ally. Maybe I should tell him about it. After all, if it means he loses out on allies, he deserves to know.

He shakes his head. "It's more like she's against your patron god."

I'm so used to being unlovable—thank you, Zeus—it takes me a second to catch up with the fact that I'm not the problem this time. "She doesn't want Hades to become King of the Gods."

He pauses as if he's not sure he should tell me the next bit. "She looked...terrified of the idea. Went all pale and shaky, just rambling about how you were going to win and it would be the end of us all."

I snort. "Based on what evidence? You did all the winning in the last one."

"Thanks to you," Zai insists, expression taking on a stubborn cast as he puts a hand over mine on the bench.

Hades' taunt about Zai falling at my feet whispers in my head. Pretending like I'm simply shifting positions, I turn sideways to face him directly, which breaks the contact. "Okay. So let's talk strategy. I was thinking, since we're already breaking virtue ranks, maybe it would help to get at least one champion from the other three virtues."

Zai nods and narrows his eyes, clearly putting that big brain to work. "Neve and Dae are both Strength and seemed to be working with Dex today. I don't know about Samuel, and I couldn't see the others to know if they've formed strong alliances within their virtues or not."

"Me neither."

"But the Courage champions are down one. Maybe we start with one of them."

"Which one?" I ask.

"Well…Amir is obviously strong and courageous, but he might be too young and immature. He can also be arrogant."

I guess I'm not the only one who's been paying close attention.

"And we still don't know how injured he was from his fall today," he adds.

I don't want that to be a factor in choosing allies…but it is.

"Trinica seems smart, capable, and calm in the middle of a crisis. But she's a little older and maybe isn't as strong as the others," Zai mentions. "She's a school principal, did you know? For teenagers."

I raise my brows. "Sounds like she can handle a lot. How about we approach both together? That way they don't have to choose between us or them."

"That could work," Zai says slowly.

"Do you want to—"

"Well look who we found," a voice sneers to our left.

As one, Zai and I turn our heads and jump off the bench as our gazes collide with Dex's glaring face—and he's not alone. Rima isn't with him, but Neve is. So are Dae-hyeon and…Samuel. That answers that. Strength and Mind are teamed up.

After Samuel's help in the first Labor and the way we worked well together, that strikes harder at my heart than I'd like to admit, and I have to look away.

Which is when the mistake Zai and I made becomes glaringly obvious.

No. Fucking. Powers. Including the sandals to fly us out of here.

Felix would be apoplectic if he saw how badly I failed to ensure I had multiple outs.

"Why are you such an asshole, Dex?" I sneer right back in an attempt to not let him see how badly I'm shaking right now.

"It's nothing personal, Lyra," Samuel says, but his eyes won't meet mine. "Hades would be the worst King of the Gods in the history of histories. We all have families back home we have to protect, and we can't let you play, let alone win."

They're still up some of the steps. Can we get out of here before they get to us?

I grab Zai's hand and tug him toward the rail at the edge of the landing. I say just loud enough for Zai to hear over the roar of the water, "We have to jump."

"Jump?" His eyes go wide. "We can't. No sandals." He shakes his head. "Besides, they can't hurt us here anyway."

"We're outnumbered and outgunned. Dex and Samuel wouldn't even need help. They can drag us off the temple grounds and then kill us."

"That's violence."

"Do you really want to put that theory to the test?" I look over the edge. "If we hold on to each other, your sandals should work after not too far, right?"

"I guess—"

"Any other ideas?"

"You want to live, Aridam? Switch sides now," Dex says, stalking forward.

"See." They're almost to us. We have seconds at most. "Zai, come on!" His face takes on a hard cast. "Let's go."

We both climb up on the rail and balance there. "What is it with drops off mountainsides today?" I mutter under my breath.

Zai holds my hand tight. "Go!"

Faith and a whole lot of trust go into the leap. I almost feel as though we hang in midair for a second before we plummet, my stomach surging up into my throat at the drop.

"Fuck me, they jumped!" Dex exclaims as we fall away.

It becomes clear very quickly that I miscalculated two things when I hatched this brilliant escape plan. The first was Zai's arm strength. I should have hopped on his back, because the second he engages the sandals and his fall stops, I jerk out of his grasp so hard my shoulder screams with the wrench it gets. I reach for him futilely but only grab air, watching horror fill his face as I keep falling.

Zai dives after me.

And that's when miscalculation number two rears its ugly head.

Because Hades' waterfall isn't nearly as far below us as I thought and sticks out of the mountain farther than I realized.

I hit the surface and am instantly sucked under by the force of a raging river of black water.

45

DOWN TO THE BOWELS

As the river sweeps me toward the gaping hole leading into the mountain, I am violently tossed around by rushing rapids so turbulent, it's all I can do to not go under or get slammed against boulders along the banks.

Twice I catch sight of Zai somewhere above me, following in the air, frantic, face splotchy and yelling. Not that I can hear anything. I go underwater and tumble until I'm not sure which way is up. The water is so black, light doesn't penetrate.

It holds me under. My lungs burn until I can't take it anymore, but just at that moment I'm flung back to the surface, where I gasp and choke and flail. And somehow, through my hair and the water in my eyes, I catch sight of Zai flying right at me.

With one desperate heave, I kick my legs and throw myself up toward him, one hand outstretched. He's reaching for me so hard, and I think maybe...

But then the water drags me back under and his face disappears.

The next time I come up spluttering, it's pitch-black, and I know where I am—in the tunnel that leads down to the Underworld, a tunnel that leads to the River Styx.

Please, gods, let the water have a way through that's not going to kill me. I'm picturing underground caverns that the water fills up to the top, leaving no air. I'm picturing white water rapids that will pulverize me against jagged boulders. I'm picturing a tunnel so narrow I can't fit through.

Just as those images strike, I'm tossed off a steep drop, hollering a screech that could wake the dead. I plummet with the water, battered and confused, with no idea if or when I should brace or what else I'm going to hit on the way down. I plunge, and it feels like the current sucks me even deeper, tossing and turning. When I'm pushed to the surface once more, I suck in a mouthful of air, right in time to be tumbled over again.

I don't know how long this will last or how deep the river runs. I'm just trying to hang on. It's got to slow down somewhere, right? I'm definitely not letting myself think about the fact that the River Styx is supposed to be deadly to mortals.

At one point, the current becomes less violent, and I shuck my heavy, waterlogged jeans, which are weighing me down even more than my relic. I've hit the walls—or maybe big boulders? Who knows—so many times, I'm pretty sure my head is bleeding.

But the worst part is the exhaustion.

I can't tell which is more dangerous, the roiling waters or my failing muscles. At this point, instead of fighting, I do the least I can to just keep my head above water, letting my body be thrown around like a broken, sopping rag doll.

I am near to breaking. The closest to giving up and letting the gods take me that I've ever been.

It would be so easy to just close my eyes and go. But I can't. I won't. I keep swimming, keep sucking in as much air as I can every time I come back up.

I practically pass out from shock when I burst into a new cavern— one where the waters calm quickly and I'm finally able to swim without being tossed or dunked.

I catch my breath in the total darkness, waiting for the next horrible thing to come at me, which is when it occurs to me that I have a way to create light. I draw a finger down my arm, and my animals come to sparkling life. "Don't leave me," I tell them. "Just help me see where I'm going."

I hold up my arm, casting their rainbow glows across the still water so I can get my bearings. It looks like a massive underground lake. The shore is so far away I'm not sure I'll make it, but I don't stop, rolling over to float on my back when I feel like I can't take one more stroke.

When my hands finally brush solid ground underneath the water, I almost sob with the relief that barrels through me so hard I shake. With plodding, scraping, crawling moves—anything I can make my limbs do—I manage to heave myself out of the water and collapse on the shore. Rocks the size of giant beetles dig into my stomach, and I don't give a shit.

I didn't die.

All I can hear is my heaving breaths, which gurgle, a little waterlogged, but that's a problem for later. I don't know how long it takes, how long I lie here before my body finally slows, catching up with the air I didn't have for what felt like eons.

"They should put *that* in the fucking Crucible," I mutter to myself.

Then laugh. Possibly a tad hysterically.

I pride myself on not giving in to despair. Ever. That would mean Zeus wins, with his curses and fits, and I refuse to let that asshat beat me down. But at this moment, with no one else watching, it's so tempting to give in to the sensations rolling through me, as if my emotions were left behind in the trauma of the water and just caught up to me, tumbling me over and over for a second time.

I couldn't name what I'm feeling if I tried. Mostly, I guess, grief. At all my life could have been.

I roll to my back and force my eyes open because if I let myself succumb to the oblivion of exhaustion, who knows what will happen to me. I'm still stuck somewhere in the Underworld and need to find a way out.

What if I'm trapped down here?

I slam my hands over my eyes, pressing my palms down, holding in tears. I am not crying. Not about this. Not when I lived. Not when Hades' kiss protects me down here. Crying is for sad things only, damn it. And even then, I'd rather not.

"What are you doing, tiny mortal?" a silky, serious voice asks in my head.

I squeal as I jerk my hands away from my face to stare directly up into the three massive, terrifying, precious, beautiful faces of Cerberus.

46

SAFE PASSAGE

"Not dying," I tell Hades' three-headed monster dog on a groan. "That's what I'm doing here."

Thank the Fates for whatever they did to ensure Cerberus met me *before* I landed here, and not after, no matter what Hades says about the mark on my lips.

"Then you are doing well," Cer says.

Ber lifts his head to glance around. *"How did you get down here?"*

My arms are too tired to even lift a hand to point. "I fell into Hades' waterfall in Olympus."

Fire and brimstone. That sounds ludicrous even to my ears, and I lived it.

"You fell..." All three heads give a harsh bark that I think might be a laugh. *"You are pulling our legs."* Rus even bark-laughs again.

I groan. "I'm afraid not."

Cer noses me gently. *"You speak the truth."*

"Yeah."

Ber gives a little growl of disbelief. *"No one could survive that except a demigod."*

"Color me lucky." Take that, Zeus. Don't need love to survive that trip.

"I do not know the meaning of that," Cer says, *"but assume it is sarcasm. Hades also enjoys sarcasm."*

I huff a laugh. Because Hades does. "I'm better at it than he is."

I swallow, and my throat feels like someone scraped razors down the inside of it. "Is there any way you could help me get back to Olympus?"

I mean...Cerberus poofed in and out of Hades' home on a wave of smoke, so why not?

"Not from this part of the Underworld."

"Great," I mutter and fling an arm that feels like a deadweight over my aching eyes. Then a small part of my brain engages, and I lower my arm to peep at him. "Wait. How did you know I was here?"

"Hades' mark." Rus draws his lips back in a fearsome grin. *"It tells me every time you enter the Underworld."*

"I will always be able to find you, tiny mortal," Ber says. And I think he means it as a warning, but to me, it feels like a promise. Protection.

Other than Hades, no one has ever protected me. Not even the Order, despite the fact that, to them, I'm an investment. And to Hades I'm a means to an end.

"You can call me Lyra."

Cer and Rus bob their heads, but Ber cocks his as if he's not sure about that. In unison, they speak. *"I can't get you to Olympus, but I can take you to a better place than this."*

Then he puts a paw on top of my chest. A paw the size of a small table with onyx claws straight out of nightmares, and he's not the gentlest about it, so I grunt. But the sound of it is lost in the silence of traveling. I have no idea what we travel through—space, time, or otherwise—and I don't care.

Gods, monsters, and magic.

We reappear in a blink, and smoke dissipates rapidly from around us, but because I'm lying on the ground it fills my nostrils and sets my already tortured airways to seizing. It takes me a minute to stop coughing.

I'm still underground, *deep* underground, but there are lights above me dotting the ceiling—bright blue and luminescent. I don't know what is making them. Glowworms, maybe? Whatever. They look like stars in a velvety night sky against the black rock of the cavern ceiling.

"Thank you," I say to my tattoos and send them back to sleep.

A lapping sound, rhythmic and soft, has me forcing my battered, limp body up onto my elbows to find that I'm lying on a dock at the bank of a wide river that glows the same color blue as the points of light on the ceiling.

I lean over the edge of the dock to peer closer. The water doesn't glow. It's like the currents deep in the river stir to life glittering specks of light that swirl and dance, creating pattern after pattern, like a kaleidoscope.

I whisper Hades' words out loud. "It's not black in the Underworld."
It's mesmerizing to watch.

"Styx?" I ask Cerberus.

"Yes," Cer answers. *"Don't touch, or it could kill you."*

I frown. "I thought the waters that brought me here feed this river."

"Yes."

"Then why didn't they kill me before?"

Cerberus makes a sound deep in his throats that sounds so much like
a dog's version of "ruh-roh" that I almost laugh.

Oh well. Chalk yet another thing up to gods and magic. That list is
getting long fast.

A noise somewhere between a keening wail and a foghorn—a sound
I'm familiar with, living in San Francisco—rises over the water.

"Here he comes!" Rus jiggles in joyful anticipation.

"Who? Hades?"

All three heads shake. *"Charon."*

Charon.

It takes a solid few seconds for that to sink in. Longer than it should,
but I'm still dealing with fuzzy-minded fatigue. "The ferryman of the
dead?"

Three nods.

Cerberus brought me to Charon? My stomach flips over. I've heard
so many descriptions—some say he's all bones with no flesh, and others
say that his eyes will haunt me if I look directly at him, and even more
reference horns and a tail and bloodred skin. But *all* the descriptions of
this god share a single theme...he's scary.

"Couldn't you just go get Hades?" I ask.

Cerberus shakes his head. *"I was told that any time you showed up
here, I should never leave you alone. I am your safe passage."*

Oh.

"And Charon wants to meet you."

Charon wants to—

Elysium save me.

47

THE FERRYMAN

Before I can ask another question, a boat appears at the end of the dock out of nowhere, and by that I mean it wasn't there, and now it is. No slowly-rowing-across-the-river bullshit. And no tiny boat that seats ten or fewer people. This thing is as big as a pirate ship and similarly styled.

A gangplank drops down to the dock with a *thud* I can feel from here, and people start walking out. Dazed-looking people who are... I stare a little harder as they near where I'm lying. Yup. They are see-through.

Dead souls. I'm looking at freaking dead souls.

Cerberus moves off the dock to the shore, allowing them room to pass, and several give him wary, wide-eyed stares and an even wider berth, but he just stands there, Rus panting. The souls don't look at me at all, like I don't even exist.

They walk onto shore and up to a series of steps that seem to disappear into the cavern wall. The first to reach the steps stops until all of them are lined up, and I can't help but laugh. "I guess you have to wait in line even when you're dead."

Then the soul in the lead climbs to the top, and the moment she touches the cavern wall, a crack in what I thought was solid stone opens up with a grinding of rock on rock, revealing a gated entrance with traditional Greek fluted columns to each side and scrolling carvings across the top. And beyond...

I can't help the gasp that escapes me.

It feels like I've been gasping a lot lately, but I'm only mortal, after all.

Besides, the view is worthy of a gasp.

Because beyond, even still seated where I am, I can see the beginnings of the Underworld, and it's nothing like I imagined. Stairs—lots and lots of stairs—lead up a mountainside into a world that isn't fire and brimstone. Not here, at least. Here is...enchanted.

Against what looks like a night sky but is really a cavern roof thousands of feet above, *everything* glows—the same as the river and the ceiling where I am, only more intensely. It's all blues and purples and greens and whites and pinks. There are flowers, trees, and vines, and pathways lead up into mountains a thousand times more magnificent than Olympus.

I catch only the barest glimpse from where I am, but that's all I need to know why Hades doesn't live with the other gods. Why he prefers to stay here.

"It's so..." I can't find the right word. "Why did Persephone hate it here?"

"She didn't."

I whip around to find a man standing at my feet and have to tip my head back to see all of him.

This can't be Charon. Can it?

He's...really hot.

I mean, not like Hades. But this being who is described as all things hideous is anything but. Tall and lean, he has sandy-brown hair that looks almost blond against fawn-colored skin and laughing eyes somewhere between blue and green. He's not the brooding kind of handsome I'd expect, given the "Ferryman of the Dead" title and all. Instead, he comes off as...approachable...with kind eyes and the type of open face that invites you to grab a beer and have a chat.

He tips his head with a warm smile that makes me want to smile back. "I've been curious about you, Lyra Keres."

"Um...same." I shake the hand he offers, but I can't make myself get to my feet. I'm still too wiped from my bodysurfing experience.

He must see that, because he drops down to sit by me, resting his wrists on his raised knees. Which is when I notice that he's wearing jeans like Hades does. Jeans and a light-green boatneck button-down that's otherwise plain.

"I have a feeling Hades will be here soon to fetch you," he says.

"I doubt that. He has no idea I fell in that damn waterfall to begin with."

Charon's lips pull into a big grin. "Cerberus told me about that."

"He—" I turn to look up at the hound. "When?"

"Just now."

I turn back to find the ferryman studying me with open interest. "I can see what he sees in you."

"Sorry?"

"Hades. You're fearless in a way he would…admire."

I lean back slightly. "It's not fearlessness. It's poor judgment and an appalling lack of filter." And a lifetime of getting through it on my own. "And judging by how much he yells at me about those particular traits, I'm not sure you know Hades as well as you think you do."

Charon laughs. "I do. Since I don't have much time, I need to tell you a few things quickly. Okay?"

Seriously? "How could a person with any sense of curiosity refuse an offer like that?" I prop my elbows on my knees.

His eyes twinkle. "First, a question. Why didn't you use one of the pearls when you were in the river?"

It takes effort to maintain a neutral expression. "I don't know what you're—"

"Persephone's pomegranate seeds." He cuts me off like he doesn't have time for a game of who knows what and is willing to admit it. "Hades can't tell you about them because it's interfering, but I'm not restricted by that, since I'm not an Olympian god."

I stop trying to pretend I don't know what he's talking about. "They're in my vest, and I was busy drowning."

His expression is that of a disappointed schoolteacher. "Don't make that mistake again. They will take you anywhere you want to go."

I blink. "I thought they'd only bring me here?"

Charon shakes his head. "Picture the destination clearly in your mind—a place or a person, either will do—then swallow one pearl."

Could I use them to go back to the Overworld? Not that there's anywhere I could hide there.

"Use them only if you have no other option," Charon warns, like he could read my thoughts. "You're already in trouble with relics."

That much, I'm well aware of.

Charon leans closer. "You'll be punished if the Daemones even discover you have those. I mean it. Only if you have no other option."

Hades didn't tell me that bit. "Okay."

He frowns at me. I stare back.

"What's the other thing?" I ask to break the awkwardness.

Charon tips his head, searching my expression like he's trying to determine if he should tell me or not. "Hades values loyalty above all else."

"Loyalty." I glance away, letting my gaze skate over the fluorescing waters and ceiling. Loyalty sounds like Hades.

"He doesn't give his trust easily." That has the tone of a warning. "He's had two friends in his entire existence, and one of them is me."

"*Three.*" All of Cerberus' heads correct Charon in unison.

Charon flicks the dog an amused glance. "Three." He gives Cerberus' paw a pat, and the hellhound snorts a small flame out of Ber's nostrils but relaxes.

I notice through all this that Charon doesn't mention the other friend. I'm guessing Persephone. "Why are you telling me this?"

"Because Hades is a total dick—"

My brows lower, and my spine cracks straight as I glare at him. "Yes, he is, but as his supposed *friend*, I'd expect you to have more—"

"Loyalty?" Charon cuts me off to ask with a delighted grin.

Was he testing me?

I'm still buzzing with whatever ill-advised snap of anger overtook me just then. Why would I give a flying flip what Charon says about Hades? "I don't like tests."

Charon shrugs. "I'd have been more subtle if I had more time. And I'm telling you because I suspect Hades could...come to think of you as a friend, too."

He might as well have slapped me. The impact would have been the same.

Then he glances over my shoulder and smiles. "Isn't that right?"

"I don't need your help finding friends." Hades' distinct growl slides through the darkness and over my skin in a delicious shiver that skims and caresses and awakens as it goes.

He kneels in front of me, running his hands over my body like he did after Poseidon's Labor. This time there's an underlying disquiet to his actions and his pinched expression. "Are you hurt?"

"Probably."

"I'm not in the mood, Lyra. Answer the question."

"I'm serious. I think I'm in shock. Nothing feels like it's critical, though."

He grits his jaw, but he nods, still checking me over. He works his way up my arms, then brushes my wet hair back and hisses. And that's when I see it. Concern. Real concern. I know because I've dreamed of someone—my parents, Boone, even Felix—looking at me like that all my life. It darkens his eyes in a way that sends my heart tumbling.

He brushes his fingertip over a spot at my temple, and I wince at the pain that slices through my head at that touch.

"Sorry," he murmurs.

But he doesn't stop, threading his fingers through my hair, checking for more places I bumped into rocks. And it takes every ounce of my feeble self-control to not let either man know what I just realized.

Hades might take up all the air in the room, and he's arrogant and bossy, not to mention secretive and closed off. Plus there's that nasty temper. And he dragged me into the Crucible. But…I like him.

I like who he is.

I like fighting with him because I know he won't hurt me and he's only fighting because he cares about whatever pissed him off. I like his sense of humor. I like the way he laughs but hides it. I like the way he stands alone against the world and all the other gods. I like the way he breaks rules to help me. I definitely like the way he kisses.

And I would actually *like* to be his friend.

In the history of horrible ideas, that one is a doozy.

"You probably have a concussion." He finally meets my gaze.

"Yeah," I whisper.

I don't know what he sees in my eyes, but it makes him blink, and then he slowly withdraws. His hands untangle from my hair as he leans back, and any hint of worry is gone behind the indifferent mask he's so very good at projecting.

"Do you need a friend, my star?" Hades' voice is still that silky drawl, but now it's tinted with laughter, and I think I also hear a supreme sort of satisfaction there.

I take it back. Charon was right. Hades is a dick.

The only way I can think to react is to go on the offensive, so I sigh. "You're like a damned predator with all the sneaking up."

Sure enough, that brings out the arrogance. "I have been likened to a panther—"

"No, that's not it." I tap a finger against my lips, pretending to study him, then snap my fingers. "An octopus. That's what you're like."

There's a snort that might be a laugh from one of Cerberus' heads. Hades eyes me. "An octopus?"

"Uh-huh. It's uncanny." I offer him a sunny, innocent stare. "The smoke is like tentacles as you ooze your way into the room unseen and unheard. Definitely an octopus."

Charon chokes on a laugh. "Oh my gods, Phi, she's right."

Phi?

I don't get a chance to ask because Charon's still laughing. "I'd never noticed before, but—"

He cuts himself off when Hades slices a glare his way.

"What?" I demand. Once you've got them annoyed, keep going. "Octopi are quite intelligent and cunning. You should be flattered."

Hades grunts, looking downward as if he might find peace in that direction. After seeing both Olympus and now the Underworld, I understand why he looks down instead of up to the heavens.

"Your ally, Zai, came running straight to me and told me about your trip down the river," he says. "You're lucky I'd already returned to Olympus."

"Ally?" He's going to stop fighting me on that now?

Hades nods. "He's earned it with that show of loyalty to you."

Zai facing Hades alone to tell him he'd lost me down the River Styx had to have taken some guts for sure. "I'm glad. Because he's coming to live with us."

Cerberus and Charon both make choking sounds.

I expect Hades to immediately protest, but he doesn't. He regards me with narrowed eyes before giving a resigned nod. "Makes sense. He can't live with Dex if he wants to survive."

"I was expecting an argument."

"Me, too," Charon murmurs.

Which earns him a speculative glare from Hades.

Then Hades leans back on his heels, mercurial gaze roaming my features. "Adding to your collection?" he asks me softly with a glance at both Charon and Cerberus.

I roll my eyes. "Are you admitting you're jealous of your best friend and your dog right now?"

Charon laughs. "I agree, Cerb. I like her, too."

Hades rises to his feet and tosses his friend a cold stare. "You'd probably like a fungus, you've been down here so long."

"Did you just compare me to a *fungus*?" I scramble to my feet, ignoring his outstretched hand, even as I wobble a bit. I jam my hands on my hips, about to give him what for when he interrupts.

"Not now, Lyra. The third Labor is about to begin."

Oh. Every word I was about to say goes up in smoke, leaving behind a haze of fear.

The third Labor. Already.

This time I don't hesitate to reach for his outstretched hand as my stomach pitches like I'm still in the river and Hades is my only shore.

48

DIONYSUS' LABOR

"**W**elcome to your third Labor," Dionysus announces in a jovial tone an hour later, his deep voice bouncing off large cavern walls at least a quarter mile away in every direction. Dressed to impress, the god is basically the epitome of hedonistic playboy with too much time and Daddy's money.

I look away from him to check our surroundings.

Based on the vegetation, we must be in a rainforest except it's in a massive cave. One with humidity, and the *drip, drip, drip* of trickling water. There's a small, circular opening high above us that allows sunlight to spill inside.

I had just enough time to take a quick shower and change into my uniform before I started to fade again, but the humidity has my uniform sticking to me in very unfortunate ways. I glance around, pinching the fabric away from my legs to ease the discomfort.

Next to me, Meike claps her hands at the sight of her patron god. She looks to be around thirty, but her eyes shine bright like a child's right now as she stares adoringly at Dionysus.

"Do you know what's coming?" I whisper to Meike.

She shakes her head, bangs flying with the movement, a smile tilting the corners of her mouth. "He insists we play by the rules, and he wasn't allowed to tell me," she whispers back in her thick German accent.

The god of wine and festivity just went up a few notches in my book.

The other champions are here, too, dressed like me in their tracksuits by virtue color. I didn't have much time to get a look at everyone's uniforms during Poseidon's Labor before. Strength are in deep green with oak leaves embroidered on their chests in glittering bronze thread.

Courage wear purple, of course, with gold thread depicting dogwood flowers. Turquoise for Mind with copper redwood trees. And Heart in wine-burgundy with silver embroidery in the shape of cherry blossoms.

Then there's me in black with rose-gold butterflies. No wonder Hades was irritated that day in the kitchen. He knew they'd shafted me with that half-assed gray ensemble with prison lettering.

Never let it be said that the gods aren't petty.

"This splendid place"—Dionysus holds his hands out, looking around him—"is the Lost Cave."

I've never understood the gift of natural charm, but Dionysus has it in spades. He gives us all a smile filled with such warmth, his blue eyes sparkling as if we truly are about to have a little fun, that I find myself relaxing just a skosh. Maybe we really *are*.

"Mortals have yet to discover this cave system," he says, "but the gods here have been kind enough to lend it to us for our revelry."

The other champions visibly perk up.

Revelry sounds promising.

"As you can see." He points to the hole in the cavern roof. "This is a doline, made by the collapse of the ground above into the cavern below. It has allowed a unique rainforest ecosystem to thrive here. It even has its own weather system.

"This Labor will test your Heart." He spreads his arms magnanimously, and cases appear before us in a shimmer, as if they are materializing from mist.

With a frown, I peer closer. We all do.

"Vodka?" Samuel asks, tone dubious.

Not just any vodka, either—the high-end, super-expensive stuff.

Dionysus grins. "Your task is to get from this doline to the far waterfall in the second doline. The champion carrying the most fluid ounces of vodka wins the Labor."

I think every single one of us blows out a breath of disappointment. If that's his idea of revelry, he can keep it.

"How far is it?" Meike asks her patron.

"About a kilometer." He points in the direction of a dark tunnel entrance and purses his lips. "But don't expect it to be easy. In fact, you may want to work together with a team on this. At least in the beginning."

He looks around us with a bright expression, as if he's expecting us to be equally thrilled with the "fun" he's concocted.

I mean…at least there aren't any monsters or immediate plummets to death.

"The prize for the winner is the Unending Cup of Plenty. You have until break of day, but beware the night." Dionysus spreads his arms again, this time like he wants to hug us all. "Best of luck, champions."

The god of wine and parties disappears in a silent blink.

I'm not the only one who turns in place, looking the cave over. A kilometer isn't far, but it's rough terrain. Carrying only two bottles won't win us anything, either. That little, almost casual slip in about nighttime makes me think faster is better, but if I'm going to lose this damned curse, I need to win soon. And this one seems easy enough to try.

"First things first," Dex interrupts my debating.

I tense, able to guess what's coming. Sure enough, he stares directly at me, and the rest of the champions either stare with him or glance between us in question. Only Zai scoots over to stand beside me.

"We can all agree that Hades can't be king, yeah?" Dex asks the group, never looking away from me.

Some nod. Some don't.

I tilt my head. "He can hear and see you. You know that, right?"

Based on the way Dex's dark eyes narrow, as well as a few others'—Amir, Dae, Samuel, and Neve—I already know that threat was the wrong way to go.

"What do you want?" I ask Dex directly. "I can promise to not win." Never mind about losing the curse. I'm used to it anyway, and I can't do much without it if I'm dead.

"We don't believe that," Dae says, running a hand through his glossy black hair. "Rima said—"

Rima cuts him off, pink tingeing the naturally warm, brown skin on her cheeks. "That you're dangerous," she says.

I peer at her more closely. The way she did that felt…suspicious. Like she didn't want him to say something in particular.

She does offer me a small wince, which might be an apology. "Hades has already shown he'll break rules to help you. That axe isn't mortal. It—"

"Was the relic that came to me over ten years ago when I hit a certain level as a thief," I tell them. "All thieves get one eventually." Of course, I never made it to actual thief, but they don't need to know that.

They glance between one another, doubt etched into their features.

"And the vest, before you ask, is also mine from before." Granted, Boone brought it to me after I was named Hades' champion, and it's for any pledges, not me in particular, but that's just quibbling. "I'm not the only one who brought mortal tools into this."

Other than the backpack I think Dae lost, I'm actually not sure that's true. But they *could* have, and that's the point.

"Lies," Neve hisses, shoving her red hair over one shoulder. "They are cheating, and we all know it. For sure."

Fuck. This went sideways fast.

"Side with us," Dex announces to the others. "We take Lyra out of the equation tonight, and that eliminates Hades from the Labors. It's the only way."

I take a jerking step back, already looking for which way to run.

Samuel clears his throat. "I don't condone killing—"

"I didn't say we have to kill her," Dex says.

"Well, that's a relief," I mutter.

"Not helping," Zai whispers at me.

Dex ignores us both. "As long as she's too injured to compete, she's out. She can't get healing unless she wins the Labor."

They stare at me, and I hold my breath.

They're really thinking about it. All of them.

Should I be running right about now?

Desperation surges, raw and sharp, as my eyes dart from one champion to the next, and I wonder who will attack first.

49

TO RUN, OR NOT TO RUN

"I have a tip about Aphrodite's Labor," I blurt out.

Dex scowls. So does Neve. "More lies," she snaps.

I shake my head and look straight at Dex. "She told me the day you tried to attack me on the road."

Doubt flits across his features, there and then gone behind a reinforced scowl. "I don't believe you."

I shrug. "Anyone who doesn't hurt me…or any other champion… during this Labor, I'll tell you the tip after we're all out of the cave."

Dex's hands form fists at his sides, but it's Rima who speaks. "If any of you help Lyra, we'll assume you're on her side."

I see the way Dae reaches over to squeeze Rima's arm and the subtle nod she gives him in return.

"I didn't say to help me," I announce. "You don't have to be my ally. You just have to not try to hurt anyone, me included. I think that's fair."

Dex opens his mouth, but Rima beats him to it. "If you're going to join us," she tells the others, "come with us now to strategize. We'll return for our vodka."

After she gives him a little prod, Dex lets Rima lead him away from where we're all standing. Neve and Dae go with them. Samuel, too, though he gives me a long look before he does.

Is he having second thoughts? Not enough of them to go against Neve and Dae, his fellow Strength virtues, I guess.

"Sorry," Jackie says as she backs up, gathering her long, blond hair into a ponytail. "I've spent most of my life as a target for assholes. I don't know why he wants to win so badly, but I can't be on Dex's shit list. I'm not joining anyone. I already told Diego and Meike I plan to do the

Crucible alone." She gives her two fellow Heart virtues an apologetic look. Where Neve manages to turn a Canadian accent menacing, Jackie's warm, Aussie vowels make even this rejection feel friendly.

With that, she bends over a case and digs out two bottles, and then, out of nowhere, massive, white-feathered wings appear on her back. She spreads them wide and leaps into the air, flying for the passage to the second doline.

Diego stares after her, hands on his hips, then hangs his head and sighs.

"I'd like to stay with Lyra and Zai," Meike says.

Zai and I both do a bit of a double take. We haven't had a chance to get to know the other champions. Not enough time. I can already hear Hades' arguments against her, given her small stature and general cheery demeanor, but I'll take any help I can get.

Diego considers her a long moment, then, with no rancor in his face, nods. "I think I'll go this Labor alone as well."

With that halo of his, he has the best shot of doing okay solo. I don't blame him for that choice.

Meike crosses to Diego and wraps her arms around him in a hug. "Take care of yourself, D," she says.

He hugs her back, also grabs bottles—four, which he has to juggle awkwardly—then gives the rest of us a wave and heads into the forest the opposite way from Dex and the others. Before he's out of sight, he disappears entirely, using his prize from Poseidon's Labor.

That leaves only two. Amir looks at Trinica with his good eye—the other is still swollen shut from his fall, along with bindings wrapping his ribs, a medical boot on one foot, and scrapes and bruises that disappear into the neck of his shirt. That look says he'll do whatever she does. After losing Isabel, they are the only two Courage virtues left.

She considers Zai and me with a hard stare. Not unkindly—more like she's weighing all her options.

"I'm not saying we're allies," she finally says, "but Amir and I will stick with you for this Labor. Safety in numbers, and any hint, no matter how small, we can get about future Labors is worth it."

"If you don't hurt anyone, I'll tell you anyway. You don't have to stay with us."

I glance at Zai. If he were Hades, he'd be pissed, but he just gives me a nod.

Trinica's expression softens. "I appreciate that. Safety in numbers still stands, and you have that vest on again, which I assume means you have more tools."

She's right about that. I grin, and she raises her eyebrows in return, a tiny smile lighting her eyes.

"Let's figure out a way to take as much of this with us as we can," Zai says.

Together, the five of us start discussing options with no clue what walking vodka through a cave has to do with testing our hearts.

But at least I'm not beaten to a pulp.

Chalk today up as a win...so far.

50

DON'T TOUCH

I swipe my sleeve over my face, wiping away sweat. Not that it does much good. It's not really hot in the cavern, but the humidity is like soup. It has only been maybe twenty minutes, but the sunlight is already dimming above. That nighttime warning is hanging over us as we work as fast as we can.

With a swing, I bury the blade of my axe in a stalk of bamboo, missing where my last strike was. Damn. Throwing my axe? I'm great at that. I can hit a target exactly where and how I want. Chopping with it, not so much. But we decided to make a pallet to drag our half of the vodka, so I keep trying.

A small vine falls in front of where I'm hacking, and I reach out to tug it back.

"Don't touch that!" Meike yelps.

I yank my hand back like I was bit by a snake as she runs over. She points at the plant. "That's poison ivy. See the group of three leaves and how shiny they are? Don't touch those, Liebes."

Behind Meike, Trinica's eyebrows inch up. "Do you know plants?"

"It's one of my gifts from Dionysus." She offers up this information like it's no big deal.

Am I the only one wondering what that could mean for us today? It seems the gods would give gifts that might help their champions in whatever game that god had devised. But knowledge of plants doesn't seem all that handy, even if Meike *did* save me from days of itching.

"Right. No touching three shiny leaves." I nod. We all do.

I look up into the skies as a shadow passes overhead. Zai is using his Talaria to literally get a bird's-eye view—partly to try to stay out of nature and partly to keep watch. He has the Harpe of Perseus in his hand. The famed sword used to cut Medusa's head off is one of his original gifts from Hermes. Just in case.

Dex and his team came and carried off half the vodka—after a heated argument that we wouldn't let them take it all. I hope they're also prepping. Strength, though. Samuel could probably carry a whole pallet all by himself.

But…one of Dae's gifts, it turns out, is some sort of super sense that allows him to sneak up on us—apparently that's how he tracked Zai and me down in Olympus. So Zai is keeping watch for him in case they attack. The bigger fear is that Dex uses his helm. It makes sense to injure us so we can't carry much. Zai wouldn't see him coming at all.

Every rustle, every scurry of tiny feet under a bush, every whisper of wind and all of us tense.

Only what if they're already far ahead? What if we're wasting time? And what in the name of Hades happens at night?

"Did you hear that?" I call up to Zai.

He doesn't look away from whatever has his attention but tosses me a thumbs-up. I go back to hacking sticks of bamboo with my axe.

"I'm telling you, taking this long is going to get one of us murdered," Amir says from behind me in a tone riddled with arrogance. I don't know if it's coming from being a teenager, being a rich kid, dealing with fear, or all three, but his constant brand of critical commentary has made the thirty minutes we've taken so far even longer than it had to be.

Amir is seated on a log, his booted foot stuck out, helping Trinica strip the leaves off vines and tie the ends together to make rope. The twine I had stashed in my vest only went so far. She bumps him with her shoulder. "Not much longer."

Amir makes a face. Gods save me from sixteen-year-old boys.

"Why don't you gather more vines," Trinica suggests, holding up the one she's working on.

Amir looks from me, to Trinica, then back to me. "I'd rather chop up bamboo."

I can practically hear Hades growling at me to not hand over my weapon, *my* relic, to one of my competitors. Even my own common sense says it's a bad idea. But Trinica and Amir took a risk by sticking with us for this Labor. And building trust needs to start with the first stone.

"You'll probably do a better job of it, anyway."

I hold my axe out to him.

Amir blinks, and Trinica sits back just a tad. Clearly, I surprised them. But Amir recovers quickly.

"Well…" he says as he takes it, solemn as a temple priest, "the gods blessed me with all these muscles for a reason."

I can't look at Trinica or Meike or I'll laugh, and I don't want to hurt his feelings.

Amir starts hacking at the bamboo, doing a better job than I was, as expected. I look over my shoulder and catch Trinica watching. She shrugs. I shrug.

"Verdammmt!" Meike exclaims in a harsh whisper as she stumbles back from the stream where she was getting a drink of water.

All of us freeze. "What?" Trinica asks.

Meike plunges her hand into the river, whimpering a little. Trinica and I rush over to her just as she pulls it back out. A hiss escapes me at the sight of an angry red blister the size of a silver dollar rising on her palm.

"What the hells happened?" I ask as she sticks her hand back in the water.

Tears trickle down her cheeks, her face tight with pain, but she manages to point at a plant. More poison ivy peeking out from under a broad leaf. "It's not normal," she says.

Fuck me. I knew this Labor couldn't be this easy. We've just been lucky that we haven't already tangled with the stuff.

"Be very careful!" Trinica calls out to Amir. "The poison ivy causes terrible blisters. Don't touch it at all costs."

Then she pulls a roll of self-adhesive bandage out of a pocket. Noticing my stare, she shrugs. "Mortal tools."

After that, we work more carefully. But the damn ivy hides everywhere, and by the time Zai finishes assembling the entire pallet with the bamboo, twine, and vines we gathered, he's the only one who doesn't have at least one blister somewhere on him. Mine is on the side of my neck and feels like acid is eating its way through my skin.

Daylight dwindling, we load up and start dragging, swapping out to share the work. Two at a time can use the bamboo bar that extends wider than the pallet on either side.

It takes about five minutes to realize that this is going to suck worse than we thought.

It's rough going, having to stop to hack through underbrush, maneuver around increasingly large patches of poison ivy, and lift the pallet over larger rocks. Sometimes we have to unload it completely to get over obstacles, then reload on the other side. One kilometer is going to take for-fucking-ever.

And every second, the cavern we're in gets dimmer.

But we keep going, plodding along toward the darkened tunnel or cave Dionysus pointed us to, the entrance to it growing larger and larger as we get closer. Until we crest a fall of rocks and can see down into it.

"What in the Underworld?" Trinica snaps as we stare.

The tunnel to the second doline is a fall of rocks that leads from where we stand to a small underground stream that shouldn't be too deep. I can't see what the other side looks like, but there's a circle of dim light far off in the deep darkness. That has to be the other doline.

But that's not what we're staring at.

Poison ivy is...everywhere.

51

BUILDING A TEAM

"Well, at least the poison ivy is only on the ceiling and the walls," Meike says.

Trinica side-eyes her. "Are you *always* this cheerful?"

Meike shrugs. "I decided a while ago that I can go one of two ways in life. Become angry and bitter, or deliberately choose to look at each day as an adventure. I chose the latter." She winks at Trinica. "And this is certainly an adventure."

Is that what we'd call this?

The light shifts around us, dimming even more, as if the dying sun is reminding us to hurry up.

"Let's get this over with," I say. We'll be lucky to reach the bottom of the rockslide before dark.

Zai quickly adds a long bamboo rod to the back end so four of us can lift the pallet together as we navigate the rocks. We struggle down the rockslide with a lot of grunting and swearing and negotiating. It doesn't help that Meike is so petite and Amir is all scraped up. Zai is wheezy, but at least he has the sandals to keep him from falling.

Working our way down a steeper boulder, I'm on the bottom end with Trinica, taking the weight, Meike and Zai above. "Hold on," Trinica says, voice strained. Taking the bar onto her shoulder, she leans over to check underneath. "I can't see."

A light beside me suddenly comes on, and I glance around to find Amir holding up his cell phone with the flashlight on. "Thanks," Trinica says. "It's caught on a lip of rock."

Together, we heave it a little higher, my muscles already shaking. Then we move with shuffling steps. With way more resting in between rounds of lifting, and changing out who is taking the weight, we finally hit the floor of the cavern. The small stream burbles happily beside us.

After a breather, like we all silently agree that we need to keep moving, we set the pallet back up to be dragged by two. Here, where the cave floor is rock instead of dirt, the pallet makes a terrible screech, which means we're all glancing into the dark before and behind us, worried about the others finding us.

We cross the shallow stream that winds back and forth in our direct path for the third time. By now my feet are freezing from the cold water and squelching in my shoes. Just as I hit dry land, Trinica's feet slip out from under her, and the pallet lists to the side.

"Watch it!" Meike cries out.

One of the cases goes sliding, and she tries to grab for it. Only she grabs it from an odd angle, and one side of the box comes undone. A bottle slides out and smashes on the rock, shooting shards of glass everywhere.

We all pause, and I'm still holding my corner up. "You okay?" I hear Zai ask. Not sure if he's asking Meike or Trinica, though.

"You should see this," Meike says, and Amir's light swings her way.

I set my corner down to move around it. "Holy crap!" The words pop out of me as I catch sight of her. Meike is holding up her pants and showing us how the blisters there are healing. "The vodka splashed me," she says.

No. Fucking. Way.

We glance at one another, then Zai pulls another bottle out of the opened box, screws the lid off, and splashes a little onto his hands. Immediately, he sighs. "It works."

Tricky god, Dionysus.

The prize we're carting to the finish line is also the cure to the poison. We're going to have to choose pain over winning.

"We reserve this one bottle," Zai says.

And we all nod, then pass it around, treating our various blisters. After an initial sting, the blisters become blessedly cool, turning from red to a less angry color. No more acid.

It takes most of the bottle just to do that much for all of us.

Whatever we do, we need to stay away from those damned vines. In here, that's not hard. Hopefully they're not everywhere in the second doline like they were in the first.

We get moving again with Amir in the lead, lighting our way. Trinica, who is none the worse for wear from her slip, goes back to dragging the pallet.

Several minutes pass before Amir asks, "Are you really a thief, Lyra?"

I hesitate. Only because, until now, we've mostly been saving our breath as we navigate the longest kilometer on the planet. I shrug and sidestep the question, not wanting to admit I might not have a skill the group would find useful and keep me around for. "Well..." I puff with effort. "My parents bartered me to the Order when I was three to work off our family debt."

Amir stops to look over his shoulder at me. "I—" He coughs. "I thought a string of nannies followed by boarding schools was bad."

"Amir," Trinica whisper-hisses, and he looks at her, wide-eyed.

"What?" he asks.

I chuckle. "It's okay. I made peace with it a long time ago."

Mostly. Although lately I've started wondering what my parents would do if I showed up after winning, my curse removed. Would they finally love me? Accept me? Or at least give me a place to stay while I figure out a new life?

"Is that why you hum?" Amir asks next. "Is that part of your training?"

I shake my head. "Actually, they tried to train me *not* to do that. They teach us to work in silence. Noise, even soft noise, could give away my position."

As if a mouse heard me, there's another rustle off to our right. We all peer into the growing darkness. It's difficult to see now that we're this far down. When no monsters and no one from the other team appears, he keeps going, returning to his questions. "So do you do it when you're scared or something?"

"No." Hades is probably, wherever he is, watching this and yelling at me to stop telling them stuff right now. "I do it when I'm focused."

But I should really try harder to control it. It is a tell, and that could get me in trouble in these Labors.

At a flicker of shadow, we all look up just as Zai lands to take a turn pulling the pallet. "As far as I can tell, no one is close," he says. "Keep alert, though."

THE GAMES GODS PLAY

The last bit makes all of us straighten a tad.

I study Zai surreptitiously, not wanting to seem like I'm mothering him. He's wheezing a little. I beckon him closer. "How are you doing?"

He flicks a glance at the others and tugs his collar up, which tells me he doesn't want them to know.

"I have my inhaler," he whispers back. "And I brought an EpiPen for if things get really bad. Left zippered pocket on my pants."

I nod, and he grabs the left cart pole, lean muscles straining as he takes Meike's place.

It's quiet for a while as we go, but eventually Meike breaks the silence. "So…it's clear Dex wants to win this thing. I'm sure he has reasons. Are any of you hoping to win? Maybe you have family needing a blessing?"

We all pause, staring at her. Does she think we're going to become friends?

She blinks right back at us. "I can go first, if it helps. I have a roommate I've lived with for years. My best friend. But we're happy with what we have." She shrugs. "So I have no interest in winning."

"No other family?" I ask.

Her eyes get a faraway glaze, and I know she's not seeing me anymore but memories. "My parents are gone, and I was an only child." Her smile makes my heart ache just a little.

"I'm sorry," Zai offers.

"Me too," I say.

Trinica moves closer to squeeze Meike's hand. "I've also lost my parents, and I've been divorced for ages. My ex and I are amicable. We were good co-parents, but our son is grown now, so I don't see much of the ex anymore. But my son, Derek, is getting married." She smiles to herself as she glances up at the dark, poison-ivy-covered ceiling. "I'd love to win." Trinica's smile widens to a grin. "I'd want to use my boon for the grandbabies."

"What about you, Amir?" Trinica asks.

He goes back to hacking at underbrush, and we all take that cue to continue pushing forward. "My parents are both alive, but we've never been close." Amir says this so matter-of-factly, if I hadn't been looking right at him, I would have missed the droop to his shoulders. Nannies and boarding schools. He must've been—

"That sounds lonely," Zai says, stealing the word right out of my head.

If anyone would understand being lonely among family, it's him.

"I wouldn't mind winning if it means a fresh start," Amir says without addressing Zai. "I don't think my family cares one way or the other."

It's suddenly sunk in even deeper that these champions the gods and goddesses have picked aren't just fighters in the same ring. They are real.

Real people with hopes and dreams and loved ones…lives they've been stolen away from. We are—all of us—just trying to get home alive.

Well, maybe not Dex.

We must all reach the same thinking because we grow silent, other than the huffs and puffs of the people dragging the pallet and the tinks of glass on glass made by the bottles of vodka. A vaguely less dark circle ahead of us—the other doline—is getting closer. And I'm suddenly hopeful that we'll make it out of here.

"My turn," Amir says a minute later.

Almost like an omen, the second we set the pallet down to take a breath and swap out, darkness consumes the cave.

Night has fallen.

Something off to my right rustles.

"What was that?" Amir whispers.

"Just a small cave toad or a mouse or something," I say. And I hope I'm right. In the distance, I see a small glow moving ahead of us. Diego?

He shines it around, but the only thing I can see is a single vine of poison ivy draped across a nearby rock.

I didn't realize there were any parts of it this close to us.

Amir hands Trinica his phone and takes over from me. I'm taking a single step to move ahead of them when something snags at my foot and I lurch sideways. I try to stop myself, but the ground here is all loose rocks, and I tumble end over end away from the others.

Right into a patch of ivy that feels like it closes over me, clinging like spiderwebs.

Fiery pain immediately explodes all over my body.

And, somewhere ahead of us, someone starts screaming.

52

IT'S THE CATCH THAT WILL KILL US

I fight to be free like a wild thing, but I can't get out of the vines. It's like the more I struggle, the more they cling. The pain is blooming all over, even under my clothes.

Vaguely, I'm aware that whoever is screaming ahead of us cuts off. Now only my cries as I struggle fill the cavern.

It feels like forever. Minutes before someone grabs me by the ankles and drags me away using more haste than care, rocks scraping up my back. The vines still grab at me even as we go, and I think I hear Zai swear. But finally we come to a stop. No more vines. I almost don't care because I'm too busy going fetal. My throat is closing over, my breath coming in painful wheezes.

Not enough air.

I'm not getting enough air down my throat. Like it's suddenly ten sizes too small.

Panic sets in, and I look frantically around my team, my gaze landing on Zai and holding.

"Oh my gods," Trinica mumbles. "It's killing her."

I sound like I'm barking with every attempted breath, my head starting to swim.

Meike's beside me in a flash, dumping vodka over me, and the pain eases…but not enough. I was in the vines too long, I think.

I shake my head, turning frantic.

Zai lunges forward, and I see the glint of a cylinder in his hand. He expertly tugs a tab off one end, and my eyes go wide as my mind catches up. His EpiPen. He rams the tapered, orange end against my leg, then holds it in place for what feels like forever.

But then…it's like the muscles of my throat start to relax, more air making it to my lungs.

I feel a bit dizzy as the effects take hold, but the longer it goes, the more I can breathe. The pain recedes, too. With a hand behind my head, Zai sits me up, his face in mine, warm brown eyes worried.

"Look at that," Amir says.

I pull my gaze from Zai to look down and gasp. The blisters are shrinking. Slowly, but the pain is going with them.

It worked.

But then it hits me, and I jerk my gaze back to his. "Was that your only EpiPen?"

The length of his pause tells me all I need to know before he shrugs.

Fuck.

He did that for me.

No one does things like that for me. He could die out here without that medicine.

"Zai," I whisper, shaking my head. Then wince, because that still hurts.

His lips tilt. "We'll figure it out."

"Ouch!" Meike yelps.

Amir swings his light around just in time to see vines of ivy wrapping themselves up her legs. Like they're…alive.

"Oh gods," she whispers. And has just enough time to look up at us with horror-filled eyes before the ivy yanks her off her feet and drags her away.

Zai takes off after Meike, his Talaria making a frantic sound like hummingbird wings. But the darkness quickly swallows them.

We can hear her cries, hear him call out, but we stand there staring into dark nothingness, twitching at every rustle and checking the ground for more ivy coming at us.

This is what happens at night.

The vines.

A flash of movement, and suddenly Zai is flying a foot above the ground back toward us, Meike in his arms. Amir's light shifts above Zai for a second, and my stomach clenches hard. Vines are reaching for him from the ceiling, thrashing and lowering. He makes it to where we're waiting.

He lands beside us, laying her down on the ground. Zai has more blisters on his hands and face, but Meike…

"Watch for the vines," he says.

I grab my axe and spin to face the darkness barely illuminated by Amir's tiny light and keep checking over my shoulder. Meike's out cold, covered in masses of blisters that go under her clothes, but she's still breathing.

Those vines go for skin. Hells.

"What do we do?" Amir asks.

"We sacrifice more vodka," Trinica says grimly.

And none of us argue. Wasting no time, Amir and I keep watch as Trinica and Zai grab two bottles and start working on Meike.

Suddenly, screams rise and echo through the cavern. Not just one person—several, and coming from behind us.

"That's Dex's team," Zai says.

I nod. "The vines must've gotten them."

The screaming keeps going and going. Have they not learned about the vodka cure?

I exchange a bleak look with Zai.

Is he thinking what I'm thinking? That we now know what makes this Labor about Heart. We could abandon our fellow champions to anaphylactic shock, or we could go back and tell them the solution.

"I could fly to them," Zai says.

"No," Trinica replies. "Meike might need you to fly her out of here."

Amir can't move fast with his booted foot and broken ribs and needs to keep hacking a path with my axe. Trinica was already struggling more physically than I was. But I have the epinephrine in my system now, which, I tell myself, will keep me protected.

"I'll go," I say.

Zai gives me a single nod.

"Here." Amir shoves his phone at me. I take it and run into the darkness alone.

It doesn't take me long to get to Dex's group. I have to duck and jump several times to avoid the vines, which are like whips reaching for me over and over. Luckily, the group wasn't that far behind, and the screaming leads me straight to them.

I find the champions at the edge of a pit full of poison ivy. Dex is on his stomach at the lip, pulling a teeth-gritted Dae out as the vines try to drag him back down. Meanwhile, Rima, Neve, and Samuel, even with his strength, are writhing on the ground.

I run to them first and help yank Dae the rest of the way out. Then I rip open a case of their vodka.

"You're seriously stealing from us?" Samuel demands on a groan, wide-set eyes accusing in the beam of the flashlight.

"Bitch," Neve mutters and tries to push to her knees, maybe to come at me.

A vine slithers out of the darkness, reaching for her.

I ignore her and twist the top off the bottle, then splash it on Dex's head.

"What the fu—" The instant the healing effect hits, he bites off the words. Then, "Shit."

I shoot him a grim smile as I kneel over a wary Samuel next. "That's right. I'm your savior today."

It takes almost half their bottles to get them to a point where they can function, especially because vines keep coming at us, leaving behind more blisters to treat. But at least none of them passes out like Meike.

"Can you run?" Rima asks her team.

Samuel lifts the crate above his head, Superman-style. "Go."

We take off through the cavern.

Not having to drag a pallet helps, but the vines are getting more aggressive. I can hear them in the cave now, rustling and moving…to get to us. Like a den of snakes coming at us from the walls and ceiling.

We manage not to stop until we stumble over my allies, and I trip over my feet at the sight of Meike still unconscious on the ground. Some of the welts are healed, but some still look rough. Empty bottles of vodka litter the ground.

Trinica looks up at me with pained eyes. "She's not getting better," she says. "We used it *all*."

53

NO CHOICES LEFT

Rima drops to her knees beside Meike, quickly checking her over with sharp, professional movements. Right. Neurosurgeon.

I know it's bad when she whispers to herself, "Merciful goddess."

A vine comes out of the darkness for her, and Samuel knocks it back, giving a hiss of pain at the contact.

Rima looks from him to me. "Meike's not going to make it if she doesn't get help now."

"Godsdamn." I think Dex is the one who says it behind me.

Neve stomps on another vine. "If we stay here, we're all dead."

Meike's breathing is getting noticeably worse. Her body is reacting to the poison, and we're out of options.

Samuel could carry her, but we need to move fast, and he can haul the most vodka. Which we all need now. Not to win—to survive. Jackie's already flown away, or I'd enlist her help. But even if Zai flew Meike out of here, it wouldn't fix her condition. Not until the rest of us cross the finish line and end the Labor.

I squeeze my eyes closed. I can't let her die here.

Fuck me.

I think I'm the only one who can help her. If I use a pearl.

"Damn," I whisper.

I'm predicting another round with Hades when I return to Olympus. Charon warned me not to do this, but I don't hesitate. "I can get Meike out of here."

Sorry, Hades.

"How?" Trinica asks.

"You'll see. But..." I pause. "I'm not sure I can take even one with me. I don't—"

Amir taps me on the shoulder. "Take Meike. We'll get through."

I look directly at Dex. "They'll need to use your vodka if—"

"Go," he snaps. He's clearly not happy about it, but it means I can leave them with him.

I look back to find Zai staring at me, earnest and urgent.

"Zai—"

"Go," he says. "I have extras in the top drawer in my room."

EpiPens, he means. I nod and slip a pearl out of the zippered pocket in my vest.

The Daemones' roars blast through the cavern, and I swear the sound alone shakes the ground. They're coming for me. I know they are.

I shove the pearl in my mouth and grab Meike. The last thing I see as I swallow the pearl is the enraged faces of the Daemones flying at me out of the darkness.

Immediately, it's like someone throws a lasso around my waist and drags me through time and space in a wind tunnel that blows so hard I can't open my eyes to see and so loud I can't hear. I hold on to Meike with a bruising grip, terrified the wind is going to claw her out of my hands.

Meike has almost slipped from my hold when the wind abruptly stops whipping around us. I open my eyes to find I'm kneeling in the middle of Zai's room in Hades' Olympus house.

Meike's head lolls to the side, her breath rasping in and out, lips turning blue.

"Shit."

I run to the drawer and find the medicine right on top. Having watched Zai do it to me, I'm back to Meike and plunging the end against her leg, then holding...and waiting.

I watch her chest, her face, for any sign that it's working. Finally, when my panic is at a fever pitch, she takes a long breath.

And so do I.

"Lyra," a voice snarls above me.

I jerk my gaze up to find Hades towering overhead, his face a storm of rage.

"I—"

Shock ricochets through me a second time when he drops to one knee by my side. "We don't have time. They're coming for you."

He yanks me up against his chest, both arms wrapped around me, and we disappear.

When we reappear, I find myself standing on the shore of the River Styx, still wrapped in Hades' arms. Before I can absorb that or the fact that Charon is here, too, Hades lets go and frames my face with his hands, leaning down so we're eye to eye.

"It's not going to take the Daemones long to track us." The way he's talking is not like the Hades I know at all. He's…worried. I mean scared-for-me kind of worried. I can see it in the tension around his eyes and feel it in the touch of his hands. Even his speech is clipped and rushed. And I wish I had time to let myself feel what it's like for someone to be scared for me.

I swallow hard. Charon warned me. "They're coming for me?"

Because I used the pearl.

Hades nods.

If he looks like this… "Is it going to be bad?" I ask.

Hades searches my eyes almost frantically, then leans down and places his lips to mine in the softest, sweetest kiss that feels like heaven and an apology at once. Maybe even more powerful than our earlier kisses because it feels like he means it this time.

He stills against me, his head coming up. He looks over my head at Charon. I can't see what passes between the friends, but I know a question was silently asked and answered, because Hades nods.

Then his gaze is back on mine, eyes black as onyx, and the look in them sends my already thundering heart to a whole new speed. "Hades—"

Anything I would have said gets trapped in my throat as he feathers his thumb over my cheek, then winces. "I shouldn't have brought you here, my star."

Everything about me goes dead still, even my heart, which was just on overdrive and now has stalled. What does he mean? Brought me to the Underworld or…the Crucible?

I'm so lost right now. It feels like he's saying goodbye. Is the Daemones' punishment going to be *that* bad? I can't even make myself ask the question again.

"I should have found another way," he says. "I shouldn't have listened to…" He swallows hard. Then determination steals over his features. "I'm not going to let them take you."

He shoves me toward Charon, who catches me just as the horrendous sounds of four Daemones rip through the cavern, bouncing over the walls and the ceiling.

The Daemones appear in midair before us, massive black wings sending the waters of the Styx eddying under them as four sets of fury-filled eyes land on me.

"Lyra Keres," they say in unison. "Come with—"

Hades shoves his hands in front of him, his wrists held together. "I offer myself in Lyra's place."

"What? No—" Charon yanks me back when I try to run to Hades.

"*I* broke the rules," Hades says without looking my way. "Take me."

With battle cries to wake the dead, they fly at him. So fast. So violent.

"Don't do this," I yell. "It's my fault—" I reach a hand out like I can get to him, stop them somehow.

They take him by the arms. When they jerk him off his feet, flying him away from me, Hades finally looks straight at me again.

"Please," I say. Beg. "Don't—"

"It's already done."

And then they're gone.

54

FAULT

Charon and Cerberus greet me at breakfast the way they have the last two mornings since Dionysus' Labor. Zai is sitting at the other end of the table on the terrace, far away from them. Cerberus might scare him more than Hades does. That could also be the allergies speaking.

He made it out with the others. Barely. They had to use all the rest of the vodka to do it. Diego also used all of his. Which made Jackie, with her two bottles, the winner.

Hades, however, hasn't been home since the Daemones took him. Today is no exception.

I stare at the chair where he should be seated. The swirling pit in my stomach is a new constant companion. It's more than worry about not being able to get through the Crucible alive without him. It's much more.

I don't *want* to feel more, though.

"Any word yet?" I ask as I set my axe, which Amir returned, on the table.

Charon is watching me closely, like I'm a grenade that might explode at any second. "Some."

Not bothering to grab food from the sideboard, I drop heavily into the seat beside him. "What?"

Charon hasn't said, but I'm pretty sure Hades being absent from the Underworld for days is causing all sorts of chaos. And yet he chose to be taken anyway. Away from the thing that makes him who he is.

"So...what have you heard?" I ask again.

"You should know the Daemones already came for him once before this," Charon says instead of answering. Cerberus nods all three heads.

"What?" I sit up. "When?"

"When you used the dragon teeth and the axe," Cerberus says.

Exactly like Hades warned me would happen. Only he didn't say they'd come *for* him. That sounds…more serious.

"He convinced them they were relics you already owned and brought with you."

"Those *are* mine," I say. "Why didn't you mention this before?"

Charon leans back in his chair. "He told us not to tell you."

Of course he did. "Why are you telling me now, then?"

"Because he's being a stubborn prick."

I latch on to the important part of that. "'Being'? As in you've seen him? Talked to him? Is he—"

"He'll be fine," Charon assures me.

My stomach bottoms out. "Which means he's not fine now? What did they do to him?"

Charon exchanges another glance with Cerberus.

"He had no choice but to explain about giving the pearls to you with the tiara before the Labors officially started and not telling you what they did," Cer says. I think he's trying to be gentle, though it's hard to tell in that rusty voice. *"They threatened to kill you because he bent the rules."*

They threatened…

I can feel the blood drain out of my face.

Charon speaks slowly, as if choosing his words carefully. "He convinced them no rules had been broken and to give him a lesser punishment in your place."

"Holy shit," Zai mutters, then grimaces. "Gods, right?"

I return my attention to Charon and whisper through stiff lips. "What punishment?"

He looks away. "They cut his palms with the Dagger of Orion. For mortals, it creates a wound that never heals. For gods… He'll heal, but it will take another day or two."

I swallow hard. "Why didn't he warn me?" I'm asking myself more than them.

"I warned you," Charon says, turning harder than he has been with me until now.

"Not enough," I snap. "You said I'd be punished. I was thinking restricted meals or solitary confinement or something. Not this." I look down at my own palms, picturing the slices, and my stomach sours.

"Would you have not used the pearl if you knew?" he shoots right back.

I can't hold his gaze because I don't know. Meike probably would have died if I hadn't. "Hades should have told me. All of it. Why is he doing this, anyway? The real reason."

"You'll have to ask him," Charon says, holding my gaze.

I shake my head. "Why is it such a big, almighty secret?"

The ferryman makes a face. "Mostly because the more people who know a secret, the harder it is to keep. But also, partly to protect you from the backlash…"

So there *is* a reason. "And partly something else?"

Charon runs a hand through his hair. "He wouldn't admit it, but after Persephone, Hades holds his emotions and reasons and actions even closer."

I don't like the way my heart pinches—for Hades' loss, but also because…

No. I won't give what I'm feeling a name. Naming it gives it power. "He must have loved her very much to be so devastated."

"He did." Charon tilts his head. "But not the way you seem to believe."

I frown. "What?"

"They weren't lovers. She wasn't his wife."

"But…she was his queen." The histories and acolytes of the temples didn't get that wrong, did they?

"Not through marriage. He signed a pact with her, giving her power over a portion of his realm."

Is this true? "Which part?"

"Elysium."

And now Hades has to rule it again without her.

Charon smiles. "Persephone had the softest and sweetest of hearts."

Exact opposite of me, then.

"And she is the reason Hades made sure flowers bloom in the Underworld, so she never had to miss the spring when she was there."

"That sounds like someone he loved to me."

Charon and Cerberus both shake their heads. "He saw her as a friend, even as a younger sister."

My heart contracts and then seems to expand with this knowledge, giving a hard *thump*. It shouldn't. I shouldn't care. It makes no difference to me whatsoever. Caring would make me a fool a thousand times over.

"My advice is to give your trust to him…" One side of his mouth quirks. "And a whole lot of patience. Stop asking questions. The Fates will take it from there."

I already handed over my trust. And patience? Years of working off debt teaches you that shit real quick. But stop asking questions?

I drop my gaze to my feet, kicking at the base of the table.

Hades' continued absence is starting to scare me because I think I've begun to lean on him more than I realized. Sure, he's got his challenging points—arrogant, argumentative, dragged me into this shitshow of a competition.

But since the very first day of the Crucible, I've never been afraid of him. And there is one thing he absolutely is—constant.

Steady. I can trust steady. It's inconstancy that makes me wary.

"Excuse me. Lyra?" One of the satyrs appears at my side. He's holding a silver tray with two letters. One with my name.

With a small frown, I pluck the golden, gilded envelope from the tray and open it.

"What is it?" Charon asks.

"It's an invitation to the next Labor." I read back over the glittering words, then glance at Zai, who is reading his. For the next Labor, apparently, our presence is requested at Apollo's home at a prescribed time.

We compete in another Labor. Tomorrow.

And Hades is still being punished. In my place.

"Shit." I look up at Charon, trying not to panic. "Is he even allowed to be there?"

55

THE TWINS

Apollo's home in Olympus is...sort of perfect.

I was expecting all golds and suns, with music and philosophy references thrown in, which is true of the outside. But inside is like walking into an Italian villa, or the closest that I've come to one, which is pictures on the internet and California's version of that style.

I'm having a hard time taking it in, though. Not because I'm about to enter yet another Labor, which should be the only thing on my mind—possibly *dying*—but because Hades wasn't at breakfast again this morning.

And I don't like how tight my chest still feels.

Bright-white walls with the occasional elaborately painted mural of pastoral scenes are set off by tile floors with intricate geometric designs. Following the satyr escorting me, I spot a common room that is all things elegant comfort, with deep couches, throw pillows, blankets, books, and a massive fireplace that could warm an entire city.

But that's not where the satyr takes me.

After waiting in the hall until the exact time on my invitation, she leads me into a chamber that reminds me of historical TV shows that depict ancient communal baths or steam rooms. White marble benches along the walls are lined with gods, goddesses, and their champions. I guess my appointed time was last. Figures.

Zeles stands to one side like a silent prison guard.

I walk right up to him before I can rethink it and mimic his posture, crossing my arms. "I want to see Hades."

"No." Not even a flicker of emotion.

"You know no rules were broken."

"I'm well aware," he says through gritted teeth.

"But you punished him anyway?"

Finally, he looks directly at me. "To set an example."

I scoff, and somewhere behind me, Zai hisses my name—a warning I don't bother to heed. "You should make tighter rules if you don't want the gods finding loopholes," I point out. "That's not his fault. It's yours."

I don't give Zeles a chance to respond, plopping my backside down on the only empty spot on the nearest bench, next to Zai and Hermes. I don't nod at Trinica and Amir. They aren't official allies. The last Labor was about safety in numbers, and I won't make things worse for them with Dex and his group. I hope they know that.

"Sometimes," Hermes murmurs, "bravery isn't actually bravery. It's just foolishness wrapped up in a pretty package."

"Sometimes," I say, "the gods are just ass—"

Zai claps a hand over my mouth, muffling what I was going to say.

A door opens, and Apollo appears. Zai sighs in relief and drops his hand.

The god makes the room feel like his home, radiating warmth and light. Apollo is darker than his twin sister, with rich black skin. He has an almost tangible glow that makes me want to bask in him a little bit, but it's his eyes that fascinate me most—pure gold, as if while driving his sun chariot through the skies, he's captured some of its rays within him and the light is trying to escape. I'm so caught up in him I almost miss the fact that Artemis steps through the doorway behind him.

Apollo smiles, and it's impossible not to be drawn to the god. "Welcome, champions, to your fourth Labor!" Apollo's smile widens as he looks to Artemis. She, unlike her brother, is not a smiler.

"*And* your fifth Labor," she announces.

"What?" Neve is the one to protest. Rather loudly. "No one said anything about two at once."

Ares sits stoically beside her, but judging by the tightening of his features, I think he's not too happy about her outburst.

Artemis spears her with a single, unimpressed look, and Neve quiets, though she doesn't stop glaring.

"No one said anything about not having two at once, either," the goddess says in a voice that tells the rest of us that arguing is pointless...

and noted. "We are twins. We have done everything together since the womb."

Dae, sitting by Rima on the bench, crooks his ally a smug little smile. I look away quickly so no one notices that I saw, but I can't help but wonder if there is a rift among that group of allies.

Apollo waves at the door they came through. "In order to make it to Artemis' Labor, you must first complete mine."

Two in one shot? Sure. Why the fuck not?

I'm way past fear or silver linings and have hit the fuck-them-all phase of the Crucible, I guess.

"For my Labor," Apollo continues, "you will each individually have two minutes at a time in the room behind me. Your goal is to find the trigger that will open a door—it might be physical, and it might not. If you don't find the answer in your allotted two minutes—"

"Let me guess," Neve grumbles. "We die, eh?"

"Do you wish to die right now?" Ares asks her in a low aside that sends rigid tension crawling up my own spine, and he's not even talking to me.

Neve closes her mouth and shakes her head, red curls bouncing.

Apollo smiles. "No. You will return to this room. You will each take your turns in an order I specify, and you may try as many times as you need until you figure it out."

Which means those who answer faster will get a head start on Artemis' Labor.

"You may discuss what you find in the room with any of the champions you like but not with your god or goddess," Apollo says. "They will be taken elsewhere when this begins."

"What if we never figure it out?" Zai asks.

"*Then* you will die." The answer is given in the same tone Apollo might use to announce that a sumptuous meal had just been served. As if this is a pleasant end.

After getting to know Hades, I'm starting to agree with him.

I blow out a frustrated breath through my nose, and it takes my total concentration to keep all my body parts still. Yet another Labor that is geared to unlevel the damned playing field. No wonder Hades finds loopholes.

"How do we win this Labor?" Rima asks, her delicate surgeon's hands clasped in her lap.

Apollo gives his champion a nod like he appreciates that at least one person is playing to win. "If or when you find the answer—and no, it is not a riddle—you will be given something, and a door will open to let you start Artemis' Labor. The first person to do so is the winner of my Labor. You will receive your prize at the end of both."

He steps back so his sister can describe hers.

That's it? That's all there is to his? Find the answer and open a door?

"For your fifth Labor," Artemis says, "as my brother explained, you will be given something when the door is opened. That *something* is four flags that you will wear on your body—one for Strength, one for Mind, one for Heart, and one for Courage."

Her eyes linger on me. I'm getting really tired of being the only champion with a different thing.

Artemis pulls her gaze away from mine. "These flags will appear clipped to your person where you think they would—on your arm for Strength, over your heart for Heart, on a headband for Mind, and to your spine for Courage. Your job will be to not lose your flags as you run an obstacle course."

Obstacle course. I deflate like a punctured balloon. I suck at those.

"Do we try to take one another's flags?" Dex, of course, asks that.

Artemis shakes her head. "There will be creatures waiting in each of the obstacles. They will try to take your flags. If they manage to remove one, you'll know. If they take your Mind, you will experience confusion. If they take your Strength, pain. Heart, exhaustion. And Courage, fear."

Always with the twists.

You have to give the deities points for creativity and their flair for bloodlust.

"If you lose all four flags, there is no possibility you'll make it through any of the remaining obstacles," she says. "You'll be too overwhelmed. If you do make it through, at the finish line, you must find and touch your patron god or goddess, who will be waiting there for you, and give them your remaining flags, if you have any left to offer. The champion to finish with the most flags wins. All champions must cross the finish line within an hour of the first. Those who don't make it by then... We let the monster at the end have you."

So, extra ways to die today. Awesome. "I was just thinking I hadn't felt challenged by the last Labor," I mutter under my breath.

And maybe, just maybe, Hephaestus has to cover a laugh while Dionysus shoots me a hurt pout.

Apollo and Artemis take each other's hands. "The Labors start—"

"Wait," I say.

Artemis' face screws up with irritation, but Apollo merely lifts his brows at me.

"Hades is still gone." I shoot a bitter look at Zeles. "Who am I finding at the end?"

"Your patron should have thought about that before exploiting the… loopholes," Artemis says.

Then, in unison, the twins say, "The Labors start…now."

And in the next instant, the gods and goddesses disappear. The door swings open, and a gold-and-silver satyr stands there with a scroll in her hands. I can't see much beyond her—only a room with more white marble and a lot of light, but otherwise, it appears empty.

"First up," the satyr says. "Zai Aridam."

56

APOLLO'S LABOR

Zai doesn't move right away. Instead, he looks at Rima. We all do. She is Apollo's champion. Why isn't the god of the sun sending her first to give her a head start on the rest of us? Rima looks back at us owlishly, and I can't tell if she is surprised or not. Either way, she doesn't look upset.

Zai takes a deep breath, then looks to Meike and me, giving us both nods before he walks into the room and the door closes behind him. Two minutes later…he walks back out. Not a good sign.

"Neve Bouchard," the satyr calls.

Zai, meanwhile, huddles with Meike and me in a corner. "There is a harp in there," he says. "Not doing anything, just sitting. It's a bit grotesque, actually."

"Grotesque?" Meike asks.

Zai nods. "I didn't want to get too close."

Okay…

"But otherwise, nothing else. I felt every part of the western and southern walls I could reach to try to find a hidden lever or button, or even a door, but I ran out of time."

The door opens, and Neve comes out fuming and heads straight for Dex, Dae, and Rima. Not Samuel.

I narrow my eyes on Dex, who is listening intently to Neve.

"Meike Besser," the satyr calls.

Zai and I wait. Two minutes later, Meike returns, too.

Trinica is next.

Meike hurries over to us. "I felt the other two walls. Nothing."

"I guess I'll check the floor." They both nod. "Zai, is there anything in your book?"

He shakes his head. "I already tried."

Meike leans closer and lowers her voice. "I have the Mirror of Ariadne, my other gift from Dionysus. It's supposed to reveal the way to go. Maybe it can show me the way out." She pauses, forehead wrinkling. "I should have used it on my first try. Sorry. I was just thinking about covering what Zai hadn't."

I'm tempted to pat her hand just for sharing that with us. She didn't have to. "The harp has to be in there for a reason." I glance around. "Something to do with music, maybe?"

"I'll try playing the harp on the next round," Zai says.

And then we wait. You wouldn't think two minutes each would feel so long, but it does.

When Dex comes out from his shot at it, face pinched with irritation, I can't help myself. "Looks like that forewarning gift isn't as helpful as you'd think."

Dex startles.

Behind him, Neve's lips pinch. "You didn't tell your allies, but you told *her*?" She flings an accusing finger in my direction.

Dex's face drops into a deep glower. "How the fuck did you know about that?" he asks me.

I don't bother to hide my grin. "I didn't. Not for sure. But now I do."

He starts toward me, hands fisting.

"Touch her and reckon with me," Samuel says. He doesn't move, doesn't raise his voice, but Dex stops dead in his tracks. I was right. They lost him as an ally in the last Labor. I don't know what swung it, but I'm glad to not have him as an enemy.

I give Samuel a nod. He may have been with Dex and the others at the beginning of the last challenge, but we're square now.

After a moment of visibly wrestling with his anger, Dex stomps away to his allies. We resume the rotation of champions through the Labor. I, of course, am dead last. Apollo could at least have slotted me in the middle to mix it up a bit.

The first thing I do when I get in the room is roll up my sleeve and awaken Hades' tattoos. I send the fox sniffing around the room and the tarantula climbing the walls, looking for any possible way out, while I feel the floors.

My two minutes are up fast, and, tattoos back in place, I come out with nothing. Zai is up next with the harp. Not more than ten seconds in, there's a loud yelp, and all of us jerk our gazes to the door.

Disappointment rolls through me when he comes back out. The others, though, all smile quietly to themselves.

We huddle back up. "That damn harp bit me," he whispers. Hunching over so the others can't see, he shows us his hand, which has teeth marks across the back and palm. Human teeth marks.

"Bit you with what?" I ask.

"That thing is…" He makes a face. "It's made up of human parts—a breastbone, and I think the strings are hair. When I plucked one, the crown grew teeth and lunged for me. I think it was going for my throat."

He was right earlier. Grotesque.

It's Meike's turn again, but her mirror shows her nothing. As each of the others goes with no success, and then all of us go a third round, the waiting room grows more and more quietly desperate.

They wouldn't kill all of us if none find the answer. Right?

Even Zai isn't coming up with any more ideas to try—his book of answers, either. At least we're not the only ones getting frustrated. I think Dex might pop a vein any second.

"Lyra Keres," the satyr calls.

Round number four for me. I step into the room, and this time, rather than looking, I close my eyes and try to make my heart stop hopping around so I can concentrate.

At first, I don't even notice I'm doing it, but about the time I realize I'm humming, there's a small *snick* of sound, and then I feel bands wrapping around my head, chest, and arm.

My eyes blink open to find a thick marble door swung wide, exposing the entrance to what appears to be a cave. *Another* cave. Much smaller than in the dolines. I'm now wearing bands that secure my four flags to my body.

My jaw drops.

Music. The harp doesn't want to be played—it wants to *hear* music.

"I did it." The words fall in a whisper from my lips. Elation slams into me like I just stole the best score ever, and I have to swallow back a crow of delight.

I won!

I mean, not on purpose or anything. This was just a happy accident. But I don't usually have happy accidents.

Oh my gods, I won.

I fucking won a Labor.

Hades is going to be over the damned moon—or his version of it, at least. Four Labors in, and I'm not dead, *and* I'm tied for victory with Diego, Zai, and Jackie. For the first time since Hades named me his champion, I feel a rush of confidence that I can survive this. Maybe even lose my curse.

And be loved.

Happiness blazes through my veins and has me bouncing on my toes with the energy of it fizzing warmly through me. It's probably a good thing Hades is *not* here, because I'm pretty sure I'd throw myself into his arms.

I peek through the door, not wanting the watching world of the gods to see what I'm feeling in this moment.

After a deep breath, I step into the dark and creepy cave.

57

SORRY, NOT SORRY

After only one step into the cave, I falter.

Zai and Meike are still out there. So are the others.

I have to make a decision. The thing is, if any of them don't figure it out, they die. If that wasn't on the table, I'd tell Zai and Meike and leave the others to figure it out for themselves.

My arms flop to my sides as I close my eyes and release a frustrated groan. But I can't *not*. Opening my eyes, I look upward, knowing that, however they do it, all of Olympus is watching me go through this.

"I'm sorry, Hades," I say, loud and clear.

There will be many hells to pay whenever he gets out of god jail or wherever they're holding him, if he's talking to me at all.

I'm actually looking forward to arguing with him about *anything* again.

Focus, Lyra.

I step back from the marble door leading into the cavern and close it, and maybe thirty seconds later, the satyr opens the door to the waiting room. The moment the others clock that I'm wearing my flags, they all jump to their feet in a jumble of exclamations and more than a few curses.

I raise a hand to shut them up. "Each and every one of you has to swear, on your lives, that if I give you the answer, you will not harm or hinder any other champion in completing either of today's Labors." Trading information for safety worked for the last Labor, right? Then I hesitate. Consequences have a different meaning to me now.

I glance at Zeles. "Is that against the rules?"

"No."

"Good." I face the champions.

A litany of expressions stare back at me—shock, dubiousness, anger. But the proof that I know the answer is on my body in the form of four flags. "Promise me, or I'll only tell my allies and the rest of you can risk ending up in the Underworld."

"What are you doing?" Zai mouths.

"I'm sorry," I mouth back at him and Meike. Meike at least shoots me a thumbs-up. See. She gets it.

Neve stares at me like I'm a bug she'd like to squish under her shoe. "Why the hells would you tell us the answer, hoser?" she says, her Canadian accent even thicker than usual. "You could've just told your allies and let the rest of us fail." Which leaves us all in no doubt that that's what she would've done.

"Let's just say I'm not a fan of death as a punishment." I hope the gods and goddesses are all listening. *Take note*, I'm telling them silently. *I'll ruin your fun by doing this every damned time.*

Then I look at one person and one person only.

Dex.

Staring back at me with his dark-brown eyes narrowed, he works his jaw for several seconds before, lips tight, he gives a jerking nod. "I swear it."

After a surprised pause, the others follow suit—each and every one of them.

There. At least I got something out of it that should help me and my team. Dex and his allies won't be coming after us today.

"Music," I tell them. "Make music—hum or sing. Don't try to play the harp, though. She bites. Do it until the door opens." I look at Zai and Meike. "I'll wait for you at the start of the next Labor." I won't have to wait long. Zai is right after me in the order we go, and Meike shortly after him.

I turn to go back through, but the satyr steps in front of me. "I'm sorry, Lyra Keres, but the rules are clear. If you come back out, you have to wait your turn."

"Ha!" Neve crows. "Serves you right."

"Shut the fuck up, Neve," Dae snaps. "She just saved your damned life."

A blush mottles up the sides of her face, and Neve opens and closes her mouth a couple of times.

"She's not really like this." Dae looks at the rest of us. "At least I don't think so. Ares' gift was a competitive spirit, and it seems to have made her…" He waves a hand at her. "This."

Dex smacks him on the back of the head. "Don't tell them shit."

Dae's jaw sets at a stubborn angle. "It's not going to help them, but at least they won't hate her for it."

"Zai Aridam," the satyr calls.

Zai stops in front of me before going in. "Meike and I will wait for you."

I shake my head. "I'm last. All of the champions are between us. With your winged sandals, you've got a shot of getting through the obstacles. You should try to win."

Someone—Dex, maybe—gives a derisive snort.

I ignore him. "Don't wait for me. Help each other, and if I can catch up, I will."

Zai looks behind him to Meike, who, after checking my expression, gives a reluctant nod. With no warning, he wraps his arms around me in a hug. "You make it through safe, okay? I don't need another death to feel guilty over."

My heart squeezes so tight it hurts. He feels guilty leaving me, and he's hugging me to make me feel better. How is it even possible? My curse should make him…indifferent at least. I soak it up like a dry sponge finally hitting water.

"I will. You be safe, too," I whisper and hug him back.

With a grin for me and one for Meike, he goes inside.

Two minutes later, the door opens to an empty room.

58

ARTEMIS' LABOR

I am the last to walk into the cave for the next Labor.

I pass through the doorway onto a damp rock surface and pull up short when Diego steps out of the shadows. He went right before I did, so he hasn't been waiting long, but...

"Why are you still here?" I ask, eyeing him warily. He swore, same as the others. No harm or hindering.

Except his gaze is as warm and kind as his smile, which soothes a bit of my tension. "We haven't had a chance to talk much, but did anyone tell you I'm a father?"

I stare at him, then shake my head. He's in his mid-forties, though, so I'm not surprised.

He nods. "Two. Marisol and Gabriel. They are ten and twelve years old, and they are my life."

And I can't help the twinge of liking starting to grow for this man who is my competition.

"Even though they may never find out what happened to me..." His shoulders go back. "I want both of my hijos to be proud of their papá, no matter what. I will play these Labors with integrity."

My heart twists. Because to yank a father away from his children, one who clearly cares for them... How could Demeter have done that when she's recently lost her own?

"You earned the right to start this Labor before me," he says. "That's why I waited."

Oh. He really, really means it—about competing with integrity. "I know they *are* proud," I tell him. "You are a good man."

"Muchas gracias." Then he grins. "But you only think that because

Demeter's blessing for me is charm."

She made him likable. Must be nice.

I shake my head. "I know when people are good versus likable."

He sobers a little bit and offers me a sincere smile. Then he takes a deep breath and steps back, ushering me ahead of himself.

Which is when I finally get a good look at the start of Artemis' obstacle course. What I see is a cavern lit by lanterns hanging from stalactites, illuminating a series of tiered balance beams. I glance down to see that it's only about a twenty-foot drop, but it's onto thousands of stalagmites that look like teeth.

No Daemones in here—not that I can see, at least—but that doesn't mean much.

"Pretty sure that fall would end me," I murmur to myself, but Diego laughs.

"Don't take too long," he says. "Bats. That's what comes for your flags in here. Small ones and some nasty-looking larger ones that could knock you off if they wanted."

So I get to dance with Dracula-makers? Shudder. "Great."

I look down again.

"Did anyone else—" I cut off the question. I don't want to know. I just won't look down, so I don't have to see a body if anyone did fall.

"Not on this part," Diego says. "But I've heard—"

A howl of pain shoots out of the other end of this cavern, and I'm pretty sure it's Samuel. What on earth could make *him* sound like *that*?

"Screams," Diego finishes. "From the next part."

This just gets better and better. I blow out a long breath and take the first step. The beam doesn't move and is solid. It's also only about six inches wide.

Don't think about that.

If I pause, I'll trick myself into falling, so I try to be quick across the beams, doing my best to handle the sharp turns right and left and the changes in height. Only a few wobbles and one windmilling-arms maneuver, but I'm still up here. Footsteps right behind me tell me Diego's keeping pace easily.

We're about halfway across the cavern when a distinctive squeak is followed by another, and another, and the sounds of flapping, and then Diego shouts, "Pick up the pace!"

My heart is pounding in my chest as I glance to my right, and I make out a swarm of bats blocking the light of one of the lanterns. Then another lantern, closer. And another. And the squeaks of their echolocation fill the room.

I go. I go as fast as I can, only having to pause once or twice to not fall during transitions between beams. We're almost to the end, where the last beam stops at a ledge that leads to a small, round tunnel.

Almost there.

With a flutter of wings, the bats swarm us. I stumble when my foot hits solid ground, and I go down, smacking my knee into the rock. I grunt but don't have time to worry about it because two strong, invisible hands pull me to my feet.

The bats whirl and dive like a tornado, trying to get at our flags. Diego practically shoves me into the tunnel, which looks like a drainpipe made of corrugated metal. It's small enough that we have to drop to our hands and knees to dive in.

The second we're both inside the pitch-black darkness, the bats stop. I mean really stop, not just give up and fly back to their roost. It's more like the instant we got in here, they ceased to exist.

"That's one." Diego sounds annoyingly chipper. I can't see him. He's clearly wearing his ring.

One down. Unknown number to go. "Did you lose any flags?"

"No."

Really weird, talking to nothing.

I blow out a silent breath of relief. I'd hate it if I was the reason he did. "Good. Me neither." Then I turn to face the nothingness in front of me. This kind of darkness is...suffocating. Like you'll never see light again. But I've lived underground most of my life. Darkness is one fear I don't deal with.

Inertia is the real killer. That much, I learned the hard way. Starting at my knees, I quickly feel up the rounded sides of the pipe.

But when I get only six inches from the bottom, a shock zaps through me, and I yelp, jerking my hand away. The electric charge lights up what is definitely a drainpipe. I shake my hand, breathing through the pain that is turning to a burning on the side of my palm where it struck. "Don't touch anything but the bottom," I tell Diego.

I assume that even though he's invisible, he can still touch.

"Got it."

We get moving.

My knee, already bruised from that rough landing off the beams, is not appreciating this at all, but I grit my teeth and try my best not to notice. Not like I have options.

Maybe ten feet in, something grabs me from the side, and I scream as I jerk away from it, right into the side of the pipe. Another zap shoots through my shoulder. The spark lights up the tunnel, and horror sucks the air from my lungs. There are holes in the tops and sides of the pipe and hands sticking out of them to grab our flags or push us into more pain.

"Fuck," I mutter. "Did you see that?"

"I saw what got you."

I describe the rest, and Diego groans. "How about this," he says.

Suddenly, the entire tunnel illuminates, the brightness coming from behind me. Diego's grin is audible in his voice. "Sometimes the glow comes in handy."

Thanks to his halo.

I laugh. "I bet sometimes it doesn't."

But he has the ring to go invisible, so he's covered. That halo really works.

"Let's go fast," he says.

Fast seems to be the theme here. "Yeah."

And we go. Even with the ability to see the hands reaching for me, I lose count of how many times I'm shoved into the wall and shocked. I thank my lucky stars for my short hair, which they keep trying to grab but can't. It's hard to tell, but Diego seems like he's faring much better.

I can't say how long we crawl before light appears ahead of me.

"Almost there!" I shout and go even faster because I want the hells out of here.

Almost there. Almost there.

The light widens as we get closer to the end. A hand shoves at me, and my cheek smacks into the metal on the other side. The shock feels like it melts my cheekbone under the skin, and I can't help the guttural yell, but I keep going.

Until the instant I feel the Courage flag rip right off my spine with a hard tug, and fear crashes through me so hard and fast that my muscles lock up and I face-plant.

59

FEAR IS MY FRIEND

The terror that wants to rip my guts out through my mouth on every scream is crippling, but I manage to take a breath. And then another.

"Did you lose a flag?" Diego asks.

It takes me at least two more breaths before I can force words through a jaw so stiff I could be a corpse. "Give me…a second."

I focus on breathing. I can see the end of the tunnel, where there is a small light. We're almost out. And my experiences—years in a place where I was forced to manage my fear or appear like the weakling all the other thieves thought I was—kick in harder with each breath. Thank the gods. Because fear isn't debilitating. Not when you lean into it. Not when you listen to it for what it is. It's a warning, your body's way of telling you to live—to fight or flee or even sometimes freeze so that you survive.

Fear is a tool.

One I've been learning to use my entire life.

Granted, this fear is more than I'm used to, and it's not coming from me, so I take the extra time to breathe through it. To let the adrenaline of it fill my muscles and instead of paralyzing me, galvanize me.

"Lyra?" Diego asks.

"I'm okay. I'm going to keep moving."

"Okay."

I position my body so that I can surge to my hands and knees and move fast. And when I do, that adrenaline is there, pumping through my veins, driving my muscles, and dulling the pain from all my bumps, bruises, and electric burns.

I keep crawling, and I don't stop until I burst into the light. I still don't stop, giving Diego enough room to get all the way out before I collapse to the ground, shuddering. I can see him as he drops next to me—he must have removed his ring.

The fear hasn't stopped, even now that we're safely out of the cave, resting in a small clearing. But I can contain it. I still have control. Sort of. I mean, my hands are in fists and my chest feels like there's a boulder on it, but I'm not screaming or in a fetal position, so I consider that a win.

I guess if I had to lose a flag, that was the best one for me.

I roll my head in his direction. "You okay? Lose any flags?"

Diego shakes his head, then breaks out in a huge grin. "That's two!" He holds up two fingers.

I laugh and groan at the same time, then roll to high-five him, only to grunt when he smacks one of my scorch marks.

He frowns. "I'm sorry."

Come to think of it, every time that tunnel lit up, it was because I got zapped. "Did you get shocked at all?"

He gives a sheepish shake of his head.

We push to our feet and take one look at the next obstacle, and I have to pitch forward, hands on my knees, to contain the unnatural fear all over again.

The next obstacle appears to be a giant scrapyard with an obvious path right down the middle. Piles and piles of junk of all kinds. Metal scraps, crushed cars, tires. Mountains of them. There is a rusted metal arch indicating the entrance to this part of the challenge.

Something bad is going to happen the second we step inside. I just know it.

Honestly, if death wasn't the result of not finishing this Labor, I'd cop a squat right here and wait until it's all over. Tempting. Really tempting. But not today.

"Let's keep going," I say.

Diego nods.

I take a deep breath, readying for whatever horror is going to jump out at me from the billion hiding places in the junk mountain, and a swath of deep purple catches my eye from behind a rusted-out truck hull. Careful not to enter, I walk to the left leg of the arch to get a better view of Amir crouching behind the truck as he stuffs something in his mouth. Something white. He's rocking as if he's in horrible pain.

But before I can call to him, he jumps to his feet and sprints down the path. I guess I was wrong about the pain. He's moving just fine, even with his boot on.

"Let's go." Diego tugs on me, and we enter the obstacle together.

I knew it. The second we pass through the arch, there's a terrible screech like metal on metal. Not one screech...hundreds coming from all around.

Birds. They're crawling out of the metal all over the junkyard, sort of the way my tattoos leave my arm, only they are peeling away from the scraps, leaving gaping holes. And not just any birds...

Stymphalian birds.

Not as big as recorded history says—maybe the size of crows. The metal of their snapping beaks catches the sun in a hundred flashes of light, as do their tails and longer wing feathers that they can turn into bronze at will.

As they break loose, they take to the air, then, in unison, dive straight for us.

An extra shot of adrenaline fires my blood. Thank fuck.

"Run," I scream.

Heart pounding, I sprint down the path between the mountains of scrap until my legs burn and my lungs ache. I almost lose my footing as I look back over my shoulder to see how close the birds are, but I catch myself and come to a stop.

They've vanished.

"That was close," I say to Diego between gasps. Not that I can see him, thanks to his ring. But I realize in the silence now that I can't hear his footsteps or his breathing like I could before.

"Diego!" I call out softly, and then again when he doesn't answer.

Maybe he passed me. "Great," I mutter. I'm on my own now.

Wait a minute. When did I start to need other people to get through shit?

The metal around me screeches as more Stymphalian birds struggle to break away from the scrap.

Not my flags. Not today. Pumping my legs, I sprint between heaps. But a flash of a green uniform and red hair snags my attention as I dash past, and I double back, scanning for the birds, who haven't caught up with me yet.

I find Neve huddled by a heap of crushed cars.

She's on the ground, knees drawn up to her chest and rocking, whimpering in pain and babbling the same thing over and over. "Nora dies if I don't win. She dies. She dies."

I probably only have a few seconds before the birds track me down. I try to take her by the shoulders, but Neve screams and jerks away. Her Strength flag is gone, which means she's drowning in pain the way I am in fear. Only she's not controlling hers. Maybe because she's also missing her Mind flag...confusion *and* pain.

At the sound of a bird rending itself from the metal right by us, she screams. "The birds. The birds." Then she starts to crawl away through a tunnel in the junk. "Have to hide," she mutters.

I frown as she crawls out of sight. Do I stay? Or abandon her and run, already having lost time?

"Fuck." I drop to my knees to follow her.

And that's when one of the birds rips my Strength flag off my arm.

Pain—like someone took a blowtorch to every nerve in my body—scorches through me, and I cry out. But I still have my wits, and, with every move an excruciating torture, I force myself to crawl after Neve.

Fear is telling me to give up. To just lie here and die from the agony ripping me apart.

Drawing deep, I force my hands and legs to move, and I don't stop until I find her. She's huddled inside a metal dumpster turned on its side, back to rocking and babbling about whoever Nora is, tears trailing down her face.

I crawl inside and hold very, very still. If I don't move, the pain isn't quite as bad. But as the birds continue to shriek outside, the fear builds, swelling within me as questions start to swarm. What if we're both stuck here in pain and fear and confusion? What if the birds never let us leave? What if I can't get myself out, let alone both of us?

I might start rocking and muttering myself in a second. I close my eyes and hum, focusing on a single image.

Hades.

As suddenly as it started, the metallic screeching outside stops, and I crack an eye. Are the apocalypse nightmare birds gone?

Every nerve screaming at me to stop, I manage to flip over and start crawling, grunting with every move, but Neve grabs my ankle. I immediately cry out, and it takes all I have not to vomit. She jerks back with a hiss, shaking her hand. Yup. Touching hurts like a son of a bitch for both of us.

"Not yet," she whispers.

Is she working her way through that confusion?

I wait. But she stays quiet.

"Ready?" I whisper.

She blinks at me like she forgot I was here and has no idea what I'm talking about.

"Can you follow me?" I ask.

Another blink, and maybe that competitive thing Ares gave her kicks in, because her blue eyes clear just for a second and she nods.

And we crawl.

Once we're back on the path, I force myself to stand, though my entire body shakes with the effort. "Don't be seen," she says in jerking words.

With a deep breath, she shoots her fisted hands out from her sides, and armor—bright bronze, speckled with stars—covers her chest and shoulders down to her hips, along with reinforced silver ankle and forearm protection. She cries out, probably at the touch of it against her skin, but starts moving regardless.

I follow.

Instead of running, which I'm not sure I could do anyway, we walk carefully, staying close to the heaps and piles, using the shadows and crevices as cover. I clamp a hand over my mouth both to stop myself from humming and to keep quiet, because after the second time a whimper of pain escaped me, Neve turned to glare at me. She is one of the Strength champions for a reason, that's for sure.

Eventually, I can see it.

The end of the path.

It opens into a field with tall, brown grasses that will stand well above my head.

What next?

That terrible metal *caw-caw* screech of the birds comes from behind us, and my heart tries to explode. No choice now. "Run!"

With a yell that comes from the pit of her, pure determination, Neve propels herself forward. Damn, that woman is fast with her long legs, even in agony. I can't keep up with her. She bursts into the grasses and disappears.

She left me.

She left me here to die. Like everyone does. Everyone leaves me.

Fear tries to grab at my feet and slow me down, stop me. But the metallic racket from behind me is enough to force that same fear to drive me forward, and I run into the grasses. They hurt. They brush against my skin, and it feels like I'm being scraped with razors over and over.

I have to stop and breathe through the pain, only to watch in what feels like slow-motion horror as a hand reaches out from the field and, before I can even think to get to my axe to defend myself, plucks the Mind flag right off my head.

Immediately, confusion joins the fear and pain—a heavy fog of it.

For a second, I'm lost. Like something dropped me in the middle of a nightmare and I have no idea why, and everything combines to an overwhelming pitch.

I slam my hands over my ears, which only makes the pain worse as I drop into a crouch, and I let out a scream to wake the dead. An immediate answering roar goes up not far away, and I cover my mouth. A second roar makes the grasses bend under the force of a smoky wind.

And panic pummels at me.

The grasses are so high, they should block my view, but I still see the purplish-black wings that rise and fall not far from me. Fear, believe it or not, blasts a hole in my confusion, clearing it like sun burns away fog.

A dragon.

I have to run from a *dragon*.

60

DEATH BEHIND AND BEFORE

Dragons mean fire, and fire in a field of tall, dead grass is a death trap. Somewhere close by, Neve screams again, then streaks by in a blaze of color, plowing a path through the field, and in her wake, I see them. The sources of those hands that took my Mind flag.

Leimakids. Nymphs of meadows.

Not trying to harm, just get those flags. They dance and flit and disappear into the tall grasses themselves.

As I pull out my axe, the confusion creeps back in, and my head swims.

Then fire erupts overhead.

The blast of heat is so unbearable, I drop to my stomach and wrap my arms over my head. It feels like my clothes just got singed off my back. Pain rends me, and I shake so much my teeth are chattering despite the heat. My heart pumps so hard, I can hear it in my head. This has to be the end.

There's an unmistakable crackle of flames behind me. Fire in the fields. Fear clears the confusion again, and without bothering to think, I'm running. Another hand reaches from the grasses, and I whack it with the flat side of my axe. It disappears with a yelp.

I should have thought of that earlier.

Thought of what? I stumble but don't fall. *Where am I?*

A nearby blast clears my mind enough to remember and keep going. With no warning, I burst into a wide-open field. A thick layer of hazy smoke sits above the ground like a dense fog. The grasses are short here — nothing to hide in. Still brown, though. Tinder waiting for…

What? What needs tinder? Where am I?

A *thump* sounds behind me, then another, and a shadow falls over me.

That's right. A fucking dragon.

I don't even look. I don't want to look. If I do, I know the fear will paralyze me and it's over.

Run!

I take off. The dragon's roar is so loud and close, it rattles my bones. The smoke is so thick, I can't see and I can't breathe. It clogs and burns my throat and the inside of my nose until I'm coughing with every breath. I keep running.

Fire scorches a wide swath of grass to my right. My eyes water like faucets, and I have to squint. But at least my pain and fear are holding the confusion in check.

Up ahead, Charon's face is visible for just a second, and my heart plummets to my feet. Charon is here, not Hades. Will that work to end the Labor?

A massive claw lands to my left, and the ground vibrates. I swear I can feel the dragon breathing down my neck. The terror ricocheting through my insides is trying to drag me to the ground.

I grit my teeth and pick up speed.

Any second now, that fucking fire lizard is going to roast me alive or snap me in half with the giant teeth I'm sure are in its fire-breathing mouth.

Hades.

I see his face. Just a glimpse in a swirl of smoke. Directly ahead. Or am I imagining things?

I scream in agony as a blast of fire grazes my arm.

Please, gods, let it be Hades.

That one thought is enough to keep me on my feet, and I run through the pain.

I still can't see him, and the fear rips holes in the hope that he's here at all.

"Hades." His name escapes my lips on a puff. Almost a grunt.

A plea.

"I'm here." His voice surrounds me in the smoke, like he's everywhere. Like he's touching me. But he's not.

Fear urges me forward despite my body's violent protests. Whimpers pour from my lips. Tears roll down my cheeks. And out of the smoke that billows away in the wake of the flames, I see Hades.

All of him.

Can't he run to me?

Obviously not. His lean body is rigid as he remains firmly in place. His eyes lock on mine.

I can't hear his voice, but his mouth forms the words, "Come on, my star."

Then his gaze jerks up, right above me, eyes widening slightly before shooting back to mine, and he gives the tiniest jerk of his head to the left.

I dodge that way without hesitation, just as the dragon's mouth chomps down on empty air where I was a second ago. The monster jerks back with a frustrated roar.

And I know it's coming again.

I'm not going to make it.

Hades' gaze shoots above me once more, and I know this is my last chance.

I put on an extra burst of speed.

And Hades' arms snap closed around me.

In an instant, the dragon and smoke and the overwhelming doses of fear, confusion, and pain all disappear. Lightheaded, I'm vaguely aware that we're now standing in a field of lush, green grass with the most beautiful blue skies above. My arms wrap around Hades' neck, and he holds me so that my feet dangle off the ground, his face buried in my hair.

He's breathing hard, like he ran that race with me. "Fuck, Lyra. You scared the shit out of me."

A laugh tumbles out of me, more from shock than anything. It cuts off, and I realize I'm shaking. "I thought you wouldn't be here." The words come out as a harsh whisper. "I was so scared."

He runs a soothing hand over my hair. "They couldn't keep me away."

Eyes still closed, I breathe him in. Bitter chocolate. I might associate that smell with safety for the rest of my life after this. "I only have my Heart left to give you," I tell him. I'm talking about the flag.

He makes a sound that might be a laugh or a groan. "I know," he says. "That's all I need."

PART 5

TRUST MUST BE EARNED

Are we having fun yet?
Not asking for a friend. Asking for me.

61

THE GODS HAVE THEIR EYES ON ME

I glance over Hades' shoulder—straight into speculative blue eyes.
Zeus is watching us.

Beside him on the ground, Samuel sits very, very still, his face ashen, staring at the dirt like he saw a ghost and is trying to pretend he didn't.

Athena is here, too, eyeing me the same way Zeus is, and so is Hera, to her right.

"Put me down," I whisper to Hades. "They're watching."

Hades stills against me. "I don't care."

"I do." For a thousand reasons.

He sets my feet on the ground, pulls his arms from around me, and steps back. His expression has taken on the mantle of my enigmatic, arrogant, taunting god, but I also know, without a doubt, that it's for them. Not me.

"You came in dead last, my star." He says this in a voice that sounds angry, but with his back to them, his eyes are laughing.

Laughing?

"I gave the other champions the answer to the fourth Labor. You're not angry—?"

He lifts a single brow. "What do you think?" His mouth crooks, and one dimple winks at me. Flirts with me, even.

What is happening right now?

I huff a laugh. But the adrenaline must be leaving my system fast, because several truths slam into me all at once.

The first is that I survived the fifth Labor. Only seven more to go. Almost halfway.

The next is that I came in last on this one, but… "The others?"

"All made it." He grimaces and nods in the direction of the champions. "Some in worse shape than others, but alive. Samuel lost all his flags but still made it to the finish line. Rima used a cloak of phoenix feathers and pretended to be a baby dragon, which was smart, but Dex managed to cross first while she was distracting the dragon."

"Oh no—"

Hades shakes his head. "He didn't win. Dae had a hard time with the Stymphalian birds and was fourth to cross, but he was the first to come through with all four flags, so he wins this one. Zai and Meike are unharmed."

Between my relief and all the energy I expended—physically, mentally, and emotionally—I'm suddenly drowning in exhaustion. Exhaustion and...pain. Except the Labor is over. I frown. Why am I feeling pain?

"Lyra?"

Hades' voice sounds far away. I hardly hear him as agony rips through me. It's like my relief gave my nerve endings permission to come back to life. My arm throbs so hard I can feel it everywhere.

I drop to the ground, legs giving out, body shaking.

"Asclepius!" Hades barks.

Immediately, the healer is at my side. "She won a Labor," Hades snaps. "Heal her."

"I know," Asclepius says in a soothing, fatherly voice that only makes Hades' glowering scowl—a real one now—deepen.

"If you know, then fucking heal her."

This is not going to help those speculative looks from the other gods and goddesses at all. "I'm fine," I say through gritted teeth. But hells, even I don't believe me.

"This burn is deep," Asclepius says, then shakes his head. "Dragon fire."

That was real?

"What does that mean?" Hades demands.

"I'll need to take her to be treated."

"First, though!" Apollo strides across the field, leaving a wiped-looking Rima where she sits in the grass. "Your prize."

"Later," Hades snarls.

Apollo's eyebrows shoot up, and he glances between us, eyes turning

If I wasn't trying to hold in screams, I'd grimace at that. I don't need more reasons for the gods and champions to not like me.

Ignoring Hades, Apollo goes down on one knee before me. His golden eyes are even more striking up close. "For soothing my poor harp, I present to you the Tears of Eos." With a flourish, he holds out a small, clear glass vial that contains an iridescent liquid that shimmers like rainbows over crystal-clear waters—only a few drops.

Hades grumbles and takes it, shoving the vial into his jeans pocket.

Apollo's teeth glint in his face in a wickedly teasing smile. "Those tears are from my daughter, the goddess of the dawn, and when dropped in your eyes will allow you to see in the dark and past glamours, spells, and magic. I have a feeling you, of all the champions, might find this handy."

Oh, I get it. Hades. Darkness. Despite the agony still tearing at me, I manage to roll my eyes. Apollo winks at me.

"But be careful," he warns. "They last only a short while, and when they stop working, the darkness will be overwhelming until your eyes adjust again. Some mortals have been known to go mad at the effect."

"Of course I get a gift with a punishment for using it," I grind out.

"Use them wisely," Apollo advises.

The words are hardly out of his mouth before Hades touches my uninjured shoulder and we disappear in a blink with Asclepius.

62

HEALING

The sound of the TV—showing all the mortal celebrations and speculating ad nauseum about the games and what could possibly be going on with the gods and their mortals—is not the distraction I think it was intended to be.

I'm lying on a pristine white bed with pristine white sheets and covers.

My bed in Hades' house.

He also hasn't left the room except when Cerberus or Charon insist on it. Even then, it's not for long. Right now, he stands at the window, hands stuffed in his pockets, shoulders rigid while Asclepius examines my arm.

Medical instruments were brought in to monitor me, despite Asclepius saying it wasn't necessary. But it has still taken the healer three days and four rounds of that glowy thing he does to repair my arm. Apparently, a mortal body can only heal so much at a time, even accelerated. The first two days were... Let's just say I never want to go through that kind of pain again. Those burns were *deep*. Dragon fire, it turns out, continues to burn until quenched. Basically, it's like being blasted by sun fire and magma and acid at the same time.

We're on the fourth round now, which is mostly itchy.

A twinge in my arm makes me grunt, and Hades' back stiffens again. "Watch it," he grumbles over his shoulder. Poor Asclepius keeps sliding Hades little worried glances.

This isn't Hades angry, or bored, or even conniving. This is Hades... something else. Something that makes me want more.

But more would be dangerous.

Wouldn't it?

"I was thinking about who we should reach out to as allies next," I say conversationally to distract him. Distract us both, really.

He *hmmm*s, so I know he heard me.

"Dex is going to be even more competitive with more champions collecting one win each, and he has none so far," I say.

Another *hmmm* from Hades.

"Did Charon tell you Meike is our ally now?"

That gets him to swing slowly around. "No."

One word and yet so very ominous. I smile. "She has the Mirror of Ariadne. That should come in handy. Right?"

"Yet another runt." Hades mutters the last bit under his breath.

"Rude. Size has nothing to do with capability," I point out. "Simmer down and let me make my own decisions."

Beside me, Asclepius makes a choking sound.

I blink up at Hades. "We've already met to talk through strategy."

We couldn't wait for him to get back. Zai, Meike, and I have met a few times while he's been gone.

"Of course you did."

"You were gone," I point out, and I immediately regret it when a muscle at the corner of his mouth ticks. "I didn't mean that as a dig," I say, quieter.

I shoot a glance at the black glove on Hades' hand at his side. He's refused to tell me about his punishment, but he's still healing. He did that for me.

Hades meets my gaze, and his softens slightly. "I know."

A nerve ending decides to fire in my elbow, and I pause, squeezing my eyes shut through it. When it fades, I open my eyes again to find Hades has crossed to my bedside.

He sends Asclepius a glare. "Why is this still hurting her?"

"Almost done," the healer answers.

"Not fast enough—" Hades cuts off when I tug on his sleeve to get him to look down at me.

"He's not trying to hurt me," I say. "I'm fine."

His jaw works for a second before he hooks a chair closer to sit down beside me, storm-cloud eyes skating over my features. "Stop saying you're fine when you're not. You always do that."

I roll my eyes and give Asclepius a smile. "Hades apologizes."

"You trying to manage me again?" Hades grumbles.

"You need a little managing."

"Pretty sure that's you, not me."

"All done," Asclepius says. The relief in his voice is so palpable I have to swallow back a chuckle. "Stay in bed one more night, and then you can go."

Hades rises to bend over me, inspecting the wound with narrowed eyes, and I swear the healer holds his breath.

"The scars?" Hades demands. My arm is covered in sort of silvery purple and shiny skin from shoulder to wrist.

Asclepius winces. "I did the best I could."

I elbow Hades with my good arm.

"What?" he asks.

With a nod toward Asclepius, I say, "You did amazing. It feels fine. Better than fine." Especially compared to even just this morning. "Thank you."

I elbow Hades again.

"Yes," he says. "Thank you."

The way the healer's eyebrows climb practically into his hairline, I'm guessing gods don't use those words often. His cheeks turn a little rosy, and then he nods and hurries from the room.

"Poor guy," I murmur. "I think you scared him."

Hades glances toward the door. "He's fine."

"Yeah, well, be nicer next time. He's helping."

Hades sits back down and runs the gloved hand over his face. "There better not be a next time."

When he catches me staring at the glove, he tucks it in his lap.

"I want to see," I say.

He shifts in his chair. "There's no point. It's almost healed."

"I get you not wanting to upset me while I was healing, but I'm better now." I hold my palm out. "Please. I'll just imagine worse things."

One eyebrow raises, but he puts his hand in mine. Carefully, I peel his glove off, then suck in sharply at the multitude of slashes across his palm. Not open wounds. Not anymore, at least. Actually, they look a lot like my arm does now. But still angry and red, and still healing. It's been *days*.

My throat grows thick, and I clear it. "Merciful Olympus," I whisper.

He tries to tug out of my hold. "It doesn't matter, Lyra."

"It damn well matters to me." He took punishment in my place. No one has ever done anything like that for me. Blinking rapidly, I run a finger softly over the smooth scars.

Hades gives a low growl, and I look up into eyes that have turned from heavy storm clouds into swirling silver.

"Why?" he asks.

I can't look away. "What do you mean, why?"

"I dragged you into the Crucible. Why would you bother to cry over me?"

I have no answer to that question. I'm sure psychologists would give it some kind of label. A syndrome of some sort. I hate labels like that—putting me into neat and tidy boxes. Life, emotions, humanity—none of that is remotely neat and tidy. We are, all of us, just trying to do the best we can, and fuck anyone who says otherwise.

I just never realized until now that that might include the gods.

"I could ask you the same thing. Why do you care? Actually…" I shake my head. "How are you able to care? Because you shouldn't feel a damned thing for me."

His jaw goes so impossibly hard, I'm surprised his teeth don't crack.

The TV breaks the silence between us. "I am here with Brad and Jessica Keres, the parents of Lyra Keres." I whip my gaze around to stare at the screen, my heart pounding in my ears so loud I'm not sure I'll be able to hear a word they say.

A young reporter shoves a mic into the faces of two people I've never seen before in my life.

At least…I don't think so.

"What do you think about your daughter being chosen by Hades this Crucible?" he asks them.

63

YOU CAN'T CHOOSE YOUR FAMILY

I narrow my eyes, trying to make the faces on the television connect to a memory. Any memory.

"We are so worried about our little Lyra," the man says.

I sit straight up in bed, tightening my grip on Hades.

The man has an arm wrapped around the woman's waist. Her smile seems wooden.

"What in the—?"

The man is the right age to be my dad. Tall with broad shoulders and an equally broad belly, he has the same black hair as me…I guess. Brown eyes, though. And the shape of his face is different than mine. He beams straight into the camera. I don't remember my dad's face, but I don't remember beaming smiles, either.

The woman is petite in the same way Meike is. Her brown hair is graying at the roots, but she does have green eyes. Like mine? Is there gold at the center? She's too far from the camera to tell.

Do I even recognize her? I mean, my family's faces are blurry in my head after all this time. I was only three when they dropped me in Felix's lap. My memories of them include eating a lot of peanut butter sandwiches and a hazy recollection of my mother singing to me, but otherwise I just have the vague knowledge that I had parents once.

"They never called me Lyra," I say. More to myself than Hades.

Lyra wasn't my name before I joined the Order. I don't remember what my name was, but that wasn't it.

"We understand Lyra is working off a debt for your family as part of the Order of Thieves," the newscaster says. "It is also said that the Order is getting threats. It seems many do not want Hades to become King of the Gods. What do you think of that?"

I shoot Hades a frowning look. "Is that true?"

"Are you surprised?"

No. Not really.

I missed my parents' answer, but I catch the next question when I turn back to the TV. "Did Lyra volunteer to pay your debts? From the little we've managed to learn about her background, she doesn't seem like the type who would."

I scowl. The world thinks they know me, huh?

The man who is supposed to be my father lets his expression droop from suitably sad to remorseful, and I curl my hands into fists, not buying one scrap of it. "She asked us to let her go," he says.

When I was fucking three years old?

"She's always been brave and selfless that way. We are allowed no contact with her, of course. Those are the rules of the Order." He wipes at his eyes. "They don't want their pledges distracted by outside influences while they work."

"Bullshit," I mutter under my breath.

That man is spewing so many lies that I can't even keep count.

"But the Order has kept in touch over the years," he continues, "and we know that our debt is almost paid and soon our Lyra can come back to us."

"Call me Lyra one more time, asshole." It's a good thing he's on the other side of the screen, or I don't know what I'd do.

There's a dinging in the background—one of the medical instruments hooked up to me. But I'm not paying that any attention.

"What age was she when she went to the order?" is the next question.

"Lyra, you need to calm down." Hades' free hand cups my face, but his voice is coming from a tunnel a long way off. All I can see and hear are my supposed parents.

My mother opens her mouth, but my father squeezes her waist, and she closes it again.

"We signed something that does not allow us to disclose," he says, "but old enough to make up her own mind."

"Liar!" My axe has somehow made it into my hands, and I hurl it at the TV. It hits dead-on, lodging in the center. The screen splinters out from the blade, and the image disappears.

Hades sits on the bed beside me, and all I can see is his face. His gray eyes are darker...with what?

Anger?

At me? He should take it out on those two people—

He uses the pad of his thumb and wipes away tears I didn't even realize had leaked out of my foolish, betraying eyes. Those people aren't worth crying over. Period. End of sentence.

After what I just saw, I'm not even sure they ever had a debt in the first place. The clothes they were wearing, the generally well-fed look of them, the latest-gen iPhone in my father's hand—it doesn't seem like they've been suffering.

Hades says my name.

The beeping of the machine now penetrates, and it's going in time to my rapid heartbeat. I'm looking at Hades, but I'm not really seeing him or hearing him. I'm just replaying those few questions and answers on the TV over and over and over in my mind. I'm shaking my head a little bit, as if rejection of all that is coming out in movement. If I don't let it out somehow, it's just going to build and fester. Maybe I know that.

I dash a hand across my eyes.

"Do you want me to smite them for you?" Hades asks.

That gets my attention. My gaze meets his, and I blink several times. "Could you?"

The look that he gives me is one not of admonishment but patience and...warmth. And I twist my lips and shake my head at the same time.

"No. Don't smite them."

I'm pretty sure he knew that would be my answer in the end. I dash my hand across my eyes again. Why won't I stop watering like a poor, pathetic gray cloud that doesn't stop drizzling? "They sent me to the Order when I was *three*." The words come out softly.

I look away from Hades. His gaze is too full of understanding. Empathy just makes me want to cry harder. "Those people are not worth my tears. Of course they're not worth it."

Again I don't realize I'm saying my thoughts out loud until he answers.

"No, they're not."

I pick at the thin blanket covering my legs. "The Order wouldn't have told them that I am close to paying off their debt, because I paid it off years ago. I just had nowhere else to go. No one knows that." I glance at him. "Except you. Every word out of that man's mouth was lies. How could I…" I stop, shaking my head again.

"How could you what?" Hades asks.

"Come from liars like *that*?"

"Could be worse," he murmurs. "You could have been swallowed alive as a baby by your Titan father."

But I'm still in my own head, spinning like a tornado sucking up more and more debris. "And my mother just stood there saying nothing. She didn't believe him. You could see it in her face. But she just said nothing. Is that what she did when he wanted to make me work off their debt at three years old? She just…let him?" I give myself a shake. "I know one thing for sure. I'm *not* going back to them."

He tucks some hair behind my ear, his fingers gentle and soothing. "You don't have to. You're well past legally being an adult in the mortal world. They have no claim over you."

My heart is still beating hard, the *ping* of the machine matching its rhythm. I wish Asclepius had turned that off. I wish my heart would just stop beating.

They're not worth it.

Easy to think, harder to truly absorb. Maybe if I keep repeating it…

"I don't have any family." I whisper this to myself more than to Hades. "I don't have anyone."

Hades pulls me against him, tucking my head into his shoulder. "There is a saying you mortals like to use." His voice is a deep, scratchy rumble under my ear. "It goes 'blood is thicker than water.'"

I frown into his shoulder. "Are you telling me to forgive them and reunite?"

That at least stops the tears.

"No." Hades leans away, holding my gaze captive. "I'm saying that if you use that phrase to define your family, then you shouldn't be surprised if sometimes they try to pull you under." He says this next part slowly, as if he's considering each word. As if he's trying not to poke at a sore spot. "But you can find a family and make them yours. A family that lifts you up, helps you float. One not made of blood."

I swallow and stare at him. It's possible if I win. If he takes away that curse. "Are Charon and Cerberus your family?"

"More than my brothers." He shrugs.

"And Persephone?" I don't know why I asked. I expect him to do what he always does when her name is brought up... Shut down.

Instead, he glances away—I think maybe toward the heart monitor, which has slowed down, I realize. My heartbeat is steady now.

"Yes. And Persephone," he says. Slowly again. Not reluctantly, though. He's deliberating what to tell me, I think. "But not the way mortals believe. Not even the way most of the gods believe."

Like Charon said. "Does it hurt to talk about her?"

The sadness that darkens his eyes to a flat, gunmetal gray is unmistakable. So is the stab of jealousy in the region of my heart. Maybe I shouldn't have asked. What if I don't like the answer?

64

SEE BEYOND THE MASKS WE ALL WEAR

"Yes," Hades says. "It hurts to talk about Persephone."

I was right. I don't like that answer.

"She was amusing and sweet." He's still talking. "Goddess of spring. How could she be anything but?"

That sounds like love to me.

"I didn't fall in love with her, though."

I blink, and he chuckles. "I can read your face like you're speaking your thoughts out loud, my star."

That's a big problem. One for later. I reach over and unplug the heart monitor.

"I loved Persephone," he says, taking the cord from me and draping it across the top of the machine, "but like a sister. Like a daughter, even. Hers is the softest, most caring heart I've run across in all my years as King of the Underworld. Losing her devastated us all."

The more he talks, the more I can see it now. The difference in the sadness coming from him. She was precious to him in her own right. Not as a wife or a queen or a lover but as herself. I wonder what it's like to love someone that way.

"I'm sorry she's gone," I whisper. "Is she why you're participating in the Crucible this time?"

Hades doesn't look away, but something in his face shifts. "I need to become King of the Gods. It will give me a certain added power."

"To do what? Take revenge? Unleash the hells?" I don't think he would, but I need to know that much.

"To set certain things right, but no. No unleashing."

"I believe you."

"You believe me." He echoes my words with a hint of displeasure in his voice. Hades leans into me, eye to eye, his sinful scent winding in and around me. "You trust too easily, Lyra."

"Maybe," I agree. "But *you* definitely avoid your feelings too much."

I'm starting to learn this about him. That cold veneer he presents to the world is exactly that. A front. It's not that he doesn't care—he just doesn't want that caring to be used against him.

Something I understand all too well.

Now he's glowering again, but I'm not frightened. Not of him. Maybe of me. Of the way I feel, sure, but of him? Not even a little.

"She was your friend," I say. "Like a daughter. Would she want you to hurt like this?"

Hades' glower falls away, and his gaze meets mine. "You don't want me to hurt?" The words come out as a guttural whisper. His voice is sandpaper and bass, rubbing at my own emotions until I feel raw.

"No." Maybe I shouldn't be this honest. "I don't want you to hurt."

"Why?"

"Because…" I say slowly. Then sigh. "This is how I'm a friend."

"A…friend." He says the words slowly, like he's tasting them.

"Yes." Charon said Hades needs one. "And a friend would say that underneath all the intense, godly bluster and the need to be in control all the time, and despite making me compete in the Crucible like an asshole, I still see who you are, and…" I shrug. "I like you."

His eyes turn molten, swirling with a hundred shades of silver and gray and even black. "Who do you think you see, my star?"

Forget sandpaper. His voice is raw silk again, and my belly turns squishy at the sound.

I smile. "I see the same person you saw in Persephone. A soft heart that cares too much. More than the world sees, because you make sure of it. Because the world should never know, or they'll take advantage of you."

He snakes his free hand upward, brushing lightly at my throat before threading his fingers in my hair to cup the back of my head, drawing me toward him.

"And you, Lyra?" he asks. "Would you take advantage of me?"

He's so close, lips a whisper away, eyes swirling with a heat that reaches in and around and through me. And I'm suddenly *very* aware that I'm in a bed, wearing flimsy clothes. Thank the gods I undid that monitor, because it would be beeping wildly about now.

"Not if I could help it," I whisper back.

"Damn. I wish you hadn't said that." On a groan, he dips his head, claiming my lips in a kiss I'm more than willing to give him. Freely offered.

That one touch tumbles me into a vortex of sensations—the softness of his lips sweetly sipping mine, the warmth of his hand in my hair, which tightens against my scalp on a twinge of pain that only feeds the heat. As if that previous kiss marking me to wander the Underworld unhindered is still there, in my skin. My lips tingle, and I moan.

He pulls back slowly and puts his forehead to mine, eyes closed, heart pounding under my palm. "Falling for me is dangerous," he whispers.

I stiffen. Is he reminding me of my curse or that he's a god? Pride snaps into place. "Who said anything about falling for you?"

This is *not* that. I don't know what it is. Attraction, obviously. Curiosity, definitely. What would it be like to simply find pleasure in someone just for the sake of pleasure? Knowing even friendship can't really happen, wanting anything more would make me a fool.

I already have the jester's hat after years of crushing on Boone.

He opens his eyes, staring into mine, doubtful.

I grin and hope I'm hiding the small amount of panic fluttering around inside me. "I just like the way you kiss."

Instead of laughing, he narrows his eyes. "You don't know—"

"Well, well, well," a distinctly feminine voice interrupts from the doorway. "Isn't this…lusciously naughty."

I freeze, then duck, burying my burning and likely bright-scarlet face in his neck. He's blocking me from view, the way he's leaning over me. "Go the fuck away, Aphrodite," he growls without turning around.

"I would, my darling. You know I would love to let you get back to whatever this is with joy. I'd join in if I thought you'd let me, but alas, I can't."

"What do you want?"

Irritation enters Aphrodite's voice. "Zeus never did like to play fair, and we all heard Lyra's healing was going slowly. I wanted to give her enough time to be ready."

"For what?" Hades snaps.

Pressed up against him, I can feel frustration vibrate through his body. Subtle, but it's there. I made him feel that. I smile into his neck. He is still so hard against me, and if he's anything like me, right now his body is screaming to finish what we started. I shift against him, press into him just a tiny bit, and he grunts. I smile wider.

"Oh my," Aphrodite breathes, and I can picture her fanning herself. "I might orgasm just from the energy wafting off the two of you. Better not let the others catch you, though." That's a warning from her. Dead serious.

"What did you want to give Lyra time to be ready for, Addie?" Hades asks through clenched teeth.

"I've been informed by Zeus that I must start my Labor in one hour."

Oh gods. My stomach pitches. The Labor that involves someone I love the most.

65

APHRODITE'S LABOR

"This is definitely the most unusual start to a Labor so far." I say this to Aphrodite, who gives me an enigmatic smile and flutters her ridiculously long eyelashes.

She's back in va-va-voom mode in a light-pink, figure-hugging strapless jumpsuit that looks, of course, amazing against her warm beige skin and long, black hair, which she's let hang down in luxurious waves to her backside. "It gets more unusual, I promise," she says in that husky voice that only makes it harder to put what I was doing with Hades a mere hour ago out of my mind.

What I was *feeling* with Hades an hour ago.

With Hades.

The god of death.

I'm not going to be cliché and ask myself what the hells I was thinking. I know exactly what I was thinking...that it felt fucking fantastic.

And that's all well and good, but the real question is...after this is over, assuming I survive, what could we possibly ever be to each other?

There is no future for a mortal and a god.

Besides, what I *should* be focusing on right now is yet another Labor—and not dying so I can get around to making any plans at all. Although the way this challenge is setting up, who knows how that's going to go.

Because I am strapped to a narrow bed.

Sure, it's a comfy single bed with pink silk sheets—this is Aphrodite, after all—and what's strapping me down are fuzzy hand and ankle cuffs, also pink. The cuffs connect to a scrolling iron headboard and footboard. I would think this was Aphrodite's way of having her wicked way with me if the other champions weren't here, all strapped to similar beds, like an odd rainbow made of our uniforms, as we're lined up by virtue. Black at the end, of course.

"Welcome to your sixth Labor," Aphrodite purrs. "This time, *your* survival isn't the focus. Love is. Today, your task will be finding someone special."

The one I love most.

A fact that creates an ache in my chest I'm trying very hard to pretend isn't there.

What will happen when no one is waiting for me? Or—and this might be worse—someone is, and it's humiliating.

An image of Hades taunts me.

"Two gods will be aiding me today," Aphrodite says. "Hypnos will put each of you into a deep sleep. Then Morpheus will send you into dreams. In your dream, you must find the mortal you love most in the world."

Mortal. I almost laugh my relief. No awkward conversation with my patron god in my future.

I focus on Aphrodite. This sounds too easy for the others, who probably already know their someone, at least—so clearly, the twist is coming. If I could, I'd cross my arms and settle in to wait for it.

"They will be trapped in their own dreams in a place particular to them. So to find them, you must figure out who it is and think only of them. Your dream will take you to them. It may not be who you think."

That's worse than I thought. I have to think of them?

"When you find them, telling them you love them is what will release you both from the dream. Bring them back to Olympus to end the Labor. If you don't return with them before sundown tonight, they will die."

See. There's always a twist. Always with death on the line.

Aphrodite's smile turns sly. "If you do wake them successfully, this person will then play in the next Labor with you...as a partner."

A second twist? Oh goody, and lucky us. I suppose Aphrodite must, if anything, outdo the other gods just to prove she can.

She holds out a hand, and, with a shower of pink sparks, two objects float in the air above her palm—a bow and a quiver of arrows. "The first person to free their loved one wins the prize of Eros' bow and arrows. These arrows only induce a temporary adoration, lasting a few hours at most. But in those few hours, that creature—man, beast, or…" Did she just glance at me? "…god…will not be able to resist you or say no to any request you make."

Assuming the winner can aim a bow and arrow and hit a target properly, that should be fun to watch.

Aphrodite looks at each of us in turn, making direct eye contact, and just that much is enough to make me relax a little. As if she has the power to reach into my soul with a single glance and tell me that everything will work out.

"Now…" She waves a theatrical hand. "Dream and go find love."

Hypnos looks exactly like you'd think—pale skin, long, straight hair of a deep purple that is near black, and beautiful like all the gods except for his creepy-ass eyes that are pure white. He moves silently from bed to bed, pressing a glowing palm to each forehead, and when he does this, the champion's eyes flutter closed and their body goes lax. As always, I'm last, so I get to watch this many times over, but it's not until he gets to me that I see his palm is marked with a swirling symbol and that's what glows bright white.

If Morpheus is present, I don't see him.

Then it's my turn. The glow of Hypnos' hand feels like the rays of the sun when you tip your face up to it in the winter, when it feels good just to keep your eyes closed and lean into the warmth above.

Only when I open my eyes, I'm still lying on the bed.

Um…did it work?

I don't think it worked.

Aphrodite isn't here. Hypnos isn't here. I turn my head to find all the other champions still lying in their beds, eyes closed and sleeping.

A swirl of emotions drops into my gut—disappointment, embarrassment, and a few others I don't want to put names to.

See. I was right. No one is waiting for me.

I expected this. I knew it was coming. And yet it still feels like someone just speared me through the chest.

I'm broken.

I get to just lie here and wallow in humiliation until the others return.

"Come with me, mortal." A bronzed man, and I mean all bronze— his skin, his hair, his eyes—with wisps of a sparkling bronze…smoke, I guess?…swirling off of him is standing beside my bed.

I had heard the myth of the sandman was based on Morpheus. Now I see why.

He holds out a palm to me, and despite the fact that I'm still strapped down, I lift a hand to take his anyway. Mine is…translucent. He helps me stand from the bed, and I look down to find my mortal body still strapped there. My soul is leaving it behind to travel wherever Aphrodite and her helpers have me going.

"Each of the champions will get to their loved one in a different way," he tells me. "For you, my mistress chose something fun."

Morpheus walks me through a small doorway and down a hall of black-and-white-checkered marble floors and pristine white walls decorated along the top with a simple black molding. At the end of that hallway, double doors lead out onto a balcony, and there, a pegasus waits. The pink one I admired. She nods her head at me a couple of times in what I think is a horsey greeting.

I'm so entranced by the thought of getting to ride a pegasus that I almost forget I need to focus on the challenge.

Think of the person I love most, and the dream will take me to them. *Start with the easier part. Get on the horse, Lyra.*

I've never ridden a horse before, so let's just say that I'm the source of great amusement for a lot of immortals watching me struggle to get on right now. And then the pegasus takes off, and I clench my thighs against her waist as I wrap my arms around her soft neck. And squeal.

Riding the pegasus involves a lot of hanging on for dear life as I try not to slide off one side or the other. This has to be harder than riding a regular horse, right? Because she's surging forward like she's running, which jostles me forward and back, but her whole body is propelled by her wings, which bounces me up and down.

Thankfully, once she gains altitude—not too high—she levels out, and it's easier to sit up and hold on with my hands now wrapped in her mane, thighs still gripping tight.

The pegasus tosses her head, eyeing me.

Think of who I love the most.

I know who it's not. Not my parents. Not Felix. Not… Well, that was a short list. But I remind myself there are all different kinds of love. And three faces immediately flip in my head.

I close my eyes and focus.

One possibility is busy right now, and another is not mortal, which only leaves…

My pegasus surges under me, and I have to open my eyes again to hold on. She flies us up and over a mountain and then spirals down into the clouds that surround the base of Olympus. They remind me of the fog that rolls into the bay in San Francisco, damp and chilly and hard to see through, and I'm used to that. When we emerge from the clouds, that's exactly where we are. San Francisco. Impossible to miss the soaring columns of the Golden Gate Bridge.

Instead of turning to the city, though, my pegasus flies me away, across the bridge, over the Minos Headlands, past the city of Sausalito, and on to the massive redwoods of Muir Woods.

I've never been here.

Maybe I was wrong?

Now with every flap, I'm second-guessing who it could be…or that it's no one and this is all a terrible joke.

The pegasus drops down between the towering, red-barked trees with their deep-green foliage. She tips this way and that, avoiding their broad trunks and far-reaching branches as she descends.

As we near the ground, the pegasus rears back, flaring her pink wings wide to catch the air and slow herself down. She hits the ground at a run, and I'm thrown forward, grasping around her neck all over again.

After slowing to a trot and then stopping gently—for me, I'm sure—she shakes her body, fluffing out her wings, and I take it as a signal that I should get off. Again, not great with horses, so my getting off is more like falling off, but at least I land on my feet. Then she nods her snout toward more trees. Toward a shadowed part of the forest.

What? Am I supposed to go in that direction?

She nods again, more vigorously, shaking her rose-colored mane, so I shrug and start walking. But after I crest a small hill and the winged horse is out of sight, I realize the problem. How am I going to find my way back to her? This all looks the same. The same the same the same. Guaranteed to get lost in this place. I'm a city girl who navigates by landmarks.

Pushing back my sleeve, I wake my tattoos, breathing a sigh of relief when they spring to life. "Maybe you can help me get around," I say to the fox. With a touch, he leaps from my arm.

He smiles with sharp teeth visible, then sits for a moment, black ears pricked, and sniffs with his dark little nose. Then he wags his fluffy, black-tipped tail and starts trotting—prancing, really—in the direction the pegasus had indicated. I follow.

I'm glad I asked the fox, because he takes a different route than I would have, right into the heart of the dark trees. Over the rise of another hill, I see it—a tiny log cabin that looks ancient and has seen better days. It sits in a clearing between two of the biggest trees I've seen so far, the bases of their trunks almost as wide as the cabin itself.

And it's guarded by two massive spiders.

66

THE BOY I LOVED BEST

I shout up at the sky. "Are you kidding me? You didn't say anything about nightmares."

Which this clearly is. Though maybe not mine, because I don't have a thing about spiders. Or at least normal-sized ones. These are something else. Their fangs could lop my head off in one snap.

A wet nose against my hand draws my attention. The fox whines, then noses the outline of the tarantula on my forearm. The large, fuzzy red spider wiggles and then lifts both her front legs and waves them.

"Can you do something about this?"

The fox gives a high-pitched yip while the tarantula waves her legs again, both of which I take as a yes. So I touch the tarantula, and she crawls out of my skin, and I hold very still while she tickles her way down my arm and onto the foliage-covered ground. While I stand well back and watch, my tarantula scuttles across to the spiders that could squash her without a thought.

With lots of creepy clacking and more eyeballs than are necessary turning my way, the creatures seem to have a conversation. Then, finally, the nightmare spiders move back into the trees. Not far. I can still catch the sun reflecting off their eyes.

My tarantula gives me a little wave. Not taking a chance, I run the rest of the way and try the door, which is unlocked, and burst into a room.

A single room.

And lying on a bed against the wall, eyes closed and perfectly still...

My heart flies, then drops, because for a second, I thought it was Hades.

But it's not. It's...

"Boone." I whisper his name.

It makes sense, but at the same time, it doesn't. I mean, I knew I had a crush. I knew I admired him, craved his attention. But love? Is that really love? Or is it that I had no one else?

When I get to his bedside, I crouch down. I don't take his hand, because that feels wrong somehow. We've never touched like that.

Instead, I grasp his forearm and give it a shake, but he doesn't open his eyes. I can see by a trail of glittery bronze dust across the top of his pillow and forehead that Morpheus has been here.

"Boone?" I frown and shake him harder. Still nothing.

Which is when I remember what I have to do. At least it will be easier with him asleep.

"I have something I have to tell you."

"Oh my gods, you're dead," a low, horror-filled voice blurts out from behind me.

With a yelp, I jump to my feet and spin to face where Boone's voice came from. A translucent version of him stands in the opposite corner, which was empty just a second ago. Do I look the same to him? Like a ghost?

Then his gaze falls to his body on the bed, and if it's possible for a dream ghost to pale, he does. "Wait…" His voice sounds sort of hollow and echoey. "Am *I* dead?"

"No!" Both my hands shoot up. "Not dead. I just… We're both alive," I assure him quickly. "Just…um… We're dreaming right now."

His brows draw together as he looks from me to his body on the bed and back to me. "You sure about that?"

"Yes."

After a second, he nods. He's taking this surprisingly well. "I don't understand. If we're dreaming, why are we in my cabin?"

That has me leaning back, then looking around. "Yours?"

He shrugs. "I bought it a while ago."

My eyes go wide.

But it doesn't matter. Not for the labor. "I'm guessing your dream took us to a place that's special to you. I had to find you."

Now for the hard part. And by hard, I mean squirm-worthy awkward for both of us.

Oh gods. I have to say it to his face. I mean, he's already heard the rumor, but that doesn't make it true. Not until I say...what I'm about to have to say...out loud. "You've been pulled into the Crucible with me for a few days," I start out. Yes, I'm stalling. "I have to tell you something... important...and then take you back to Olympus with me. Okay?"

He crosses his arms, feet planted wide, and an intrigued grin pulls the corner of his mouth up. "As long as I'm not dead, yeah. Okay. What's this important thing?"

Right. Time to say it. I open my mouth but close it again.

Just say it, Lyra. It's just words.

Open. Close. Nothing comes out. Because it's not just words. It's vulnerability.

I give my head a shake. Maybe it would be better to ease into it. "Remember when—"

No. I should just cut to the chase. Band-Aid-rip-style.

"I'm supposed to—"

"Hey," Boone says, dragging my attention off the floor at my feet to him. "It can't be that bad."

A quick laugh punches from me. "I love you."

Those three short words string together in a rush, and I blow out a sharp breath at the end, hands going to my hips as I drop my gaze from his eyes to his feet.

Only that doesn't feel right. Or maybe never was. Except we're here now.

He doesn't say anything. For a very long time. Long enough that I start shifting my weight.

And he still says nothing.

Oh gods. This is worse than I thought it was going to be.

I peek at his face to find him staring at me with a confused frown. Like my words and my face don't quite belong together. Apparently, I can blush in my dreams, because heat crawls all over my skin, and I'm tempted to wave my hand in my own transparent face to cool off.

"I don't understand," Boone says slowly.

I thought getting the words out was hard, but I guess it can get worse. "You need me to explain it to you?"

He frowns harder. "Not the love part, just why you had to tell me that."

Oh.

I close my eyes and sigh. So very, very much worse. Without opening them, I say, "I had to find the person who…" I can't believe I'm going to admit this. "Who I love most in the world and tell them. It's the only way to wake you up."

Except he's not awake. Did I get the wrong person? But no. He's here. So obviously, right person.

More silence.

I crack one eye open, then the other, and my heart slowly drifts to the soles of my feet like an autumn leaf dropping from a tree.

Because Boone's scruffy face is all things regret and exactly what I feared…embarrassment. He won't look at me.

"I'm sorry," he says. "I…" He shakes his head. "I don't feel the same."

I swallow around a heart that should be slowly cracking. Except… "I know. It's okay."

"I mean…I'm flattered, Lyra-Loo-Hoo, but—"

"Stop." Oh hells. I drop my head in my hands. "Seriously, you don't have to. I had to tell you. It's how this Labor is played. We can forget about it now."

Please let's forget all about this. Forever.

"Labor?" he asks.

A tiny tapping noise has us both turning to the window, where I can see the outline of my tarantula waving her legs.

"You've got to be kidding me," Boone mutters behind me.

Spiders. He hates them. Not many know about that. I only do because it's in his file and I'm his clerk.

The tarantula taps again, and I hear the fox give his high-pitched yip outside. And that's when realization strikes me between the eyes and my lungs seize. Evening is falling, the purpling shadows in the trees growing longer by the second.

How?

We started this in the afternoon. I had hours before sunset. And it didn't take that long for us to fly…

I pinch the bridge of my nose. Because if it took that long to get to Boone, the one-way journey is longer than it felt. What if I don't have enough time to get him back to Olympus?

I'm getting really tired of night as a deadline. Or deadlines at all. That word has taken on a whole new meaning for me.

I reach for one of the pearls tucked into my vest and realize that while things feel real here, they're not. The tattoos are part of me, but the pearls, the real ones, are back in Olympus.

And Boone is still a ghost.

Why? I confessed my very embarrassing feelings. He should have woken up.

"We don't have time," I say, hurrying across the room.

I grab his hand and tug him to the door, which I fling open, but the two giant arachnids scuttle out from the trees to crowd into the doorway. Boone reaches over my head and slams the door, having to put his shoulder into it. The door surges and rattles as the spiders try to push their way inside. He's breathing hard by the time he gets it shut.

"This is bad," I say.

"You think?"

"No." I shake my head. "I mean I think your dream turns into a nightmare that won't let you leave while you're still asleep."

He glances at the window and startles. Probably because a bunch of eyeballs are now pressed up against it, watching us. "So wake me up," he demands, slowly backing away.

"I tried. I told you what I was supposed to tell you."

The front door shudders.

"Tell me again, then," Boone urges. "Maybe I was too shocked to really hear it. Or tell *that* me." He points at his body on the bed.

Again? I have to say it again? Fuck me.

Crossing the room, I kneel beside him and take his hand. I have to clear my throat twice. I'd better do this right. "I love—"

My heart pinches, and I swallow the rest of the words. That *still* doesn't feel right. Not the way I was going to say it.

So I change it. Just a little. Still the truth. Maybe more of the truth than I've been willing to admit, even to myself, until now.

"I've had a crush on you since I was fifteen," I say, my words tumbling over themselves. "You're the only person who has ever shown me a lick of kindness. It's pathetic. I'm well aware. And you don't have to feel anything for me." I know he won't. He shouldn't have to deal with guilt for it. "Just know that I'll always love you a little, for making my time in the den even the tiniest bit easier."

Boone's body doesn't move, doesn't blink, nothing.

I look over my shoulder, but…he's gone.

Gone. Gone. Not just that I don't see him. It's a single room. He'd be hard to miss.

"Boone?"

I whirl to face his body. Does he look paler? I glance at the window, where the outside world looks dark, but we're in a forest. Did I take too long?

"Oh my gods!" The whisper rips through my throat as my hands fly up to cover my mouth. "Oh my gods, it's too late. I've killed you."

67

HERA'S BLESSING

I squeeze my eyes shut, unable to make myself face what I've done. My hands, still over my mouth, start shaking, and the quiver travels down my limbs and into the rest of my body.

I killed Boone. I killed him. I took too long. Oh my gods, I—

"Open your eyes, mortal."

I know that voice. My eyes fly open to find Morpheus standing beside me. And on the bed, lying next to Boone's body, is mine. No longer chained to the bed in Olympus.

The spiders are still pounding to get into the house.

"Come." Morpheus takes me by the hand and helps me lie back into my body. Like when he pulled me out, there's no sensation to it. You would think that it would feel like drawing in or out of something or sinking into quicksand, maybe. But it feels like...nothing. I lie down. I close my eyes, and when I open them again, I'm mortal and Morpheus is gone. So are the spiders.

"Hey." A hand lands on my shoulder, and I yelp as I jackknife up in bed.

Only to stare into laughing warm brown eyes.

Solid, no longer translucent.

My own go wide as I take him in from head to toe—sitting next to me, living, breathing, not-dead Boone.

"But you were—" My gaze shoots back to him. "Gone. You were dead. I took too long—"

Boone must hear the hysteria rising in my voice because he suddenly swoops me up in a bear hug. "I'm here. I'm here, and you didn't kill me."

I didn't kill him.

The reality of that is starting to penetrate the bone-deep horror of what I'd thought happened. "You're okay?" I whisper.

He shakes against me like he's laughing and is keeping it silent to not hurt my feelings. "I'm really okay."

He lets go of me and takes one of my hands to flatten my palm over his heart, which beats steady and calm. "See. Alive. Not dreaming. Not a ghost. Not dead."

I realize what we're doing and tug away from his grasp. "I'm glad I'm not a murderer."

And in my head, I wince. Because what I should say is I'm glad he's not dead. It's what I'm feeling. But I'm still a jumble of confusion about Boone, so the words come out the way they always do with him. Snappy and sarcastic.

Instead of shooting back, though, he just grins at me.

Outside, the fox's yip sounds frantic. He's in a hurry. We should be, too. We have to get back to Olympus.

"Come on."

I drag us both out of the house. The spiders are all gone, except mine, and now the pegasus is standing in the yard.

"Whoa," Boone whispers.

"Hey," I say to the winged horse. "Were you too afraid of the spiders to come closer?"

She rears up a little.

Right. Hurry.

After recalling my fox and tarantula into my arm with a murmured thanks, I'm about to do my awkward-attempt-to-drag-myself-on-top-of-a-horse-with-wings thing when two strong hands wrap around my waist and lift me onto her back. Before I can protest or say thank you—I'm still debating which—Boone is up behind me. He slides his arms under mine, his chest pressing against my back.

And I'm trying to ignore all of that when we launch into the skies.

"Tell me what the hells is going on," Boone immediately demands. "Details, Lyra."

Because he doesn't know anything beyond being dragged into something about the Crucible. Well, and that I love him. But the Crucible is still a total mystery to him. I fill him in quickly and succinctly, well aware that he turns more and more grim with every word I say.

"If I could kill the god of death, I would," he mutters ominously when I finish.

Which is when we burst through the clouds and Olympus comes into view, the sun's rays barely reaching over the peaks by now.

I feel the way Boone sits up straighter, but it isn't until we come over the mountaintop that he gets his first good look. "Amazing." His low voice rumbles against my back, breath tickling my ear. "I've never…"

"I know," I say. "And the Underworld is even more."

He goes rigid, gripping the pegasus's mane tighter. "You've been to the Underworld?" His voice is laced with more than anger. Concern? I can't tell. Apparently, my emotional antennae are broken.

I point at the three heads and waterfalls. "I fell in the black river, which leads down to the Underworld. But it's okay. I'm fine — "

Our pegasus suddenly tilts and spirals down to drop us off on the balcony of Aphrodite's house. The instant her hooves hit the stone, I breathe a little easier.

We made it.

Before I can say anything, an agonized scream tumbles down the black-and-white hallway and out the open doors to the balcony where we stand. Boone on my heels, I run to the room with the beds and skid to a halt just inside the door.

Aphrodite is sitting beside Dae's bed, holding his hand, tears streaming down her beautiful cheeks. I didn't know goddesses or gods could even cry.

Maybe even worse, the four Daemones are standing in the four corners of the room, hands clasped before them, heads bowed and wings lowered so their feathers drag the ground in an attitude of forlorn, profound sadness.

Dae's mortal body is on the bed, not strapped down, but it's obvious he's *still* asleep, caught in what has to be a nightmare. Several of the other champions fill the room along with their rescued loved ones. All of them, actually, now that I glance around.

Amir is standing farthest away, against the wall, facing out a window in a manner that reminds me of Hades in my bedroom earlier. A tiny woman in a blue sari with rich, deep-brown skin and dark-gray hair worn back and loosely covered is patting Amir's shoulder with a weathered hand, murmuring softly.

Dae screams again, so hard his chest lifts off the bed.

Why doesn't he wake up? Get up? What's holding him down?

Zai leaves a woman who is a smaller, softer version of him to come to where Boone and I are standing. After a quick glance at Boone, Zai stands beside me, facing Dae. "Amir's blessing from Hera has apparently shown itself."

"And it's making Dae scream?"

Zai nods. "Hera's blessing is vengeance. Dae is the reason Amir lost his Strength flag in the last Labor, and her blessing is that any champion who hinders or hurts Amir during the course of the Crucible will reap the consequences in the next challenge."

Dae screams again, so long that his voice runs out but his mouth remains open.

I flinch.

"Easy," Boone murmurs to me.

And Zai shoots him a frowning look.

A curse from the gods. I feel the blood drain from my face, leaving me lightheaded. "Is he in pain?" I whisper.

Zai's expression fills with reluctant concern. "No. The curse trapped him in his body. It's not Amir's doing. He has no control over it. It just…is." Zai glances out the window. Evening has almost swallowed the light of the sun, turning the sky dark blue except at the westernmost horizon, where it is still changing from deep purple. "Dae can't go save his loved one."

"Who is it?"

"His grandmother."

I close my eyes against the knowledge and sight of what that's doing to Dae. His grandmother, who he loves most in the world, is going to die, and he can't get to her. He can't save her.

The fervor and timbre of Dae's screams heighten, and the sort of bolted-down thrashing of his body only escalates, growing worse and worse, tears leaking out of the corners of his eyes, until suddenly he goes quiet and horribly still.

A quick glance shows that the sun is gone, taking the day with it.

It's too late.

Dae's grandmother is dead.

He blinks his eyes open slowly, looking up at the ceiling for a long, silent moment. Then he puts his hands over his face and sobs.

68

ME...AND THEM

"**I** see you survived." Hades is waiting in the center of the foyer of his home when Boone and I walk in. He stands with his hands loosely in his black suit pant pockets, the sleeves of his silver button-down shirt rolled up. Why is he dressed like that?

His tone and gaze are back to calculating, lethal-edged steel. No hint of the man who shared small parts of himself with me in my bedroom.

"Both of you."

I've never seen Boone go so still as when he stares down the god of death. "So, you're the asshole who put Lyra's life in jeopardy by making her play in these fucked-up games."

Hades doesn't react with so much as a twitch. "So, you're the thief who thought he made it in and out of my home without notice."

Boone frowns, glancing at me, then back to Hades before his expression turns sly in a way I am more than familiar with. He's up to something.

"Caught that, did you?" Boone snakes a hand around my waist, giving me a squeeze. "Just trying to help."

"I know." Hades doesn't even glance at that arm around me. "It's why I let you live."

Oh, good grief.

I shrug away from Boone's touch, which he doesn't really mean. He's just fucking with Hades. "Why don't you two get acquainted while I change."

"No time." Hades snaps his fingers, and Boone and I are wearing new clothes.

Now both men are wearing black suit pants and crisp button-downs, except Boone's shirt is white. This is the dressiest I've seen him. I'm wearing a conservative black pantsuit with loose legs and long sleeves, with a butterfly made of glittering thread over my heart.

I glance from it to Hades, but he's still closed off. Giving away nothing.

"We have a...party...to attend," he says.

A *what*? "You've got to be joking."

Hades just shakes his head, and we follow him out the door and over one house to Zeus' home—yes, with lightning and clouds adorning everything and a lot of glitz, flash, and over-the-top decor. The god would do well as a designer for Vegas casinos.

In a large ballroom—and yes, Zeus has a freaking ballroom, with a mural of nymphs and cherubs serving him and only him painted on the ceiling—we are led to chairs at one of two long, beautifully decorated banquet tables that face each other. We're at the very end of ours, near the open doors that lead out onto a terrace. Ares, Neve, and a girl who is apparently her sister are to Hades' left, then me and Boone to Hades' right. I'm stuck in the middle, so to speak. Dae, of course, isn't here. Artemis is seated at a table by herself with no champion and no loved one, conspicuous as hell. And Aphrodite isn't seated with Jackie and the young man with her. Her brother, I think.

This is a nightmare.

Maybe I didn't rescue anyone and Hypnos and Morpheus still have me trapped in my sleeping body.

Zeus enters the room with Samuel and his loved one, a woman around his age. Even Boone sits back slightly when the god of thunder appears.

"On Aphrodite's behalf, I welcome our new guests," Zeus booms. The god is in his element, hosting people visibly in awe of him. "Aphrodite has taken the result of her Labor hard," he explains.

"This is the Crucible," Hera murmurs in a tone that sounds suitably saddened, though it's paired with an expression that is anything but. "She knew the risks when she set that Labor up. She didn't have to make the end so dire."

Beside Hera, Amir's face turns beet red. He can hardly make himself look at his patron goddess, facing instead to the older woman seated to his other side. One of his nannies, maybe? Given what he said about his family, I don't think it's his mother.

I move my gaze back to Hera.

The thing is, as cruel as it sounds, the goddess isn't wrong. Aphrodite didn't have to make death at the end be part of the rules. I get that the gods and goddesses love their ticking clocks, and death is certainly an incentive, but there are other ways. As for Hera's blessing for Amir...now that we all know the consequences, no one is going to risk touching him. *That* right there is a brilliant move on her part.

The goddess's timing in pointing that out could have been better, though.

Zeus shoots Hera a chastising look. "I will host in Aphrodite's place. We would have postponed, but after all, our 'guests' are here only three days before the next Labor starts."

Days only again? Ugh.

I mean, I guess they have a bunch to get through and only a month to do it, but still.

"First, I would like to congratulate Neve for winning today's challenge, as she was the first to return with her sister."

He offers her a smile that doesn't reach his eyes.

"Your prize for winning this Labor—Eros' bow and arrows—is already in your room."

"Thank you," Neve says politely. Though I'm guessing by her expression that the good manners are sticking in her craw hard.

"Now," Zeus continues, "as we enjoy the sumptuous spread, I would like each champion to introduce their loved one." He waves as he sits.

Awesome. My personal nightmare is reaching torturous levels— public speaking *and* trying to explain who Boone is to me. In front of the god I was kissing just this morning.

"Must we?" Hades drawls, leaning back in his chair indolently, expression bored.

Zeus glares first at him, then at me. "Can't you do something about him, Lyra?"

The fuck you say. That was a calculated remark to get a rise out of one or both of us, and probably Boone, too.

Deliberately, I mimic Hades' indolent posture and tip my head, looking not at Zeus but at Hades as if I'm studying him. "I don't know. None of *you* have been able to do something about him in the several millennia since he was released from Cronos' insides," I say.

Hades' mercurial eyes pin me to the back of my chair with a wild flash of satisfaction so violently fast, the only reason I know I saw it is the way I'm still reeling.

I clear my throat and force a steady gaze to Zeus, who is scowling petulantly. "I don't know why you think I, a mere mortal, would have better luck."

Zeus sits down hard. "We shall start the introductions," he says with a dismissive shrug. "As you know, Dae's person was his grandmother."

The callous delivery drops the words into a vat of silence.

She's sitting near enough to me, so I catch Rima's whispered, "I'm not sure if that's better or worse than Dae's boyfriend."

Not hearing her, Zeus waves at Samuel, who gets to his feet.

Luckily, I'm not the only one not all that enthusiastic about this. The room has a subdued weight to it as the champions each quickly make introductions. Most aren't too surprising. Samuel's long-time partner is here, and Jackie's older brother. Meike has her roommate. Trinica rescued her son. The woman with Zai is his mother, like I guessed. Diego's wife is no shock, and Demeter, showing her mothering side, assures us their two children are being cared for by Diego's parents. Rima's husband is here as well.

Neve gets to her feet. "This is my younger sister, Nora."

I slowly lean forward to look around Hades at the woman sitting directly beside him. She's probably in her mid-twenties, so only a little younger than Neve. *The* Nora? The one who Neve was muttering about how she was going to be killed?

Boone gives me a low whistle—one the others don't even notice, let alone understand. He's using a pledge's signals to ask me what I find interesting.

I whistle back the signal for *nothing or not important.*

Not true, of course. Nora looks a lot like her sister, only her hair is a darker red and her eyes more green than blue. Somewhere in between. She also has a sweeter smile…or smiles at all, come to that.

Neve's chin tips up. "Our family are…important business owners in our community. Ares informed me that someone from outside the family has threatened Nora's life if Ares becomes king, but now that I have her back from them…" Her eyes narrow, determination stamped across her features. "They will pay for that mistake."

Wait. Is Neve's business-owner family some sort of crime family, Canadian style?

Hard to imagine that accent being used during criminal acts, but that would explain a *lot*.

Boone taps a finger on the back of my hand to get my attention and raises his eyebrows in question. I shake my head.

He sits back as Dex gets to his feet and waves at the boy with him. "This is Rafael…Rafe," Dex says. "He is my nephew, my sister's son, and he's only ten."

Ten? So young. I want to wrap the kid up and hide him away somewhere, or ask Hades to hide him, until the next Labor is over. Amir is already too young at sixteen. A ten-year-old shouldn't be exposed to this.

"My dad died before I was born, and Mom is…sick." Rafe speaks up earnestly, looking at Dex like the man is his hero. "Tío Dex helps raise me."

I'm having trouble reconciling the image in front of me now. I mean, Dex might as well be wearing tights and a cape. How does that fit with the competitor Dex has been so far?

But the affection in his eyes as he ruffles Rafe's hair is unmistakable and real. Until the Crucible, I thought I read people well. Am I reading Dex wrong now?

Boone leans over to whisper in my ear. "What are you going to say about me, I wonder?"

Not that I've had a huge crush on him for years. "That you've been a pain in my ass?"

"Stop. You're going to make me blush."

I chuckle.

Then pause. Something feels…different with us. Easier.

A glance shows me that, on my left, Hades is leaning away from me, talking to Nora. He even smiles at her. No dimples, but still, he's charming enough that she smiles back widely, visibly starstruck. Apparently, he *can* put some mortals at ease.

Neve is pretty, but I have to say Nora is drop-dead gorgeous, her creamy skin flawless against that abundance of auburn hair and a smile that could compete with Aphrodite's. What's more, she seems unafraid of Hades.

I bet he'll appreciate that about her.

I pull my gaze away to fiddle with the stem of my wineglass. "Lyra?"

Boone nudges my foot under the table, and I look around to find Zeus staring at me and all eyes except Hades' and Nora's already on me.

Oh, I guess it's my turn. How many times did the god have to call my name?

I stand, the same way the others did, wincing as my chair scrapes loudly against the marble flooring. "This…" I wave awkwardly to my right. "Is Boone Runar. He is a pledge in the Order of Thieves with me."

I go to sit, and my butt is halfway to the chair when Athena slides a question my way. "Friends?"

The goddess's brown, bobbed hair has golden highlights picked up by the fires in the braziers, and she's smiling warmly like I can trust her. But her high brow and intense, deep-brown eyes give the impression of an intelligence that misses not a single detail. The indent in her chin smacks of stubbornness, and I've noticed before that she moves with the prowling grace of a fighter. She's the goddess of both wisdom and war. Not to be trifled with.

Where is she going with this?

I pause, then stand back up. "I—"

"Yes, we're friends." Boone's grin is all things Boone, and it's no surprise when at least half of the group grin back at him. He's always had that effect on people. A lot like Dionysus that way, despite the rough-looking exterior.

I don't say anything. I can't.

"The person you love most in the world is…just a friend?" Athena clearly has an agenda here. I think I'm starting to see what. "What about your parents?" she asks. "They seemed so caring on TV."

What. A. Bitch.

"Is that really where you want to take the evening, Thena?"

I thought he wasn't listening, but Hades is now looking directly at Athena.

Unfortunately, that only makes Athena's eyes brighten with interest. She studies me. "Lovers?"

"Excuse me?" I ask.

Her smile turns sly. "You and Boone, of course. What did you think I meant?"

That same spark of irritation that got me into it with Hades when we first met at Zeus' temple in San Francisco rears up. "I thought you meant Hades." I smile back at her sweetly. "We're not."

The flare of surprise in her eyes is worth it. Hades, however, doesn't react because he's turned back to Nora like he can't be bothered.

"Yet," I clarify, just to see what he does.

Nothing, it turns out.

He's clearly engrossed in whatever he's discussing with Nora. To the point that Neve catches my eye and then looks deliberately between them before shooting me a smug smile.

I'm tempted to point out that I saved her ass two Labors ago. I don't. "Boone is the most talented of our pledges," I tell the room at large, "and a bit of a cheat. You might want to lock up your valuables."

"Hey!" Boone protests. But I know that he's protesting me warning them, not the veracity of the claim itself.

Nora laughs suddenly, but everyone else—other than Hades—is still focused on Boone and me.

"Well, that's too juicy to ignore," Dionysus says, joining the conversation. At least his interest seems genuine. "Got any stories?"

Hundreds, but only because I've been paying attention. I raise a single brow at Boone. "Which one should I pick? There are so many."

Instead of getting irritated or even embarrassed, he laughs right back at me. "How about the time I followed Lakshmi into that museum and took the piece she'd come for before she knew I was even there?" He turns to the room. "I got back to the den with it, and Lyra about blew her top at me for snatching a score from another one of our pledges." He just shrugs.

Grins turn to laughs, and what the fuck? How did we become the entertainment tonight?

Nora laughs again. At Hades.

Hoping that's it, I lower into my seat. But Boone tugs my chair closer to him as I do, and I don't miss that or the fact that he leaves his arm draped across the back. I have no idea why, other than helping me save face here. I'll ask him later.

Boone grins. "Lyra was so pissed about the bank, she made sure—" I step on Boone's foot, and he stops talking, looking at me with interest-bright eyes.

I forgot to tell him that only Hades knows that I'm just a clerk, and he was about to reveal that I put the earnings from that score under Lakshmi's name, not his. Part of my job. Guaranteed to bring up questions.

"Made sure what?" Meike asks. Seriously, she and Dionysus could be twins.

Boone clears his throat. "She called the police, letting my sorry ass cool off in jail for a few days before sending another pledge to spring me."

"Maybe she should have learned from you instead," Dex says. He sounds reasonable. Beside him, Rafe nods along with an eager face.

But I'm close enough to hear the way the back of my chair creaks with the sudden strength of Boone's grip, and his grin disappears behind a look of anger so stark I blink. I've only ever seen him look like that once, when one of the apprentices was accidentally killed because of a mistake a visiting master thief made.

"Lyra was angry with me for a reason," he says. "I broke two cardinal rules with that stunt, ultimately putting other pledges of the Order in harm's way. She was teaching me a lesson *I* needed to learn." He leans forward, eyes so sharp they could slice flesh. "And while I'm at it...the gods may not be allowed to interfere in the Crucible, but I'm not bound by the same restriction. I hear that gift of foreknowledge you received doesn't work all that great. You might want to watch your back while I'm here."

Dex's face goes so tight he looks like a pissed-off plastic doll. "It works well enough that I'm still alive and in it. We all have different ways of playing. My home could use the gods' blessings, and I have a family to"—he cuts himself off, glancing down at Rafe, then continues—"to get back to."

"The same as everyone else," Boone snaps. "Are those the excuses you tell yourself for being a dick? Good luck living with your actions and decisions when it's over." He glances significantly at Rafe. "Someday, he'll be old enough to see for himself through eyes not looking with rose-tinted innocence." Then Boone hooks a thumb at Zai, who is sitting at the other table. "Ask him if you're curious. He grew up with a father who played the Crucible the same way you are."

Clearly, I told Boone way too much on that pegasus flight. I whistle softly. The signal for *stop now*.

Boone straightens to blink at me, and I can see the struggle in his eyes. He really would go after Dex if Rafe wasn't right there. I have no doubt. And my chest tightens with reaction. If I didn't know better—if I wasn't carrying this curse—I'd think he really cared.

I whistle again, the signal for *all fine*.

His lips flatten, but finally he nods.

The others are all still staring at us in fascination. Well…Dex is glaring.

"What was that?" Athena asks. This is the first time I haven't seen the goddess in calculating mode. Her entire body seems lit up with curiosity. *There's* the thirst for knowledge we all expect from her.

"My thieves use whistles to signal one another." Hermes is the one to answer—rather smugly, too. Then again, as the messenger god, I can see how he'd like that elegant solution.

"Lyra's idea," Boone tells the others. "We had our crypticodes but needed something for in the moment. At the time, we were using hand signals and sign language, but that meant needing line of sight. She came up with the whistles when she was just six."

My only true accomplishment, as far as the Order is concerned.

I can't help the heat creeping up into my cheeks. No one has ever in my life bragged about me. Not once.

It feels…nice.

Nora's sudden laugh breaks the silence around us and sends me sitting straighter, which only makes me lean closer to Boone. A knowing light enters his eyes as he glances past me to her and Hades, then back to me. But he doesn't say anything.

Then Zeus, no doubt needing to reclaim the center of attention, claps his hands. "Welcome again, guests. Let us all enjoy the feast."

Not likely.

69

COME BEARING GIFTS

The soft knock at my door doesn't exactly wake me up. After the party, Boone said he wanted to explore Olympus and Hades left with the other gods and goddesses, so Zai and I walked home with his mother together. She, by the way, is a sweet but definitely timid woman.

I've only had time to change into pajamas and brush my teeth. The party lasted well into the night, and the stars still blanket an inky sky outside my window in pinpricks of light—so many we don't need the moon to illuminate the lands here.

Frowning, I open my door.

Boone stands there, leaning against the frame, one ankle crossed over the other, and in his hand, presented to me like a gift, is the Helm of Darkness.

"Holy shit!" I grab him by the arm and yank him into my room, looking both ways down the hall and almost expecting an irate Dex to be barreling after Boone. He's not. The hall is empty, and I close the door before whirling on him. "What in the hellfires are you thinking?"

Boone's self-satisfied smile fades, turning to something like accusation aimed directly at me. "I'm thinking I'm a fucking thief, Lyra. What about you?"

I stand firm, crossing my arms over my thin pajama top, not completely unaware that I'm not wearing a bra right now. "What about me?"

He steps closer. "Your skills may be rusty, but the second that dickhead Dex tipped his hand that he's gunning for you, you should have taken this." He holds up the helm. "And you know it. That's just the way the world works, even here."

He tosses the helm on my bed.

"I'm not going to play like that." I lift my chin.

"Dex can survive without the helm." His hands curl into fists. "You might not, given the way he can use it to get close to you. You'll be dead before you realize."

"I already have more tools than the others," I say. "Hades has been punished once for it. I'm not taking away someone else's just because I don't like them."

"Don't like them?" Boone is practically yelling. "He wants to *kill* you, Lyra."

My mouth drops open, and I know I'm staring, but the way he's yelling...

Boone must catch my confusion, because he calms a little, eyeing me. "What?"

"You sound like you care."

"I do."

I give my head a hard shake. "That's not possible."

Tension steals through his shoulders, and he glances away. "I don't care like *that*—"

Oh hells. "No," I rush to stop him from saying one more word. "I mean care enough to worry about me like this. Zeus cursed me the day I was born. I'm unlovable. I can't be loved or cared about."

Boone goes thief-still, his gaze taking me in like he's never seen me before. "Is that true?"

I shrug.

"Unlovable," he murmurs more to himself, like he's trying to wrap his head around the meaning. "That really...sucks."

He surprises a laugh out of me. "Yeah. It really does."

"Who else knows?"

"Felix. Hades. My parents." So-called. "That's it."

Boone's brows draw down. "That can't be right."

"I assure you it is."

He still shakes his head. "I've always admired you."

He has?

"You're smart, and you see things others don't—like, every detail. It's what makes you such a good clerk."

Boone thinks I'm a good clerk. A bubble of surprised happiness expands in my chest, but I pop it. "Admiration isn't caring."

"Sure it is," he insists. "I've even wanted to partner with you on a few scores."

I rear back. "The hells you say."

He grins. "I mean it. But you've always put this wall around yourself with a giant *'stay the fuck away'* sign at the gate. You kept all the pledges at arm's length, so no one has had a chance to get to know you. To be your friend."

Did I do that? I don't think so. "The curse—"

Boone leans down—he really is very tall—so that we're eye to eye and I can see the sincerity in his. "I may not be in love with you, Lyra, and maybe the curse did that. But I'd like to be your friend."

Oh.

"Really?" I whisper.

His smile is slow and sweet and doesn't contain an ounce of pity. "Really."

I'm not sure I believe this. Maybe he feels this way because we're in Olympus. Maybe this place lessens the effects of curses. I don't know. Look at how Zai wanted to ally with me. Or at how Meike isn't any different with me than she is with anyone else. And I'm definitely not invisible here. Although that could be because of Hades. He doesn't exactly blend in.

Whatever the reason, the part of me that has been craving a friend since I understood that I couldn't have any, the part that I've silenced and ignored and stuffed deep down, feels this. It's light, like I could float away.

"Okay," I say. "Friends."

Boone's smile widens, turning cocky. "Good. Now, about Dex…"

I roll my eyes, giving him a shove. "We're returning the helm."

"Hear me out." Boone holds up a hand. "Dex sees you as his strongest competition with a dangerous god as your patron. His sister is dying of cancer, which I'm guessing he'll ask to be healed if he wins."

I blink. "Wh—what?" Is that right? "How do you know that?"

He gives me a look.

Right.

"In his mind, you are the person between him and saving his family," Boone says. "Sure, he wants to help his people, but even more, winning means he gets to give his sister and nephew *everything*." He points to the ground. "Luxury, longevity, blessings…you name it."

Instead of riling me up, his words deflate me like pricking a balloon with a needle and listening to the whistle as the air slowly leaks out. I picture Rafe and the way he looks at his uncle. "In other words..." I say quietly, my chin sticking back out. "He has an honorable goal that he'll do anything to reach."

Boone stares at me a long moment before spinning on his heel to stalk across the room, then spins back, hands going to his lean hips. "Fine. I'll return the helm. I know better than to argue with you when your chin does that jutty thing."

I almost tuck it back in, but this is important. "Good."

His eyes spark with mischief, and I find myself confused. What just happened?

"Let's at least take this baby for a spin first. The gods are meeting to discuss something important. We should listen in."

This is typical Boone. Jump right in with both feet, no planning, just the absolute confidence that it will swing his way every time.

I know he catches the doubt dragging at me when he tilts his head, gaze intent on mine. "You know you want to, Lyra-Loo-Hoo."

I roll my eyes. "I hate that nickname."

"I know." He chuckles. "I started it so you'd have one."

Just like I thought.

"But then I realized that it makes you adorably irritated and usually lets me pull a couple of your strings."

I snort. "I doubt that." But I cross to the helm and pick it up. Brass and formed with a nose plate dividing two slots for the eyes, it's surprisingly heavy. "But this time I'll give it to you. Let's go listen in. Maybe we'll learn something useful."

Boone takes the helm from my hands and slips it over his head. Immediately, he disappears. I reach out and encounter a solid, muscled stomach covered by a shirt, and the instant I touch him, I disappear, too.

I yank my fingers back, and I rematerialize. "Wow. That's handy."

"Makes this tougher, though." His voice comes from close. Really close.

"What?" I ask.

There's a heartbeat before his lips press against mine. The kiss is sweet and chaste. I jerk back on a squeak of shock, and his low chuckle sounds, still close.

"Jeez, Boone," I grumble. "What was that for?"

"I just…wanted you to have that. As a thank-you for loving me." His voice has gone serious now, and I wish I could see his face. "Even if it's just between friends."

Before Hades named me his champion, that qualification would have hurt. Instead, all I feel is…affection. Like Boone gave me something precious.

I smile at where I think his face is. "I knew I was right to have a crush. You're just a solid guy, aren't you?"

"Shhh… I have a reputation to uphold."

"Yeah, yeah. Come on."

There's a small silence, and then he suddenly appears again, helm in his hands, brown eyes darkly intent. "One other thing, before we go. Do you know what they're saying about you and Hades all over Olympus? That you're *lovers*."

That word takes on an edge.

I swallow down a groan. If the gods could have seen what Hades and I were doing just this morning, they'd know for sure that I'm not opposed to that idea. And the moment when I walked into Boone's cabin and thought it was Hades has been nagging at me all night. The thing is, feelings for Boone aside, future or not, I want the god of death. Even if it's just for a quick, mutually satisfying tussle, I'll take that memory with me after.

"So what?"

"The gods are all already opposed to Hades as King of the Gods. So are the mortals, for that matter. You're giving them even more reason to hate you." He sighs when I don't say anything. "Is there any truth to it?"

My eyes narrow. "None of your business."

"So there is." He tucks the helm under one arm. "Now that we're officially friends, you should know that I'm not just going to sit idly by and watch you end up with the god of *death*. There's no future with him, Lyra."

"I know that."

He tips my chin up with a gentle finger, so I have no choice but to look him in the eyes. "Maybe more than anyone else in the world, I understand your background, your past, who you are, and what you've had to overcome. What you'll go back to after the Crucible is over."

Where is he going with this?

"I'm just saying, now that you have a friend, maybe it will be easier. You have a future to look forward to in the Overworld."

A future to look forward to. I had plans. But maybe not alone anymore.

He searches my gaze. "Just think about it, okay?" The helm goes back on, and he disappears from sight. "Let's go."

He grabs my hand—his large and warm and curling around mine protectively—and I'm gone, too.

70

PLEDGES

Walking around invisible is strangely freeing. As in it makes me feel invincible. Nothing and no one can see us, and that means they can't hurt us, either.

Hand holding mine, Boone guides us unerringly through the houses, not toward the town but to the other end, to the very last house in the row. The place itself is huge—bigger than many of the others, even—but otherwise unassuming in a boxy way and made of simple dark-gray stone. A carving of two crossed forger's hammers graces the lintel of the gate into the courtyard.

Boone's signal is a soft whistle. *This way.*

He tugs me around the side of the house and to the rear, where we climb stairs that lead up a series of terraces until we enter through the back. No wonder they don't bother with locks here. These places are wide open.

Then again, who would dare rob from a god or goddess anyway?

I almost snort a laugh. Boone, that's who.

He must have already come here to know the way like this. Clearly, he was quite busy while I walked home and brooded. He leads me through the rooms, which remind me of mountain cabins, or rather, wealthy-people mountain cabins—lots of timber beams, gray granite, and oversize woodsy furniture.

This is Hephaestus' house, after all.

The god of blacksmiths, metalworking, carpentry, craftsmen, artisans, and fire has always been one of my favorites. Probably because I think of him as the underdog god, the one the others tend to consider last, maybe because he's so quiet. But he's the reason Zeus has his lightning bolt, Hermes has his helm and sandals, Achilles had his armor, and Apollo has his sun chariot. Even Eros' bow and arrows are thanks to him.

Hephaestus is brilliant.

He's also brave. There are many accounts for the reason Hephaestus' feet are turned backward, giving the god a distinctive gait when he walks. But the one I believe, even more so having seen him in person now, is that as a child he protected his mother—some say Hera, others not, but definitely one of the goddesses—from Zeus' unwanted advances. Zeus threw the child out of Olympus. Hephaestus fell for a full day before hitting the earth so hard it almost killed him. His immortality saved him, but his rapid godly healing accidentally went too fast, and his feet healed backward.

Another whistle sounds. The signal for *all silent.*

I squeeze Boone's hand, indicating I understand.

Boone takes us through a door that leads to a landing, and then, our steps as silent as we can make them, we creep down the balcony that runs along the entire side of the house. Light streams into the night from several tall windows.

We inch our way forward until we reach the first window. We peek around the frame to find the four Daemones standing in the corners of the room and all thirteen gods and goddesses, even a puffy-eyed Aphrodite, seated around a massive, perfectly round slab of stone serving as a conference table. No head or foot.

Zeus must hate it.

"We're not here about your Labor," Poseidon is saying to Hephaestus.

The mountain man of a god is leaning back in his seat, muscled arms as big as logs crossed over a broad chest. He fits the vibe of his home— tan, like he works outside all day, every day. Then there's his dark-brown hair worn short but sort of shaggy, matching the scruffy beard that might be several days' unshaved growth or could be a deliberate look. Keen green eyes don't stray from Poseidon.

"Then why have you and Zeus gathered us?" Hephaestus asks, his impassive demeanor giving nothing away.

The two brothers exchange glances, but Poseidon is the one who speaks. He's the only god with a champion no longer in the hunt, so I'm surprised he cares enough to be here.

"As we all know," Poseidon says, "this Crucible has been somewhat... chaotic."

You think? I roll my invisible eyes.

"Well, we all know why," Demeter snipes.

Each of them turns to the man seated to Hephaestus' right. Hades lounges in his chair, foot propped on his knee, looking even more bored than he did during the party. He lifts a single eyebrow at them. "What do I have to do with any of the chaos?"

"You entered this year," Athena points out. "Never in the history of the Crucible have there been thirteen champions, and one patronized by the King of the Underworld, who already rules a realm. That creates chaos on its own. But that's not all. There is the matter of your champion."

Hades doesn't move a single muscle.

"Lyra is one of the few playing this farce of a competition with any integrity," Hades says in that quiet way he does when he's truly pissed.

Athena is the only one brave enough to lean forward and address him. "But you have to admit, chaos seems to follow her footsteps."

At that, Hades appears to relax. "That's not my fault."

The others ease a tad as well, but they shouldn't. How I know that, I'm not sure. It's just...obvious to me.

"Why does that little mortal interest you so much?" Zeus asks.

Hades' expression darkens, and I think the others collectively hold their breaths.

Both Athena and Dionysus cast concerned glances out the window, past where Boone and I stand, over the beautiful lands of Olympus.

For the first time ever, I wonder exactly who among them leveled this place during the Anaxian Wars.

"It's too bad your own champions can't stay out of her way," Hades says. Doesn't even bother to address Zeus' question. I secretly grin. "But these Labors were designed to be brutal—to fulfill your mirth for bloodshed. Don't complain now, and definitely don't blame me or Lyra."

Hades pushes to his feet slowly, and he towers over all of them, even Zeus, in a way that makes them seem small and petty.

"Hephaestus isn't going to share what his Labor is going to be. The rules aren't going to change, unless you want to allow me to add my own challenge to the mix." He glances around the deities and the Daemones. No one takes him up on that. "Then I suggest you stop worrying about my shit and figure out your own."

Then he lifts his gaze directly to mine. Spears me with that look. Right through the heart.

He knows I'm here.

Fuck me.

71

CLAIMS HAVE BEEN STAKED

With the gods scattering all over Olympus, heading who knows where, Boone doesn't remove the helm on the way back to Hades' home, and neither of us speaks. All the way, I feel as if we're being watched, which is impossible. But if I'm right and Hades knew I was there spying on them, it's only a matter of time before he shares his displeasure.

We go around to the back, the same way we did Hephaestus'. If anyone saw doors to the front courtyard opening and closing on their own, they'd wonder.

The second we reach the top terrace leading into the house, Boone lets go of my hand to remove the helm. Immediately, we're both visible, and he runs a hand through his hair. "This helm is terrible for my beauty," he says.

Such a Boone thing to say. Instead of hiding my laugh, I chuckle right out loud. Funny how knowing someone cares about you changes your perception of them. "You should return it." I nod at the thing.

Boone looks down at it, then back at me with a twinkle. "You sure? It is a pretty handy gadget." He makes a face. "Way better than dragon teeth."

"Those already saved me once," I say without thinking.

"Really? How?"

I cross my arms. "I'll tell you after you get back."

Boone sighs. "You never let yourself have any fun. Are you sure?"

"I'm sure. Before anyone notices."

Boone's eyes narrow. "You mean before *Hades* notices."

"Yes." A harsh rasp of a voice comes from the darkness inside the house. The lanterns immediately flare to life, illuminating a Hades who is all cold control, despite the dark smoke wrapping around him in swirling tendrils. "That is exactly what she means."

Boone does maybe the worst possible thing and steps in front of me, blocking me protectively from Hades with his body, tension radiating from him so much the air around me heats. He's holding the helm with one hand, but the other curls into a fist at his side. "This was my idea."

"You don't say," Hades drawls.

I wince at the tone. He's getting quieter.

Boone's shoulders draw back. "I won't let you hurt her."

Would now be a terrible time to hug him just for that? Probably. I can't see Hades, but the dead silence from his side can't be good.

Needing to put a stop to whatever this is, I step to the right, but Boone scoots with me. So I put a hand on his arm and squeeze. "He would never hurt me, Boone."

He tips his face toward me without looking away from Hades. "You don't know that."

"I do," I say. "It's one of the few things I'm certain of."

That's enough to get Boone to look at me instead of Hades. "You've never been a trusting fool before, Lyra."

An animalistic growl comes from the god across the way. An otherworldly sound that makes the hairs on the back of my neck stand.

"I'm not being one now," I tell Boone. "Return the helm while I talk to him."

His face takes on a stubborn look—jaw clenched and eyes hard—that I recognize. "No way in all the realms of the Underworld am I leaving you with him."

Perhaps a poor choice of words. "Go." I give him a little push toward the stairs, not that he budges. "I'll be fine."

"No—"

A rope of smoke whips around Boone's chest, and suddenly he's dragged across the room—or flung, more like, his body sailing through the air to hit a wall, then drop to the floor. The *thud* of impact hits at the same time as the metallic *clunk* of the helm on the marble.

Faster than a blink, Hades is across the room, his hand curling around the back of my neck, eyes ablaze.

"Lyra!" Boone shouts, and out of the corner of my eye, I see him jump to his feet.

Another otherworldly growl comes out of Hades, his eyes turning as dark as thunderclouds. "Don't hurt him," I say in a rush.

Hades blinks at me just as Boone sprints toward us. A wall of fire as tall as the ceiling ignites between us and him. The blast of heat against the side of my face, the immediate roar and crackle of the flames nearby—they're nothing compared to the god staring me down.

But Hades didn't hurt Boone. I can hear him through the flames, though it's impossible to see him.

"What the fuck were you thinking?" Hades demands, and the growl of his voice is so low, so feral, I shiver.

Fires of hells, I was right. He did know we were at Hephaestus' home. I lift my chin. "I was thinking that a thief should use the skills they have."

"To steal gifts and spy on gods. Damn it, Lyra. They could have *killed* you tonight."

"That would be interfering. The Daemones wouldn't let them."

"Not if they deemed you to be breaking the rules, and trespassing in a god's home is breaking the fucking rules."

My own anger rises, matching his, and I curl my fingers around his wrist, though I don't pull his hand away. "Boone is damned good at what he does, and tonight he wanted to get information to help me. And another thing—weren't *you* the one who first suggested I use my boon"—I gesture to the menagerie hidden along my forearm—"to spy on the other champions and their patrons, *the gods*?"

He huffs an unamused laugh but doesn't respond to anything I actually said. Jackass. "Does he know about your curse?"

I give him a flat look. "Yes."

Hades' gaze narrows, glittering at me in silvery slits. "I would always tell you any important information that might help you survive the Crucible, Lyra."

He almost sounds...hurt...that I'd think otherwise. "I know. That's why I had to do this. You've already been punished for me once."

He pulls back a smidge like that answer surprised him. Then his fingers spread out from where he's still cupping my neck, spearing through my hair, and my body reacts instantly to a touch that's now familiar. Something behind his eyes changes, the heat morphing from anger to...oh wow. "You took a risk to protect me?" he demands.

I'm not ready to admit that. "I used the opportunity available. That's all."

He stares at me, still anchoring me to him with that one hand, as if he can plumb the depths of my mind and heart with a look.

Then his gaze slowly lowers to my lips, and I swear silver fire flares in his eyes. "He kissed you."

72

WHAT SCARES ME THE MOST

Oh...my...gods... Can he *see* Boone's kiss? In the mark Hades left on me with his gift? Feel it somehow, maybe?

What I want to say is that it was a kiss between friends. But there's still enough pride inside me to stay the words. It's none of Hades' business who I kiss, the same way it's none of Boone's. Yes, I was just kissing Hades this morning, but we both know that's all it can be.

All I am to him is a champion he hopes will win him the Crucible. That's it.

So why am I not moving out of his grasp? Putting some distance between us? Insisting he not touch me? He would listen to me if I asked. I know he would.

Gaze never leaving mine, Hades slowly lowers his head, and everything about me, every single piece of me, focuses solely on him. On him and the swirl of desire inside me, the *wanting*.

I want this. Again.

Gods, I shouldn't. But I do.

He brushes my lips with his just barely, then groans deep in his throat. His fingers curl into my scalp as he kisses me harder. Harder and hotter. This is a claiming. A plundering.

He catches me about the waist and lifts me onto the table where we eat breakfast in the mornings, parting my legs so that he can pull me up flush against his hard body, never once taking his lips from mine, and the flames at my back match the heat we're generating together.

"This is all I was thinking about during that farce of a meeting," Hades groans against my lips. Then kisses me again, hard. "Tasting you again. Making you light up for me."

His lips feather across the line of my jaw to the sensitive spot behind my ear. "Because you do light up, Lyra. Stars are made of fire. Meant to burn."

His hands are at my hips, gripping me, pulling me against his heat, even as he sucks at my neck, and I moan. I'm holding on to him and tipping my head to give him more access.

"I wanted to get back here. To do this again. To you. With you. I wanted—" He jerks his head up. He's glaring at me now, his expression a battle of both anger and need, all of it scorching. "And then there you were, outside that window. I could *feel* my mark on you. *My* mark. And you were with him. When you are mine."

The accusation wakes me up a little from the haze of need I plunged into so readily. I blink, then take a deep breath. "Temporarily."

He rears back. "What?"

"Only while the Crucible lasts. Isn't that right?"

His expression shuts down, turns dark, and the stars in the sky outside might as well be chips of ice dousing me in a chill. "I will never force you into something you don't want," he says in a voice that scrapes over my skin. "But make no mistake, Lyra. I want you to be mine. Not a champion. Not a thief. Not a mortal. *Mine.*" He snarls the word. "And no one else's."

He gives me one more hard, claiming kiss, and when he raises his head, Hades looks over my shoulder, directly into the flames keeping Boone away from us—flames I assumed were too high and too deep for Boone to see through—and Hades smiles.

A darkly triumphant challenge of a smile.

My own confusion, lust, need, heat, and whatever else has been poured into the cauldron of emotions roiling inside me burn away in an instant flare of anger. It was all for show. I shove Hades away from me and hop off the table.

"You want me to be yours?" I demand. "I don't think you know what that really means. How could you? A god," I scoff. "Your power means you get what you want, when you want, forever, but it's made you a spoiled ass. Yours?" My voice is turning a tad shrill, and I don't give a damn. "If you really meant that, you wouldn't kiss me for him. To show him. You'd kiss me because you can't *not* kiss me. Because *I* am the only thing you can see."

I've had a long, long time to imagine exactly what that would feel like.

An answering fury that matches my own curls his lip. His shoulders square and his chin lifts, and suddenly he is the arrogant, seething, powerful god he shows less and less around me. "You have ideas about things of which you know nothing."

He stalks away from me. The wall of flames snuffs out the second he reaches it. As he prowls past Boone, he snaps, "Keep your fucking hands off my champion if you know what's good for you. And return that helm before anyone figures out it's gone. You. Not her."

For a second, I think Boone might punch Hades in the face, but instead he rushes to my side. "You okay?"

Relief that he might not have seen anything doesn't unknot the emotions twisting inside me like a den of writhing snakes. But I nod.

Boone glares at Hades. "You act like I'm the one who's done something wrong here, but I'm not, and neither is Lyra."

Hades stops, back to us, as Boone continues.

"This is your fault. There's no reason for you to have taken her away from her life and put her in danger like this."

He's right. This *is* Hades' fault.

And as for a reason... Hades doesn't do anything without a specific goal in mind. For the first time since he assured me that he had reasons for picking me that he didn't want to share, I feel that I need to know what they are. That I *deserve* to know.

Hades speaks over his shoulder, barely turning his head to the side. "Watch Lyra's back in the next Labor, Boone."

Why? So I can win for him? "I can watch my own damned back."

Mid-step away from us, Hades whirls, glaring at me. "I know you think that, but it's what makes you dangerous."

I glare right back. "I am *not* dangerous—"

"You scare the shit out of me, Lyra." He's gone deadly quiet now, but not with anger. This quiet frightens me a thousand times more. This sounds like defeat. "You," he says. "Not the other champions, not the challenges, not the gods or what they speculate about us, not even this guy. *You* scare me like nothing I've ever experienced before. And that's saying a lot."

Then his face contorts with a new anger—a burn I think is directed inward, at himself for admitting that. With a shake of his head, Hades disappears deeper into the house.

And I let him go.

73

HEPHAESTUS' LABOR

We've been in Olympus three days. Three days without Hades. I think he must have taken himself down to the Underworld, because when I ask the satyrs, they merely shrug and say that god is not among us.

Doesn't he know that after the Daemones took him, I was terrified I wouldn't see him again? Disappearing on me now feels like that all over again. I understand that he's mad at me, but I can't handle him taking the time for an almighty sulk.

When Trinica and Amir came to us, asking to join our alliance officially, we accepted. I expected Hades to show up and argue me out of two more people to worry about, but he didn't.

He still hasn't.

Which means that today Boone and I got ready for my next Labor, the one we'll go through together, without Hades here.

Clothes appeared in Boone's room, matching mine. Only instead of the butterfly in the center of his chest, a chrysalis is embroidered on the mock neck. Boone's own vest and tools also appeared in his room. We dressed. We ate an early dinner. And then, with the other eleven champions and their loved ones, we gathered in Hephaestus' home.

I pretend an awe I don't feel as we walk through, putting on a show as if I've never been here before. I stop when I catch sight of Dae's pale face. He is subdued today, quiet, keeping to himself. Dex pats the champion's shoulder, murmuring something I don't catch, and Dae pulls away.

Dae isn't hiding his heartbreak. I don't think he should. Maybe seeing that will make the gods rethink the Crucible. Probably not, though. Isabel's death didn't.

"Are we all present?" Hephaestus asks.

None of our gods have gathered with us, which is interesting. Not that Hades is around to fucking gather.

With a satisfied nod, Hephaestus raises his hands, and, starting at the ground, a glimmering, watery line rises higher and higher. As it does, his home transforms into a different world. It's like a mirage, slowly consuming our surroundings to reveal new ones. When the mirage line passes over our heads, it disappears in a shower of sparks like a hammer hitting heated metal, and we find ourselves within a circle of large stones in a forest so dark and empty that even the wind through the trees sounds lonely.

"Well… That was something," Boone murmurs. I raise my eyebrows at him, and he shrugs. "I know you told me about the other Labors you've completed so far, and I was already in one with you, sort of. But it feels different when you're *really* in it."

"No kidding."

Pine trees surround us. Not as tall as the redwoods in Muir, these are skinnier and shorter but dense enough to obscure the light of the sun.

At the top of the circle, thick wood posts support a horizontal stone slab to form a gateway. The lintel stone is carved with two hammers and between those, words.

BE BOLD. BE BOLD.

I frown. Why do those words sound familiar?

Hephaestus looks like the template for a fairy-tale woodsman, with his scruffy beard and all those muscles. He only needs a red-and-black flannel shirt, thick logger boots, and an axe to complete the picture.

I pat the back of my vest to check for my own axe.

The god crosses his arms and sets his backward feet wide, which makes him tilt away from us. "Welcome to your seventh Labor, champions, and welcome, guests."

He says this in his quiet way, which has the group leaning toward him, trying to catch all the words.

"First, I would like to congratulate you. Having lost only one champion, you have set a record for having lost the fewest by the halfway mark of the Crucible. Well done."

My throat tightens. I still see Isabel's horror- and pain-filled eyes when I go to sleep at night, and I'm not sure Dae appreciates his grandmother being excluded from the list of losses, judging from the way his lips thin and he looks away.

I don't know what Hephaestus expected. Cheering or clapping, maybe. We all stare back at him silently. That doesn't seem to faze him, though. "Today, you and your partner will compete solely on time and time alone."

That's a new twist, at least.

"It's a staggered start. The course won't allow the champions to interfere with each other."

"An obstacle course?" Boone whispers at me. "Easy."

"You didn't see the last one." After Artemis', I can't say I'm all that eager to face another. Although Boone doesn't know about the burn. He hasn't seen the silvery scarring on my arm.

He shoots me a cocky grin. "I'll get you through it."

I roll my eyes.

"This is not an obstacle course." Hephaestus stares at the two of us sternly.

I do my best to look suitably chastised.

"You will find your way through these woods to a tower," the god continues. "Inside, on the first level, you will find one of my automatons. You must defeat it to move to the next level, where another automaton will be waiting for you. Each is different. Some, you will fight. Some will require other skills."

"Sounds like a movie I saw one time," Boone leans over to whisper to me.

Hephaestus shoots us another admonishing look.

"Shhhh," I hiss. "Always getting me in trouble."

"Not me," he says. "That's you. Trouble magnet." He waves his hand, indicating where we are and what we're doing.

"Do I need to separate you two?" Hephaestus demands, voice all things fed up.

I clear my throat. "He'll be quiet now."

"Always blaming me," Boone whispers. Then straightens at Hephaestus' stony glare.

The god finally looks away. "When you defeat one level, the door to the next level will automatically open. The best time wins."

Boone meets my eyes and winks in that confident, cocky way, but I don't return his smile. There's more to this. There's always a twist.

"When a team has progressed sufficiently, the next team will be allowed to start. If you are unable to complete the course within the four hours allotted to each team, you don't die," Hephaestus says. "You're simply disqualified from the Labor."

Well, at least death isn't an extra incentive this time. See, I knew I liked this god.

"The levels are deadly enough as it is," he tacks on.

Never mind. I take it back.

"Two heads are always better than one, of course, but you *do* have a choice," Hephaestus adds. "The champion and their guest can collaborate and compete as a team, or the champion can go it alone."

Every person in the circle shifts on their feet, already turning toward each other, questions in their eyes. *The levels are deadly enough as it is.*

Hephaestus looks at Dae, expression softening. "You have no choice, Kim Dae-hyeon, I'm afraid. You must compete alone."

Dae gives a jerking nod.

Murmuring rises among us, but Hephaestus holds up a hand. "You may discuss your choice in a moment. First, a final reminder. All you have to do is make it to the top fastest. How you do that, regardless of the challenge you face at each level, is up to you. But you cannot progress from one level to the next without defeating or outsmarting each level. And as an added challenge, your gifts will not work beyond the course, so you cannot go around it, either." He lowers his hand. "Now, make your decisions. The first pair will start in five minutes."

I turn to Boone, mouth already open with points and arguments I've been composing in my head, but he puts a finger to my lips. "Don't even consider going alone."

74

TWO ROADS DIVERGED IN A WOOD

I scowl over Boone's finger, tempted to bite it. Instead, I pull away. "We don't have to *both* take the risk," I point out.

"No."

I glare. "Don't be stubborn."

He snorts. "Said the most stubborn pot in existence to the most equally stubborn kettle. Besides, I told you I've always wanted to work with you."

I let out a sharp breath. That was a low blow just to give me warm fuzzies and get me to agree, and he knows it.

"You could save yourself. I'd feel better—"

"If something happened to you, how would that make me feel? Especially when I'm good at shit like this."

Now he's appealing to my logical, clerk side. He's definitely not going to let this go. "Fine. Put your life on the line. See if I care."

Boone's slow grin makes my stomach flutter. Just a little. Not like Hades, but still, when Boone chooses to be charming, he's hard to resist.

Hephaestus holds up a hand, signaling for quiet. "First up is Amir, starting with his guest, Zeenat."

But Amir and the woman we've all learned was his nanny are arguing. She's small but mighty, and I can tell she still expects Amir to listen to her the way he did as a child.

"Amir?" Hephaestus demands.

"No, ayah," Amir snaps with a swift glance in the god's direction. "I will *not* listen to you. Not this time. I didn't save you in the last Labor to lose you now. I—" His voice chokes a little, and he looks away, swallowing hard. "I couldn't take it."

Zeenat searches the face of the boy she's known and obviously loved since infancy, then reaches out and pats his hand. "All right. I will wait."

Relief hunches his shoulders, and Amir bends over to give her a hug. "Thank you. I'll do better if I'm not worried about you."

"Always such a kind heart, my Amir."

He smiles. The arrogant boy who at first I thought was used to getting his own way in everything has turned out to be someone else entirely. With a kiss on Zeenat's cheek, he leaves her and walks through the gate and into the woods.

After that, it's a waiting game. For me, at least. Hephaestus doesn't say specifically, but as names are called, I have no doubt Boone and I will be last. As usual.

Amir isn't the only one who chooses to compete alone to save their loved one. Zai does the same for his mother. Meike, too, for her roommate, who I think is older than her by at least a decade.

And Rafe argues with Dex right up to the last second. "I'm strong."

Dex's face is a study of regret and determination. "I know you are, sobrino, but your mother would never forgive me—"

"She'd want me to be the man of the house. The gods picked me to help you, Tío Dex."

They go on and on in circles until Hephaestus calls Dex's name.

Rafe bolts for the gate, but Dex grabs him by a skinny arm. Every one of Dex's thirty years is suddenly etched into his scowling face as he marches his nephew over to the god. "Hold him for me?"

To my surprise, Hephaestus scoops the boy up under one arm, like a football, ignoring the pounding of ineffectual fists as Dex nods his thanks, then runs into the woods.

"Dex!" Rafe's call after his uncle would wrench even the hardest of hearts.

And those are, I think, the easier decisions among us. Everyone else argues for even longer. Trinica is determined that her son must get married and provide her some grandbabies, and he can't do that if he's dead. She doesn't win that argument. Neve doesn't win her argument with Nora, either.

Diego, in the end, does win his heated debate with his wife, Elena, by insisting that their children need at least one parent in their lives should something go wrong. The kiss those two share before he heads off without her… I have to look away, give them their privacy. But their love is something precious. Something rare. Something worth fighting for.

A feeling Zeus stole from me.

Actually, every goodbye today makes my heart both whither with sadness and warm at the evidence of love in the mortal world. The cruelty of our gods and goddesses is highlighted with every word, every glance, every embrace.

I wish the fucking world was watching this and taking notes.

The guests not running the course are escorted away by the Daemones, no doubt to wait for their champions to finish and find them. *Please let them all survive this.*

Selfishly, I don't think I can watch the loss that Dae went through only a few days ago all over again.

The wait gets worse with every team that's called. My heart won't quit tripping over itself. Not for me but for Boone. And for the others. There is no signal when anyone finishes, no way to know if they made it to the top alive.

"Lyra," Hephaestus says. "You're up."

That was fast. Trinica was only called a few minutes ago. It was much longer between teams with the prior rounds. But then, it makes sense, I suppose. She told us her blessing from Hephaestus was invention, the ability to see and understand mechanisms. Like automatons. Her patron certainly gifted his champion a leg up for his Labor. A small smile plays around his mouth, so I know I'm right.

Boone swings around to face me and holds out his hand. "Ready, Lyra-Loo-Hoo?"

I've wanted to be on his team for years. Years of watching others get to work jobs with him while I sat back and handled the paperwork.

But I didn't want it like this.

I have to at least try one more time. "You could wait for me—"

"Nope." He starts walking, tugging me along behind him until we're through the gate and can't turn back.

All that's around us is the stillness of the forest broken by the occasional whisper of the wind through the pine needles. I take deep breaths and try to tame my heart, try to find a calm I can't quite reach. We don't have to win. We just have to make it through alive.

A turn in the path takes us into a deeper section of the woods. Not gloomy but almost enchanting, filled with fireflies that flit around us. And soon, we come to another gate. This one leads onto a drawbridge

THE GAMES GODS PLAY

suspended over a dark-watered moat surrounding a single castle-like tower with a crenellated top.

Like the first gate, the lintel stone has carvings. Hephaestus' hammers again, and new words.

BE BOLD. BE BOLD.

BUT NOT TOO BOLD.

"Well…" Boone says. "That's ominous."

They're not words of encouragement—they're a warning. And the last warning carved into stone didn't go so well.

As we stare at the words, I remember where I know them from. One of our pledges once nicked a book of Celtic fairytales that we passed around. There was a story about a man who murdered women in his castle, and his fiancée discovered this horrible truth. She learned it because she was curious about the castle he talked about but never showed her and went looking for it on her own.

In the end, curiosity saved her life.

At least, that's how I always interpreted it. I think that's why I remember it. It also means that I'm not surprised at the words carved over the tower door itself when we get across the moat.

BE BOLD. BE BOLD.

BUT NOT TOO BOLD.

LEST YOUR HEART'S BLOOD SHOULD RUN COLD.

"Cheerful," Boone mutters. But his humor has dropped away, and he's in full get-shit-done mode.

I pause with my hand on the old-fashioned door lever and look up, inspecting the stone tower. I don't see windows or slits or anything from this side to indicate how many levels there are. "What do you think?" I ask. "Seven or eight stories?"

"Sounds about right to me."

Seven or eight levels to survive. But even if we don't make it to the top in time, we don't die. That's something, at least.

The lever creaks in protest when I press down, and together, Boone and I step inside.

75

WIN, LOSE, OR DIE

I don't know what I expected Hephaestus' first automaton to be like, but for damn sure it wasn't a tiny child made entirely of gold standing at the center of the circular room.

The door shuts behind us, leaving the space lit by lanterns and a single window on the opposite side. The automaton kid, who looks like he's about three years old, slowly lifts a wicked-looking butcher knife, and his sweet bow of a mouth stretches into a smile that's pure evil. His tinkling, delighted laugh fills the room as he runs right at me, slashing wildly with the blade.

"Holy shit!" I yelp.

I grab for my axe, but I'm so rattled by the murder-child that I miss the pocket for it. Fumbling around, I dodge and run. Boone gets between us and punts the metal kid across the room. The automaton hits the wall but gets back to his feet and giggles before charging us again. By this time, I've given up on my axe. There's something about chopping a child, even one that's an automaton, that I just can't stomach.

Dodging the homicidal, laughing demon-toddler, I pull the wire twine from my vest that Zai returned to me after Dionysus' Labor.

Boone sees what I'm doing and, without a word, works with me.

It takes another punt from Boone and both of us working in tandem, dodging the automaton three more times before I finally manage to tackle the thing from behind as he chases Boone. I wrap the twine around him until his metal arms are pinned to his sides. The second he stops squirming and drops the knife with a clatter, a hidden door to our right swings open.

I see now why running this course alone would be a disadvantage.

"Not bad, Keres," Boone says.

He's not even winded. I am.

Inside, we find a winding staircase of stone weathered by the tread of centuries of feet leading upward. When we reach the next level, the door is already open.

Inside, we find a brass owl perched in front of a chess board.

I laugh.

Chess is the only game the Order keeps in its dens. In fact, they insist all the pledges learn how to play and play well, claiming that learning to think strategically is a key tool for all thieves. Good thieves, at least.

I'm actually good at this. So is Boone.

Ha!

Boone and I study the board, which is already mid-game. Then we sit in the chairs provided and start working. Four moves in, he gently covers my mouth with his hand. "Sorry, but you've really got to get a handle on that habit. It could get you killed one day."

I wrinkle my nose at him, then pull away. "I know."

It takes longer than I would have liked for us to finish the game — mostly because Boone and I have to stop to argue strategy — but we finally manage to put the owl in checkmate in seven moves. Another door swings open.

Boone grins. "Damn, you're good. When we get back to the den, I'm asking Felix to partner us."

He says it so casually, so matter-of-factly, I know it's not calculated or said out of pity. He really wants to work with me. He just checked that dream off my list without even knowing he was doing it.

Only...

Why is it suddenly hard to picture myself back in the Overworld? Away from Hades.

"Good game," I say to the owl.

Gears inside it whir as it spins its head, then gives a tooting little hoot that makes me smile. Two levels in, and I'm feeling more confident now that survival at the very least seems assured.

I head for the door, but just as I get to the bottom of the next set of spiraling stairs, a familiar whistle sounds behind me.

I spin to find Boone sitting — yes, sitting, like he doesn't have a care in the world — on the wooden window ledge, his legs dangling to the outside and a grin on his face.

"What are you doing?" I ask as I run over.

I look past him to the drop below. We're on the third level, so it's only about thirty feet to the ground, but the moat doesn't come all the way to the tower walls. There is a spit of land between the wall and the water, and it's covered with spears planted in the dirt. Hundreds of scary-looking spikes shooting straight up into the air, like the quills of an angry porcupine.

Boone swings one leg over, unconcerned. "Hephaestus said it didn't matter how we got to the top. Just that we get there." He looks up the wall. "I think we've been going the hard way."

I lean out the window to look up with him.

Damn it all to hells, he's right. I see that there are seven levels, now that I can count the windows, and the walls of the castle are easily scalable, made of rough rock that protrudes all over the place—plenty of ledges and grips to make it to the top.

It's definitely faster, especially for Boone, who is, of course, a fantastic climber, and it's much safer than facing the automatons. That's assuming I can make it. I'm not the worst at wall-work, but I'm not the best, either, and we have no ropes.

Boone must read my mind, because he winks. "I'll make sure you get to the top."

He means it.

"Move over." I wave him back impatiently.

With a chuckle, he maneuvers so that he's no longer sitting on the windowsill but scaling the wall off to the side. I sit and swing my legs over, then look for the best foot- and handholds. In seconds, I'm also hanging from the side of the castle, looking up, trying to remember my training and map out the first set of moves.

"To the left?" I ask.

"No." He points. "Right. See that larger outcropping?"

"Got it."

We start climbing. My heart is pounding so hard, I can feel the blood pump in my ears and temples. At least once, I see a glow from one of the windows near the top. Diego's halo, I guess, or maybe Dae's necklace. And a few yells come from various levels. I'm careful and slow, trying to keep most of my weight on my legs, not my arms, as we make it past one window. We're just coming to the next windowsill when Boone whispers, "The humming."

I cut the sound off in my throat. "Sorry."

Quietly, we split and make our way to either side of the opening.

When the sill is about hip height on me, I pause to look for a different handhold. As I turn my head to search, a flash of something silver lashes out from inside the tower. A blur, it's so fast. All I know is Boone lunges so that he's between me and whatever is coming at us from inside.

I see the way he takes the impact, his big hands curling around the windowsill as his body jerks. He grunts. Hard.

Then, without a pause, he reaches for me. Trying to move me out of the way or make sure I don't fall—I'm not sure which. It all happens in an instant. When he turns away, I suddenly can see the stain of red already seeping into the tear in his shirt, a wide gash across his chest.

But the silver thing from inside comes at us again before I have a chance to so much as gasp—and then Boone's in the air.

His face contorts with shock as he wheels his arms, and I reach out a futile hand for him, grasping nothing as he falls away.

"No!" I think I scream it as I watch him drop.

It feels like time has slowed and the fall takes a lifetime.

Drops of blood follow him down like rainfall, and Boone's horrified eyes never leave my face, even when he hits the spikes. I hear the *thud*, crunch, and gurgle of the impact, even from up here.

"Lyra." I can't hear him, just see his lips move. Then he coughs up more blood.

A tiny firefly strays from the safety of the trees to flicker in front of him curiously, and Boone sees it...and smiles. Then he looks up, seeking me out like he wants us to share that moment and not the reality of what's happening. His gaze stays on mine, then, even as the life oozes out of him. He doesn't look away once, not until his head lolls back and his entire body goes limp around the spikes skewering his chest, shoulder, and leg, holding him aloft.

"Boone!" I'm screaming for sure now as time catches up in an almighty rush. My next scream lasts what feels like an eternity, and I don't stop until my voice is raw.

I take a quick, hiccupping breath. It cuts off abruptly with a jolt of pain as a blur of silver strikes at me from inside the room, nearly knocking me off, too. I see it this time—through a blur of tears and anguish—a whiplike tentacle made of metal, with a lethal-looking sharp-tipped end.

That thing is what knocked Boone off the tower wall.

I have my axe in my hand in a flash, just as that tentacle shoots out again.

I slam my axe down on top of it, and the blade penetrates, pinning the thing to the wood of the windowsill. And then I climb.

I have no choice.

I don't let myself look down. If I see Boone's mangled body again, I know I'll lose it. I have to reach the top. A shadow flies by overhead—probably one of the Daemones, but I don't look. Avoiding the windows, I climb and climb and climb until I'm at the battlement wall at the top. I manage to use the narrow slits between stone blocks to pull myself up and over, muscles burning, heart aching.

The second my feet hit the roof, I spin around to lean over and look for Boone. But before I can see him, arms wrap around me from behind. Hades. I'm sure of it. He doesn't give me time to look at Boone again or react at all before we disappear.

Not to end up in the forest. Not to go wherever the others who have finished or are waiting for loved ones to finish have been taken. Not to return to the third floor to start all over like I semi-expect, given the cheat to get to the top. Not even to Hades' house in Olympus.

When we reappear, I'm standing in the circle of Hades' arms, my back against the warmth of his body. We're in a library. Columns, not fluted or Greek but inlaid with turquoise and gold, bracket a divided staircase winding on both sides up three stories to a glass dome showing a velvety sky that's not a sky outside. And books everywhere.

I'm standing with him in the Underworld.

In his home.

I'm sure of it.

He drops his forehead to the back of my head. "Lyra." His voice is a quiet murmur. Hesitant. Not like Hades at all.

And that's what finally punctures the numb bubble I wrapped around myself in order to get up that fucking tower. It's when the image of Boone's face as he fell, the twisted sight of his broken body on those spikes, finally hits with the reality that, unlike the last Labor, I can't wake him up this time. There is no magic. He's really gone.

I crumple.

And Hades catches me.

PART 6

DEAD LOSS

What could have been will now never be.
That's what hurts the most.

76

WHAT HAVE I DONE?

Hades scoops me up and sits on a huge leather chair, pulling me onto his lap, curving his body around mine as though to offer shelter. A stillness has taken me over.

Not numbness.

The pain is right here, eating at me. But I don't want to move or speak, and I definitely won't let myself cry. I know, somehow, it will get worse if I do.

"Lyra," Hades murmurs. He strokes my hair softly.

I breathe. I try to breathe through it.

"Don't hold it in, love."

If anything, I clamp down tighter. I don't want to feel this. I don't want to let it in. But the one thing I can't stop are the memories.

Moments of Boone over twelve years. Moments I'm seeing through different eyes.

That cocky grin taunting me from around every corner. The way he used to sidle up next to me in the food line, usually to snatch something off my tray. "Whachya working on today?" he'd say.

He had a particular craving for pancakes. I've never seen someone smother anything in that much syrup. And he'd laugh when he got in trouble for using too much — our den wasn't big on condiments — so he'd just go steal some more.

The time he stole that damned painting from under Lakshmi's nose is there, too, fresh in my mind after he brought it up the other day.

New memories as well. *I'd like to be your friend*, he said.

Even this morning, just having breakfast together.

He was with me *this morning*.

My throat clogs.

Breathe.

He didn't share this part of taking that painting with the gods the other night, and at the time I thought he was just making fun of me, but now the memory might haunt me for the rest of my life. "I took it for you, Lyra-Loo-Hoo. Won't it look pretty on your bedroom wall?" Was he trying to be my friend even then? How had he known that I secretly coveted the beauty of that scene? I never shared that with anyone. Then he pointed at another one he'd taken, too. "That one, we can fence." Not that I believed him, and not that Felix let him keep anything.

Oh gods. *I* did this. He's dead because of me. My humming alerted the automaton inside that room and...

"Lyra." Hades' voice has taken on a thread of worry.

"I don't want to let it out," I tell him, my voice as small as I feel.

"Why?"

"If I sit here and cry, if I give in to it, I don't know if I'll ever get up again." And that's not me. I'm the person who gets shit done, who never stops moving, who figures out a solution to the problem in front of me, because they never stop coming, and then the next and the next until one day all the problems will be solved.

Only I can't solve this one.

Hades' arms tighten around me, and we sit in silence. I don't know how long. He doesn't push me to let go again, and the memories are coming faster now. I can't make them stop.

It's like discovering the fabric of my past was sewn into a tapestry that I couldn't see until I stepped back. A thousand different moments that I disregarded or wrote off because of my curse.

A thousand missed opportunities.

My mind goes all the way back to the scrawny kid who showed up when I was eleven and Boone was thirteen, all elbows and knees but with hints of the man he'd become. He took one look at me, grinned, and said I was too small to be a thief and maybe the Order should throw me back.

Gods, he's such a tease.

Was.

Sorrow grips my heart and squeezes hard.

Boone *was* such a tease.

Not anymore.

How would things be different if I hadn't put up the walls he said I built around myself? If I'd tried harder?

We'll never know now.

Boone is dead.

I can see his face as he falls off the tower.

It keeps cropping up between all the other memories, hitting harder every time. He never looked away. He watched me until the very end.

He didn't die fast enough. Not right away. He *felt* those spikes—

Why can't I stop reliving all this? I need to stop. I need to shut it down.

Oh gods...

"Boone." His name whispers from my lips.

I curl into Hades, gripping his shirt, squeezing my eyes shut.

"I'm sorry," Hades murmurs. "I'm sorry." He runs a soothing hand over my hair. "I'm sorry."

His words are like a ribbon of warmth wrapping around my heart, not taking away the pain but soothing it, gentling it. It slows the memories I don't want to relive.

I stay tucked in against him. "Can you find B—"

My throat clogs around his name.

Breathe.

Start over.

"Can you find his soul a good place in Elysium? Like you did for Isabel?" I whisper, my voice thick. "I know he's a thief, but—"

"Don't worry about that. He'll be taken care of."

Is Boone down here already? Is he crossing the Styx on Charon's boat? Is he walking into the Fields of Asphodel alone?

"Can I see him?"

Hades stiffens against me slightly. "No. It's not good for souls to see loved ones so soon after. It confuses them or causes them pain, makes them want to go back. That's how souls get trapped in the Overworld and become spirits."

"Oh." I pluck at his shirt. "Thank you."

"Don't... Don't thank me, Lyra."

His statement is the first thing that's made the memories completely stop. I should be grateful. But I frown against his chest. "Why?"

"He was right. This is my fault. You're here because of me. He was here because of me. I did this." His voice is weighted with guilt. "I'm so sorry, Lyra."

I lift my head. Dull gray eyes look back at me, and my heart squeezes. It took me getting roasted by a dragon and then losing Boone for Hades to realize what entering me into the Crucible really means to me. But the thing is...

"I'm not angry with you," I tell him.

He can't hold my gaze and looks away. "You should be."

"You told me about Persephone." I take a breath. "You may not want to tell me how the Crucible is involved, but I know you didn't do this to me on a whim."

His gaze cuts back to me, searching mine. For what? The truth in my words? The anger he thinks I should feel?

"You don't do anything without a specific reason, Hades. A good reason. Am I wrong?"

Don't tell me I'm wrong and you're as petty as the others. I don't think I could take it.

Hades swallows hard. "Someday, I'll tell you the rest, and I think you'll agree it was a good reason. In fact, I know you will. But I'm not sure now that it's good enough for what *you* are having to pay. I didn't know."

I knew it. Deep in my heart. I'm not here because some capricious god is toying with me just for shits and giggles or greed for a throne. Boone won't die for no reason at all.

At the mere thought of him, tears burn, and I close my eyes and screw up my face, stuffing them back down. I try to focus on Hades, on the distraction he's providing. "Why can't you tell me now? Maybe it will make me feel better."

Hades shakes his head. "It's too dangerous now. But if you win, I'll..." He trails off.

I force my stinging eyes open to study the underside of his chin. "You'll what? Tell me?"

He straightens against me, expression suddenly intent. "If you win." He looks directly at me now, and I can feel the emotions vibrating through him. "If you win, I can save Boone."

77

THE POWER OF A SOVEREIGN

My eyes go wide. "What?" The word rips from me. "What did you say?"

"The King or Queen of the Gods, and only that god or goddess, has the ability to make new gods out of mortals. If you win the Crucible, I'll—"

"Be king," I whisper. "Wait. You're already a king. Couldn't you do it anyway?"

"I'm King of the Underworld, not King of the Gods. I would have to transfer all my godly powers along with my title to a mortal in order to save them."

I slump. *Well, that's out, then.*

He smooths a lock of hair from my forehead. "But if you win, I could make him immortal. I could make him a god. Samuel won the Labor today. All winners only have one each, including you. You would only need one or two more. There's time."

Hope is a peculiar, terrifying, painful thing. It floods me in a rush. Hades could save Boone. He could save him. All I have to do is win.

Hades lets out a sharp breath, murmuring words that I don't catch but sound a lot like a prayer. Which can't be right. Who would Hades pray to?

"Okay," I whisper.

He goes still. "Okay?"

"I'll win." Trying is for people who expect to lose. I don't have a choice. I have to win now. For Boone. Maybe I can harness a little of his cocky confidence. I could definitely use it.

I wish he was here now to show me how.

Hades' arms tighten around me as he lifts his head, searching my expression. "You're sure? Winning is a dangerous journey."

"I know. But for Boone…and for whatever reason you have, too, I can do it."

He searches my face again, like he doesn't quite believe me. "Even with me not telling you why?"

"Yes." That part is easier than it probably should be. "I trust you. You've shown me who you are, and I trust you."

His brows draw together fiercely. "Fuck, Lyra. I—" He shakes his head.

Hades with no words is a sight to see. I want to wrap that lock of pale hair around my finger, brush it back from his forehead. I don't. "Just… promise me you'll save Boone if I win."

"I swear on the River Styx that if you win, I will bring Boone back," he says solemnly.

An oath I know means a great deal to the gods. Unbreakable. "Good."

Hold on, Boone. I doubt he can hear me, but I tell him anyway. *We're coming.*

Which is when it hits me… Zai, Meike, Amir, and Trinica. My allies. What do I do about them? Together, we were trying to just survive. It wasn't about winning.

One problem at a time. Tomorrow is soon enough to figure that out. Maybe they'll understand if I explain.

"Thank you." I go to hug Hades, but the instant I lift my right arm, pain slices through my abdomen. I cry out as I hunch over, my hand going to the spot.

"Lyra?" Hades' voice is urgent. "What's wrong?"

"I—" I pull my hand away from my stomach, and it's stained in bright-red blood. I stare at it blankly.

"Fuck." Hades spits the word. "How did you get wounded?"

"I'm hurt?" I ask at the same time. I don't remember being injured— maybe that sting when the automaton almost pushed me off, too—but nothing felt real after Boone started to fall.

In a blink, Hades has me lying on the couch that was across from us. I can't straighten my legs because that pulls on the wound that I guess adrenaline, shock, and then grief were masking. Not anymore, though. He gently tugs my shirt up, then swears again, and I stare in horror at the gaping slice across my abdomen. Hades checks my back, and all it takes is a single grim look from him to know that the tentacle must've pierced me all the way through.

"I'll get Asclepius," he says.

"No!" I grip his wrist, but mostly because I don't want him to leave me. "He can't heal me. I didn't win this Labor."

The string of curse words that comes from his mouth would make a demon blush. "Fine," he says. "I have souls down here who were once doctors. Charon!" he barks even as he rips a blanket off the back of the couch and rends it in half.

The part of me starting to go a little hazy from the blood loss mentally notes that they have blankets in the Underworld. Which seems odd. Isn't it already warm here?

In an instant, the ferryman is standing in the room with us. He takes in the scene in a single, quick look.

"Asclepius can't come." Hades presses the cloth to my wound, and I cry out at the lancing pain. "Get her every godsdamned doctor down here if you have to," he orders.

Charon doesn't ask questions. He just goes.

And that's the last thing I see before oblivion drags me under.

78

WHICH WAY IS UP?

I know it's coming. I know, and I can't stop it.

Because ever since I blacked out, I've been trapped in a nightmare, reliving the same moment over and over, and even though some part of me knows this is just a dream, it feels real. Every time.

I move my head to see a flash of something silver that lashes out from inside the tower. A blur, it's so fast. All I know is Boone grunts, and then he's in the air.

His face contorts with shock as he wheels his arms, and I reach out a futile hand for him, grasping nothing as he falls away.

"No!" I think I scream it as I watch him drop.

Hands at my shoulders shake me. "Lyra!"

But I don't wake up. I'm still caught in the nightmare.

"No!" I scream as I watch him drop.

It feels like time has slowed and the fall takes a lifetime.

Boone's horrified eyes never leave my face, even when he hits the spikes.

"Lyra!" Another rough shake yanks me out of the nightmare, and I'm back in the here and now. My own harsh breathing rasps in and out, with sharp pants as the horror of that moment ebbs.

"Boone," I whimper.

"Lyra?" Hades' voice is coming from a long way away.

I frown. I know I'm awake now. Where am I? In my room, asleep? No, not there.

But my eyes won't open, like sandbags are holding them down.

"You're going to feel a prick," his voice tells me through the darkness and confusion and fuzzy sort of awareness I'm trying to navigate.

There's a tiny sting in my arm, followed by a wave of pain, as if that prick reminded all the other nerves in my body to wake up, too. My side aches dully but horribly, and the rest of my body… "Ouch."

"Are you in pain?" Hades asks me, I think. Then, "Why is she in pain?" demanded in a very different voice, hopefully to someone else.

"Mmm…hot." Why am I so hot? I'm sweating so much, my body feels sticky, and my hair is soaked.

A cool cloth presses against my face. "I know," Hades says. "You have an infection, and it's causing a fever."

Infection? From what?

I must ask that, because Hades answers. "The thing that pushed Boone off that wall must've gone past you to do it."

The thing that…

Boone.

It's real. It wasn't a nightmare. He's dead. Tears leak out of my still-closed eyes even while I'm trying to hold them back. "No, no, no." The words are slurred, and I try to curl up into a ball.

But those hands are at my shoulders again and won't let me. "Don't move, love. You'll tear your stitches, and you're all wrapped up in wires."

Wires. Stitches. Because I got hurt.

I remember now. The blood. The pain. Hades in a panic.

I force my eyes open and find a bleary view of the underside of a heavily stubbled jaw. "You…need…a shave."

"What did she say?" another voice in the room asks.

I frown and reach up to tickle his chin. "Do…gods…shave?"

Hades lowers his head to inspect me, brows practically meeting over his eyes, and I stare back in misery. "She's delirious."

"Says who?" I demand. Or try to.

Gray eyes crinkle at the corners, and he shakes his head. "If gods could be killed, you'd be the death of me, my star."

"I like it when you call me that." Did I say that out loud?

The frown is back. I guess I did. "She's definitely delirious," he says.

Am I? I actually feel better. Just the sight of him helps. I sink into my pillow and keep my gaze trained on his face. And then the memories come following on the heels of the weight of exhaustion. "We can…save him?" I mumble.

That was real, wasn't it? If I win, Hades can save Boone?

He lets go of my shoulders, taking my hand in his and pressing his lips to my knuckles. But he doesn't quite look at me. "Sure. But first, we need you to get better."

Why does that sound off?

Sleep is dragging me back under again, heavier and heavier and heavier. "We need...to save...Boone."

Hades' face blurs out, and I go under.

⚡ ⚡ ⚡

"No!" I scream as I watch him drop.

The fall takes forever.

Boone's horrified eyes never leave my face, even when he hits the spikes.

"Boone!" I shout again.

"Lyra!" Hades is calling me, pulling me back to him.

Hades, who has been here with me every time I come out of the nightmare into a different one. Hades, who hasn't left my side.

I stop thrashing in my sleep, still breathing hard, but the worst is over. I don't know how many times I've relived it now. It feels like a thousand. And, gods, I feel like shit.

"Boone is dead," I manage to whisper around a throat as dry as the Mojave Desert.

"I'm right here, Lyra-Loo-Hoo," Boone says from somewhere close by.

I whimper at the sound of that voice saying that name. My heart tumbles over itself. I'm dreaming. Hallucinating. Or Morpheus is playing a cruel trick, taunting me.

"I'm real," Boone says. "Don't be a coward. Open your eyes and find out."

It takes gargantuan effort, as if my eyelids are welded shut, but I manage to pry them open. I'm in a dimly lit room. Mortal machines are hooked up to me and beeping. My body is still on fire—not the good kind—and still hurts like hells, and generally I feel like the walking dead. Or supine dead, as the case may be.

But I don't care.

Hades is sitting beside my bed, holding my hand.

And Boone is standing at the foot...looking right at me with that big, cocky grin of his. "Hey," he says.

79

TRY EVERYTHING

A laugh bursts out of me, somewhere between relief and shock and joy. Only it sends a jagged pain through my belly, and I wince. "Don't make me laugh."

He snorts. "All I said was *hey*."

"And grinned." My face twists all up, holding back tears. "I didn't think I'd get to see that again." I glance at Hades. "Did you get Zeus to make him a god? I don't have to win now?"

The look I get in return is a thousand layers of regret. "I asked. He wouldn't do it. The Daemones said it was interfering in the Crucible," Hades says.

I frown. "But—" I look closer at Boone, and… Oh gods… He's see-through. Not like dream Boone. This is different. He's a ghost. A soul.

He's still dead.

"You said it wasn't good if he saw me now." The whisper comes out harsh, an accusation aimed directly at Hades, but I don't take my gaze off Boone.

"You needed me." Boone tips his head. "You kept calling out for me in your sleep. So I came."

"But what if you get confused? What if you want to go back and get trapped?" I need to get up and push him out of the room.

"I'm fine," Boone says.

Hades makes a gesture off to the side—hiding it from me, I think— and Boone glances his way. "I can't be here much longer. I need you to listen."

After a moment of fighting back my overwhelming tumult of emotions, I manage to nod.

"I need you to do something for me, Lyra."

I nod, the movement making my head spin. "I know. Win."

"No." He shakes his head. "I need you to fight, for *you*. I don't want to see you down here with me. Not yet. Do you hear me? Stop worrying about me. I'm fine." His smile is both real and forced. "Better than fine. But you're going to die if you don't let me go and try to live."

"No—"

"Let me go. I'll see your face again in about eighty years, after you've had a long life." He's fading away.

"Boone—"

"Promise me you'll live, Lyra." His voice is coming from far away. "Promise."

"I promise." I swallow. "And I'll see you sooner than eighty years. I'll win the Crucible. It's in the bag."

He shakes his head again. I think. I can hardly see him now. "You live for both of us. That will be enough."

I can't see him anymore.

"Eighty years, Lyra-Loo-Hoo." His voice whispers around me. "I'll be counting down the days."

And then he's gone. I feel it when he goes.

I clamp my free hand over my mouth, holding back the sobs that want to break free.

Hades nods at someone, and for the first time, I realize there's another man in here, one I've never met. He inserts a needle into my IV line and depresses the plunger. Immediately, warmth hits my blood, working its way up my arm to my chest, then to the rest of me.

I turn my head, staring at Hades, even as my eyelids grow heavier.

"Why?" I whisper.

His face twists. "Maybe now you'll let yourself sleep and heal...and fight."

For me. He brought Boone here for me.

"Thank..." I'm not sure I get to "you" before I'm out again.

⚡ ⚡ ⚡

The nightmares don't come anymore now. It's more like I'm trapped in my own body, drowning in heat and pain. Every so often, I manage to swim back up to the top for a breath. Whatever they're trying, it's not working. I'm not getting better.

But I'm holding on now, at least.

Hades' voice is my anchor.

His touch. Even when I'm deep under, I can feel him here. When I'm closer to the surface, he's never far away.

One of the times I manage to swim up and open my eyes, he's arguing with someone. Charon, I think, though the other person is standing backlit in a doorway. Another time, he's asleep sitting in a chair, head lolled back. He looks awful. Exhausted, with purple bags under his eyes. I didn't know gods could exhaust themselves. I reach toward him, but I'm already sinking again.

80

THE ONLY VOICE I HEAR

Sensation flushes through me in the dark and pulls at my consciousness. "What…" I hear myself from far away.

Like a cool breeze off the bay after a hot summer day, the sensation moves through me again. Breaking through the heat of the fever. Not eradicating it. But this is the first hint of relief I've felt since I've been trapped in my own body.

Worry wriggles through the relief like a worm. And I think I frown, because why would I worry? This is…relief.

"Is it working?" Hades' voice comes from a long way off.

Is what working? Are they trying another medicine? Another treatment? "Not the ice bath again." I try to say the words, but my lips won't move.

That was agony. Fire and freezing at the same time.

Another flush of cool, like the relief is inside me. In my veins.

Then another, but this is more like a wave moving through me, and I sigh my relief. Audibly. I know because it's loud in my head.

And yet a dark emotion coils in my stomach. Doubt? Dread? Hope?

I don't think I'm the one feeling those things.

"I think it's working," someone says. They're closer now.

Or I'm closer to consciousness. The lessening heat and pain is buoying me up to the top. Please don't let this stop.

"Lyra?" Urgency lines Hades' voice.

I want to answer him, tell him I'm okay. More than okay, but I'm still having trouble making my mouth and eyes work.

"What's wrong? Is it killing her?" The panic in his voice would be adorable if it didn't seem to be wrapping around my heart and squeezing hard. Like his panic is feeding into me.

I try to reach for him, for his hand, but I can't move yet. The sick exhaustion is still trying to drown me.

Another wave of that blessed cool.

I manage to make my mouth work. "Hades."

"I'm here." His voice sounds…tortured. "I'm here, Lyra."

His hand wraps around mine, anchors me to reality, and that single, simple touch is heaven.

"It's getting better," I try to say. I'm vaguely aware that the words come out as gibberish.

Another bolt of worry hits.

"Help her!" he orders someone in a voice that is all King of the Underworld. So much authority. So much power.

"We have to let it work," someone says in a voice that quavers. "My apologies, Lord Hades."

So much fear from them. Because of him. Him trying to protect me.

"Hades," I whisper.

He lets go of my hand, and I whimper a protest. Then his palms cup my face. "I'm here," he says.

That touch, the closeness of him, that voice… It's all I need.

A final rush of that relief-giving sensation flows into me, through me, and it feels as though my body is being soothed and cleansed and rebuilt from the inside. Starting from my bones and working its way outward.

Followed by…fear.

Not my fear. I'm not afraid. I'm relieved. What is happening?

"Elysium save me," I hear him whisper. Feel his breath brush my lips. "Is she—"

"I feel…better," I mumble, exhaustion already reaching for me. But a different kind. The type of sleep that heals instead of traps you in your own tortured body. "Much better."

That odd sensation has receded, so the emotion that barrels through me isn't that. And it definitely isn't mine. I'm sure of that now.

Shock and relief and dawning realization are followed by worry-tinted, supremely masculine satisfaction.

It moves like a lightning bolt through my chest—there in electrifying clarity, then gone, leaving me buzzing.

Not *my* feelings…
That was Hades. I felt what he was feeling.
How?

81

I PROMISE YOU

I frown, Hades' hands still on my face. That can't be right. Feeling Hades' emotions like that. Am I hallucinating? More dreams?

Someone in the room coughs. "I'd say that worked remarkably well, Phi," they say. A low, male voice. Charon, I think. He's the only one I've heard call Hades Phi.

There's silence.

"Lyra?" Hades says, still close to me. "Can you open your eyes?"

I really don't want to. My body is drifting away, the exhaustion easing into something more like comfort.

"Please." Hades never begs, but he's begging me now.

I force my eyes open, squinting against the light of the single lantern in here, and his face comes into vague focus.

He releases a small breath that probably only I hear. "Thank the Fates. I didn't want to do this until you woke up."

"Do"—I have to clear my throat because it's like talking through gravel—"what?"

He holds up a bronze chalice where I can see. It's simple, with his symbol of the bident and scepter engraved on it. "I'm trying something dangerous."

That doesn't sound good. I frown as his face sways before mine. "What?"

"You're not getting any better, Lyra. So I gave you some of my blood."

My lips hitch in an attempt at a smile. Ichor, the golden blood of the gods, famed for its ability to do…just about anything, as humanity tells it. "I'm…a goddess." Then it hits me what he's saying, and my eyes widen as much as they can while I'm barely keeping them open. "Oh. That was... why...I'm better now?"

He shakes his head. "No. That was so you can survive the next part. Hopefully."

Next part? What's he talking about?

He holds up the cup again.

Oh. Right? What about it?

"Water from Styx."

I blink as my mind tries to glom onto what I know about that. "Poison," I whisper.

"That's why I gave you my blood."

Now it's coming together vaguely. Only a few mortals have survived touching the Styx. Achilles was one of them. It made him invincible everywhere except his heel where his mother had held him when she dipped him in the waters, and that part didn't get wet. That one entirely mortal spot became his only weakness.

Did Achilles survive because he had a deity's blood in him? His mother was Thetis, a sea nymph. Did that make him enough of a demigod to survive it?

Hades must be desperate.

"I'm...that...bad?" I ask.

He hesitates, then nods.

I search his face. "You...look terrible."

Hades' lips crook. "You should see yourself, my star."

"Wow." I take a labored breath that shudders through me. It's getting harder to stay here with him. "Guess you...better...do it...then."

He doesn't, though. He hesitates visibly. It's got to be pretty damned dangerous. "If you die, I'll take care of you," he tells me. I get another lightning bolt of emotion from him. I'm sure it's from him, now. Desperation this time. "I promise."

He is tearing himself apart with guilt. Can't have that.

"Seems like..." I lick my cracked lips. "You're...taking care...of...a lot...of souls...these...days."

His expression alters, and my heart thumps heavily at the odd combination of exasperation and tenderness on his face. "I hope you're not rubbing off on me," he says. "Always running around trying to save other people."

"Heavens...forbid." I try to chuckle, but it turns into a cough that racks pain through every part of me. "But...don't...worry about...mine."

"What?"

"My soul. I...like it...down here."

"Fuck," Hades mutters darkly.

"If you're going to do it, Phi." Charon's voice reaches through the shadows. "Do it now, before the effects of your blood wear off."

Cool hands lift my shirt. The air is oddly cold against my skin, and I glance down and grunt at the sight—my wound not only hasn't closed, it's a pit of black flesh, like acid has eaten its way through me. Like Isabel. Only different. Black spider veins crawl out of the wound into the graying flesh all around it in every direction.

I'm no doctor, but even I know that's bad.

"This is going to hurt—" Hades doesn't bother to finish warning me before he pours the contents of the cup over the wound.

Agony and fire. A thousand times worse than the dragon burn. I've never screamed so loud in my entire life, the sound torn from my throat, my body bowing off the bed as if it's trying to escape itself. He doesn't stop. He's pouring more and more. Then he rolls me to pour more on the exit wound on my back.

I scream until my voice goes hoarse, and then the darkness reaches up and yanks me down so fast it's like that wild rush down the river from Hades' waterfall in Olympus.

"No! Lyra!" I hear Hades shout at me.

But I'm too deep, and in the darkness, for the first time, I find total, true oblivion.

82

HIS STAR

When I open my eyes next, my head isn't muzzy anymore, and while I'm stiff and achy from lying here so long, I feel no other pain. Also, they've removed most of the tubes that were stuck in me, so that's better, too. Charon sits at my bedside instead of Hades, reading a romance novel. I smile. I didn't peg him as the type.

"Good book?" I croak.

He lowers it and grins at me, and I blink. Gods really are extraordinarily beautiful.

"I've been debating if we should call you Sleeping Beauty or Snow White."

I guess the River Styx did its work, and Hades' blood kept me alive. Barely, it felt like.

It took several more days, or...however long. I'm not exactly keeping track of time. I only remember patchy pieces, but at least most of them didn't involve pain or fever or even delirium. Just exhaustion as my body mended.

"Weren't both of those fairy tales a sleeping death?"

"Hence the debate." He puts his book on the table beside his chair. "Given how pale you are and the raven-black hair, I'm leaning toward Snow White."

"Hephaestus could be the huntsman."

Charon laughs at that. "And Aphrodite the evil queen?"

I shake my head. "She didn't mean for things to turn out so bad." I saw how she'd cried herself puffy over Dae's grandmother. Those emotions were real.

"Hmmm... And prince charming?" His gaze turns sharp, curious—

not in an idle way. "Seems like you have a few options."

No use denying it. "One is a ghost who doesn't love me more than a friend. And one is a god. Doesn't seem like either prospect has much of a future."

"Not to mention the ally," Charon says.

"Also just a friend." While these games are played, at least.

What I don't tell him is that Hades was the rock I held on to through all of it. Boone's visit helped ease my guilt, helped give me a goal to work toward and something to live for. But Hades?

He was my peace. He was my strength. He was my haven.

Definitely didn't see that coming. Though I probably should've.

"I've never seen Hades…distraught before," Charon admits. Not like this."

For a minute, I worry that I spoke my thoughts out loud or that he could read them. But then his actual words sink in, and heat flushes through my face. I try and fail miserably to be casual. "Was he?"

He searches my expression. "Enough that it scared me."

I stop tracing a pattern on the blanket to look at him more closely. "Scared?"

Charon shrugs. "He's king down here, but I couldn't make him leave you. For *days*. This is the first time he's been out of this room since he brought you here, and I still had to force his hand. If he loses it…" Another shrug.

But I get the idea.

The heart monitor beats a little faster, the sound of it pinging and obvious. I really hate those machines. With a flick, I remove the gadget from my finger.

It flatlines, and Charon turns it off with a not-so-secret smile. "You don't think you have a future with him? Why? Because he's a god and you're mortal?"

I really don't want to have this conversation, so I say nothing.

He doesn't let it go, though. "You don't seem the type to let details get in your way."

"What are you saying?"

"What has he told you about Persephone?"

I press back into my pillow. Where did that come from? "He told me she was like a sister to him. How losing her devastated him."

He glances away. "There's that, at least."

"What does that mean?"

He shakes his head. "It means he's being up-front with you." He pins me with a pointed look. "Hades only shares information for two reasons—either you're in his very small circle, or he's using it to get something from you."

"Which am I?"

He runs a hand around the back of his neck. "I'm hoping the former."

"'Hoping' doesn't sound promising."

Charon huffs an unamused laugh, and yet he seems to want me to give Hades some kind of chance.

Mine.

Hades' claim, his word, bounces around inside me.

But the way he takes care of me feels like more than possessiveness over his champion.

I try to push up in the bed, and Charon grabs a pillow and stuffs it behind my back gently. Just getting situated takes all the fight out of me, and I close my eyes for a second. I don't want to go back under. I've had enough of that.

When I make my eyes open again, he's still here. Charon asks, "Did he tell you—"

At the click of the door, I look directly into mercury-gray eyes.

The second Hades sees me sitting up, it's like all the tension drains from him. And a memory strikes. A real one, I think. I stare at him as I recollect.

A moment in the middle of the night when I swam to the top of consciousness, after the Styx fix, and Hades' face blurred into view.

"You can leave me, you know," I remember slurring. "I'm not going to die now."

"That's debatable." Then he frowned. "Or do you want Boone again instead?"

Both irritation and a genuine offer laced his words.

I tried to shake my head, but my body just wasn't cooperating. "No. You."

"You want me?" His face did that supremely satisfied thing. When it's not annoying, his arrogance is slightly endearing. "Good. Get well and I'm sure we can figure something out. I have plans."

I don't remember what happened after that. I probably drifted back off.

But what's sticking with me now is the way he said he had plans. *Mine. My star. Plans.*

For me? For us? Does it have something to do with the Crucible? Or was he just teasing?

He steps farther into the room and into the light of the lantern, and I gasp.

"Fuck." Charon's on his feet. "That bad?"

And I don't blame him. Hades looks awful, visibly somber, which I think might be Hades' version of shaken. His lips are pinched, eyes sunken into the pallor of his face. He looks like…well, like death warmed over.

Hades lifts a single eyebrow at Charon. "What do you think?" he asks in a voice devoid of all emotion.

The ferryman winces.

"Did I interrupt something?" Hades asks, flat tone turning silky.

Charon doesn't look at me. "Not really. I was just about to fill her in on what she missed."

What I missed? My mind is moving at the speed of a sloth, so I'm not entirely keeping up with this conversation.

"I'll do that," Hades says.

A distinct doggy whimper comes from the hallway, and behind Hades, one of Cerberus' heads leans down to look into the room with one eye.

"Hey, buddy."

"Are you okay?" This is Rus, and it makes me smile.

"Doing much better. Give me another day or two, and I'll be back in the Labors again."

"We don't like that." I can't see the other heads, but Cer is the one talking.

Me neither. But I have more riding on winning now than just me. A lot more. My gaze slides to Hades, and suddenly all I can see is a man who would do anything for the few people he loves most.

Hades doesn't change his expression by so much as a flicker, but a flare of dark suspicion sizzles through me—a flare of clarity and knowing that isn't mine. It's coming from somewhere else.

Oh wow.

It takes everything I have not to gasp, not to let the shock show on my face.

That was real? The emotions I got from him earlier. Those weren't hallucinations or wishful projections. Those were all *real*.

Because of his blood? It has to be. Maybe it will wear off. Does he know?

Why is he suspicious, though? The Crucible? Or maybe about what Charon was telling me? Not that he got a chance to tell me much.

I shift my gaze to Charon, who won't look me in the eyes. "Better get back to the boat," he mutters. He gives my leg a squeeze over the covers. "Good to see you lucid finally, Lyra."

He and Hades exchange an inscrutable glance as he leaves. "Come on, Cerberus. Let's give them some privacy."

Cerberus grumbles as they walk away.

But I'm too busy studying Hades to care. "Where were you?" I ask.

83

TOO LATE

"The Stygian Marsh."

The crossroads of the Underworld. Where souls are judged and sent to different destinations depending on how they lived their lives in the Overworld. It's said Hades has to judge the best and worst cases and render blessings or punishment. Given how he looks, it doesn't take a genius to guess which he was just deciding.

"Want to talk about it?" I ask.

Knee-jerk denial ripples over his features, but then he pauses and leans in the doorway. "The judgment wasn't the hard part. This soul was a sociopath and tortured and killed many people without mercy or remorse." He shrugs, but I can see the weight of whatever they must've been like in the action.

I wait quietly for the hard part.

"But his mother is a soul in Asphodel, and…" He drops his head back against the doorjamb. "She begged for his punishment to be lessened, told me about his abusive father. I saw it all, of course."

"Was it bad?"

Hades comes off the door and drops into the seat where Charon just was, pulling it closer. Then he takes my hand in both of his, tracing the lines of my palm. "No soul is born evil. There are proclivities, leanings, but like carbon is compressed and fired into a diamond, pressure and pain can transform a soul into something terrible."

The empathy Hades hides from the world is showing. He felt for this person and what made him into a monster. For his mother, too.

"I can see alternate futures when they come to me, sometimes—what could have been if things had been different."

"And this could have been different?"

He nods. "So many lives ruined."

This is what the King of the Underworld must endure. "I wish I could help."

He searches my eyes, a small smile playing around the corners of his mouth. "You do?"

Warmth blooms in my face, but I leave my hand right where it is. "Yeah."

His dimples peek at me for a quick second. "Yeah." He takes a long, slow breath, then releases it in a rush. "Let's change the topic."

I get needing emotional space, so I try not to be hurt by the distance threading his voice. But I pull my hand back and scratch an itch on my arm. "Were the other gods mad about having to wait for me?"

Hades groans. "How about something else?"

That's not a good sign. "What happened?"

"They sent Asclepius and the Daemones down," he says. "They understood after they saw the shape you were in."

His voice isn't right.

"Tell me the bad news. Go ahead. Rip it off like a Band-Aid."

He leans back in his chair. "I've never understood that expression."

The casual pose doesn't fool me at all. "Then you've never worn a Band-Aid that got stuck to hair or part of the scab." I pin him with a hard look. "You're stalling, Phi."

"Uh-uh." He shakes his head. "You don't get to call me that."

I frown. "Charon does."

"Yes."

"Then why can't I?"

He crosses his arms. "My star…has anyone ever called you stubborn to your face?"

"You're still stalling."

He looks bored, reminding me of the night we met.

"Fine. I won't call you Phi. But back to the Band-Aid… I'll imagine much worse things. It's better to tell me now and get it over with."

He glances to his right at a window with curtains drawn across it. "They didn't wait."

My heart plummets to my gut. "They went ahead with the next Labor without me?" Shit. "Who won?"

"Diego."

Double shit. Now he's won two, and Boone's counting on me.

"Start from the beginning, and tell me everything," I demand.

Hades runs a hand through his hair, the pale lock flopping onto his forehead, making him appear disheveled. "Damn."

"What happened to your poker face?" I tease with a wan smile. "Now I really need you to tell me."

He looks away, and I can tell he's debating it, but eventually his expression flattens to something grimly resigned. "Fine."

I exhale deeply. He really could have said no.

"Samuel won Hephaestus' Labor, beating Trinica by only two seconds. His prize was a compass Hephaestus made that will always point the correct way to go."

"Three Strength virtue wins in a row," I say. "Do you get the feeling the Labors are rigged?"

Hades lifts a single eyebrow. "When have my siblings ever played fair?"

Good point.

"Demeter's was the eighth Labor," he continues. "She had them run through the Fields of Forgetting. If they succumbed and got lost, storms would chase them down." After a pause, his voice is gentler when he says, "Neve didn't make it."

My stomach turns over, then over again. Another of us is gone?

I swallow around a throat thickening with grief but nod for him to continue.

"Diego won, and his prize was the Protective Mark of the Algea—he can't feel pain. Physical or mental. The ninth—"

I hold up a hand. "Wait." *No. Tell me they didn't.* "They've completed more than one Labor while I've been out?" I ask slowly.

He nods.

We're fucked. "How long was I out?"

"Almost two weeks."

"Two—" I feel the blood drain from my face. I thought it was days. Suddenly, Hades is standing by my side, tipping a cup of water to my lips. I swallow some, which helps. Before my injury, the Crucible was being run with only a few days between Labors at the very most. Almost two weeks?

Hades sets the cup down and takes my hand in his, a lifeline of steady strength.

"How many did they get to?" I ask.

"You're upset, and you should be resting. We can talk about this later—"

"No. Now." I spear him with a glare.

The zap of emotions when it strikes this time is a mix of regret and reluctance. "Three Labors—the eighth, ninth, and tenth."

"Three," I whisper.

Three Labors. There are only two left. "Tell me the rest." I'm not sure I really want to know.

"The ninth was Hera's. As the goddess of the stars, she put a new constellation in the skies. The champions had to figure out which one. The world remained dark until they did, and she unleashed Deimos and Phobos on the champions to make it harder."

The gods of fear and panic when it's pitch-black? "I bet that was a treat," I mutter.

"Rima and Zai figured it out together."

I allow myself a small moment to smile at that. "Tied?"

He nods. "Hera gave them separate prizes. Zai has a stone that, when eaten, will ward off poison. And Rima was given a single vial of dragon fire."

I shudder. I only dealt with a glamoured dragon, and that was enough for me.

But the good news is that gives Zai and Diego two wins each. I could still beat them. I just need to win the last two.

"And the tenth?" I ask.

"Ares," he says.

I wince. Of all the Labors, Ares' was the one I'd dreaded the most. I can't say I'm all that sorry to have missed it. "A battle?"

"As he's the god of war, you'd think so," Hades says. "But he reminded the champions that in the ancient world, almost every god of war was about protection of their community, their people. His Labor was centered around that. Each of them was given a baby chimera. They had to get it back to the nest without being mauled by the baby and without the mother destroying Larissa, Greece, where her babies were taken."

Interesting.

"Samuel was severely injured."

My breath catches. "He's not—"

"No," he says. "Not yet. I loaned Zeus the doctors who worked on you."

Which means none of the Strength virtues won that Labor, or Asclepius would have healed him. "Thank you for that."

I pause, studying him. I'm not sure Hades would have done that on his own. But for me...

No. Silly idea, Lyra.

I force my mind back to the Labors. I almost don't want to ask the next part.

"Who won?"

The way he hesitates, he doesn't have to say it. I already know.

"Diego."

Oh gods.

"His prize is a spear that telescopes down to pocket-sized." Hades' voice sounds like it's coming down a tunnel.

I close my eyes to hold the panic at bay, pushing the desperation and terrible truth down where they can't hurt me. Where I can think.

Zai won one. That gives him two. And Diego...three, now. At the very most, with only two left to play, I could tie for the lead, and I'd have to beat Zai to do it.

"What do they do if there's a tie?" I force my eyes open for the answer.

"It depends," Hades says slowly. "But they don't allow two winners. There can only be one ruler of the gods."

Fuck.

I want to scream the word. Scream at the unfairness. Just...scream.

No. I curl my free hand into a fist in my lap. There's too much riding on this, and I don't have time to wallow or lose it. I have to think. "I have to try anyway. A tie is still a chance."

Hades' scowl could strip concrete off rebar. "You can barely sit up."

I scowl right back. "Then you'd better get your ass back up to Olympus and buy me a few more days. I'm doing it."

He shoves a hand through his hair as he's up off his chair, whirling away from me. Even his rigid shoulders look like they're considering all the ways to get me to not do this. "Don't make me put you through more," he says in a voice I've never heard from him before.

Can't he see? If I don't, I'll hate myself.

"Hades." I say his name quietly, and his back goes even more rigid, like he's ready to snap. "Please. I *have* to."

"Fuck," he mutters. His hands go to his hips as his head drops forward, and his shoulders rise and fall. "Fine. I'll go talk to them."

84

IF TRUST WON'T WORK, TRY BRIBERY

When you have everything to lose, you start coming up with the shit
that will get you smited.

That's what we're doing tonight. Any minute now, in fact.

Fates, please be on our side and let this work.

We have to be very careful in how we do this to avoid the "no
interfering" rule for Hades. So, at my request, Hades is bringing...
guests...to his home. Charon about fell on his ass when Hades told him.
How they can come and go from the Underworld without a mark similar
to the one Hades gave me, I don't know, and I don't ask. But as far as
anyone else is concerned, this is a "hooray I'm better, let's catch up on
what I missed" party for all the champions.

Given the size of Hades' home down here, you'd think entertaining
was common. "Mansion" doesn't really cover it. "Castle" is closer. I've
been encouraged to walk a lot by the ghost doctors attending me in
committee, and so I've explored.

At this point, I'm pretty sure I've only covered about fifty percent
of the grounds, and I've cataloged at least thirteen bedroom suites, two
dining rooms—one formal and one informal under a skylight. There's
a sauna, a massage room, the library where he first brought me after
Boone's death that puts the fairy-tale Beast's to shame, three separate
indoor living spaces, and at least three more outdoor—one up on the
roof, where I am now, one by the pool, and one in a garden that stole my
breath. Two kitchens inside—one for Hades' personal use and a massive
one for the staff who serve here—and one kitchen outside. Indoor pool
and gym, outdoor pond, but also an outdoor pool that is more like a series
of pools incorporated into the lush landscaping that swirls and eddies

from unique feature to feature, with bridges, grottos, and even one with cabanas on islands surrounded by water.

Suck it, Olympus.

That's what Hades' home in the Underworld screams.

The other champions are in for a surprise when they get here. I almost smile as I picture their reactions. The opulence and luxury are both in your face and understated. Just like his penthouse, it's eclectic. A mix of elements from all around the world.

But what's different is the lived-in feel. The rooms and decor aren't untouchable, uncomfortable, or showy. Every space here is…cozy. I want to tuck myself into each nook and cranny and just enjoy—read, take a nap, watch TV, plan a heist.

Hades is there with me in every one of those fantasies. I can't quite seem to get that to stop.

I'm waiting in the rooftop living area. From here, I have a three-hundred-and-sixty-degree view of the mountain the home is built into and the lands beyond with their ethereal hills, fields, and rivers covered by a cave ceiling so high, it might as well be sky. There is a sort of daytime and nighttime here, mimicking the Overworld, but the colors are more vibrant. Especially at night.

I sigh as I drink in the view for perhaps the last time.

Tomorrow, we go back to Olympus for the eleventh Labor. Hades bought us the time. The Daemones helped, coming back down to inspect me and agree that the final challenges should wait for all the champions still living to participate.

Hades hasn't told me any more about the three Labors I missed, despite me bothering him nonstop—a bad sign that I won't like what I hear, but it doesn't matter. I'll find out tonight regardless.

A breeze ruffles my hair and caresses my skin.

There's a breeze in the Underworld. I'd pictured a roasting wind to go with the burning fields, but not here in Erebos, the Land of Shadows. Here, the breeze is cool and perfect.

I'm wearing a sundress, of all things, in a cheerful yellow. I have no idea how Hades knew I'd always wanted one. Pledges wear utilitarian clothes or clothes to blend into the environment where we have a job, but we don't get to keep those. And I never got to that level anyway.

I stare out over the vistas and sigh again because I think I could stay here forever and never miss any other place. But maybe that has something to do with the god who calls this home.

I *feel* Hades before I hear or see him move up next to me at the rail. Not from his emotions. I haven't felt those again in the extra days he wrangled for me to rest and recover.

But there's this tension now.

Like a thin wire has been strung between him and me, and if we get too close…sparks travel that wire and we both risk getting scorched. So we've been moving around each other carefully.

We don't touch.

We don't glance or stare.

We don't share a room alone for longer than a few minutes.

We don't breach the invisible walls of personal space, like glass bubbles around us.

We don't imply. Or tease. Or tempt.

And thanks to all of those unspoken "thou shalt not" rules…I fucking smolder with unrealized need.

"You're still determined to go through with this?" he asks.

All of our discussions since I stopped sleeping all the time have focused on strategy. How to win the Crucible.

"Yes." For Boone. For me. For Hades, too.

"Lyra!" Meike's cry has us turning to find her, Zai, Trinica, and Amir coming up the stairs that lead to the rooftop.

I don't have to look, because I already feel that Hades has disappeared. He's not supposed to be here with the champions. Any of them. Not for what I have in mind.

With hurried steps, Meike runs to me and pulls me into a hug. "Thank the gods," she says. "We thought…" She grimaces as she pulls back.

"Thank Hades, because he's the reason I'm still alive."

She glances around as if she'll find him here.

By now, Zai has joined us, also giving me a hug. "We didn't know what happened to you."

"I'll fill you in."

Trinica hangs back, watching warily, Amir at her side. It's not like I've been present for most of the Labors they've been officially allied with us for. "I'm glad the four of you had one another while I've been gone," I say.

"We missed you," Amir says, offering me a boyish smile.

Trinica just nods, but she's lost the wariness.

I lead them to one of the large outdoor couches that horseshoe a firepit. "We don't have long to talk," I tell them. "The others will be here in about fifteen minutes."

Zai leans back a tad. "Others?"

"I invited all of the champions here."

The four of them exchange glances.

Meike frowns. "That doesn't seem like a good idea." And usually she is the optimistic one.

I half laugh but can't help pulling a face. "Yes, all. Even Dex. There's a reason." I clasp my hands in my lap to keep from fiddling. "We don't have much time, so I'll lay it out for you plainly. All right?"

They nod.

I glance behind them toward the stairs, then start talking rapid-fire. I tell them about Boone. About how Hades can make him a god, but only if I win and he becomes king.

"Why are you telling us?" Zai asks slowly, strategic mind at work. I can see in his eyes that he's already tracking where I'm headed.

There's a bit of a distance between us now. All of us. Not palpable or bad, just…there. I'm not sure if it's because they survived three more Labors without me, or something else.

"Because I'm going to propose something to the entire group of champions, but you are my closest allies. So, I wanted to tell you first."

Movement on the stairs has me glancing over them again. The five of us get to our feet as first Jackie and then the others all make their way up to where we are.

No Hades. No Charon. No other gods or goddesses.

Just us.

85

A GAMBIT

As they arrive, most of the champions look around in open-mouthed wonder, and I smile as I give them a chance to take in these surroundings. Okay, yes, their reactions are even better than I imagined. It feels almost like this is *my* home and I'm proud to show it off.

Blast and brimstone, Lyra. Get a grip and get started.

"Thank you for coming," I say.

"What the fuck is this about, Keres?" Dex demands.

I guess his blessing of foreknowledge only applies to the Labors. Although he was right when he told Boone that he may not be winning but he's still here.

"Please sit down. I promise I'll tell you everything. After that, you can return to Olympus regardless."

"Regardless of what?" Jackie is the one to ask slowly, searching my face not in suspicion but concern.

We all sit, some more reluctantly than others. I nudge Zai. "Congratulations, by the way."

He shoots me a smile that's just a little bit lacking.

"What was the constellation Hera made?" I ask.

They all look to Dae, who tips his head back like he can see the stars here. He can't—or not the same stars, though I pick out shapes in the bright spots that glow on the ceiling—so he slowly lowers his gaze. "It's called halmeoni," he says. That isn't English, and I don't think it's Greek. I raise my brows in question.

"Grandmother," he says quietly. "In Korean."

For him? My throat closes around an ache. Maybe Hera wasn't quite as hard-hearted about that as she seemed.

Dae meets my gaze, and in his eyes, I can see an understanding. A mutual sort of wound. We both lost the people we love most. "Maybe she'll give you one for Boone, too," he says. He even smiles a little, kindness there in his eyes. "She could call it the thief."

I smile back, dropping my gaze to my hands, which are now tangled in my lap. "I think he'd love that."

I glance around at the others. "Where's…" I almost don't want to ask. "Samuel?"

Meike takes my hand. "What did they tell you?"

I look from face to face. "They told me about each game and who won. And about…Neve. She died in the Fields of Forgetting?"

"That's one way to put it," Dex mutters darkly.

I frown, and Jackie says, "She wore her armor as protection—after the last Labor involving fields, she said—and when she got lost and the storms came, it attracted lightning. It was—" She has to stop and swallow.

"Gruesome," Trinica says, stone-faced. "It was gruesome."

I glance around at the others. Now that I can take a closer look, it's more obvious. They are, all of them, shell-shocked. That's the only way to describe it. As if the worst has been thrown at them and they've come out different on the other side.

"Oh gods. I'm so sorry."

"She was a competitive bitch," Dae says fiercely, and then his lips pull up in a bitter smile. "But she was *our* bitch."

Dex looks away. So does Rima.

Dae studies me. "Nora was devastated when Neve's death was announced in the Overworld."

I look down into my lap again, trying not to replay the image of Boone falling away from me.

"Artemis took me to her so I could speak with her," he says, and I lift my head. "Tell her the details of how it happened."

I like Dae more for having done that. Artemis, too, for that matter.

"And Samuel?" I ask again. "He's not—"

"He's still alive." Dex is the one to speak. "Barely. He was trying to hold off the mother while the rest of us returned the babies. Turns out that band of metal he wore around his wrist was Aegis, the shield. He used it to protect himself, and it got stuck in the mother chimera's serpent-tail mouth. He couldn't get it off. The lion head—" Dex grimaces.

"It ripped his hand right off."

My stomach turns queasy. I've seen videos of what lions do to their prey.

Which is when I notice that, while the others are visibly upset, Diego is sitting and just sort of smiling.

Zai must catch the drift of my thoughts, because he gives Diego a nudge, and Diego frowns in confusion at first, then a dawning sort of frustration. He's hardly spoken tonight. Maybe because he not only survived but is in the lead now.

"Sorry, Lyra," he says. "My prize for winning Demeter's Labor makes me feel no pain, physical but also mental. Including grief."

Oh. I have no idea what to say to that.

"Anyway," Dae says, "Samuel is still healing."

"I'm glad. He is a good man." I glance at Diego. I know he is, too, despite that mark.

"Is memory lane why you dragged us down here?" Dex demands harshly. "So you could catch up on all the things we've been put through while you've been taking a break—"

I lift my dress, not worrying about flashing them my underwear, and he blanches at the sight, the rest of his accusation pittering away.

Styx left its marks on me. It healed my flesh, but the solid black spiderweb-looking pattern is scorched into me for all to see. Front and back.

"You weren't the only ones fighting to stay alive." I hold his gaze until he glances away.

"Gods, Lyra." Zai shifts in his seat.

Rima folds her hands in her lap. "So why did you ask us down here?"

I lower my dress, smoothing it over my knees. Now for the hard part. "I have a story to tell, and then a...proposal to make to you all."

Dex surges to his feet. "If you think we are going to ally—"

I hold up a hand, cutting him off. "That's not the proposal."

86

SHOW ME WHO YOU ARE

I say what I have to say, then stay on the rooftop while the other champions return to Olympus. After they've gone, I drop to sit on one of the comfy couches and draw my knees up to my chest, wrapping my arms around them and staring sightlessly out over Erebos.

A shiver steals up my spine.

Not because of the breeze that ruffles my hair. It's perfect here. But because I don't know if I just handed my enemies a weapon against me... or not.

I gave them until tomorrow to think about my proposal.

"How did they take it?"

I jump a little at Hades' voice but don't turn my head. "Hard to say."

He comes around to sit on the cushioned ottoman facing me, with his elbows propped on his knees. "You told them that I would swear on the River Styx to honor my part?"

I nod.

His part. This was all my idea, or the Daemones would be down here ripping him a new one.

He promised me that if I win and he is made the King of the Gods, he will make sure all those who've perished in the Crucible will be given a choice. They can either be given a home in Elysium or, if they choose, be brought back from the Underworld with Boone. This applies to Neve and Isabel, as well as Dae's grandmother and anyone else who might die before this is all over.

If I win the next two Labors. *If* I make him king of the Overworld, too.

Being king of both will give him the power to cross souls between worlds.

"I know Dae's other gift now," I tell him. "He used it. That pendant on a chain around his neck is the Lantern of Diogenes."

Hades is silent a moment, considering. "So they all know you were speaking the truth."

"Yes."

"Then they'd be fools not to take your offer." He clasps his hands together. "All of them win this way."

I shrug. "Mortals."

Which makes his lips twitch. He's been doing that more lately. Smiling. My heart lifts a little at the sight.

"What fools they be," he murmurs. Shakespeare, I think. Not my best subject.

I prop my chin on my knees. "Gods aren't much better."

"You'll get no argument from me."

He lowers his gaze, staring at the floor, the streak through his hair falling over his forehead. I so want to brush it back, but that would be breaking one of our unspoken "we don't do that" rules.

"I want to show you something." He glances up, studying my face.

"Okay."

He hums—not amused, more surprised—and shakes his head a little.

"What?"

"Just so...trusting."

"I already told you I trust you. Why are you surprised?"

"I guess I'm not used to it from many people." He straightens slowly, and something in his face turns cautious. Then he sort of shakes himself out of it and gets to his feet, offering me a hand. "Come on."

I stare at that hand, warmth fluttering through my body to settle in my chest.

Touching. That breaks the unspoken rules.

He grunts impatiently, and I force myself to casually stand and put my hand in his. I try not to make a sound that gives away how good that single, simple point of contact feels.

A connection.

My vision and hearing blink out, only to blink back in faster than usual, and I find myself standing in a place even more beautiful than Erebos.

"Elysium," I breathe. He doesn't have to tell me. It's that obvious.

This part of the Underworld is also called the Isle of the Blessed—the place reserved for the most deserving of souls—the heroic, the pure, the kind. The champions, now, hopefully, no matter when they die. Although a few of them would be…interesting additions.

This place is beyond time, beyond measure, and beyond any words someone like me could ever hope to craft. Even poets would struggle.

"Want to see more?" he asks.

"Is it okay?"

His eyes twinkle back at me. "Yes. I think you'll find it interesting. Elysium is, for each soul, their perfect place."

"How?"

"Because I allow it." He's all arrogant mystery again. "Here. I'll show you."

We're suddenly standing on white beaches, looking out over crystal-blue waters, and there's a home made of glass that stretches out into the ocean. Then we're in a city. Paris, I think. It glows sort of pink in evening sunlight.

"Some see their homes from the Overworld. Some see the purest parts of what their imaginations can create."

We leave Paris, and what greets my eyes next makes me laugh out loud in wonder. "Wow," I whisper.

He grins, dimples in full view. And now I'm struggling to breathe right, because he's entirely himself in this moment. Who he was meant to be—the King of the Underworld who truly feels for the souls under his care. That he's letting me see him like this…

"It's a recreation of the game Candy Land," he says. "The little girl who lives here loves that game a lot."

Still reeling a little and reluctant to glance away from the openness of his face, I force myself to look back out over the view. I didn't get to play board games as a kid—chess or nothing for us pledges—but I've seen it. It was one of those things I imagined doing with friends someday, back when I still bothered to imagine such things. In this living version, I see the Peppermint Forest with what I'm guessing is Licorice Castle in the distance. "I bet the Gumdrop Pass is something."

He nods.

"Can I see what it would be like for me?"

THE GAMES GODS PLAY

Hades sighs. "A mortal's vision of their ideal place changes throughout the course of their lifetime. It is only solidified when their soul arrives in Elysium."

"Oh." It would have been nice to know. "Are you able to see what it could be if I died now?"

"Don't—" His throat works around a swallow. "Don't think about dying yet, hmmm?"

I offer a soothing smile. "I'm not planning to."

"Good."

"What about you?" I ask next. "Do you have a perfect place? I mean, being a god already and all."

He looks out over the lands and shrugs. "I see many things."

I'm not entirely sure that's an answer.

I take a last, long look, then turn to him. "Why are you showing me this?"

"Because whether the champions accept the proposal or not, this will be their home at the end, regardless of if they die in the Crucible or in old mortal age. And I'll make that true of every champion retroactively and moving forward. I promise you that much, Lyra. And..." He turns his head, looking out over Elysium, jaw clenching slightly. "If you don't win either of the next two...I wanted you to see that Boone will be fine."

Fine. He'll be fine. More than fine. In his own version of paradise. So will the others.

"What about their loved ones?" I ask. "They shouldn't be alone here."

"I can arrange that, too." Amusement filters through his voice.

"Can the souls here interact with one another?"

Hades sort of pauses. "Yes."

"How, if they're in their own versions of paradise?"

"If someone else has a similar or same paradise. There are whole families here together. Lovers, friends."

But only if it's the same paradise? So I might never see Boone's face again, and he knows it. He knew it when he visited me as his spectral self.

"You and Persephone made this place as incredible as I've ever seen," I say, still looking out. "And as lonely." That tells me a lot about both of them.

Hades goes still beside me. Did I hurt his feelings? Offend him?

"What *do* you see?" I ask again.

His shoulders ease slightly. "Maybe I'll show you one day."

But not today. He doesn't have to say it.

"Can we go back?" I ask.

"Of course." Immediately, we blink away, and when we arrive at his home, we're standing in the garden near one of the grottos. The small waterfall that hides the grotto fills the night with a soft gurgle. I've always loved the sound of running water.

I glance toward the lights of the house. Why'd he bring us here instead of there?

"I thought seeing Elysium would make you feel better." He's searching my face, or the side of it he can see.

"It does." I may not get to see him ever again, but Boone will be okay either way. That makes it...easier. I frown. "What if Boone doesn't want to leave there?"

It's paradise, after all. And he's more than just safe. He's well cared for. Why would he want to return to our world—

"I asked him."

"You...asked him." Slowly pivoting, I stare at Hades. I know I'm parroting his words, but they don't quite make sense.

Hades lets go of my fingers and shoves his hands in his pockets, and I can tell it's supposed to be a casual move. It's anything but. "When I brought him to you while you were sick, I asked him if he wanted to stay in Elysium or gain immortality as a god if that option became possible."

He asked him. Hades asked Boone, who he doesn't like very much, what he wanted. He offered to make him an immortal god if he wanted, if he could.

"Why did you ask?"

A shrug. "No soul should be forced into something they don't want or didn't earn. Especially if it has permanent consequences." He glances away with a muttered, "After all this time, I learned that the hard way."

Is he talking about...me?

I'm still hung up on the fact that he asked Boone at all.

He asked *for* me. And maybe it's incredibly conceited to assume, and I'm sure the whole no-forcing-a-soul thing is also a reason, but he did this for me. Unlike his helping Samuel heal, this time I know that thought isn't silly. I'm sure of it. He did this because I was hurting. And yet, he wanted to make sure that my selfish pain didn't override what Boone would choose for himself.

Hades is still trying to play it casual, but I can see the way his hands are fisting in his pockets.

An earthquake of tenderness for this god shakes my very foundations.

Forget the unspoken "don't"s. I'm about to break every single one of them.

87

I OFFER YOU A CHOICE...

I step into Hades, right into his personal space that we've both been so careful not to breach, flattening my palms against his chest. He goes so rigid, he could be a cold, carved marble version of himself. I ignore that as I go up on tiptoe and place a kiss right at the corner of his mouth.

A tiny, soft grunt escapes him.

Lowering, I don't take my gaze from his, holding his stare, which is all things wary but also watchful, taking in every nuance of me.

"Thank you," I whisper. "For all of that."

Never looking away, I back toward the pool behind me. At the same time, I slowly lift my yellow sundress up over my head, then drop it on the stone path of the garden. I'm not wearing a bra, and the perfect night air caresses my skin.

His gaze goes first to the black spider scar on my side, and I swear he's angry—it's infinitesimal, but I see it. But then, as if he can't help himself, his gaze roams the rest of me with eyes turning a predatory kind of hungry, changing from mercury to cut steel.

"What are you doing?" His voice is low, wary.

Those silvery eyes tell a different story. He's devouring me with his gaze. The heat of it is licking at my skin, even as he holds himself so fiercely still.

I smile. "I'm changing the rules of our game."

He takes a jerking step forward, hands coming out of his pockets to fist at his sides, frustration rippling over his features. "This isn't a game between us, Lyra."

I'm at the edge of the pool now, and I kick off my sandals. "I know. That's why I'm changing the rules."

THE GAMES GODS PLAY

He shakes his head. "I'm leaving."

Only he doesn't move. Not an inch. Not even turning his gaze away.

I turn my back to him, facing the water, and slip my panties off, kicking them to the side. My heart is pounding against the cage of my ribs so hard, he can probably hear it from way over there. I may be a smart-ass and a cursed thief. I may stand up to gods and do what I think is right at any moment, even if the consequences are not all that great for me. I've been called a fool by more than one person in my life.

But this is different. This is *true* vulnerability.

Not just because I'm exposed physically, but because I'm putting *me* on the line. I'm telling him in no uncertain terms that if he wants me, I'm his. Forget the impossibility of the future. I'll take what I can get in the here and now.

The Crucible has taught me that much.

It's Hades' choice now. He can still leave, turn away, reject what I'm offering.

That's going to hurt like a son of a bitch if he does.

But some risks are worth the painful consequences. This is one of them.

I glance over my shoulder to find him still standing. Watching. Jaw clenched and looking like a strong shove could shatter him. Forget trying to flirt with him outrageously. That's not me, not who I am. Instead, I offer him a sincere smile. Unlike every day of my life in the den, I don't hide what I'm feeling.

I let him see my need. But also affection, tenderness, and…hope.

And he flinches. Direct hit.

A muscle ticks at the side of his mouth. My god of death is holding himself back so hard. That knowledge makes me smile even more. At least he's not coldly unaffected, like I think he wants me to believe.

"I'm offering myself to you," I tell him. Just to be perfectly clear. "No deals. No quid pro quo. No expectations."

I pause, studying everything about him as that sinks in.

"Join me…or don't. Your choice." I turn away, closing my eyes against the horrible knowledge that he could very easily choose *don't*. Especially with the way he's fighting this. "But I would really love it if you joined me."

With that, I dive into the water.

Like everything else about this place, the water is perfect, cool but not cold, a rush of silk against my skin as I swim.

My heart is beating so fast, I have to come up sooner than I'd like just to take an extra breath. I'm trying to play it nonchalant as I go. I don't know if Hades is still there watching. He could have turned away.

I force myself to not look, to swim lazily along, into the entrance to the grotto. It's beautiful in here, too, the natural stone awash in lantern glow, and whatever it is on the cave ceilings over Styx that lights up like blue stars is in here, too.

But when I swim out, it feels more like I'm suspended above the Underworld in a private, fantastical floating sanctuary. And yet gloriously, uninhibitedly exposed.

And Hades isn't here.

He didn't follow.

I turn finally to look and immediately deflate at the aloneness. There's no one behind me, no disturbance of the water beyond what I'm making, no splash of sound within the grotto.

His answer is no.

He doesn't want me. Not enough.

I take a deep breath that pushes at the tightness of my chest and swim to the edge of the grotto, where the water spills over into another pool below, numb. As far away as I can get from the mountainside and him, I lay my arms across the top of the rock ledge, propping my chin on them with a sigh.

At least I picked a nice, private place to hide my hurt and humiliation. Believe it or not, I'm doing my best to focus on the second feeling and trying damn hard *not* to acknowledge the disappointment that's building a crushing sort of weight around my chest.

I've been alone most of my life. I do fine alone.

But this is different.

This meant something. More than just lust. Am I foolish to let it affect me this much? Probably. All the same arguments against giving in to this attraction are still there. They didn't disappear like dust in the wind just because he showed me a tiny piece of who he is deep down, just because he showed how he knows me, and supported me, and protected me, and took punishment for me.

And I proceeded to turn to mush.

"Damn," I whisper.

With no warning, strong arms steal around me and a bare chest presses against my back. Hades drops his forehead to the back of my head, and I hear him breathe me in. There's still resistance in him, in the inflexibility of his embrace, the unbending way he's holding himself.

"I need to know you realize what this can't be...and what it can," he growls.

A hard warning. A dark promise.

88

THE SURRENDER

E ven with Hades pressed against me, even with him fighting his desire, I need to be sure I know what he means.

"Tell me, just so we're clear," I murmur and can't help my smile.

I want so badly to lean into him, elation filling me in sharp bursts, but I make myself wait.

"I can't give you a future, Lyra," he says. "I can't care for you the way mortals need. It's not in me. But I want you."

Harsh. Direct. Real. I don't want to believe that's all it is for him, even with my curse, but I make myself. "That's clear enough."

Neither of us moves.

"You gave me a choice," he says, breath brushing over the back of my neck. "Now I'm giving you one."

I close my eyes and make my own demand. "I need to know that the only reason you're here right now is because you want me. *Me.* That I mean enough to you to make you need this even when there are so many reasons we shouldn't. Even when my curse doesn't allow for more. Even when this might be the only time and neither of us can give anything beyond this."

"I want you," he says. "Though I'm damning us both with it."

Is he still fighting this? I won't push him more than I already have. I've made my choice and made it clear.

After a taut moment of silence, he doesn't lift his head, but his arms tighten slowly, drawing me back against his flesh, which is hot enough to warm the water around us. He pulls my body flush against his, then trails a single, teasing, questing touch down my belly to the soft curls at the juncture of my thighs.

With the lightest, most frustrating of brushes, he sends that single finger over the spot that makes my body hum.

I drop my head back against his shoulder on a gasp, and a lightning flash of his emotion charges through me.

Satisfaction and need that is nearly overwhelming. And something else. A determined sort of control.

It's gone before I can hold on to it, but it only makes what he's doing with his hand, the thickness of the shaft pressed into my backside, that much...more.

Over and over, and oh gods, over again, he teases. Until I'm moving my hips to chase his fingers. Until my breath hitches in my throat. Until I raise my arms up and behind me to wrap around his neck, anchoring us together.

I might have expected this to be fast and hard. But tender and teasing—gods, I'm already coming undone.

His free hand trails up my ribs to tease the underside of my breast before moving up to cup it, and then he barely brushes over my nipple. Desire sizzles from that touch to the throbbing point where his other finger still teases.

Then that questing finger dips lower, parts me, slips inside me, testing me, and I couldn't hold back the moan if I wanted to. Not that I want to.

He stops there, finger buried in me. Tormenting me.

"Don't stop now," I demand. Mewl, even. That's what he does to me.

I sense his smile, and then he presses a sweet, claim-staking kiss to the nape of my neck that I feel like a brand. He's marking me as his. Different from the kiss of blessing on my lips. This isn't about protection.

"There are a thousand reasons we shouldn't... *I* shouldn't..." he whispers, that rough voice rubbing against my senses. "But I want you, Lyra. I've wanted you for a long time..."

He takes a shuddering breath against me, all leashed power and desire. Utter determined control.

His fingers move over me, one teasing, one sliding out, drawing a tremor from my flesh. "I want you the way stars burn." Another move of those torturous fingers, back in, but it's his words that are driving me higher. "I want you in the way a storm gathers over mountains only to give in to violent release."

Finger still buried in me, he brushes his thumb over that spot that makes me quiver. But it's his words that curl around my heart and make it beat faster. It's knowing he wants me that way—me, someone who has been invisible and unwanted all my life—that makes me quiver for him. Whimper for him.

Yearn for him.

His lips move to the spot just behind my ear. "I want you in the way the first mortals in the wilderness found their like in each other and... *hungered*."

The last word is a promise-filled purr that captures me so fully, I want to hear that sound for the rest of my short, mortal life.

"Good," I sigh into his tormenting touch, then drop a hand to slip it behind me, between us, wrapping it around him and squeezing, reveling in the way he groans against my skin. "Then we want each other the same way."

I've never touched anyone this way before, and yet it's so...natural.

The feel of him in my hand is silk-covered iron, and the way he pulses—I made him feel that.

Wondering... I pump my hand once. Twice.

The way his entire body goes rigid before he groans makes me smile my own satisfaction. "Now what I want...is for you to stop holding back."

He stills. I can hear the harsh in and out of his breath, his chest pressing against me in time. He's still fighting for control. Then, "I don't want to hurt you. If I lose control—"

I grip him tighter and revel in his groan. "I want you to fucking *break* me."

"Fuck, Lyra—"

He moves out of my grip and pulls his own hands away all of a sudden, and I barely have time for my heart to drop, thinking he's stopping this, before he grips my hips, so urgent his fingers dig in hard as he spins me to face him, and I suck in at the sight of his eyes. Molten, liquid silver.

The sight makes my heart stutter, heat and something more filling those beautiful eyes—hells, his entire being—with a light that makes every part of me hot.

I have a single heartbeat to absorb all those impressions before he captures my mouth in a kiss that turns to wildfire at the first spark of lips against lips.

A restlessness consumes me—consumes us both, I think—as his hands are everywhere, caressing every part of me, lingering when he makes me gasp. Teasing mercilessly when he makes me moan.

And with each new discovery, with the feel of his hands on me and him under mine, we both turn more frantic. If we only have what little he can give, what we can both give, then I'm taking everything I can and offering him everything in return.

But soon my restless energy isn't soothed by hands and mouth alone. I want *more*.

"Hades," I moan, winding my arms around his neck, practically crawling up his body to wrap my legs around his waist.

I gasp when he suddenly lifts me out of the water and sets me on the top of the rock ledge, which is about a foot thick. Instinct has me glancing over my shoulder. The drop behind me seems to go on forever, sheer and deadly. I cling to his arms as my stomach clenches, and when I face him again, I'm breathing hard, eyes wide, only to have my heart pound even faster at the intensity of the satisfaction on his face.

And another bolt of his emotions crackles through me.

Fascination.

"I knew it." He breathes the words. "Danger makes you fight, makes you alive, sets your senses on fire."

Because you see me.

I think he's always seen the real me. Because he's a god, or maybe the god of death, or maybe this is just who Hades is. He sees me.

The same way I see him.

He reaches up and cups the back of my head, bringing my lips down to his, as if my response only jacked his own desire up another notch. This kiss is hard, demanding. He nips at my lower lip and soothes it with his tongue, then draws back. And I'm moaning into his mouth and trying to climb back down to him.

He's right. Even now, my body feels so...*primal*. I am like our mingled breaths, like air, floating and flying and alive at his will.

He pulls away sharply, slashes of red over his cheekbones. "Lean back."

A command.

When I immediately obey, all the answering fire in him coalesces into a look that is all things wild heat and wicked teasing and tender adoration.

My heart stutters at the adoration.

"Hold on to me, my star," he warns. "And don't let go."

89

MAKE ME

Before I can guess at what he's going to do, he presses my legs apart and lowers his head. I'm leaned out over the drop as I cling to his arms, his hands holding me by the waist, and his mouth...

His mouth.

With that sinful tongue, he laps at the heart of me. He takes all the sensation we've been building together and intensifies it, ratchets it up until my body is pulsing. He slips a finger inside me, then another, stretching me, moving them in time to what he's doing with his mouth, his tongue.

And oh...gods...

The explosion of sensation blindsides me. No warning. I go off like a *bang*, and I cry out as everything about me draws in hard before rushing outward. I cry out again when he suddenly lifts me off the ledge, pulling me hard into him.

"Wrap your legs around me. Now."

I do, and, staring into my eyes, he lowers me until the swollen, jutting tip of his cock presses against where I'm slick with the pleasure he's already given me. I'm still pulsing with it. His dimples appear in full force as he offers me a wicked grin.

Then he's pressing into me, stretching me, filling me.

He pauses. Once. Letting me adjust, letting my body settle. Then, like he can tell I'm ready, he keeps going until he's deep inside me, and my world narrows to a new reality. A place where we are joined.

He buries his face in my neck, taking a deep, rasping breath. Then he jerks his head up and claims my lips again.

He kisses me until I can't breathe, until breathing seems like a secondary need anyway. But then something feels different around me. I open my eyes to find we're no longer in the water but lying in one of the beds. Sheer white curtains drift around us as he settles deeper inside me, his weight over me only adding to the sense of being claimed.

His hands, free to move now that he doesn't have to hold me, stroke along the outsides of my thighs in frantic brushes, as if he's painting me, memorizing me by touch.

"Be careful what you ask for, my star," he warns.

My body contracts at those words, eagerness billowing inside me. Satisfaction whips across his features a heartbeat before he moves.

Not slow. Not teasing. Not leashed.

If I thought he'd already let go, this is something else entirely. His movements are...ruthless. Driven. And desperate. I squirm beneath him, wrapping my legs around him to hold on. But the more he loses control, the more I do the same.

I lose myself in him. In the feel of him. The strength. In the way he watches my face to see my reaction to each move, each touch.

When I rake my nails down his back, he throws his head up on a growl of pleasure. A smile that is a warning slides across his mouth, and then he's taking my hands in an unmerciful grip, stretching my arms above my head.

My eyes go wide, and his laugh is near feral.

Then, still buried deep inside me, he lowers his head and takes one nipple into his mouth and sucks. Hard. Then bites.

And I about come off the bed.

The rough stroke of his tongue against that sensitive tip that comes next, though—I can't help but arch into it more, chasing the sensation. He doesn't stop until I teeter on the precipice. That's when he lifts his head.

"What?" I groan. "Wait. Don't stop."

Another feral grin, his hair disheveled over his forehead—from my fingers running through it, I realize. "I'm going to make you wait and want, the way I have been all this time."

Oh. My. Gods.

He positions himself on his knees, his hands at my hips lifting me, changing the angle, and thrusts.

I cry out, every nerve ending alive as he rears back, then thrusts again. Harder.

"Fuck."

And that sends him pitching forward to grab at the headboard. Straining. Gaze never straying from mine, he pistons his hips. Fast. Hard.

Suddenly, smoke rises all around us, the scent laced with the bitter dark chocolate that is just...him. By the way his eyes intensify, I know that this is his power, but out of his control. The smoke forms into tendrils.

And the tendrils...reach for me.

They touch me.

Every part of me. Soft and tender. A slide like silk. Harder, more aggressive. They touch me everywhere. As if only using his corporeal body isn't enough. As if he's so impatient to explore every part of me, bring me every pleasure possible, that this was the only way.

I don't know if it's him or the smoke that plays with the pulse point at the juncture of my thighs, but it's like having the heat of his mouth on me all over again. Moans tumble out of me as the sensation builds and builds, drawing me closer to bliss.

But it's his eyes, devouring my reactions I don't bother to hide from him, that truly catapult me higher.

With everything I am, I pour the sensations he's creating in me back into him. I pour my need back into him. I pour my heart back into him.

This might be our only time, my only moment like this with him. Is he thinking the same thing? Is he determined to revel in it, and damn tomorrow and any consequences? The edge of desperation makes me want it to be everything. For both of us.

For the woman who has always craved love.

But also for the god who stands so very alone, managing the eternity of the souls under his care with more heart than any other god has shown us mortals.

His touch, against me, inside me, and everywhere, is like fire that threatens to both consume and to renew, burning at his will.

Like Hades himself.

"Please," I whisper against his mouth. I'm so far gone at this point, I'm not even sure what I'm asking for.

But he seems to know.

We both reach for a kiss, each capturing the other's sounds of pleasure with our mouths.

For a tiny second, I think this is too much. Too intense. Too *necessary*, as if I won't be able to breathe without him after this.

Hades rears back, and his eyes go wide with a glimmering of what I think might be shock—and then their molten grey depths start to glow. "Lyra—"

A smile curves my lips. I did that. I made a god who values his control above all else completely lose it. He growls low in his chest before leaning down to nip at my neck, his hips never breaking rhythm until we *both* break.

The rush comes then and threatens to obliterate me, slamming through and cresting over me, tumbling me over and over and over. Hades gathers me closer as he follows me into the torrent on a shout. And I swear obsidian-tipped flames rise up in the smoke all around us.

Pleasure batters at us but then slowly eases, drawing us back down until we are like castaways thrown upon a shore the morning after a storm with the waves gently lapping at us.

And as the smoke dissipates, everything else about the world drifts away until it no longer exists for me—pain, fear, the past, the future, the gods and champions, the Overworld and Underworld, Olympus.

All of it is irrelevant in this moment. In this incandescent melding of bodies, minds, hearts, and souls.

Hades gathers me closer, burying his face in my hair as we breathe together. This time, his emotions, when they come, pour into me sweetly—unending, incandescent pleasure, a shattering kind of wonder, and soul-deep possessiveness.

I'm his. My heart claims him back as we cling to each other. Even if he can't go beyond tonight.

PART 7

MY ONLY HOPE

Victory or the grave.
Death wins either way.

90

THE ANSWER IS NO

To say that slipping into blissful sleep wrapped in your lover's arms on a mountainside…only to wake up alone in your own cold bed is disorienting would be an understatement.

I didn't expect cuddles and declarations of undying love. Obviously. Well…mostly. What my secret heart wants—for last night to have *meant* something—is a revelation that isn't a thunderbolt. It's soft, like butterfly wings.

This is different from my crush on Boone. That was a lonely girl's innocent feelings, someone who simply wanted a connection and his was the only friendly face in the crowd. But with Hades…it's something else.

With Hades, it's still a connection, but it's also protection, tenderness, and survival. It's danger, frustration, and all his damned secrets and trusting him anyway. It's fairness and respect and understanding.

It's seeing and being truly seen in return.

And maybe…maybe it could be more.

Which is why this morning is jarring to say the least. Yes, we were both clear about what last night was, but this feels like either running or abandonment. I mean…not even a note?

Okay. Benefit of the doubt, I tell myself. Maybe Hades wanted to give me a little privacy. Or he's asking the staff for my favorite foods for breakfast. Or he likes to shower early in the morning. I've decided that if gods eat, sleep, and fuck, then they must shower. Although that instantly-dressed-and-styled snap thing might indicate otherwise.

Or he knows today is the next Labor and I need to focus.

Except my head is entirely with Hades. And I can't make that stop while I shower and dress, which I do with more haste than care, at least until I'm checking my vest. That, I take my time to go over carefully. Thankfully, Hades got my axe back from Hephaestus for me. I'd left it pinning that automaton's tentacle in the window.

But Hades isn't at breakfast, either. Charon and Cerberus are.

I give Ber's head a scratch before I get myself toast and tea. Pretty sure my stomach wouldn't appreciate more for a lot of very good reasons.

Charon eyes my plate when I sit. "Hades would understand if you decided not to do this after all," he says, almost casually, popping a slice of apple in his mouth and chewing.

"I know."

"Boone would understand as well."

"I know that, too."

Charon breathes in and out audibly, sandy hair falling into his eyes. He's hated this plan for me to win the next two Labors since the moment we told him about it. A growled "the fuck you are" was a pretty clear indicator, which made Hades stare him down coldly. He only eased up about it when I explained it was my idea, but Charon has remained against it.

I grin. "You're a bit of a mother hen, you know?"

Rus lets out a woofy wheeze of a laugh that fills the room with the strong odor of smoke. Cer and even Ber join in when Charon pushes the eggs around on his plate with a grumble.

Then Ber swings up to look past me before nudging the other two heads. I don't need to look. I knew Hades was there before the dog did, as if my body is so attuned to him now that I could be a Hades location app.

Charon looks past me as well. "Tell Lyra not to do this."

I also turn slowly…to encounter a wall of absolute indifference.

He looks *through* me. I might as well be one of the dead souls down here, I'm so invisible in this moment. And if anyone knows what invisible feels like, it's me.

Only this is so much worse.

Like razors over my skin, leaving a thousand little cuts.

"Lyra knows what she's doing and what she wants," Hades tells Charon.

"Do *you*, Phi?" Charon demands. Then he levers to his feet, chair scraping against the stone floor with a protesting screech. "Don't screw this up just because—"

He cuts himself off when Hades' expression goes utterly blank, his voice bored when he speaks. "She is my concern, not yours. Feel free to fuck right off."

I lean back at that. I may not have spent a lot of time around them, but that is *not* how these two talk to each other.

With a lethal scowl, Charon shoves his plate across the table and then disappears. Cerberus snorts at Hades before he follows, leaving me alone with him.

His jaw might as well be hewn from granite. After a second, he looks at me like he has to force himself to. "Ready?"

That's it?

That's...*it*?

Screw that. Why is he being so weird? As far as he's concerned, we had phenomenal, consensual, no-strings-attached sex and that's all. Being a dick to me now is not required. I already understood the assignment.

"Absolutely." I abandon my breakfast on the table and cross the terrace...and I deliberately don't stop until I'm right in front of him, close enough that a deep breath would brush my breasts against his chest. Then I hold up a hand in the air, like I'm pressing it to the invisible, glass wall of distance he's erected between us, higher and thicker than before.

I wait.

I wait for him to look me in the eyes, and when he does, I smile. *Just treat me like you have before*, I'm saying with that smile.

For the briefest of seconds, his own expression gentles, and there's a lightning flash of tender need curling through me.

But in the next instant, it's all gone, scorched away under a diamond-hard determination that makes no sense. He presses his palm to mine, and we blink out of existence. When we blink back in, we're standing in the front courtyard of his residence in Olympus. But he doesn't step back. And he doesn't lower his hand.

We stand there, close together, palm to palm, and I stare into eyes that show me a mere glimpse of the battle raging within him. A battle that is well beyond the folly of a god and a mortal getting involved.

What in the hellfires is going on with him?

I open my mouth to ask, but his gaze lifts above my head and the familiar mask of the closed, brooding god of death slips into place.

"Are you here to speak to Lyra?" he asks.

I look over my shoulder, breaking the connection of our hands and feeling as if Atropos cut the line of our fates in that instant.

But I can't let any of that show because Rima is standing just inside the gate, watching.

Rima. None of the others. Not even my allies.

"Yes," she says, looking between Hades and me.

"Good luck in the next Labor," he says to me, gaze aimed at my forehead, before walking away.

I look at the ground, everything focused on the sound of his feet getting farther and farther away. I hear a small click—the door to the house opening. Then a pause.

"Don't die, Lyra," he says quietly.

After what almost sounded like a plea, the snick of the door closing behind him feels oddly final, and I can't contain my flinch.

Rima approaches, and I force myself to look at her. Focus on her. She glances between me and the door as if she worries that if she gets too close, Hades will reappear and punish her for interrupting us. The fear in her eyes is unmistakable and impossible to ignore.

"He won't hurt you," I assure her.

Her gaze, deep-brown eyes almost consumed by the black of her pupils, settles on me. She shakes her head, and I don't know if she's rejecting what I said or something else.

"I am here to tell you that we all discussed your proposal."

I figured. I can also tell by her expression that the answer didn't swing my way.

A new heaviness joins the weight that's been slowly growing since the moment I woke up alone this morning.

This weight is different, though—made of guilt, disappointment, and desperation.

"The answer is no?" I ask, and my voice threatens to crack, but I control it.

"That is correct."

"All of you?" My allies didn't want to come tell me themselves? I don't ask about that. It would show weakness.

"Also correct."

My lungs let go of all their air, and my shoulders round over as my heart shrivels. "Do you mind if I ask why?"

Her back goes ramrod straight. "Zai wanted to deliver this news himself. But I insisted I be the one to tell you. We are saying no...because of me."

I frown. "You? Why? It's a good deal for everyone—"

"My blessing from Apollo is the gift..." She says the last word with a dubious burr in her voice. "Of prophecy."

Wow.

And...okay? "I don't see how—"

"The problem is, I can't control the gift. It chooses what to show me." She makes a face. "This has not been helpful throughout the Labors because my gift shows me the same thing...only one vision...over and over."

Dread oozes through me like stagnant water through a bog. "What does it show you?"

"Hades as King of the Gods."

"I know you don't want that," I say slowly, "but it's nothing to fear. He is good—"

"In my vision, he is in a towering rage...and burning down the world." She says this starkly, with a tremor in her voice that becomes visible in her hands, her face turning pale and sort of green. Her fear is so heightened, she can't hold it in. "And no one—not mortals, not the Greek gods, not any other gods—can stop him."

91

ATHENA'S LABOR

"Welcome to your eleventh challenge, champions."

Athena stands before us, beautiful and yet still martial in a white pantsuit with shoulder pads that the fashionistas of the 1980s would envy. Her smile is more scary than reassuring. Honestly, I find Athena intimidating as fuck. I can't say that rejoining the Crucible on her round was what I would have picked. Hera's with the stars-and-constellations thing definitely would have been better.

The other champions watched me warily when I arrived, Samuel included. He's swaying a bit and ashen, but on his feet. No golden band around his one good wrist that I saw.

I nodded at them all, hoping they'd see that I understood why they couldn't take me up on my offer. My allies, though... They apologized, and I had to stand there silently sending mental *I'm sorry*s to Boone even as I reassured my team that I understood.

Which I do. I really do. But now I have to beat them at this labor, because I'm still going to try to win. Which I hope *they* understand.

They're standing beside me now, at least, which is something.

"Everyone believes Ares to be the bloodthirsty god," Athena says.

Then she makes a fist, slamming it down through the air, and a spear appears in her grasp, hitting the stone floor with a ringing, metallic clang. Immediately, her white suit changes to armor, the same that she wore the day the champions had to earn our gifts.

That seems like eons ago. A lifetime lived between then and now.

On her silver breastplate, an olive tree grows with a snake winding up its trunk. Her helm is that of an owl's head, the horned features forming slashes above her brow, and owl feathers emerge from the top and back in a warrior's headdress.

Her face is painted in runes and glyphs of glittering white. She holds a simple spear in one hand, and around her neck dangles a pendant. I'm guessing it's an image of the Gorgoneion for protection. She's known to wear it.

The goddess of both knowledge and war stands before us.

The four Daemones, positioned in each corner of the platform, immediately drop to one knee, heads bowed, fists over their chests.

"Rise," she says.

Um...weren't they supposed to be neutral for the Labors? Judges? I can't say I love this little byplay. The way the other champions shift on their feet, I'm pretty sure they're thinking the same thing.

Athena snaps her fingers, and all our gods appear at our sides. Hades puts his hand on my shoulder, and we blink out. When we blink back in, we are no longer standing in Olympus. Before I can take a breath, Hades is gone again.

Which is when the roar of the crowds hits me like a freezing-cold wave cresting over my head and forcing me under.

I try not to stumble back as where we are sinks in.

The Roman Colosseum, only not like any picture I've ever seen of the ruins.

We are standing on a podium built into the stands where I suppose Caesars of old sat with their family and sycophants, and around us, the vestiges of the original building rise. The areas where rock has been weathered and crumbled away is now reformed or filled in by...opaque glass.

The entire structure has been rebuilt this way, forming stadium seating and completing the walls with their arched doorways and windows, and a rounded roof—all of frosted glass—I'm guessing to block mortal eyes while letting sunlight filter through.

The place is packed.

The stands are teeming, but not with mortals. Instead, it appears all the immortals of the ancient Greek world—gods, demigods, nymphs, satyrs, and more—are here to watch in person. They seem to me like a pit of vipers, ready to coil, strangle, and strike. Just like we're at a football game, the immortals yell and scream our names. Some carry banners cheering on their favorite champion.

I don't see a single one with my name or Hades' butterfly on it.

Turquoise flags with Athena's symbol of an owl fly overhead, but here, she goes by her Roman name—Minerva. Her flags are interspersed with flags of the other major Olympian gods and their Roman names: Jupiter, Neptune, Juno, Venus, Mercury, Apollo, Diana, Mars, Vulcan, Bacchus, Ceres. Even a single black flag for my god, Pluto.

I'm shocked Athena is allowed to hold this here. Mortals will know something is going on. Or maybe from the outside it's enchanted to look and sound no different than usual?

You have bigger worries right now, Lyra.

The Colosseum floor, which is also glass but completely clear, allows us to see the tunnels underneath, where gladiators and prisoners used to be held before their trials and fights above. The rock columns are filled in with glass, too, making a flat surface here at the stadium level but allowing me to see what looks like several levels of floors descending into the pits that together create...

A maze.

Multiple levels of it.

I fucking have this! I've grown up living in a maze—the tunnels under my city. I spent my childhood exploring all the parts of it.

This, I can do.

This, I can win!

"No!" The cry comes from Trinica. Horror twists her features as she shrinks away from something behind me so fast, she slams into Zai and they both stumble. But that has the rest of us looking, and I have to clap a hand over my mouth to stop from vomiting up my toast and tea.

There, on spikes, are the heads of the champions we've lost, skin sallow, eyes cloudy with death, and mouths open as if they are screaming.

Neve. Isabel. But also Dae's grandmother...and Boone.

His cold, dead eyes stare down at me.

"It's an illusion," Jackie says.

She knows because she sees past illusions and glamours. I found that out because apparently she used it more openly during Hera's Labor, Deimos and Phobos having no effect on her.

I stare at the heads in revulsion. An illusion—like so many of the horrors we've endured—but the effect is no less real. Like the dragon's fire. I know Athena is playing the mental game with this move. I know it, but I just can't let it stand. Especially when Rima silently reaches for Dae's trembling hand.

I whirl on Athena in a snarl that would do Hades proud. "You're a monster."

The entire stadium gasps and, I swear, shifts back as one. Because they know. That's a statement that should get me cursed in a way only the gods and goddesses have a talent for.

"Kill her!" an immortal with a vile sense of justice yells from the now-silent crowd.

"What's wrong with Dex?" I hear Jackie mutter to my right.

Next to her, Dex is bouncing on his toes, mumbling "kill her, kill her" in a singsongy voice until Rima elbows him.

No one else takes up the call.

Athena merely smiles. "War and knowledge are both hard-won, hard-fought, harsh realities that you mortals don't seem to be able to stomach. And yet they still exist. Unavoidable, inescapable, and as necessary as breathing."

"It doesn't have to be that way," I argue. I've screwed myself already, so what's a little more? "Only monsters, fiends, the willfully ignorant, and demons make the world that way."

She tilts her chin down just slightly, eyes molten gold. "Call me a monster one more time, little mortal."

I'm pretty sure the "ignorant" part is what pissed her off most.

I manage to keep my mouth shut, but I don't stop glaring at her, my hands curling and uncurling at my sides.

Her smile turns smug. A taunt.

One that makes me mentally take a step back. Does she *want* me to challenge her? Holy shit, I think she does. She wants me to give her a reason to punish me that the Daemones can't say is interference. What she doesn't want is me competing. That's why Boone is up there.

Dex must have told her about the deal I offered...and about why.

I knew he'd be the godsdamned leak. Did he make some kind of deal with her? He is, after all, her champion.

When I say and do no more, she forms a disappointed pout before stalking past me and the others to the first of the spikes, where she picks up a large, clear, covered bowl filled with spiders. She takes the lid off and holds it under Boone's head, catching the blood that's dripping down as if he was only just killed minutes ago.

Revulsion is a slap to the face as the spiders immediately start growing. Athena dumps them into the glass maze below us, where they scuttle off, continuing to get bigger and bigger.

"Ooh, pretty," Dex says, still in that odd voice.

I glance at his face, dark eyes glossy with fervor. What is going on with him?

Athena follows the spiders with a bowl of scorpions grown with Neve's blood, then a bowl of bullet ants grown with Isabel's blood, and finally a nest of hornets with Dae's grandmother's blood.

All these creatures go into the glass maze.

Athena doesn't waste time with long explanations.

"Get out if you can. You may not use a relic of any kind to skip running the maze, just to survive it. If you can't find your way out in an hour..." She points to a massive digital clock set to sixty minutes. "Then you'll be left down there to suffocate or for the bugs to eat. The first champion out wins."

92

CREEPY AS FUCK

At the snap of Athena's fingers, I'm no longer standing on the platform. I'm in the pit of glass and rock—at the very bottom, probably, because the floor here is sandy, crunching beneath my shoes. The air is stale, unmoving. At least it feels like there's air in here, though Athena did say "suffocate," so I'm guessing it will only last so long.

The cheering of the crowd is more like a faint buzz in the background. Mostly, I hear the sound of my own breathing. None of the other champions are anywhere near me that I can tell. And I can't use my pearls to get out faster. Pretty sure Athena added that rule just for me.

A noise like feet running—no, it's more like feet scuttering over sand and rock—whizzes by. Maybe in the next tunnel, because nothing is here with me. Yet.

At another scuttering overhead, I look up to see at least ten different bugs crawling around the levels above, their many legs clicking against glass floors. I frown at the underside of the maze directly above my head. That glass looks scored. For us to run easier? Or for the bugs to?

A splatter of yellow goo from overhead has me scrambling back just in time to see the underside of Zai's feet as he runs by with the Harpe of Perseus clutched in his white-knuckled hands.

Move, Lyra. He's already trying to win. He's already gotten up a level.
I hate that I have to think that way at all.

Right or left? I choose right, and only a short way in, the path turns to shadows as it twists and turns beneath the stadium, until the light is blocked completely. I'm about ten steps into the pitch black, navigating by touch, when they come.

Spiders.

Out of the darkness.

Which is when I run into a web. Already they've laid a trap that covers the entire width of the tunnel. I manage to swallow my yelp of surprise, but my touching the web sets them off. With a tapping and odd sort of squeaking that reminds me of my tarantula, I'm covered in spiders the size of my fists.

I can't see, but they are all over me.

Thank you, Order of Thieves, for the torturous training that means bugs don't bother me. I saw the kind of spiders Athena used. Nothing deadly. Painful at this size if they bite, probably, but my flesh won't rot off.

Eyes and mouth closed, holding my breath, I form my hands into flat, closed-fingered blades and slide them along my arms, knocking them off me. A sudden sting of pain on my neck makes me flinch, and thank the gods this isn't Artemis' Labor with the fear, pain, and confusion overtaking me, because that would suck worse.

Forcing myself to move carefully, I knock that spider off, too. But then a second, less painful sting hits my ankle through my pantleg.

I frown. They shouldn't be biting me. I'm not being antagonistic. I'm not wiggling, screaming, moving, or crushing them. These aren't aggressive spiders.

I back up while I keep knocking them away. Another bite at my hip. And they keep coming. More and more of them. This is an attack.

Almost like it's planned.

My heart rate kicks up, adrenaline hitting my blood, and I have to control my breathing because they're on my face. I back away faster.

I'm still trying not to act aggressively toward them, but another bite, and I know that's not working. So I cross my hand over my chest and, in a violent swipe, throw as many off my arms as I can. At the same time, I turn and run, flinching and twitching and slapping at myself all the way.

Back into sunlight, past it, and into the darkness on the other side. Not quite as bad, though. At least I can see where I'm going.

The squeaking and clacks of the spiders' fangs and skittering of their feet on the glass behind me is the creepiest fucking sound. I don't stop running, even as two more bite me on the legs. The little yelping noises I'm making bounce off the glass. Hands flying, I knock more spiders off as I sprint down hallways, not caring where. Turn after turn. And they're still following.

This isn't working.

Yanking back my sleeve, I awaken the fox and panther, who leap from my flesh, becoming real to run with me. "Help!"

That's when the tarantula does something that feels like she's crawling under my very flesh, which, given what I'm dealing with, almost makes me lose my shit. But I look down instead to find her waving frantically at me.

She wants to be released. Of course—how could I forget Aphrodite's challenge?

I touch her, and she springs from my body. Only this time, she grows beyond the normal size of her species. The skittering behind me stops dead, the silence palpable. Enough that I stumble to a halt and turn to watch as my tarantula, now big enough to fill most of the tunnel, faces down at least thirty spiders of varying sizes, from my fist to that of a large dog. They aren't on the walls of the tunnel, just the floor, but they cover it in a moving, wriggling sea of blacks and browns, with their eyes—all those eyes—trained on my tarantula.

She moves the smaller appendages near her mouth and vibrates. A few of the other spiders move as well, like they're waving at each other. Some scrape appendages together, making a scratchy noise. Others clack or squeak, and there is a vibration in the air that I can *feel*. It slithers over my body in invisible waves.

They are communicating.

I have no idea what my tarantula says to them, but eventually, they scurry away in the other direction. She shrinks a little so she can turn in the tunnel to face me.

"I have promised them that you will not kill any spiders in this maze." Her voice is bizarre, like scratches and hums at the same time, but I can understand her. *"In exchange, the spiders will not attack you."*

I am still smarting and bleeding in a few spots, and I'll probably start itching and swelling, given the size of the bites. I nod. "You have my word."

"The other bugs down here, I cannot help with."

"Thank you." I offer my arm, and she returns.

Now I have to figure out what's next. Hopefully, my unaimed running didn't get me lost or send me deeper into the tunnels.

"Please, help me find the way out," I say to the fox and panther. "Watch out for more bugs."

They don't hesitate, loping off down the tunnel. I follow at a jog. We hit a T in the maze fairly quickly.

"Go." I point in opposite directions.

Then I wait there. I close my eyes to force my racing heart and thoughts to slow down and focus. To center on my senses. To ignore my spider bites. The air to the right is cooler and a little sweeter. Barely.

A clattering of legs coming toward me stands the hair up on my neck, and I spin around just as a bullet ant lunges.

93

CRYSTAL LABYRINTH

With a snarl, the panther leaps over my head, just avoiding the glass ceiling, and comes down on top of the bullet ant. The cat's powerful jaws sink into the back of its armored skull with a sickening crunch.

Axe in hand, I drop my arms to my sides in a sort of anticlimactic realization. My animals can fight for me as well as direct me? Hades didn't say anything about that, but I should have guessed. Very handy.

My panther comes away with greenish goo around her muzzle, which she proceeds to spit out, pawing at her own face.

Above me, Samuel runs by, looking closely at a copper disc of some kind in his hands. Hades said he won Hephaestus' Labor. The prize was a compass that always points the way to go. A lot like Meike's mirror.

With a chuff, my panther runs past me in the direction the fox went. I follow, axe in hand.

We come across the fox making his way back to us, and he turns to run in the same direction. More running and following.

We run until we come to another T, one way leading up, the other on the same level. We do the same thing, just to be sure, but this one seems obvious. Sure enough, the fox returns first, and we head upward, after the panther.

We emerge onto the second level. This one is all glass, the level between the stone maze below my feet and the top level above. Sunlight dissipates the shadows here…and I can see bugs everywhere, running this way and that. I catch sight of several of the other champions, too, and when I look up, I see faces in the immortal crowd filled with bloodlust and fascination, their cheers audible even down here.

I block all of that out and focus on only what's directly in front of me. Solve one problem, then the next. And every single second, I'm expecting to hear Hades' voice offering advice. Or maybe his butterfly showing me the way.

But I don't.

I'm standing at another crossroads when a pounding on the glass has me whirling, heart thudding harder, crouched and ready to defend. But I find Trinica standing under my feet.

I drop to my knees as she stares up at me.

"Which way?" Her voice is slightly garbled through the floor.

Because of the clear tunnels, it's impossible to tell if I've been in that section before. I point. "That way, I think. But I'm not sure."

Easy to get turned around in here with the glass.

She frowns, hands going to her hips. "You're not sure? Or you're not helping me now that you need to win?"

I give her a look. "I wouldn't *not* help you."

After a second, she looks down at her shoes, then back up at me. "Okay. I believe you."

I'm not sure she does. "You can do this. The way you should go always feels a little cooler and smells sweeter. It's subtle," I tell her.

"Subtle. Great."

I put my palm to the glass. "I'll see you on the outside."

Which is when a wicked, stinger-tipped tail rears up out of the shadows behind her. "Scorpion!" I yelp.

Immediately, she scrambles straight up, using gauntlets at her wrists and ankles to climb the walls to the ceiling with apparent ease. Her gift from Hephaestus, I assume. The scorpion scuttles by underneath her, then tries to climb up after her, only to slip on the smooth walls. It can't reach her with its tail, either.

Trinica, hanging upside down, grins at me. "Thank the gods those and the spiders can't climb glass—or the spiders not without webs, at least." She makes a face. "The hornets and the ants, however…"

Giving up, the scorpion keeps going, and Trinica drops to the ground. With a wave, she runs off in the other direction.

Which is when a sensation like being shot with a gun point-blank, like a metal bullet shredding through my flesh, strikes me in the thigh before my panther tackles the bullet ant away from me.

Already on my knees, I clutch my leg and rock back and forth as I try to breathe through agony. "Fuck," I mutter. "They weren't kidding around when they named those things."

The bug is dead in seconds, but I am dying more slowly over here. I expect to see blood leaking out of me, but I don't. Because it wasn't a real bullet, just a stinger the size of my thumb.

The panther prowls over and noses at me, as if to say she's sorry she didn't get to it sooner, but a second, still-oozing corpse to my left tells me why—a hornet, its stinger like a knife protruding from its yellow-and-black abdomen. I hadn't even heard it coming.

"Thank you," I force out through gritted teeth.

The pain isn't subsiding. It's still pounding with every heartbeat, throbbing. I can't just sit here, though.

"Lyra?"

I jerk my head up to stare through a blur of tears at Dae standing at the other end of the tunnel. Nothing separating us.

Oh gods. This is it.

He's going to kill me while I lie here in so much pain that I can't run or fight. I grab my axe, which I dropped on the ground earlier, and hold it above my head, ready to throw. I'll aim at his shoulder, try not to kill him.

Dae's wary gaze is on my panther, though, who has curled back her lips to bare her predator's teeth at him.

"If you tell your animals to let me by," he says slowly, "I'll give you the petal I took from Amir during Artemis' Labor."

Petal? Is that what Amir was eating in that junkyard? What does it do? Heal? Wait…if he had that, why didn't Amir offer it to Meike during Dionysus' Labor? Or maybe he did while I was gone helping the others.

Not a question I need to be answering right now. I stare at Dae. Does he mean it?

His gaze flicks to me, then back to the panther. "For Boone," he says. "Because I wish I could help him."

I stare at him another long second, but it's a deal worth taking. "Don't hurt him," I tell my animals. "Let him by."

Dae is still cautious as he scoots past us, but he drops a white petal in my lap as he passes. "Eat the whole thing," he says.

I nod, stuffing it into my mouth. "Take a right at the T," I tell him. "We already checked it out. I'll count to sixty before following."

I meet his stark, assessing gaze, and he nods. An acknowledgment,

I think, that *this* is how these games should be played. At least by the champions.

The petal's effects are immediate, but not healing like I'd thought. More like a shot of adrenaline straight to my heart with an added kick of invincibility. Not sure I needed that part. Overconfidence tends to get people killed, in my experience. After waiting the time I promised, I take off down the maze yet again, leg as good as new—or at least I'm not *feeling* the pain anymore.

Thank you, Dae.

I don't know how long we've been down here by this point or how many times I've gone up and down levels, the number of twists and turns, but I trust my animals. With more and more frequency, I run by bug carcasses instead of live insects.

It's not until I burst into the topmost level and the roar of the crowd rattles the glass like thunder that I know I'm close. I'm so close I can damn well taste it.

Just one win closer. Please the Fates.

I take precious time first to look at Athena's clock—fifteen minutes left. It took me forty-five to get this far? I look around, trying to get my bearings. It's easier to see the various tunnels up here, but the glass still makes it difficult to figure out which way to go.

"Move your ass, Lyra," I say to myself.

And we run again. Two more Ts, and I'm waiting at the second one, which I think must be in the dead middle of this level, when I hear the slap of feet coming at me, pounding the glass floor of my maze cage. I spin, axe ready, only to find nothing there. But the pounding of those steps is still coming.

Horror crawls all over me like the bugs in this Labor.

This could only possibly be two people. Diego, with the Ring of Gyges he won in the first Labor, but I'm pretty sure he'd identify himself and, like Dae, simply ask to pass. Which leaves only one person.

Dex.

Fuck.

94

MURDERERS & MONSTERS

Instead of searching for Dex when I know I won't see him, I stare downward at the glass floor that shows me the bowels of the maze underfoot, and I focus on the sound of his steps. Closer. Closer. He's breathing hard.

Now.

I duck and roll, and the cadence of his steps trips up as he has to jump. I come up, axe held in front of me, because now I know roughly where he is. The panther and fox are snarling and yipping, as they can sense him—smell him, hear him—but not see him.

"Don't make me do something we both regret," I warn him.

"You're going to lose." He still sounds funny. Then he giggles—like a child—and takes off the way he was already going, the slap of his feet growing quieter.

I swallow hard, allowing the fear I was holding back to wash through me, then recede. Gods, that was close. I doubt I could've killed him before he killed me, but the bluff worked, so who gives a shit. I straighten, glaring in the direction he ran.

My animals paw at me to keep going, and we're off again. Hopefully, Dex isn't lying in wait up ahead. Three more turns, and the air becomes even sweeter.

I'm close to the end? I'm almost there. No Dex, so far.

I come to another T, and we do our thing again.

Standing in one spot as I wait for my animals to return, I'm shifting from foot to foot in an impatient dance, eager to be out of this cage, when a new roar of the crowd pummels the glass. This roar has a different timbre to it. I spin and catch a glimpse of a wine-colored uniform and dark-brown hair and then the glint of sunlight on a mirror.

Meike.

No.

The truth hits me so hard, I raise a hand over my heart like I could shield it from the impact. It doesn't help, and I lean forward, hands on my knees, closing my eyes against reality.

Meike won the Labor.

She won, I lost, and that's it. No way to tie Diego. No way to free Boone. Hades doesn't get to be king. I keep my curse.

Game over.

I suck in, trying to breathe around the death of the hope I've been carrying since Boone died and Hades said he could make him immortal.

"Lyra?" That's Zai's voice from my left.

I stay where I am, watching Meike wave to the crowds, trying to make myself remember that I'm happy for her.

"What happened?" He's closer now.

I turn my head slowly. Trinica is with him. The Harpe of Perseus, in Zai's hand, is covered in yellow-and-green bug guts, but they're both alive.

"Meike won." I try to make it sound positive, but it comes out flat. Gods, I'm a terrible friend.

A sudden garbled scream reverberates not just through the glass walls but down into my tunnel, and I jerk upright in time to get a clear view of Meike being lifted off the ground by nothing. Her hands circle something invisible, and her feet kick out in the air as she fights. With one hand, Dex removes his helm, revealing himself to the crowds.

Trinica bursts past me with a scream of challenge, hurling curses like bombs as she runs. Axe in hand, I sprint after her, down the last halls of the maze, Zai on my heels.

My animals don't even have to show us the way. We don't stop running as we make the last three turns.

As we burst from the maze, the noise hits us like a solid wall.

Maybe that's why Dex doesn't hear us running at him, but with a scream a banshee would envy, I launch myself on his back. He drops Meike and goes wild under me. It takes everything in me to hold on and not drop my axe. No more sound. No more screams. The only noise coming from me are grunts of effort as I hold on to his thrashing form.

Vaguely, I'm aware of Zai trying to trip him as he and Trinica dance around us. But Dex is bucking and kicking at them and clawing at me, trying to get me off, and we can't make him stop. That's when he rolls, slamming me into the glass floor with the force of his body.

As I come to my feet, so does Dex. He rises with murder in his eyes, only to get a kick to the balls from Trinica that drops him back to his knees, doubled over on a groan. *Thank the gods.* Maybe that will slow him down. The three of us stop fighting, taking a breath.

Just long enough for him to lunge for Meike, who's still lying on the ground. Then he's back on his feet, holding her in the air by her neck with one hand. Eyes bulging, her face turns purple.

I hurl my axe, not trying to kill him, just stop him. It spins end over end and hits true, sinking into his shoulder with a *thwack* right where I intended. Only, to our disbelief, it doesn't stop him. It doesn't even slow him down. Still holding Meike up with one hand, he yanks it out and throws it away, and it clatters away on the glass.

Then he jerks her down and in and twists her neck sharply with both hands. I hear the crack, even over the yells of the crowd. Worse, I feel it in my own bones. I feel it in my heart when her body goes instantly limp before she's dropped in a jumbled heap of limbs.

Dead.

I fall to my knees as he thrusts both of his hands into the air and shouts a carnal roar of triumph. He's the winner of this Labor now. Beyond where he stands, I see Athena on the platform, and she's smiling.

Until the answering thunder of the immortals in the stands threatens to break the glass under us.

Boos.

They're *booing* him.

Because it's Meike, I realize.

He should have come for me, not her. Not the sweetest and gentlest of us.

I let Dex go.

Just minutes before this in the maze. I didn't fight him. I didn't try to kill him. I let him go, and now…

The watching immortals whip one another into a frenzy. I'm guessing only the Daemones are keeping them from doing anything to Dex, who stands on the glass top to the maze, in the center of the entire stadium, hands dangling at his sides, shock frozen on his features as the throng batters him with their screams for justice and blood.

Dex turns his head, looking at Meike, and I think maybe he says her name as he frowns in confusion. Then he raises his gaze past her, landing on me, and the feral rage that overtakes his features sends terror barreling through me.

"Oh, fuck," I think Trinica says.

And then he's on top of me so fast I don't even have a chance to get to my feet. Just like with Meike, he lifts me by the neck, his grip so tight spots dance before my eyes. I'm clawing at him, beating my feet in the air. But he's too strong. I try to let go with one hand and get to my vest, but he's jerking me around so violently, I can't get a grip on any of the zippers.

Trinica launches herself onto his back. It doesn't even seem to slow him down.

And the violence of his eyes is like he's possessed.

I catch a flash of Zai, who runs closer and stabs his sword into Dex's leg. But it doesn't stop him, like he's not even human.

Then, Dex jerks me closer to his face. "Time to die, Keres."

Trinica suddenly jumps at Dex from the side. She hits hard enough that he stumbles with all three of us.

Right into Zai's sword.

I hear the sick slide of it as it enters his body, feel him take the hit. Holding me in the air, Dex sways for a second before all three of us drop to the ground with a hollow *thud* of glass. I claw his hands away from my neck and scramble back in case he's still on the rampage.

But he's already gone.

Zai's sword must've hit something vital, because the life has already drained from Dex's face, his eyes cloudy.

I turn away on all fours, reaction making my stomach heave. I retch but manage to not vomit.

"Lyra?" Zai's voice reaches me. He sounds…small.

Controlling myself, I look over my shoulder to find him standing not far away, the Harpe of Perseus now limp in his grip as he stares in dawning horror at Dex. Then he starts shaking his head. Hard. Then harder. And his entire body starts to shake.

I can't watch him fall apart.

Part of me expects Hades to appear and take me away, like he did when Boone died, but he doesn't. I lift my head, searching for him, but he's not even among the other gods and goddesses, who are all seated up on the platform with the spikes with the heads of our dead.

The Olympian gods are, all of them, on their feet. My gaze lands on Athena.

Hades' blood is still inside me, still part of me. Maybe the rabid wrath that tears me apart at the sight of her is him. I don't care.

I jump up and point at Dex. "What'd you do? Drug him? Curse him to be more aggressive today?" I scream at her. "Well, he's dead now, and that is fucking karma, you monster." Dex was *her* champion. "You won't be Queen of the Gods now, will you?"

The four Daemones, still standing at their posts in the four corners of the platform where the gods and goddesses watch, all suddenly extend their wings with sharp, militaristic precision.

That is when Charon appears in front of me and takes me away, kicking and screaming.

95

COOL IT

The second we blink back into being, I'm vaguely aware that Charon and I are in Hades' Olympus home, but not much more than that. Fury is still eating me alive. Fury that Dex killed Meike. Fury that someone got to him and altered him somehow. That we couldn't stop him. That our hands were forced. Fury that Athena put those heads on spikes. Fury about the entire cursed Crucible.

The emotion burns me, scouring me from the inside like acid and poison, turning me rancid. So much that I'm thrashing in Charon's arms. "That bitch needs to pay! They all do!"

Charon locks his arms around me in such a way that I can't move. "Settle," he says.

"Fuck you."

Meike.

Gods, the warmest of hearts. Always smiling. All about the adventure.

"Settle, Lyra." There's so much command in that one word that despite the rage still pumping through me in hot spurts, I do.

I go dead still.

Charon doesn't let me go as I stand here breathing loudly through my nose like a bull ready to charge.

"Are you going to start back up if I let go?"

I clench my teeth but, after a beat, shake my head. Once. "I'm calm now."

He still takes a moment before he loosens his arms a tiny bit. When I don't start thrashing again, he lets go and steps back. I don't turn to face him.

I also don't start raging again.

The anger has abandoned me for something way worse. Grief. For Meike, of course for Meike. For Rafe, Dex's poor nephew, who will miss the uncle he hero-worships. For Dex's sister, who lost the brother who was trying to help her through illness. For Zai, who will carry Dex's death around with him, along with Isabel's, for the rest of his life. For Trinica, who is comforting him without me.

For me.

"Hades sent you instead of getting me himself." The words I direct at Charon are not a question.

"He couldn't come right that moment."

Couldn't come? I was fighting for my life, and he couldn't... What was he doing that was so godsdamned important? "Did he even watch?"

"He was...called away."

Called away? "By whom?"

"He wouldn't say." There's an edge to those words. Is Hades pushing Charon away the same way he is me?

No. That doesn't make sense.

My gaze skates past him and out the window at his back, looking over the brilliance of Olympus in the sun. It's all so gaudy to me now, after the Underworld.

"He wouldn't have gone if it wasn't important, Lyra."

"Don't make excuses for him. He was in my bed last night..." I'm vaguely aware of the way Charon startles, but I'm still stuck following the runaway train of my thoughts. "And today he can't be bothered to watch while I fight to win that fucking—"

I cut myself off, because the anger is rushing in on the back of resentment toward Hades, toward all of them, and the overwhelming sense that I'm even more alone than ever. It's like there's a dam I keep building up only to have it break again behind the weight of the flood. Over and over.

I force myself to move, like I'm shrugging it off, like I'd reject a touch. "He warned me he had nothing to give beyond..." I shake my head. "I just didn't realize—"

I walk away. If I don't move, the anger will drown me.

Charon goes to follow, but I ignore him, stalking out the back of Hades' house, down the terraces to the lands beyond. I keep walking through the fields of soft grasses and summer flowers toward the closest mountain. A path catches my eye, and I follow it.

I just need to not stand still.

The steps are small, forcing me to shorten my strides, and they never stop going up. And up. And up. Winding around the curves of the mountain. And with each step, I'm going over and over every single moment since I tried to throw a rock at Zeus' temple.

This doesn't feel right, Hades' rejection. The callous treatment. It doesn't feel like who he is. Who he's shown me. To abandon me this way, and just because he fucked me?

The drop to my right gets so sheer, it would make mortals with a fear of heights plaster themselves against the stone wall. I barely notice. I don't see the end of the path until I round the last bend and pause, for one small second shocked out of my spinning thoughts and emotions.

Hera's observatory.

"Wow," I whisper.

White Corinthian pillars lead up a pathway to a set of floating stairs. Literally floating, not attached to each other or the ground. Those wind up to a domed building, also floating on a bed of clouds. It's an observatory made of a pink stone of some sort—maybe pink quartz, because the glow of lanterns inside is visible. Over the top of the observatory, like a sail, is a thin, intricately carved sliver of a silver moon. It's set on rails, and I imagine that it moves with the telescope inside so that it doesn't block the view.

Even from below, from where I stand, the sky here seems so much closer. So much bigger. I imagine that at night, it would feel like I could just reach out and touch the moon itself. Feel the heat of the stars.

Stars.

Hades calls me his star.

"Are you all right, Lyra?" Cerberus' serious voice drifts through my mind, and I glance back to find the hellhound standing on the path behind me, all three heads cocked, each set of oddly colored eyes reflecting concern. *"I felt your distress."*

Am I all right?

"Not really. No." Not okay.

All that pounding, restless anger has abandoned me the same way Hades did today, leaving behind confusion and a ton of other shit, and I plop down in the grass right where I'm standing.

After a second, Cerberus lumbers over and proceeds to lay his big body down beside me, curling around me like a shield, positioned so that I can lean back against his shoulder, with his three heads hovering to my right and his hind quarters to my left. His fluffy tail flops in my lap, like a very big, smoky-smelling fur blanket.

"Hades wouldn't have slept with you if he felt nothing," Charon says.

I guess he followed me, too. He's standing now where the stairs from the mountain meet this field, looking poised to turn and walk away if I tell him to.

I sigh and drop my head back against Cerberus, looking up at the brilliant blues of the cloudless sky. Rain would be more appropriate weather for my day. Thunderstorms, maybe. "He told me that there was nothing he could give me. I knew it was…just physical."

And I convinced myself a little bit that he didn't really mean it. Because of the way he touched me, the way he looked at me, the things he said, the way he made me feel…

Charon takes a step closer.

Ber's head comes up, baring a fang. *"If you upset her, you answer to me."* He lets me hear what he's saying to Charon.

"All of us," the other two tack on.

The ferryman's eyebrows wing high. "Now I see what Hades means about changing loyalties," he grumbles. "I will try not to upset her, but she needs to hear this."

Hear what, exactly? There's nothing he can say that will change Hades' mind.

Charon approaches and goes down on one knee before where I sit, expression earnest on that boyishly handsome face. "He's different with you."

"That's true," Cerberus confirms in triple stereo.

I brush a hand over the tail in my lap. "Because he needs me to win."

"Because he actually smiles around you," Charon insists.

I frown. "He smiles around others, too—"

Charon shakes his head. "He's looser with Cerb and me. Relaxes a bit. But even more with you. And smiles? Not the calculated ones, but sincere ones… No. Never."

That can't be right. I would have noticed. Although lately, my powers of observation seem to have been glitching.

"So, I'm an amusing toy—"

"You know better." Charon leans his elbow on his knee, earnest. "He just needs time to be able to figure out what he really feels. If he could have gotten Persephone out, that would have helped—"

Out? Of what? "What are you talking about?"

Charon stutters to a halt to stare at me, confusion drawing his brows down over his eyes. "You said Hades told you about Persephone."

Trepidation tightens the muscles in my shoulders, and my hand stills on Cerberus' tail. "Pretend he didn't tell me everything."

Charon shoots an agitated hand through his sandy-brown hair, blue eyes turning squinty. "Fucking hell, Phi," he mutters to himself.

I sit up straighter. "Now you really need to tell me."

He grunts, looking at Cerberus, clearly debating what to do.

The hound shifts restlessly against me. *"Tell her,"* he says—all three heads.

I watch Charon expectantly, watch the battle of indecision cross his features. He's already told me one of Hades' secrets about Persephone, but I'm guessing this is bigger.

"Fuck," he mutters again, then looks me in the eyes. "She's not dead. She got trapped in Tartarus."

A laugh, like the shot of a gun, bursts from me.

Not a normal reaction, I know.

I'm vaguely aware that Charon and Cerberus exchange a glance, but I'm still so much in my head that I can't deal with them.

Then Cerberus growls at my back, all three heads coming up in snarls of warning, eyes trained on a single person standing at the top of the path that leads to where I sit.

Hades.

96

DON'T

The god of death, the King of the Underworld. How is it that I didn't see him coming? How did I not keep him out, like Boone says I do with everyone?

He stands at the top of the stairs leading up to the observatory, dull, gunmetal-gray gaze pinned to my face.

"You called Athena a monster?" His voice is so quiet with wrath, I actually shiver.

For a second.

Maybe self-preservation kicks in, because that shiver fades away and all I feel is cold acceptance.

Persephone isn't dead. She's in Tartarus. I'm guessing the other gods don't know that, somehow. And if that's true, then that's got to be the reason why he joined the Crucible. He thinks he needs something that only the King of the Gods has access to in order to get her out.

It all makes such obvious sense now.

He picked me to win for him. That's all. Everything else was a lie, a show in order to get my cooperation.

Did he call Persephone his star?

Oh my gods, I'm jealous.

A harsh, disbelieving laugh escapes me. That's what this burn is. It's also everything else I've already cataloged. But right now, right this moment…this is romantic jealousy.

I cross my arms, head tipped and eyes unseeing as I examine this foreign sensation. I've had twinges of it before. Normal mortal moments. But not like this.

It feels…oily. Like a thick tar that I'll never be able to scrape off me, no matter how hard I try. A smelly substance that will taint everything I touch.

What a slimy, unhelpful, crappy emotion to have to deal with.

I don't like it. I won't do it.

Whatever I thought he and I were or could be in my most secret of hearts is over. Any love I could have felt for him is a corpse at the bottom of a frozen lake.

I get to my feet, and both Charon and Cerberus follow suit, standing slightly behind me as I face Hades.

"Was I wrong?" I ask calmly.

"What?" Hades' voice is a growl of warning.

I could get used to this kind of frostiness. Like nothing can penetrate my heart now. Not love, not anger, not hurt…definitely not him.

"She put their heads on spikes," I say. "She put *Boone's* head on a spike. And she smiled as her champion killed Meike after she'd already won. She did something to Dex to make him like that. She *is* a monster."

"Damn it, Lyra!" he snarls. "She is, but you called her that twice. With the entire immortal world watching. You think she isn't going to take retribution?"

I huff an uncaring laugh. "She can Medusa me, for all I care. At least then I can turn assholes like you to stone with a single glance."

Hades rears back, eyes flaring with shock before they narrow sharply. "Leave us," he commands Charon and Cerberus.

Neither of them move.

In fact, both of them look to me. I'm still watching Hades, so I see when that registers. I catch the moment he realizes that his only two friends in this world are protecting me…from him.

And I see what it does to him. The way he absorbs the hit almost physically before slowly pulling his shoulders back, spine straightening, face going as blank as I feel, smoke swirling around him like a moat of protection.

"I'll be okay," I say to them quietly.

Neither is happy about it, but they go, disappearing from the mountain, leaving me alone with Hades.

I don't wait for him to take the lead. He doesn't get to do that anymore.

"I know," I tell him.

Black brows snap down. "Know what?"

"That Persephone is still alive. Is that why you need to become King of the Gods?"

His features go slowly stony as if I just petrified him with a glance, a word.

I was right. It's true. It's all true.

Hades takes a step. "Lyra—"

"Don't." I slowly move back, still so calm it doesn't feel real. Nothing feels real. I'm pretty sure the pain is coming after I thaw. "You don't want to come anywhere near me right now."

He stops.

"Was that what last night was about? Boosting my confidence or something to try to get me to win? You feel nothing for me. I'm just a tool."

"I—"

"That wasn't a question." I don't want to hear that it's true, and I won't believe him if he says it's not.

I take another slow, careful step back, even though he doesn't move. "I thought I could see you. The real you. But it was all a calculation."

I stare at him, still so unfeeling. And he stares right back.

I can't stand looking at him now, at that harshly beautiful face, and drop my gaze to a spot at his feet. "You made me burn for you." The words come out not as an accusation, but as a harsh whisper of humiliation and bone-deep hurt.

"Fuck. Lyra, listen to me—"

I shake my head. Here it comes. The pain. It's trickling in now. I need to be far away from him when it really hits.

"I don't want to hear what you have to say." I raise my gaze to a spot on his chin. "I lost today." I'm not even sure who won. Trinica, I guess, since she was out of the maze next, after Meike and Dex, who are dead.

"I know," he says.

"I can't win the Crucible."

No response.

"I can't make you king, so you don't need me anymore." I look down at my feet and realize—randomly—that I'm a mess. My shoes are covered in bug guts, both from killing bugs and from running through their remains. There are holes in my clothes where the spiders and the bullet ant pierced through. Blood on my shirt.

The sight is like an outward expression of what I'm starting to feel like inside.

Only pride is keeping me upright, the numbness giving way to everything I don't want to feel. What I want to do is go curl into a little ball and fall apart. I'll do that later. When no one can see. When no one can find me.

After the last Labor is over, I'm going to disappear forever. Forge a quiet new life somewhere else. Away from him.

Hades takes a step closer, eyes turning to molten silver. "The crown isn't out of reach yet."

I blink, then stare at him. For me to win, Diego would have to die. I search his face for any hint that what he's saying bothers him at all. "And you think being an asshole is going to make me want to win?"

An emotion flickers over his features, but it's gone too fast to catch. "Make me king, and I'll grant you anything you ask for that is in my power to give."

The fire he lit inside me…that's all ashes now.

"Do you want to be back with your parents? Done." He snaps his fingers. "Do you want to be rich? Done." Another snap. "Rule a country? It's yours."

He really doesn't know me at all to offer those things.

He never bothered to really know me, and I damn well don't know him like I thought I did.

"I don't want anything," I tell him.

Don't do this. Tell me not to kill Diego. Tell me not to put myself through it. Just to survive.

Stubbornness has him prowling closer. "Everyone wants something."

I back up—not in fear. I can't stand to have him near me. I don't want him closer, where he might see the devastation laying waste to my insides. "Not from you," I say.

There's only the slightest pause in his steps, and then he keeps coming. "That's pride speaking, Lyra. Get over it and take something for yourself."

I slip two fingers in the small, zippered pocket where I keep the pearls he gave me. "Come closer, and I'm gone."

He jerks up hard at that, fury and a sort of shocked denial whipping across those beautiful features.

And betrayal.

He feels betrayed by *me*? Fucking gods.

A shadow streaks by overhead, and Hades' gaze shoots past me. Another lightning flash of emotions lashes out at me from him.

A very different kind.

Fear—metallic, urgent, sharp. It hits so hard that I gasp.

97

IN THE WAKE

"**N**o!" Hades raises one hand, and tendrils of smoke shoot out from him, only to be blown back by the force of four Daemones' wings.

They land, two on either side of me, and Hades' fear becomes my own as Zeles and another Daemon take me by the arms.

Hades holds out his hand, and suddenly, his bident is in his fist—onyx and shaped like spears, the two tips immediately light with hellfire.

In the same instant, the jeans and gray T-shirt he was wearing are replaced by armor. Not intricate like all the other gods' and goddesses', and not fashioned after ancient warriors of bygone ages. This armor is gunmetal gray and...liquid.

Like his eyes.

Like a living, breathing exoskeleton, it shapes perfectly around him, even coming up over his head so that he looks inhuman. Like a futuristic nightmare of a robot with no features for a face.

"Fuck," Zeles mutters.

Zeles lets go of me, and another of the Daemones takes his place holding my arm as Zeles steps forward.

"Release her," Hades commands in a voice that doesn't boom but makes me shiver all the same.

"No," Zeles says. Does the Daemon have a death wish? "You agreed—"

Hades throws out a hand, and a blast of fire explodes from his silver, liquid armor–covered palm, only to hit an invisible wall, the flames curling back away from us.

Zeles doesn't even flinch. "In joining the Crucible, you automatically agreed to the contract, which protects the four of us from all the gods' and goddesses' powers."

Hades hurls his bident so fast, so violently, that it's across the space before I register what he did. The bident is also stopped by the invisible field. But instead of bouncing off, it penetrates a little before it's stopped.

Enough that Zeles has to jerk back or take a strike to the chest. "Damn it, Hades, listen to me."

"Release her." The King of the Underworld stalks toward us, smoke swirling around him in billows like a volcano getting ready to erupt. "Release her, or I kill you all."

"No!" I cry out.

Hades jerks to a stop. He doesn't look at me—I don't think. It's hard to tell with the weird liquid armor over his face. But he doesn't keep coming, either.

"No one else is dying because of me," I inform him. "Hurt them, and I'll hate you forever."

The liquid armor...flinches.

It's the only way I can describe it. It ripples like I threw a pebble into a still lake.

"They are going to punish you—"

"She will not be harmed," Zeles tells him.

Hades pauses, and then the armor oozes away from his head, absorbing into the shoulders below so we can see his face as he studies Zeles. "I have your word?"

"Yes. She will be kept in our prison until the final Labor and will be treated well."

"She can't even win," Hades snaps. "Why—"

"Athena requested death," Zeles says, "with a judgment of Tartarus as her punishment."

Holy shit. Death. Smite me then and there for calling her a monster to her face. No Medusa or other horrible curse. Just a one-way ticket to the part of the Underworld reserved not just for Titans but for the wickedest and most evil of souls. They go there to be punished for all eternity.

"This is a...compromise," Zeles says. "You may not have access to her until the next Labor is about to start. But Athena will also not have access to her."

Hades stares at the four of them, each in turn, as if assessing the truth of their words, then moves his gaze to mine, and I meet his eyes directly, unflinching. With a restrained violence, he yanks the bident out of the invisible wall it is buried in, then gives a single jerking nod.

The Daemones take off into the sky, dragging me away from the mountain and away from Hades.

98

PRISONER

Z eles waves a hand, indicating I should go through a door into what is clearly the Olympian version of a jail cell.

God jail.

It says a lot about my mental state that I am now fighting back a case of the giggles and tears at the same time.

"In here, please," he says.

No shoving. No anger or suspicion. Even a *please*.

The Daemones said they weren't going to hurt me, just keep me locked up until the next challenge. Even so, I've clocked the details of how we got here, the ways in and out of the building that I could see, the rooms leading here, and now this space.

Because you did such a bang-up job learning escape techniques last time, sarcastic me drawls in my head.

"Huh," I say deliberately as I step inside. "It turns out prisons in Olympus are pretty much the same as the ones in the Overworld."

Zeles frowns. "Really?"

"No." I roll my eyes. "Not really."

This prison is, of all things, pristinely clean and fancy with white marbled walls. Well-lit. A desk, a computer, and a bed with a fluffy pillow are included, along with a private bathroom inside opaque glass walls. The outer walls of the cell are clear glass instead of bars. More glass walls to deal with. At least these are bug free and with holes across the top so I can breathe. Thoughtful of them.

"You're taking this well," a Daemon I heard Zeles refer to as Nike says from behind us.

"This is the most protected I've been since I was three years old." I manage to smile up at Zeles.

This might be the safest place for me if Athena is out for my blood. And I could really use the space away from Hades.

Zeles doesn't so much as crack a crease around his eyes or lips.

Granted, our last interaction had a lot to do with me demanding Hades' release. Probably from this place. Given the trouble I've caused, I'd lay money that I'm not the Daemon's favorite champion.

Despite the luxuries, this is still a prison. It's still four walls with no contact with the outside world beyond a few scattered visitors, no way out, and a guard.

I step inside, and then Zeles turns the lock and leaves.

Nike sets herself up by the door that leads to the halls and freedom beyond and pulls out a cell phone and earbuds, proceeding to ignore me entirely as she watches something that makes her snicker every few minutes.

It looks like I will get no privacy. No way am I letting them see me fall apart.

I'm holding myself together with sheer will, emotional duct tape, and twenty years of learning how to not show my true feelings to others if I don't want to. Who knew that the harsh reality of my life would come in this handy someday?

Even so, I'm starting to shake.

Just a little.

Giving the shaking a disguise and an outlet, I wander my cell, checking out the entire thing. I give the bed a good bounce. Turns out it's a nice, thick mattress, and the sheets are some fancy cotton with a high thread count—a league better than the thin, scratchy shit in mortal cells. The toilet paper in the bathroom is also the good stuff. No one-ply tissue paper bullshit for the gods' asses, even ones in jail.

"Can I—"

Nike jerks her phone down, gaze on me hard and suspicious.

Right. Okay. She is not as relaxed around me as she looked. Yet.

I hold up both hands. "Can I get a change of clothes?" I wave at my bug-gut-and-blood-splattered clothing.

Annoyance crosses her features, but she goes to the door and asks someone outside named Craton. Ten minutes later, I'm brought a white jumpsuit.

"At least it's not orange," I tell Nike. "Makes me look jaundiced."
She frowns.

Daemones. So serious.

With a shrug, I head into the shower.

The only place I can be alone in here. I turn on the water, strip, and step under the spray, then immediately wrap my arms around my middle, crumbling over them as I try to contain my heartbreak.

I don't know how long I stay in there like that, letting the water both hide the sounds that escape every so often and wash away the evidence.

"That's enough!" Nike's voice is muffled by the walls but still distinct.

Damn.

It takes three tries to answer her in a normal-sounding voice. "Bug guts are sticky. I'll be out in a bit."

No answer, which I take as agreement.

Even so, I force myself to stop wallowing and actually wash myself off. The toiletries provided are basic but get the job done, and minutes later, I'm back out in my cell, wet hair slicked back and remarkably comfy in the jumpsuit, which is fashioned from some soft, stretchy material.

I'm holding it all in again. So tightly I feel like an overblown balloon. If I so much as brush against the carpeting wrong, I'll pop.

Meanwhile, it's still daylight. Probably time for lunch. I can't lie down and go to sleep and hide myself in the dark.

So now what?

I go to the computer. Thieves of the Order don't have email or any kind of online presence. We're digital ghosts on purpose. So there's nothing to check. Instead, I open up a browser.

And the first thing I see is a giant headline that reads, *Two More Dead as Crucible Nears the End.*

Meike and Dex's deaths immediately replay in my head in detail so distinct I hear Dex's grunt all over again, see the life leave his body. I click away from that fast but not fast enough, thanks to the renewed shaking of my hands. I close my eyes and try not to see the image on the backs of my lids.

"Are you going to be ill?" Nike asks with an indifference that would do prison guards around the world proud. She clearly doesn't want to deal with the mess.

"No."

I force my eyes open to stare at the screen, which is now showing the home page of a streaming service—the first thing I saw that seemed neutral to click on. Except the movie they are featuring at the top, the preview already running, is some bloody action film involving murders and purges.

"Nope," I mutter, then scroll and click the first thing that looks not that.

K-drama. A romantic comedy.

Right. Better.

The sound will be a shield of sorts. The computer, too. I can stare at it like I'm watching to pass the time, and she'll pay no attention to me. Maybe it will even distract me. Although I don't think so.

I'm staring down several days to sit in here and think of nothing but...

I shove his name out of my head before I can think it. I don't want to think about him.

So think about something else.

Like surviving the final Labor and getting the fuck away from this place. Never seeing him again.

Or maybe I can run now. Skip that last challenge. I can't win anyway...

I have five pearls left. How long can I keep away from the gods with those?

99

PLANS & SCHEMES

I take a bite of the mango-and-strawberry sorbet cake two satyrs made for my dessert tonight and groan. "Oh my gods, Z, you need to taste this."

Zeles grunts, staring at the cards in his hand fiercely. "Don't call me Z."

He hates it, which is why I do it.

The Daemones take turns babysitting me. They're not so bad once you get to know them, and I welcome the distraction, given that they're the only thing in here to keep me company other than the computer. Though I still haven't figured out how to make Zeles crack a smile. But he'll play card games with me, using the food slot in the glass wall to pass cards back and forth.

After three days here, I'm thinking of never leaving. Peace, quiet, entertainment, privacy of a sort—in the bathroom, at least—and meals to die for. The cooks figured out that I have a thing for fruit and have managed to work it into every meal. Like the bite of heaven in my mouth right now.

And every single second, every moment of every day, I am mentally working through how I'm going to face Hades before the next Labor and how I'm going to move on with my life after this is over.

That and trying to hold back how that makes me feel.

I shovel in another bite and pick up a card, then grin. "Gin." The word comes out garbled around the food in my mouth as I lay my cards down.

Zeles grunts, then scowls, and I laugh.

"I only needed one more," he grumbles and tosses the cards in his hands to the ground in a huff. Then he eyes me narrowly. "You've got to be using your thief skills to cheat."

"Nope. I never did master the card shark or sleight-of-hand stuff for that."

He gives me a dubious look.

I swallow my bite. "You're going to have to pick those up, you know. I can't from this side."

I'm sitting cross-legged on the floor, but thanks to the wings, he can't, so he usually stands and stalks around as he thinks.

He grunts again.

There's a knock on the door that leads into this row of about five cells, and he stomps over and swings it wide.

"Lyra has a visitor," a Daemon named Bia tells him. "He's been checked."

Even though I know "he" can't be Hades—he's not allowed— my stupid heart, which apparently can't learn hard lessons, kicks into overdrive.

I've had a visitor each day, always in the evenings after dinner. Cerberus and Charon have both come by once each. I sit up straighter to see who comes through the door.

Zai walks in.

My heart puts on the brakes.

His face is a study of both fascinated interest in seeing the inside of my prison...and guilt.

I get to my feet and wave. "Hi."

"They're treating you well?" he asks as he approaches, keeping an eye on Zeles.

I smile, trying to show Zai I'm fine. "Yes."

"Trinica and Amir would have come with me, but they're only allowing a single visitor each day."

Not Meike, though. Because she's dead.

"I know. I appreciate that. Tell them thanks."

He grimaces. "I should be the one in here. I killed..." He can't even say Dex's name.

What he's carrying is so heavy, I can feel it through my glass prison. I *knew* it. I knew he'd take that guilt and hold on to it.

"It was an accident," I say. "He would have killed me, and it just... happened."

Zai looks away. "I know."

"I'm not in here because of that," I tell him, dry as dust.

He frowns. "Then why?"

I shift into baby talk. "I called Athena a mean word and the wittle, baby goddess got her feewings huwt."

"Fuck, Lyra. You are just asking to get sent to Tartarus," Zeles mutters darkly, glancing around as if he expects retribution to strike.

With an uncaring shrug that is some of my best acting yet, I shoot the Daemon a pointed look. "Do you mind?"

He leaves us with a final grunt, closing the door behind him. At least they give me privacy with my visitors when I ask for it.

As soon as he's gone, I focus on Zai. "Anyway, *that's* why I'm in here. They don't give two shits about dead champions."

He blinks a little owlishly. "Oh."

"But it's good to see your face." I lean closer to the glass, peering at him. "How are you?"

He shrugs. "My father came to congratulate me on a good kill."

Good grief. Zai should take the Harpe of Perseus and skewer that man, too. "That's harsh, even for Mathias."

At least that gets Zai to huff a laugh. "He said he didn't know I could swing a sword so well."

"Well, he'll be mortal again soon. That and dealing with the Overworld after living basically as a god will be his own personal hell."

"Yeah." Zai ducks his head, hiding a grin I'm sure he feels is inappropriate. We are, after all, talking about his father.

Suddenly, he steps closer to the glass, as close as he can without smashing his face. "I'll try to win," he says urgently. "And if I do, Hermes has promised to make Boone a god."

My mouth falls open. "How in the name of Olympus did you manage that?"

"He's the patron god of thieves." Zai looks behind him to check the door, probably making sure none of the Daemones come rushing in if they heard that.

Not that it's breaking any of their rules, but it gives me a chance to wrangle my own reaction under control. The tears burning my eyes are welling hard, making the sight of Zai's face blurry.

"You are a good, good man, Zai Aridam," I whisper.

He shakes his head. "Don't thank me."

I frown. "Why? Did you promise Hermes something in return?" I ask, suspicion making me watch him more closely.

"No." He waves away my worry. "He came to me, actually."

The hells he did. Why would Hermes do that? What possible reason? "Isn't there anyone you would ask to bring back? Someone close to you?"

He shakes his head.

"Well…thank you from Boone and from me." I put my palm against the glass, and Zai flattens his on the other side.

What else can I say?

"Thank you for asking me to be your ally," he says. The smile he offers me is one I imagine old friends would share, full of understanding and acceptance and a need to be there for each other.

I like to think of him as a friend. Boone said I didn't have friends, not because of my curse but because of the walls I put up. I didn't with Zai, and he accepted me when he really never should have. Curse or no curse.

"I probably brought you more problems than solutions," I say.

Zai's smile widens to a grin. "I like solving problems."

His expression is so endearing, I don't bother to tell him the truth. Even if Zai wins the final Labor, I'm guessing he won't win the Crucible. Not with one of his wins being a tie with Rima. Diego wins. No matter what. But I'm not going to point that out. The gesture alone is…enough.

It also gives me an idea.

Hades won't like it. Charon, either, for that matter. It's a betrayal of sorts. But it's also the right thing to do.

"Zai…I have a favor to ask."

"What favor?" he asks. No wariness. No suspicion. Only trust.

I truly did pick the best possible ally for this nightmare. "You're not going to like it."

100

THERE CAN BE ONLY ONE

The fact that a brand-new uniform was delivered to my cell this evening with dinner was a good clue that the next Labor is soon. Tonight, most likely.

I ate. I dressed. And I've been sitting on my bed, waiting. I should rest or something, but the anxious energy of nerves and…well, too many nerves to figure out all the other emotions swirling around in there… won't let me relax.

So I pace. And sit. And pace.

And through the night and into the next day, I watch the door, anticipating one face, hoping for another. I've put Zai in a tricky position, but I have absolute faith that he did what I asked. It took convincing, but he agreed.

In the evening, the door suddenly opens—I didn't even hear footsteps on the other side—and I get to my feet, expecting one of the Daemones or maybe Hades to walk through and take me to my final fight.

Instead…a goddess enters. Dressed in a flowing pink chiffon dress, made up with glittering gold at her eyes and lips, she strolls casually through the door as if this is just a normal Tuesday.

"Hello, darling," Aphrodite trills.

She doesn't even glance at Zeles, who let her in. Instead, she looks around my cell, nose wrinkling.

"How very…drab," she comments. "You must be so bored."

"I get by."

She pins me with a gaze sparkling with mischief. "I'd be happy to give you a mental orgasm just to lighten up your dreary day."

Zeles stiffens where he still stands in the doorway.

THE GAMES GODS PLAY

Her back is to him, so he doesn't see the way more mischief tugs at her lips. She's fucking with the Daemon deliberately.

"I'm about to go into a Labor," I point out.

Aphrodite hums deeply, suggestively. "It's the best way to relax before battle that I've ever found."

Battle? Is that a hint?

She raises her eyebrows at me, eyes wide and questioning.

I clear my throat around a chuckle lodged there. "No. Thank you, though."

She twitches her shoulders in annoyance. "I can feel the unrealized sexual tension stretching from Hades' home on the other side of Olympus to here." Then she gives me a look that is insistent and pointed. "Are you *sure* you don't want my help?"

Then she glances sideways, indicating Zeles. She wants him to leave.

"Oh… Well… I guess it wouldn't hurt…"

"Excellent!" She claps her hands joyfully.

Zeles, whose unemotional face is as close to horrified and simultaneously fascinated as I think he gets, clears his throat. "I'll give you some…privacy."

He's through the door like a gunshot, and Aphrodite laughs, her face transforming to genuine humor and not something designed to elicit a specific response. In my opinion, she's much more beautiful this way. Real.

Sobering, she lets her gaze skate over me.

"Why did you come?" I ask.

"Demeter."

My eyes widen. That's the last thing I was expecting, mostly because Zai and I are the only two people who know I reached out to that goddess, through him, asking her to come talk to me. But understanding comes quickly enough, and I grimace. "She won't come?"

Aphrodite pauses, then shakes her head. "She said no pet of Hades was worthy of her time."

Stubborn, prideful, arrogant deities. I'm surprised any of them have noses left after cutting them off so often to spite their faces.

"Why did you wish to see her?" Aphrodite asks.

I study her face like she did mine a second ago. Strangely, of all the gods and goddesses, I think I trust her the most. Possibly even more than

Hades, with all his secrets and lies. Maybe it's because she's let me see the side of her that is real. I'm honestly not sure.

Sharing this secret with her, though…

I take a deep breath. Then another. *Please let this be the right decision.* "Persephone didn't die."

There. I said it. Too late to take it back now. The only way is forward.

The goddess of love and passion's eyes go wide. "That's not possible," she whispers through tight lips.

My heart beats harder at her reaction alone. Did I fuck up by telling her? "You'd better sit down."

Once we're both in chairs facing each other through the glass, I tell her the little I know. "Is it possible for the King of the Gods to release prisoners from Tartarus?" I ask.

A little frown has formed between her perfect brows. "No," she says slowly. "The only way to open Tartarus requires all seven of the gods and goddesses who trapped the Titans in there. Even for Persephone, I don't think we could convince all seven to risk trying it." The frown deepens. "How did she get in?" she asks, more to herself than me. "And why?"

Then she lifts her gaze to mine, speculation replacing confusion. "You were going to tell Demeter?"

I nod. "Diego is her champion. The Crucible is his as long as he lives through this Labor. Maybe she could figure out how to use that power to get her daughter back. You said it yourself—Hades always has a plan."

Hades should have told Persephone's mother before now, but it's so like him to play his cards close and to try to fix this on his own.

"I was going to trade this information for a promise to make Boone a god," I say.

She gives a seductive hum. "I knew I liked you for a reason." Then her expression becomes serious. "Why now? Why go to all this trouble rather than tell her after the challenge yourself?"

"Because I may not survive," I say. "And she deserves to know."

She nods, lips thin. "But I still don't know what Hades is thinking," she says. "Opening Tartarus is dangerous and not possible. Not without all of us."

Aphrodite turns her face away from me, gaze seeming to search the stark white wall opposite. Then she takes her own deep breath, a small sign that tells me how shaken the goddess is. "If Jackie was closer to winning, I would offer to save Boone for you."

I sit back slightly. My proposal to the other champions really has made the rounds.

"But not Persephone." Aphrodite returns her gaze to mine. "I won't tell Demeter this secret."

Shock reverberates through me, straightening my spine and slashing my brows in a confused frown. "What? Why not?"

"It could start another war between us, and after the last one…" Her eyes darken with pain. "I can't risk that."

A war?

Sadness lingers in her expression. "Demeter almost burned down Olympus the day Hades told her Persephone died. He was smart to tell her that lie. Kind, too. If she knew her daughter was alive and where she is—" She shrugs. Then a frown slowly tugs at her features. "I'm guessing Hades doesn't want anyone else to know?"

I say nothing.

Aphrodite lets out a low whistle. "And yet you'd trust me with this?" She stares, her expression inscrutable, then softly says, "I'm honored. Truly."

I offer her a crooked smile. "I think you're one of the good ones."

Which makes her chuckle. "We're all equally good…and bad. Just like mortals."

"Some of you are worse than others," I mutter darkly.

Aphrodite rolls her eyes. "Athena is…who she is. Zeus, too. All of us, really. We are what we were born to be. Better than the violent Titans but far from perfect."

"Well, either way, after this is over, I shall pray to you often."

Aphrodite's smile is sincere and shows the depth of her heart for just a moment. "Take care in the last Labor, Lyra. I would like to hear those prayers." She goes to the door and lifts her hand to knock, only to pause again and shoot me a devilish grin over her shoulder. "Moan."

"Huh?"

She gives me a pointed look. "Mental orgasm, darling. I have a reputation to uphold."

Oh.

It hits me what she wants me to do, which is put on a show.

Awesome.

I do my best, moving to lie down on the bed and rumple the sheets so I look appropriately thrashed, which is kind of hard to get enthusiastic about in the moment. Then I let out a keening moan, followed by a healthy, "Oh god."

"Goddess," she whispers. "Don't forget who I am."

"Oh goddess," I cry out louder. Then again for good measure.

With an eye roll, she knocks, the door opens, and she's gone.

Leaving me alone with a thousand competing thoughts.

In my short amount of time being locked up here, I've gone over every moment with Hades. Everything he's said and done. For most of the time, my own heartache had me convinced that the way he was with me—the looks, the touches, the fact that he shared parts of himself with me—was an act to manipulate me. He saw my weakness for him and used it to keep me on his side and fighting to win the Labors. I even, for a second, convinced myself that his offer to help Boone was a lie.

Except he swore on the River Styx. That's a sacred oath to the gods.

Something else he said comes to me now. *Someday, I'll tell you the rest, and I think you'll agree it was a good reason... But I'm not sure now that it's good enough for what* you *are having to pay.*

What I am having to pay.

At the time, I thought he was only speaking about Boone and the death and fear I've gone through. But...what if he was talking about more? About him.

My thoughts take a new path. Away from me. Away from the pain of my own feelings, focusing instead on...him. On Hades.

I'm a trained liar.

One of the things we're taught is to use as much of the truth as possible to make a lie feel more real. Not all of what he showed me, who he was with me, was a lie. It couldn't have been.

He was holding himself so tightly together on Hera's mountain.

But at the same time, he wasn't playing the smart game with me. To get what he wants, he should have been leaning into my sympathies, using the determination I've shown to help the other champions survive. And why, after sleeping with me, not continue to use my feelings for him against me? Instead, he seemed to be trying to make me hate him.

Was he being deliberately, brutally nasty? Why?

I can only think of one reason.

Without the stained filter of bitterness and pain and trying very hard to look at it without rose-colored glasses, the way he was with me when we slept together makes no sense in the wake of how he treated me the very next day. That night, he didn't have to tell me the things he did. He already had me.

Is Aphrodite right that Hades always has a plan? Is Charon right? Did Hades start out trying to deceive me but get tangled in his own web and grow fond of me instead? And without his brother's curse, could he feel even more?

With a click of the handle, the door swings open and Nike enters. "It's time," she says.

101

ONE LAST BLOW

It's time to compete in my last Labor. Or at least to not die, and then what? I was going to run away, but now…

"Are you able to tell me where?" I ask Nike as she unlocks the door to my cell.

The Daemon shakes her head.

"It's okay," I assure her, though she doesn't look concerned. "I figured."

"Follow me," she says.

Which I do, out of my block of cells and into a long, narrow hall that leads through what could pass for a fancy version of the front office of a police department, and then outside into the night.

"We can't teleport inside that building," she explains. "Wards."

I expect her to either fly or teleport me away, but instead, she spreads her wings wide and takes off without me.

"Hey!" I call after her. "Where do I—"

Hades appears in the silent jolt of an instant, standing several yards away. Like he can't quite bring himself to be near me. His eyes glint silver in the glow of evening light as he takes all of me in with a single, sweeping glance. "They treated you well?"

That's it? That's all he has? Would it be unladylike to punch the god I love in the face?

"Yes." I'm staring. I can't help it. I'm drinking him in after days without, but I'm also searching for a flicker of a sign he's hating this as much as I am. That he has regrets. That he's pushing me away in some misguided attempt to protect me. That he has a plan and he's trying to save Persephone and Boone…and me.

That's a lot to shoulder.

Before, I would have said that sounded like him. To deal with all that silently and alone.

Now, I don't know what to believe.

"As your god, I am required to take you to the last Labor."

Required? As if he wouldn't be here otherwise. The same way he didn't watch Athena's Game? I cross my arms. "I'm surprised they let you near me."

"They feared any other god wouldn't be able to hold off Athena if she decides to attack you on the way."

"Oh." I hadn't thought about that.

Hades crosses to me in his slow prowl of a walk, coming closer but not close enough. Then he holds out a hand to me. "Let's go."

I peer closer, but he's still a wall of nothing. Not a single damned emotion.

"I tried to tell Demeter. About Persephone, I mean…"

He lowers his hand to his side slowly. "You what?"

I flinch because that is very real anger. But I don't back down, tipping my chin up. "If Diego wins, she'll be queen. She could help her own daughter herself. She deserves to know."

Hades spears a hand through his hair, pacing away. "They won't let her. She's going to bring down everything, start a war—"

"That's what Aphrodite said."

He whirls on me and clasps his hands behind his back as if he's physically restraining himself from unleashing on me. "You told *her*—"

"She said she would keep the secret and not tell Demeter. For the same reason you just said."

"Damn it, my star—"

"*Don't.* Don't call me that." The words lash out from me. But I can't listen to that endearment. Not anymore.

He snaps his mouth closed.

"I'm not going to apologize," I tell him. "I thought I was doing the right thing with the limited information I had. If you had told me everything from the beginning, we really would be in a much better place now."

Hades glares. "There is no other way—"

I take a step forward. "Bullshit."

His jaw works. "Every person I've ever trusted has betrayed me."

I want to soften at that. I feel my insides squish a little, but I don't let him see. "You could have trusted me."

His head rears back slowly, arrogance and impatience becoming a mantle over his face. "This isn't helping anyone."

Then he stalks closer to grab me by the arm, and we blink out. When we blink back in, we're standing with all the other champions and their patron gods on the flat, cracked earth of a desert somewhere in the Overworld. Night—somewhere far from Olympus, then.

"Don't die," Hades says as he lets go, already turning away from me.

"Were you really going to make Boone into a god, or was that a lie to get on my good side?"

He pauses, then barely cants his head in my direction. All I see is the side of his face, his jaw clenched. "Finish this Labor and go home, Lyra. Forget about everything that happened here."

Then he's gone.

And I have my answer.

PART 8

THE SPOILS

Fates, curses, and prophecies be damned.

102

ZEUS' LABOR

I stare straight ahead, unseeing, as I absorb the truth that after today, it's over.

All of this is over.

Win, lose, or die.

The nine of us still alive to face this last challenge are lined up shoulder to shoulder. Zeus stands before us, surprisingly subdued. He is not dressed in armor or fancy clothes or modern clothes at all. He is dressed in an ancient traditional Grecian tunic, pinned at his shoulders and belted at the waist. Over that, he wears a forest green cloak that lifts behind him in the breeze and leather sandals on his feet. Maybe he wants to remind us of how ancient he is.

His expression isn't intense or bloodthirsty or arrogant. None of those things.

Zeus is…serene.

Blue eyes clear, brow smoothed, and an easy smile.

This is different from how I've seen him before. Like he knows something we don't.

I don't trust it.

While Samuel *is* here today, looking a little better—not quite so ashen—he can't win or even tie at this point. A gold band is around his uninjured wrist—Aegis, his shield. Zeus must've gotten it back for him. Good. Like me and most of the others, he's just here to not die.

But either way, Zeus seems a little too calm, given the best his champion can do today is a tie. I think if I were about to lose my crown, and I was an oversize god-baby like Zeus, I'd be a little more panicked.

Zeus spreads his hands wide, offering us a smile of welcome that makes me lean back slightly, because it feels like a snake smiling at a mouse. "Welcome, champions, to your final Labor."

None of us move. None of us smile back. We wait for the other sword to drop.

As usual, he's unruffled by our lack of response. Or maybe oblivious. "You have come far. You have lost allies and friends. You have suffered, but you have also fought well. We, your gods and goddesses, your patrons, applaud you and thank you for fighting in our steads as our champions in this Crucible."

Well…that's new.

None of the others have thanked us yet. I kind of wasn't expecting them to. It's not in their nature to acknowledge mortal suffering. As far as they're concerned, this is all about them.

His smile falls away, turning serious and even tinted with concern. "As is tradition, the last of the Labors is the most difficult. This will be no exception, and the gods and Daemones will not be here to step in should you falter."

I glance down the row. Did they catch that?

Did he just tell us the enforcers of the rules won't be here?

Zeus holds his arms out wide, indicating the desert around us. "This is Death Valley, in the Mojave Desert of the western United States."

I take a better look at my surroundings. The skies directly overhead are turning darker blue, already awash in stars—not quite as brilliant as Olympus but close. The sunset bathes everything around us in an orangish-pink glow that will turn darker as the sun sinks farther and more silvery in the light of the already risen full moon.

We are standing in a huge, flat area that is solid cracked earth broken by patches of rocks and larger boulders and every so often a particularly stubborn cactus that clings desperately to life.

I know exactly how those prickly suckers feel.

In the distance, to the left and right are mountain ranges. Even from far away, I can see stripes of colors that show all the different strata of rock and soil that built the peaks over eons of crushing heat. No wonder Zeus chose evening for this Labor. I'd heard once Death Valley is the hottest place on the planet. Despite a growing coolness in the still, dry air, heat wafts up from the sand and rocks around us.

"You won't be able to hide here," Zeus warns. "But running…"

Now he's being coy.

"And drumroll, please, for the twist…" I mutter under my breath.

Zai chokes on a laugh.

Zeus shoots me a warning glance, and I stare straight back at him in wide-eyed innocence. He clears his throat. "Behind me is a series of gates."

I lean to look around him, and sure enough, I can see one about two football fields away. Hard to tell in the dark, but it looks like scrolling black iron bars with the doors open. Only, what's the point? There's no wall connected to it. It's just standing in the middle of nothing. Beyond that, even farther away, is another. Are there more than two? I can't tell.

"Three gates," Zeus says.

That answers that.

"The person to pass through the final gate first wins this Labor. And…" Zeus holds up a hand, smile turning sly. "As an added bonus, this challenge will count as three wins added to your total score."

I swallow a gasp as a murmur moves through the rest of the champions. I don't dare look to my left or right.

Zeus just upped the stakes.

Anyone can win now, and without having to kill Diego to do it. Or tie him, at least, for those with no wins. But I have a win. I could beat him.

I could win.

Oh my gods, I could fucking win.

For Boone. For Persephone. For Hades—

No, damn it, not for him.

For *me*.

I just have to run the race. That's it. Get through those three gates first.

"It won't be easy, champions," Zeus warns. "You may use your gifts and prizes to defend yourselves, but you may not use them to escape or skip any portion of this challenge. And to get to each gate, you must get past some of the most terrifying monsters of all the Labors in history."

Terrific.

"Starting with…" Zeus turns, raising his hands to the skies as if he's lifting something.

Lightning strikes the ground far out in the distance. Then again, closer. And closer. And the final strike is so near, the clap of thunder sends my ears ringing. Then the ground rumbles under our feet—a small vibration at first, then bigger and more violent until we are all struggling to stay upright.

A crack forms in the earth, splitting it before us in a long gash.

I almost expect steam or lava to erupt or, since it's monsters, for something to come flying out. But there's nothing.

With a final smile, Zeus disappears.

Still nothing.

We glance at one another. No way is any of us foolish enough to go stick our heads over the edge and look down. That's the first rule in a monster movie 101 survival guide.

A snort is the first thing I hear, followed by what might be boulders falling, crashing against the walls of the crevice on the way down, and then a distinct, angry bellow.

Every muscle in my body ratchets tighter, already instinctively moving into fight-or-flight mode.

I've never been on a ranch in my life, but that sounded like a…bull.

Hands appear at the lip of the ripped earth first. Human hands, but not, with massive fingers tipped in thick, yellow claws. Then horns. Massive, bone-white horns that end in deadly points, so wide from tip to tip, the creature they're attached to must be huge.

A minotaur.

103

DON'T LOOK BACK

Zeus has unleashed a damned minotaur on us.

"It's not an enchantment, like the dragon or the frog!" Jackie hisses. "It's real."

The dragon's fire was real enough if you ask my arm, so I'm not sure if I care about the difference. And what we should be doing right now is not standing here staring.

With a bellow, the minotaur disappears, and a cloud of dust and debris bursts out of the crevice into the sky. It's having trouble climbing out.

"My compass indicates there's no one path," Samuel says. He's already tucking the copper instrument away. "But go through the gates. You can't go around them." Then he shoves something in my hands. "Here. This showed up in my room, but I know it's yours."

I look down to find the handle of my axe in my hands.

What the—

I reach into the vest pocket where I keep my relic, but it's still there. This isn't mine. This is…Hades'. The twin that completes the set Odin gave him.

Zeus *stole* it and gave it to Samuel.

It's not a relic or tool Samuel already owned, like I did with my axe and the dragon teeth.

That godsdamned cheater.

Another bellow. The minotaur is pissed. Great. Why are we standing here?

"Run." Diego beats me to it.

His glow is immediately doused as he disappears from sight. Like horses out of the starting gates, the rest all take off. Not together. Not a single one of us is sticking together. Because we can all win now.

Me too. I should be running. Instead, I drop to one knee, reaching a hand into one of my zippered pockets.

I have a few dragon teeth left. About four of them. I start digging a hole in dirt that is packed so hard it doesn't want to budge and my scratching's barely making a dent, so instead I shove the white shards of bone into one of the cracks and hope that's enough. If last time was any indication, it'll take a few minutes.

The horns are back. Fuck me, I should have just run. Two massive hands appear at the top of the crevice again. I pull out both my axes, holding them up. Not that they can do much against a thing that size, but they're better than nothing. It's coming out with its back to me. That will buy me a little more time.

I take off after the others, who are far enough ahead that they're small in the distance. Trinica is closest to me. And Samuel, maybe still weakened from his wound, isn't much farther ahead. Jackie and Zai are still on the ground, having not used their gifts of flight yet. The others are all too far away to tell.

The minotaur is halfway out, now off to my right, covered in brown-and-white mottled fur. Its bull head sits atop a human-ish body—huge shoulders, bare cowhide-covered torso. The human shape of him is rippling with muscles on muscles.

Run faster, Lyra.

The minotaur swings a leg up to the ground. The thing is wearing breeches of some sort that only come to its calves, revealing that, like satyrs, its lower half is the same animal as its head—also bull, with the same brown-and-white coat. Both hooves finally on firm ground and chest heaving with anger and effort, the minotaur rises to its full height, towering into the skies, back to me still.

But movement must catch the minotaur's eye, because it whips around to face us.

Its fur-covered face is grotesque, with a brass ring through its wrinkled, glistening nose. But of all the parts of the minotaur, including its size, the scariest are its eyes.

Cold, glassy, black eyes with no whites, as if the soul was sucked out of the beast a long time ago.

My stomach twists even as I pump my arms and legs.

I'm at the back of the herd. The obvious weak one. I am fucked.

Its head comes down, and it paws the water-starved dirt with a hooved foot, kicking up dust. Its body vibrates with rage built up from its frustrating climb, and I'm the easiest target available to take it out on.

This time, its bellow shakes the very earth.

The minotaur charges, coming straight at me. Out in the open. Alone.

Adrenaline hits my blood hard, and my heart pumps fast as I force my body across the long, flat distance between me and the gate. The ground shudders with every pound of its hooves as it closes in on me.

I know I'm not going to make it when a puff of humid, rank breath hits me in the side of the face.

With a yell, I stop and face it, but not with any real plan. But before I can make one, some invisible, magical force draws my axes up as if they are magnetized. They cross at the hilts, and the second they do, a force strikes them so hard I'm thrown to the ground, but so is the minotaur.

I don't wait around to figure out what just happened. I'm back on my feet and moving.

But it doesn't take the bull long to get up and chase me again. I got lucky last time. This time, I have no choice. I'm reaching for a pearl in my vest, thinking I'll only use it to escape him, when a streak of turquoise zooms by me and rushes the minotaur's head. The monster pulls up mid-charge. Another wine streak with white wings is right behind that, and the minotaur bats at the air with its beefy hands.

Jackie and Zai.

Zai manages to get in a stab with the Harpe of Perseus, hitting the minotaur's forehead. On another ground-shaking bawl of rage, the bull swings its head, and Zai catches one of its massive horns in the stomach—thank the Fates, not with the tip—but it catapults him through the air, the wings on his sandaled feet beating ineffectually against the momentum.

"Zai!" I yell, my stomach twisting as I watch him flip midair.

He recovers before hitting the ground, and I almost stumble in relief.

"Go!" Zai shouts at me, then flies back at the minotaur.

And I do.

Heart now in my throat for them, making it hard to breathe, I run as fast as I can for the gate. Any second, I expect to hear a crunch of bones as it hits one of them, but I don't stop. It would only keep them in danger longer.

The ground under my feet quivers. I think.

I keep running.

Up ahead, I see Samuel pass through the gate, where Dae is already waiting for him.

Another quiver, harder this time, shakes clumps of dry dirt loose. Then another shudder, even bigger, and I have to slow down because it's moving the ground under my feet.

That's when four bone soldiers the size of the minotaur erupt from the ground in a blast of dirt and sand.

My bone soldiers are formed as men, rather than merfolk like last time. They wield bone spears and shields, bone helms covering their heads.

The minotaur stops swatting at Jackie and swings around to face down this new threat.

I point and yell my orders. "Protect us from all the monsters."

Immediately, the bone soldiers crouch, shields up, spears at the ready. In a single line, they take a step toward the minotaur. Then another.

Their bones clatter when they do, the sound ominous. The sound I imagine death makes when a reaper visits.

The threat to the minotaur is clear, and the bull focuses solely on the soldiers, no longer paying any attention to Zai or Jackie. The beast paws the earth again. It also crouches, fist to the ground like a defensive lineman, and lowers its head to peer at the soldiers from eyes narrowed with fury. Its breath blows dust up off the ground as it snorts and paws. Then it does a full-body shiver, its muscles bunching before it springs into a sprint.

I skid through the open iron doors tall enough to let King Kong through, then whip around. "Run!" I yell. Trinica made it through ahead of me. She is with Dae and Samuel, none of them moving on to the next gate yet, transfixed on the stragglers trying to make it through the gate, each shouting and screaming to urge someone on.

I scour the area for any of the other champions and catch sight of Rima close by, Amir right behind her.

"Come on!" I wave at them.

Zai and Jackie dive to whip through the gate overhead, but then the minotaur clocks Rima and Amir and runs at them with a bellow.

The two bone soldiers closer to us beat him to the champions, each scooping one up.

"Close the gates!" Jackie yells.

"What? Why?" The gate stands solitary in the wide, flat valley, disconnected from the mountains far to either side. It's just symbolic, isn't it? It's not going to stop anything.

"Walls! I can see walls." She's already pushing at one door to swing it closed, but it's not moving more than an inch or two.

The rest of us start pushing with her. Even with Samuel's strength, the gates resist us. Do all of us have to get through to close them? Or die. I can see Zeus thinking that's a fun little twist.

The soldiers are almost to us, but the minotaur is faster, bearing down on them like death incarnate.

It's right behind them.

"Here! Samuel!" Diego's voice comes from nowhere, and a telescoping spear made of brass appears and tumbles through the air.

Samuel catches it and hurls it at the minotaur, his enhanced strength shooting it like a rocket. It hits the creature in the cheek, and the minotaur roars but doesn't slow. Samuel goes back to pushing the doors.

The bull lunges for the skeleton holding Amir, and it stumbles but keeps its feet. One after the other, the soldiers take diving leaps for the gate, sliding through on their bellies.

But the minotaur is right there, and the gates aren't shut.

"Please let this work," I mutter, then jump into the open space between the doors.

"What in the name of Hades are you doing, Lyra?" Trinica yells after me.

Both axes in my hands, I cross them in front of me, then try not to flinch or move as the minotaur bears down. The thunder of its hooves competes with the pounding of my heart as the other champions yell at me to get out of the way.

"Close the gates!" I yell back. It's still taking all of them pushing to do it.

Then I brace.

This time, when the minotaur hits, I see it. My axes form an invisible shield in front of me—a lot like the walls to either side of the gates, I'm guessing. The minotaur bounces off it like it rammed into a mountain. I get thrown backward. Samuel catches me, and my momentum sends us both tumbling, my axes flinging out to the sides.

"Ouch," I groan.

"Watch it!" Amir yells.

I jerk my head off the ground in time to see one of the skeletons still on the minotaur's side of the gate slam into it as it's lumbering to its feet. The minotaur throws it off with ease, but that gave the second soldier enough time to get to us. It squeezes through to our side. I guess I was right about getting us all through to close the gates, because suddenly, they slam closed in a rush.

The doors lock a heartbeat before the bull rams the entire gate with a resounding *clang*.

104

MONSTERS, MONSTERS EVERYWHERE

I pitch forward, sucking in air. "Fucking…bloodthirsty…gods," I mutter at the cracked earth.

"Here," someone—Dae, I think—says, handing me my axes.

"Thanks."

The minotaur backs up and tries to run around the gate, only to bounce off whatever invisible barrier is there. With a bellow, it's back on its feet, running back and forth to either side of the gate, testing the wall it can't see.

And maybe that's why I don't recognize the shaking of the ground for what it is.

Not until a sickly yellow tentacle curls out from the same fissure that the minotaur crawled out of. Only on this side of the gate.

No rest for the wicked, I guess.

I point at the fissure. "Go—"

Together, we take off again, and while I run, I check to my right, watching and waiting.

What in Tartarus did Zeus send us now? A few creatures from history have tentacles, none of them good. Would they do well out of water, though?

I catch a movement and, after staring hard, realize it's Dae. What in the hells is he doing, sprinting toward the fissure instead of to the gate like we are?

He grips Artemis' arrow in his hand. His prize from the fifth Labor.

That fool. He's trying to give us all a better chance. Risking life and limb, he runs straight to the tentacle and jabs the arrow tip into the writhing suckered appendage. A howl of pain that is somewhere between a whistle and a roar blasts out of the crevice, and a hundred tentacles burst from the deep crack, flinging and waving into the dark skies. They squirm as they drop back down to the land, but then, acting as one, they shove, and the creature that leaps from the bowels of the Underworld is what nightmares are made of.

Similar to the minotaur, it has a partially humanlike form, standing upright with two human legs, two arms coming from broad shoulders, and a head atop those shoulders.

That's where the similarities stop.

Tentacles of all sizes protrude from its body, becoming extra arms, and more slender tentacles form strands of its long hair. Even thicker tentacles sprout from the waist that can apparently act like legs as it slithers its way over the ground.

Its face is also far from human. It is like an octopus, but one with holes gouged through its head where eyes should be and rows of razor-sharp teeth in the maw that I guess is its mouth.

A kraken?

I bark a laugh through heaves of breath as I keep running. Of course, a kraken.

Female, I think, based on her breasts and the form of her body. The kraken is dragging one of the armlike tentacles. That must be the one Dae stabbed with the arrow. It didn't kill her. It barely slowed her down.

She tips her creepy-ass head to one side, taking in the field, and I think that hole of teeth...smiles.

Shit. "Scatter!" I yell.

Giving her a single target is a bad idea.

Dread is an icy lump in my chest, and a shudder threatens to shake my teeth loose.

From the other side of the first gate, the minotaur roars, and the kraken rears back and roars in return. They're...communicating.

Fuck, fuck, fuck.

The bone soldiers must agree with me, because I hear a crack of bones, and when I glance back, the two still with us are in that crouched stance, facing the kraken. Then the bone soldiers and kraken lunge at each other, and chaos erupts.

The bone soldiers lock their shields and absorb the hit before driving the kraken back, but she manages to plant a foot against a boulder and grab one of the shields, throwing that soldier to the ground.

And all of us champions are now running to stay out of the way on a battlefield of giants.

I sprint in one direction, only to skid to a halt when a skeleton crashes to the ground in front of me, spraying dirt into my face. Its jawbone separates and lands not a foot from me. In an instant, it's back on its feet, grabbing the jaw off the ground. It shoves it back on, then opens it wide in an eerie silent scream of retribution. Then it launches itself in the air, spear held high. When it comes down, the kraken has moved, and the spear tip slams into the ground, sending more dirt and dust up into the darkening skies, making it even harder to see.

Coughing and wheezing and blinking the grit from my eyes, I go the other way and have to hit the deck, belly to earth, as one of the kraken's tentacles flies by overhead. I glance left and see Trinica rolling in the opposite direction.

Air punches from my lungs. Gods, that was close.

Move your ass, Lyra.

As I try to circle the fighting, I'm keeping an eye on the kraken through the dust. I don't see Trinica beneath the kraken's feet until the monster is on top of where she's still on her knees and blinking in a stunned stupor. But Samuel is suddenly there, too. Arms up, he takes the full weight of the kraken as she stomps down on them. From here, I can't see if she squished them or not.

Closer to me, Rima jumps up onto a boulder. With a yell, she breaks the lid off a small glass vial, and dragon fire explodes out of it. The immediate, crackling *boom* is so loud I clap my hands over my ringing ears, the flare so bright I have to squeeze my eyes shut, blinking rapidly but only seeing spots dancing. The smell of sulfur fills the air.

That had to have killed the kraken, right?

My vision comes back in time to see the kraken stumbling around, hands clapped over the holes where her ears must be, a massive scorch mark in her chest, her dead eyes wild.

Samuel is dragging Trinica away toward the second gate. I don't see Rima. Which is when I realize the kraken is stumbling in my direction, a bone soldier attacking at the same time.

I take off again. The world seems to be a chaos of dirt and battle around me, the roars of the furious creatures and the clattering and clashing of bone and flesh filling the air. As I run, I search for anything—a rock, a boulder…I'd accept a shallow dried riverbed at this point—just for a little cover. Which is why I don't see the tentacle swinging at me through the dust obscuring the air until it's too late. I cross my axes in front of me again, getting ready to be slammed into, when something tackles me from the side. Strong arms wrap around me as I'm lifted into the air in jerking beats.

Jackie.

"You goddess!" I cry out.

She grins and flies me straight through the second gate—this one is bronze and just as scrolly as the first. Jackie drops me on the ground next to Trinica just as Amir stuffs a white petal into her mouth.

"Be right back." Jackie shoots back into the dustup.

Samuel and Dae are next through the gate, and we're still waiting, positioned to close the gate quickly, flinching with every rattle of bones and blast of the kraken, the minotaur's yells still trumpeting in the distance.

"There!" Rima points.

Above, Jackie shoots through the dust-laden skies, Zai behind her with the Harpe of Perseus drawn.

The second they're through, the doors shut on their own, and the lock clicks again.

Two down.

One to go.

"What in the name of the Underworld?" Samuel mutters.

Collectively, we all turn.

Trinica narrows her eyes. "That can't be good."

ALL THE REASONS WHY

The darkness here is so thick, the stars and moon don't penetrate. A few feet in front of me, it's like a wall of shadow has been raised, obscuring everything.

Which means not only do we have to deal with whatever creature is next without seeing it coming, we have to find the gate, too.

Trinica pulls a strange pink stone out of a pocket and studies it. The prize she won from Athena's Labor—the Stone of Imithacles, a relic none of us had heard of before but which will give one true answer a day. "Might as well put this to use," she says, then closes her fingers tightly around it. "How do we pass through this last gate safely?" she asks.

She closes her eyes, but I don't hear or see anything. I guess the others don't, either, because we're watching her and glancing at one another. All while the kraken and my remaining skeleton warriors battle on the other side of the gate.

Then she opens her eyes. "It said, *don't listen.*"

"Don't listen to what?" Rima asks.

"What does that mean?" Diego's disembodied voice asks.

Which is when I hear it. I think we all do, because each of us slowly stiffens.

Singing.

Beautiful voices raised in song.

Don't listen.

"Sirens," Zai whispers beside me.

"You're finally here," a voice as beguiling as a lover's sigh beckons from the dark. "Come play with us."

The others immediately all move forward, their gazes dreamy. Diego must take his ring off, too, because out of nowhere, he appears, then is swallowed by the wall of shadows.

Everyone but me, Jackie…and Samuel.

Jackie grabs Rima's arm, but she shakes her off hard and keeps going. Samuel reaches for Dae, but Dae's too fast, sprinting away.

"Stop!" I try to pull Zai back, but he pushes me to the ground before disappearing into the dark like the others.

Confusion is a writhing knot in my stomach. Jackie's blessing is to see through enchantments, so I guess she's protected from the sirens. But Samuel…

He stares back at us for a wide-eyed blink.

"That explains the color of your eyes today," Jackie whispers. "You've been glamoured."

In other words, Zeus did something to him to help him resist this.

"Why aren't you affected?" she asks me.

"No clue."

It doesn't matter. One of us still needs to get to that gate. Maybe if we do, the Labor will stop and they'll be okay. But I doubt it.

We all look into the darkness.

"We need to get the others across the line," Jackie says.

Not waiting for us to agree, she heads into the dark.

With a nod, Samuel activates his shield, holding it before him as he also heads off.

I extract the tiny vial from my vest—my prize from Apollo—and squeeze drops of Eos' tears into my eyes. Immediately, my vision changes—it's like looking at the world through iridescent light, as if dawn has turned the land around me blue and bronze and orange and yellow, highlighting the details.

"Here we go," I whisper to myself.

Then step into the shadows.

Even with my enhanced sight, the darkness is suffocating. It feels like I'm buried alive or drowning. The sensation is beyond unpleasant. It takes every ounce of focus I have not to give in to the panic trying to crawl up my throat.

Around me, scattered across the wide, long, flat earth, are the other champions. They seem to be walking in circles or sort of drunken, meandering paths. I move slowly, one step in front of the other, guard up for anything dangerous.

But it's just the nine of us. No monsters. No sirens. I don't even hear them now.

"Yes!" Trinica lifts her arms to the skies like a child reaching for a parent. "Take me!"

Something flashes from the sky to the ground so fast I can't make it out, and just as fast, it zooms upward.

And Trinica is gone.

"Holy shit!" I stumble back.

"What was that?" Jackie calls to me.

"I don't know." Do sirens move that fast? And where did they take Trinica?

A sound like a flag snapping in a stiff wind has me whirling around in time to see the same thing take Diego.

Then Jackie yells, and I whirl again to find her with her wings spread, fighting another winged creature that's trying to take her into the sky. The thing manages to pin her wings and arms down, and it rockets away.

Do something, Lyra.

Only there's nothing I can do except stumble around.

They're too fast.

"Where are you?" I hear a siren's singsong voice behind me and whirl to find it standing in front of Samuel, who has his shield up. Can it not see him? Is the shield warded against them or something?

"I hear you," Zai calls out, and the siren whirls.

When she goes for Zai, I have an axe ready, and I throw. It hits the creature in the arm, and the siren screams. But then two more descend, taking her and Zai with them when they go.

My axe clatters to the ground in their wake. I run over to scoop it up, only for that same sound to come down close by. When I look around, Amir is gone.

There's a flash of gold flying through the air at the siren coming for Rima. Samuel must have thrown his Aegis at whatever is after her. But he misses, and almost a single breath later, a siren takes him, too.

Then Rima. Then Dae.

And then...I'm alone.

I mean completely alone. Abandoned in the middle of the desert, cracked, dry earth beneath my feet. Quiet settles all around me. Even the kraken and minotaur, trapped behind the walls at my back, have gone silent. And the darkness feels like it's pressing in on me, growing heavier and heavier.

I can't breathe.

All the champions are gone.

I swallow.

Then jump when that flash of movement comes down right on top of me, and suddenly, a siren is standing before me.

Even with the Tears of Eos painting the details of her face and form in unique lights and lines, I can still see the beauty and deadly danger of the creature. She is all woman except for her arms, which are wings, the feathers reaching the ground. She wears a skirt of sorts, belted low over her hips and with slits up the sides that bare her long legs, and flowers cover her breasts. Her hair is made of feathers sweeping back from her face like a warrior's headdress, reminding me of Athena's armor.

I don't think her skin is human flesh. It's white, with intricate, swirling markings that look like feathers and tears at the same time. And her face and features could rival Aphrodite for symmetrical, curving perfection.

The siren lifts her chin, slowly turning her head from side to side, eyes skating past me as she seems to search around her. "I sense you, mortal. Why can't I see you?" Gods, what a voice. Like honey and music and the sound of gentle running water. "Come to me and let me love you."

I stay very still, holding my breath so even my chest doesn't move.

She cocks her head the way a bird of prey does. "I will love you better than anyone in your life," she tempts.

For the briefest second, Hades' face fills my mind. Then the siren's gaze shoots to me, and I wrap my hand across my mouth to smother my breath.

But she still can't see me.

Like I'm invisible.

And that's when I know for sure.

What Homer didn't know when he composed the Odyssey, something they now teach us in school, is that sirens don't just lure humans with their songs—they crave the human's love almost to the point of sickness, and so they steal them away to their island, where there isn't food or water to sustain mortal lives.

My stomach twists into a thousand knots, my chest so tight I can't breathe from the pain echoing in my heart.

Hades didn't choose me because he saw something special when we first met. The exact opposite, in fact.

I take a shuddering breath. Then another. Hades picked me because of what I'm not.

Lovable.

106

THE CHOICE WAS ALWAYS MINE

Hades *knew*. He had to have somehow found out Zeus' Labor, and he knew I could win it. Because of my curse.

Because I can't be loved.

And that makes me invisible to the sirens.

With no warning, the siren standing before me spreads her wings and takes to the sky. So fast. They move so incredibly fast. I can't even track where she goes.

I search the skies for any trace that she's nearby. What if I move and she sees and pounces? I take a single, tentative step forward.

Nothing happens.

And another step, and another.

Still nothing happens.

And then I blink and the gate is right before me. Not close, but with luck, I can make it there without the siren finding me. I can't tell what kind of metal the gate is made from because of my distorted vision, but I swear angels' wings are designed in the scrollwork, like they are the gates of heaven of a different god.

What they are to me is salvation. The finish line. I can win.

I could end the Labor for the others as well.

Let's end this.

Slowly, I make my way, step by careful step, to the swirling gates, the finish line beckoning. An enticement, just like the sirens. And I get there. I get to where I only have to take one step. One single step.

But I can't make myself take it. My gut is screaming at me that this is wrong.

Hands fisted at my sides, I close my eyes and try to think.

Will the gods leave their champions—who will have lost them the Crucible—to die with the sirens? Even if I end the Labor, the gods don't have to go get them. The Crucible will be over. No need for their mortal champions after today. And the gods are known for their pettiness.

Well, almost all of them.

But could Hades even save them if he wanted, once I ended the Labor? Something tells me in my bones that Zeus set this final Labor up so that there would be no champions left but his own. He just wasn't expecting me.

But if I stop now, I could lose it all. For Hades. For Boone. For Persephone.

My hand shakes as I slip my fingers into a zippered pocket, bring out one of my pearls, and study it. The thing is…I can't let the others just die. And I don't think Hades would want me to, either.

Realization stays my hand for a second as that last thought connects all the dots for me suddenly.

Hades wouldn't want me to leave them. Even hating the danger I'd be in. Even hating my losing. He'd know that I can't abandon them. That I would never choose to.

My eyes widen as I suddenly realize why he's been pushing me away. He knew what this would cost me, and he was giving me a choice.

He's always seen me better than anyone else, even myself sometimes. My memory flashes back to that moment when we first met, when he said my ability to put myself first would serve me well. I'd thought he was calling me selfish—but maybe he saw me clearly even then. That, probably in some part due to my curse and my need to be loved, I put everyone else before myself. But sometimes, I need to put myself first. Like now.

I need to make the best choice now for *me*. Not because of Hades. Or Persephone. Or even for Boone. I need to choose what *I* can live with—and that means saving my friends.

And he knew.

I remember the way Hades held me after Isabel died. The way he never left my side both times I was injured. The way he was when we came together. Those moments were real. Not him moving pieces on the chess board. Real.

He wouldn't want me to win now if it means living with the pain that

I could have saved everyone. Or at least tried to.

I know that's real, too.

Because if he already knew I could win this challenge, then he also knew I would win it for him. If I didn't hate him, then I might choose winning for *him* over saving everyone else. And he made me hate him so that I would make the choice for *me*.

In his own fucked-up way, he's told me exactly what's in his heart.

Because he was willing to sacrifice what I felt for him, even his own needs, to give me a choice. And I don't hesitate to use his gift now.

I swallow the pearl, picturing exactly where I want to go.

Using my pearls is jarring every time. The same force throws that invisible lasso around my waist and drags me until I'm standing on top of a rock that juts out over pristine blue waves that rush up against it, sending a mist of water over me. When the waves recede, I can see the details of everything on the bottom of the ocean.

Only in an oddly colored way, thanks to the Tears of Eos.

What I'm standing on is one of many such rocks, projecting from the water like spikes, that form a crown around a small island. Doors, windows, and recognizable shapes of buildings are carved out of the natural rock. And all around—in the crevices, on the boulders, in the water—are flowers bursting with color...and bones. Human bones bleached white by the weather and sun. Thousands of them.

Anthemusa. The Isle of Sirens.

But where are they? Shouldn't at least a few of them be out here on these rocks, luring sailors to their deaths? I check the skies but see no birdlike creatures anywhere.

Carefully, I pick my way across my rock ledge to the island itself. It isn't massive, but I'll have a lot of spaces to check in the carved buildings. Or get caught.

I decide to approach this methodically, a room at a time.

Before I set foot through the first doorway, though, I hear it. Singing. But a turmoil of singing, almost like listening to a pack of coyotes in a killing frenzy.

Zeus be damned, that's not good.

As quickly and quietly as I can, checking around each corner and in every door I pass, I follow the sound, tracking it as it gets louder and louder until I almost stumble into them.

Sirens, hundreds of them, are gathered in an amphitheater carved into the rock of the island itself. At the heart of the theatre, the stone forms a semicircle of tiered seats around a flat bottom, facing a stage that looks like several stories of carved pillars and doorways.

I stand in the shadow of an archway at the back, at the top of a set of steep stairs leading down into the amphitheater. A bird's-eye view, so to speak. In the flat space before the theater, also carved from rock, are straight-backed chairs that look like thrones. Five of them, in which more sirens sit. The leaders, maybe?

Kneeling before them, faces slack with enchanted wonder, are Zai, Rima, and Diego.

None of them are restrained or fighting. They appear perfectly content to sit there as the sirens seem to argue, but in song. To me, so many voices are a cacophony. I can't tell what they are saying or arguing over.

But I'm guessing it's over my friends.

Where are the others?

I scan the grounds for any sign of where they could be and pause at the sight of two younger sirens standing with their backs to a door that leads into the stage itself.

They have to be in there. Right?

Make a plan, Lyra.

Coming up with this one doesn't take long, but it's going to involve at least two more pearls if everything goes perfectly. Exactly the number of pearls I have left.

But when has anything gone perfectly in these challenges?

I'm tempted to send a prayer to the gods. *Please let me get us out of here without leaving anyone behind.*

107

CLERK, ALLY, FRIEND

I don't know how long it takes me to work my way around the amphitheater to the back side of the stage. A while. I can hear the sirens the entire time, keeping them to my left thanks to the terrain and buildings of the isle. Every so often, one takes off into the skies, and I have to duck into shadows or hide in doorways.

It's not until I'm staring at the back of Jackie's blond head that I actually believe I can pull this off.

The other champions are held in a small chamber with a door that leads to the sirens and a window—not big enough to climb through—at the back. I don't want to startle them. If they make too much noise, it'll draw attention to us.

I give a tiny whistle.

Two heads turn my way—Samuel's and Jackie's.

Jackie's ocean-blue eyes go wide. "Lyra!" she whisper-screams. And I wince, waving at her to be quiet before we both go very still, listening for the sirens guarding the other side of the door. They don't come. I check over my shoulder, and no one is in sight. But the tension already riding the muscles in my shoulders cranks down harder.

They come to the window. "Tell me you have a plan," Jackie whispers much more softly.

I show them my pearl. "I need all of you holding hands tight, and for you to hold mine."

Samuel nods. "Got it."

They work fast, Samuel carrying the others, one by one, over to the window, and Jackie lining them up with hands held. They've got Dae and Trinica in place when a ruckus breaks out inside the theater, the sirens' argument gaining steam. A few shoot up into the skies, their shadows passing over me. Then two sirens come running around the corner, out a side door from the amphitheater, and Jackie and I freeze.

Only…they don't seem to notice me.

My heart is in my throat, trying to choke me, but that's okay, since I'm holding my breath anyway…as they walk right past where I'm squatted, hand stuck through the window. Never even glance in my direction.

Somewhere, the goddess of irony has to be laughing her ass off.

Once they're out of earshot, Jackie mutters, "What in the name of Hades just happened?"

"More like in the name of Zeus." I hope that asshole is choking on frustration right about now. "Hurry."

Samuel gets Amir in place at the end of the line, and Jackie checks all their handholds one last time, then comes to the window, taking Dae's hand and mine, gripping tight.

Please, for the love of Hades, let me be able to take them all with me.

I set one pearl on my tongue and get two more ready in my hand, then swallow.

The weight of so many people with me pulls at my bad arm—the one the dragon burned—and even in the void of sound, a shout is pulled from my throat, cutting off jarringly when we land directly outside the final gate in a heap.

"Where am I?" I hear Dae groan.

Sharp relief hits me with an added burst of adrenaline. "Get across the finish line before the sirens can come for you again," I tell them.

Then gulp down another pearl.

I materialize exactly where I pictured—right behind my kneeling friends in the center of the amphitheater.

It was a risk, but I figured it's faster than sneaking in.

I hold very still and wait for the sirens to scream or attack or have any kind of reaction.

Nothing.

They are still arguing among themselves, and it's like I'm not even here.

I lean over to Zai and whisper in his ear, "Take Diego and Rima's hands."

He sways away from me, frowning a little. "Lyra?" he asks. Not whispers. Says it right out loud.

One of the sirens in the throne-like seats up front focuses in on him, frowning a little.

"Did you hear Lyra?" he leans over to ask Rima.

"Who?" She's even louder.

The siren watching sits a tad straighter.

Shit.

Think, Lyra, think.

The sirens have already shown how fast they are, but I can't hold on to all three, and I don't have enough pearls for an extra trip. I need a way to make my friends hold hands without making a scene.

Wait. Poison.

Didn't Zai get a stone that's an antidote to poison as his prize for Hera's Labor? Please, please, please let siren song be included in that. Pickpocketing skills have never come in handier in my entire fucking life. I find the tiny, lime green, pea-shaped stone in one of his pockets.

"Zai," I whisper again.

"Hey—" The second his mouth is open, I slip the antidote on his tongue, and he coughs a little. The effect is immediate. He goes dead silent, blinks, and then his eyes fly open wide.

"Don't move," I whisper urgently at him.

To his credit, Zai manages to stay still and say nothing. That siren is watching him carefully, though.

"Look dazed and happy if you can and don't say a word," I tell him. "They can't see me, but they can see you."

Okay. Now for the tricky part.

"When I say so, take Diego and Rima's hands and hold on tight." I wrap my arms around his waist.

The siren on the throne suddenly gets to her feet, prowling in our direction.

"Now!"

Like that one word sets her off, the siren coming our way suddenly screams and spreads her wings wide. The theater explodes in chaos as more sirens jump to their feet and take to the air. But at least he fucking takes Rima and Diego's hands.

And I swallow one more pearl.

When we show up in the desert, someone—maybe Diego—knocks

into me, and I end up flat on my back on the hard-packed ground, dust poofing up around me. Coughing, I scramble to my feet.

"Hurry!" I tug Zai up with me. "Get across the line before they come."

The sirens are fast. They'll figure out where we went and be here in no time.

Rima and Diego are up, all three of them confused but no longer dazed. "What happened?" Rima asks in a voice that slurs.

"Answers are for later." I grab Zai's hand and whirl away, intending to drag him with me if I have to, only to pull up short at the sight of the others—Samuel, Jackie, Trinica, Amir, and Dae—all lined up.

On *this* side of the gates.

My heart is like a trapped thing in a snare, beating to get out. "Have you lost your senses? Get over there!" I have my axes out in front of me in one hand, my back to the group in the next moment. Clearly, they're still working off the effects of siren song. Maybe I can hold off the sirens until they are all safe. Eos' tears are still helping me see, and none are here. But any fucking second... "They're coming."

"We want you to go first," Trinica says.

"What?" I cast a frown over my shoulder to find them all still there. Her words make no sense. Still holding my axes out, I start dragging Zai with me. "I don't have enough pearls to go and get you again."

Zai pulls out of my grip. "Then you'd better hurry and win."

Along with Rima and Diego, he joins the others. Waiting for me.

And my caged heart wants to burst at the show of solidarity.

For me.

They want me to win? Even after what Rima saw in her vision. Even after deciding it was dangerous. They weren't wrong to fear that future. My lips twist around the emotion clogging my throat, around the urge to wrap my arms around them all. But there's no time.

"Let's all go together." I hurry to them on the line, still facing away from the gate with my shield in front of us.

"You first." Samuel gives my shoulder a gentle shove. But with the added strength Zeus granted him, the force has me tumbling backward through the doors of the gate.

I stumble to a halt and stare at the champions.

In the next breath, everything about the Labors disappears—the

108

THE FINAL BLOW

E very part of me gets hit so hard with another burst of adrenaline, fear, and shock, my skin feels electrified.

It can't be.

I very slowly turn and find Cerberus is there before me, bigger than ever, as if he's grown to the same proportions as the other two monsters.

"Kill the mortal," Cer snaps inside my mind. He lifts all three heads and sniffs the air. *"Kill her,"* Rus snarls. Ber just growls, showing me teeth designed to rend the flesh from my bones.

Sour bile rushes up my throat, and I swallow the burn back down.

This isn't him. This can't be him. The rage pouring through his voices is…feral. Rabid. Which is when I catch sight of Ber's eyes. Black, soulless eyes. Like the minotaur. Zeus has to have them spelled. All of them.

But…the Labor is over.

We crossed the last finish line. Do all of us have to cross, like the other two gates? Except the gate is already gone. Thoughts fly through my head in a thousand directions.

Run. Hide. Help Cerberus.

Where the hells is Hades? Forget interfering. Zeus took Hades' godsdamned pet and is loosing him on me after the Labor is already over. That fucker is cheating. If the hound is killed, Hades will never forgive himself. We can't kill him. I won't let the others. But I can't let him hurt them, either.

Holding my axes up before me—a barrier between him and them—I face him. "Don't—"

A black paw slams into me from the side. I hear Cerberus growl as, on a cry, my arms flailing, I sail up into the air and back down. When I hit, my axes go sliding away in opposite directions and the wind knocks out of me so forcefully, my next breath sounds like I'm dying.

That horrible noise of trying to make my lungs work again is immediately drowned out by Cerberus' howls as he leaves the other champions behind and runs straight at me.

I see my friends scatter as soon as his back is turned, helping one another try to get to safety somewhere. Anywhere. My lungs are still struggling, and I'm swinging wildly between needing air and needing to run. The axes are too far away to get to both of them. I have my last pearl in my hand before I even think. It's my only way out. There's nowhere to hide here.

"Cerberus," I yell. He's so close. Right on top of me. "Don't do this. It's me. It's Lyra."

Cer...smiles. *"I know."*

What happens next comes so fast, I don't realize what I'm seeing until it's over. Cerberus lunges for me, and a massive spear made of bone lifts into the sky over his head, startling white with my changed sight.

"No!" I scream.

Too late.

The skeleton soldier plunges it into Cerberus' back. With a pathetic, horrible, heartbreaking yelp from all three heads, the hellhound twists around on the soldier, even as he falls to the ground.

And I have to scramble back to not get crushed when he does.

"No." The word tears from my throat. Then I'm stumbling to get around Cerberus' body to stop the bone soldier from finishing the job. "Don't hurt him," I order.

I don't care if Cerberus eats me. I can't let him die.

My protector immediately stands at attention, waiting for my next order.

"Lyra?" Cer's voice is shaky in my head now. No more fury. No more mindless rage.

"Oh gods," I whisper.

I reach out, only to jerk away at the sticky feel of blood, and Cer flinches from my touch, whimpering. His rapid pants are shallow and raspy. Ber and Rus are limp on the ground, eyes closed, unconscious and unmoving.

"I did not hurt you."

I pat his head. "You didn't hurt me."

"I could see what I was doing, but I could not stop myself." His voice is growing fainter.

"It's okay. It's okay." I'm shaking so hard, my hands keep clenching in jerking spasms, nausea rolling through me. "Can you get us to Hades?"

Where is Hades, anyway?

"Too…weak…"

"What will…fix you?"

"Only…the…" He stops, giving a pathetic little mewl. *"Styx."*

Then Cer growls, the sound broken but fierce as he looks at something behind me. The hairs on the back of my neck stand straight up, like I've touched a light socket. I don't have to look to know, but I do anyway.

Zeus.

Oh fuck. I really should have grabbed my axes before coming over to Cerberus.

The god's expression twitches with a sort of thwarted fury, but that's not what makes me backpedal. It's that, with my eyes still filled with Eos' tears, I'm seeing things now. And what I see is a shimmering veil of mesh over Zeus' face. In the odd rendering of the tears, it's all sorts of colors, like looking through a prism, and fitted to his features like it's been painted on.

What the hells is that?

Cold, heavy dread takes over my limbs, and I can't move, can't speak. I really wish freeze wasn't one of my trauma responses.

Incredulity ripples over Zeus' features. "I'll be damned," he mutters, then points an accusing finger at me. *"You* are the baby I cursed in my temple? The unlovable one?"

Shit. *Now* he remembers?

I lift my hands in the air in surrender, turning to face the god more fully.

He laughs, the sound a little out of control. Then he starts muttering and pacing. Something about, "If he knew all along, then he planned to become king."

While he's distracted, I roll my last pearl between my fingers, inching closer to Cerberus. I'll take him with me. To Styx, obviously. Maybe Charon can help him.

I slowly stretch my fingers toward Cer's head.

"No—" Zeus rounds on me, and his brows snap down in a scowl so dark, so wrathful, it transforms a face that is almost boyish in its handsomeness to twisted and terrifying. "I can't let him win."

So fast I barely register the movement, Zeus throws out his arms, and he is covered in head-to-toe armor. My mortal mind and body are too slow to react as lightning flashes from his hands and hits me right in the belly.

When the colossal *boom* and scorching flash of light recede, I'm not dead.

Not yet.

I'm on the ground, coughing up blood. The metallic taste of it in my mouth is the only thing that seems real. I don't even feel the pain yet.

Vaguely, I'm aware that the blast knocked me into Cerberus. My constricting throat makes every tortured breath an agony. I don't have to look at my stomach to know it's bad. Hands over my belly, I can feel the wide gash, the blood surging out of me with every pump of my heart— too fast. I'm losing too much blood. Weakness and heaviness invade my limbs and slow my mind.

Hades. Where are you?

"Lyra..."

Cerberus.

"I'm...still...here," I manage to whisper. I think I do. I'm not sure if my voice is working.

I'm still clutching the pearl. I close my eyes, scrunching them hard. I'm dead. I already know it, but maybe I can help him before I go. Even the Styx can't heal me from this one. Not fast enough. Not without more of Hades' blood first, and we don't have time for that.

Cer noses at me weakly, then falls back. And that's when I shove the pearl in his mouth, my hand coming away covered in thick, sticky drool. "Think of the Styx."

"No—"

But he's already gone.

I go limp on the ground. That took everything I had left. Now...I'm just going to lie here and die. At least I did something good with my last precious seconds of time. I stare up into the brightening sky and picture the Underworld. I'll be there soon enough.

Hades.

He's going to blame himself for this when he finds out. A tear squeezes from the corner of my eye.

Then Zeus' feet come into view directly in front of me. Probably to finish the job.

Honestly, I'd rather go fast than sit here and bleed anyway.

I smile. "Bring it, asshole."

109

THE GOD OF DEATH

Maybe I'm a coward, despite my bravado, because I close my eyes as I wait for the final blow.

"Don't. Fucking. Move."

My already struggling heart stutters. I *know* that voice. That sinful voice of darkness and soot.

Hades.

I'm in love with him.

Persephone isn't dead. I'm about to be. And I'm in love with Hades.

What a stupid, horrible, gods-awful time to figure that shit out.

I force my eyes open, and even through the spots still trying to steal my vision, I can see Hades standing behind Zeus. He's dressed in his liquid armor, his bident in his hand, the murder in his eyes as sharp as cut steel.

I squint, trying to make my spotty vision clear.

I don't have time to force my fuzzy mind to focus. Rage contorts Zeus' face a heartbeat before he launches himself at his brother.

I think I scream.

But what comes next happens so fast, my already dwindling mortal senses can't track it. One second, Zeus is rushing Hades. The next, he's on the ground, bleeding from the ears, and Hades stands over him, bident at his brother's throat.

Zeus' entire body vibrates with fury…and also visible fear. It turns him even more pale, red splotches mottling his skin.

"Are you going to kill me, brother?" he spits at Hades.

Hades leans closer, eyes so cold they look like silver frost. "You and I both know I easily could."

Zeus tries to move, then stops, probably realizing that if he does, he'll cut himself on the bident. "I won't let *you* have the throne."

Even as hazy as I am, it's obvious that Zeus is terrified of that possibility. This isn't just him throwing a fit at losing. This is something else.

Does he truly fear Hades that much?

"Aphrodite told me. About Persephone," Zeus says. "You're going to use the box to try to free her. Go around the seven wards. That's why you need the throne."

I don't know what box he's talking about, but the rest of it clicks right into place with what I already know.

"You can't," Zeus insists. "You'll unleash the Titans on the world again."

Hades' smile is one of pure determination. "Maybe I'll just unleash them on you."

"You cheated. They'll never give you the throne."

Hades barks an unamused laugh. "The one who cheats, who has always cheated, is you. In this Crucible alone, you've done so much—arranged extra sea dragons for Poseidon's Labor, killed Neve with strategically aimed lightning, glamoured Dex into a murderous rage, added new rules to your own Labor, and gave Samuel a glamour against the sirens, as well as my axe."

"Lies!" Zeus spits.

"He's telling the truth." Is that Zai?

A wavering form is standing just beyond Zeus. I try to focus, and he comes into clear view for a second. He's holding out the Lantern of Diogenes on its chain—Dae's gift—and Dae is standing right behind him.

The lantern is glowing.

I want to be horrified that Zeus did that. Disgusted. But I'm too numb. I'm almost gone. Lying in a pool of my own blood.

Then a familiar horrendous chorus of sound rends the night, louder even than the earlier turmoil of the monsters fighting. The Daemones appear in that whirlwind of feathers and fury. Hades stands back, and they take Zeus by the arms, forcing the wrathful god into the skies. They drag him away kicking and screaming.

"No!" he shouts. "Hades cheated, too. He knew about the sirens. He shouldn't have been allowed to play at all."

They ignore him, flying higher and higher. The last thing I hear is

Zeus' desperate cry. "He'll be the death of us all!"

Then, suddenly, Hades is with me.

He's with me.

His face is inches from mine, features blurry but unmistakable. "Lyra."

I manage to prop my heavy lids partially open. "You're...late."

"I'm so sorry. My brother locked me and the Daemones in the prison."

It feels like we've done this too often before—me dying while he tries to fix me in a panic. Being mortal really sucks. I groan, my eyes fluttering shut as he pulls my hand away from my stomach. "Fucking hells..."

Well, that's bad. I was pretty sure I was dying, but now I know for certain.

His hands come up to bracket my face. "Stay with me."

I train my gaze on his, trying to center on him and only him, the weakness, the pain, and everything else fading to nothing.

Just him.

"You made me...not love you...on purpose—" I cough. Too many words, and my body isn't going to let me say them.

"Yes," he replies in a tortured voice. "How did you know?"

I want to reach up, to cup his face, but I can't. "The sirens," I say. I need to explain more, but it would take too much effort. We don't have much time left.

"Do you get to...keep the throne...even if...I die?"

"No."

That sucks. "You'll find...another...way."

"Lyra—" Hades' deep rasp of a voice breaks over my name.

I catch his shuddering breath more through the one hand still on my face than the sound. "Not like this," he says. "Not—"

His face blinks in and out, the angle changing as I can't hold up my head. "Visit me...in...Elysium."

"Fuck." He's shaking so hard, I can feel it.

Rima's vision comes back to me. "Don't—" I can barely get words out now. They're so slurred, I hope he can understand me. "Don't...burn... down...the...world..."

The grave drags me into oblivion.

The Underworld waits for me.

110

AND THEN...

Light pierces my consciousness, waking me from nothingness.
I feel myself frown at it. They say this is common at the end, no matter what gods you follow.

The light is only a pinpoint in the distance at first, and then nearer. Not like a tunnel I need to go down, though. This light is coming to me. It grows and grows until I am awash in it, everything around me radiant. It parts the darkness like it's digging me out of it, and then...it touches me.

Warmth.

Glorious, perfect, soothing warmth. It's everywhere inside me, all parts of me, and yet not of me.

The warmth turns to...heat. Not searing heat. Not unbearable.

Just everywhere.

I still can't see anything but the light.

Then...a pulse of power.

It hits me so hard it's like a jolt of electricity.

Did Zeus just strike me with lightning again? What a dick. Doesn't he know I'm already dead?

Another jolt. And in the distance somewhere, a voice is calling. Faint.

What are they saying?

Another jolt. This time, an extra sizzle fills me with fear. The emotion is so strong it makes me want to run and hide.

My fear? What am I afraid of?

Another jolt. Then desperation.

"Come on, Lyra!"

Hades. That's Hades.

"Come back to me, my star."

Another jolt, and despair creeps into the emotions battering me.

Which is when I come back into myself in a *whoosh*. Into my body. And yet not. Because I feel no pain, no weakness, only vital, incredible, pulsating...life.

Life!

Another jolt—this one inundated with a sudden, searing hope—and I realize what I'm feeling is...him. His emotions.

"That's it," he whispers, as if he can't make his voice work anymore. "That's it. You can do this. Stay with me."

Always. I want to stay with him always.

"Open your eyes, Lyra."

And I do.

No fluttering. No struggle. I just open them.

To find that we are still in the desert. I am suspended in midair above the ground, upright, and Hades is standing below me, looking up. The champions are behind him, staring in awe.

And the light...the light is coming *from* me. Is me.

Hades smiles, dimples in full view, face covered in tears and every emotion he was keeping from me, holding back from me, stubbornly refusing to give to me before—it's all there in his eyes, in that smile that is for me alone.

"I can't believe that fucking worked," he says.

Incandescent happiness is like an explosion inside my chest. The light draws inward, as if my body absorbs it, consumes it, becomes it. And as it disappears, I lower slowly to the ground until my feet touch the packed earth.

Then the light is gone, and we are standing staring at each other.

"Hades?"

His smile turns serious as he searches my face, and then he's across the space between us, his arms wrapped around me so tight, it's hard to breathe.

And I don't care.

I don't care, because he's trembling and he's real and he's holding me. "I couldn't lose you," he says in a voice that breaks.

"What happened?" I whisper into his chest. "I died. I know I died." But before he can answer me, I close my eyes in terrible comprehension, tightening my arms around him. "Tell me you didn't—"

"If you mean I didn't give you my crown, it's too late to take it back."

I gasp. "Oh my gods..." He gave me the thing that means the most to him in the world, that makes him who he is? I died. He won't be crowned King of the Gods, either. He gave up *everything*. For me. "Why?"

"I couldn't lose you." He shrugs like it's no big deal. "I actually wasn't sure it would work."

I stare into eyes that harbor no doubts. "I'm...the Queen of the Underworld now?"

"Yes."

Holy shit. Holy shit. Holy... "Fuck me," I whisper. "I'm a goddess?"

The dimples flash again. "That too."

"Goddess of what?"

He huffs a laugh. "Probably curiosity and trouble," I think he mutters. Then, louder, he says, "It takes time to manifest."

Vaguely, I realize I'm in Hades' arms—surrounded by the other gods and goddesses and their champions. I glance at my friends, tears on their faces as they smile at me.

I turn back to Hades and shake my head. "I can't believe you did that—"

He cups the back of my neck with his palm, holding me closer.

I curl my hands into his shirt, burying my face in his chest, breathing in bitter chocolate. "Why? Why would you give that up for me?"

"Do you know what I see in Elysium?" He's smoothing his thumb over my cheekbone in rhythmic circles.

"What?"

"The two of us there. And you as my queen. I've seen it for a long, long time." He swallows hard. "I just thought it was only something I'd get in the afterlife someday. But now that I've had you there with me, I won't wait that long. Being King of the Underworld without you at my side is an eternity of my own personal hell."

He shudders against me, holding nothing back now.

He lifts his head, hands threading into my hair so he can stare down into my face. "Be the queen there. Keep me at *your* side."

Even though I can't turn back from being what he made me now, he's still giving me a choice.

This is what it feels like. To be loved. To be wanted.

To have a someone.

I always wondered. I always dreamed about how some day... But I never really believed it. Not even the night we shared ourselves.

I can't contain the smile that wants to burst from me. "No more games?"

I know Hades understands what I'm asking when his mercurial eyes spark with silver. "Only the fun ones."

111

THE MAKING OF SOVEREIGNS & GODS

I've been called many names in my twenty-three years in this world—criminal, cheat, bitch, unloved, cursed, champion—but those are just what happened to me. Not who I am. Especially now.

I have new names.

Better names—friend, goddess, survivor, lover...

Turns out being made a goddess knocked the curse right off me, although Hades claims that he broke it just with his charm alone.

"This is ridiculous," I mutter out of the side of my mouth at him.

"I agree, my star." He raises our clasped hands and presses a kiss to my knuckles, lifting his head with a smile.

And I melt a little.

He's been sweet like this these days following the Crucible while we've hidden out in the Underworld, reveling in the new world that we've started building together. Even Charon and Cerberus—the Styx healed our dog just fine—have hardly been allowed to visit us, and only on order of not telling us what's happening elsewhere. We'll deal with reality soon enough. In between...other things...Hades has been teaching me how to rule the Underworld. It's not easy.

But it feels worthwhile.

"Put up with the ceremony," he tells me as we walk down a long hallway in a building in Olympus I haven't been in before. "They'll gloat that we lost. But I don't think we have, and I'll show you why when we get home again."

A sizzle of his emotions—something that hasn't gone away yet—courses through my blood. Desire. But also a wonderous contentment that makes me giddy. Charon says it's disgusting how happy Hades is.

And that's despite our worry over not having solutions to help Persephone or Boone yet. She's still stuck in Tartarus. And Boone…well, Hades no longer has a crown to give up to make him a god. We're not even sure who won the Crucible, since the finish line disappeared after I crossed it. Probably Diego, seeing as he had the most wins before that.

In the days following the final Labor, Hades and I have talked. We talk now. About everything.

And we talked about this in detail. We decided that if Diego is the winner, the plan is to talk to Demeter—we'll help her get Persephone out of Tartarus. Although that's the second thing Hades hasn't told me specifics about yet—what being the King of the Gods had to do with it. Zeus said something about a box.

What I did discover is that it's connected to how Hades found out about the sirens being part of the Labors. When I asked, his expression took on a wicked glint filled with laughter and…a suspicious sort of knowing. "I have an inside source," he said. "Someone who can see the future."

I raised my eyebrows at that. "An oracle?"

There hasn't been an oracle born in centuries.

He shook his head. "I'll tell you someday soon. Just know that this person can see multiple futures. She is how I knew about the sirens. She is who told me to break your heart when I did."

"I'm pretty sure I don't like this source," I muttered darkly.

Which made him laugh.

"She's who told me to make you my champion. And the reason I trusted that you'd come out unharmed is because she also told me I'd be the King of the Gods. Which meant you'd win."

"And you *believed* her?" I crossed my arms and glared at him then. "But you're not king. I'm not so sure this source is trustworthy."

He shrugged, seeming unworried when what I would have expected him to be is suspicious or pissed. "I told you. She sees multiple futures." Then he pulled me into him, holding me tight and resting his chin on the top of my head. "As long as I have you, we'll figure out the rest."

So now, all we have to do is get through this crowning ceremony for whichever god or goddess won, then figure out a plan to help our friends. The new ruler better not be fucking Zeus. In fact, if he's there at all, I'm not entirely sure what Hades will do. He's gone smolderingly silent any time I bring up his brother.

With an irritated sound, I twitch at the dress I've basically been sewn into, which I have already been complaining about.

Hades is dressed in black again, mostly to see the way I would laugh at him, I think. A modern suit, designed to match my dress. Two butterflies facing each other, their wings forming a larger butterfly, are embroidered over his heart, right in the center of a black threaded star.

His symbol for the two of us.

Meanwhile, I am trussed up in a diaphanous gown of the unique, glowing blue of the Underworld. A sort of modern take on ancient Greece—slim fitting, it has a strap over only one shoulder, and the skirt splits into panels with long slits up to my hips. The material is sheer, and because of the slip that matches my skin so well, I look like I am naked underneath. Butterflies of many-colored iridescent threads are embroidered along every hemline. A gold band at my waist, more at my wrists, and a gold neckpiece that means I have to keep my chin up or pinch my skin in it are all sources of added irritation.

Aphrodite made me this gown. That's the only reason I am putting up with it.

"You go in here," he says. "Nike will escort you to where I'll be in a few minutes."

"What?" Is it silly that I don't want to leave his side? My heart shrivels a bit. I'm still traumatized after everything that happened, I guess.

He runs a finger down my cheek, and I shiver in response. "I'll be close, my star. I promise."

When I nod, he presses a kiss to my lips, then ushers me through double doors, closing them behind me. I pause just inside as I find all the other champions standing in a large room with no windows.

Zai sees me first, and he goes still, a slow smile breaking out over his face.

"Lyra!" Trinica is first across the room to pull me into her for a tight hug. "Oh my gods," she said. "We didn't know what happened to you."

By the time she lets me go, the others have made it to where we are, and I find myself being passed from hug to hug, laughing as I go.

When we finally stop all the hugging, I sober a little. I've been wanting to tell them this for days. "You should know that I've seen the others—Isabel, Meike, Neve, and Dex—they're all in Elysium now." I reach over and squeeze Dae's arm. "Your grandmother, too. She said to tell you to take care of your sisters and…" I repeat the Korean words she taught me, hoping I get it right.

His eyes turn a little glassy. "That means 'my family is my strength and my weakness,'" he whispers. "She used to tell me that when I got annoyed with my sisters." Then he gives me a small bow. "Thank you."

"Are you seriously a goddess, Lyra?" Amir asks.

I find eight pairs of eyes trained on my face. "Yes."

"Of what?" Zai asks.

I laugh. "We don't know yet. Still figuring it out."

"Well, don't expect me to pray to you," Zai says with a grin. And I laugh again.

I never thought I'd have this. Laughing with friends. It feels… amazing. Better than I imagined.

I wish we had more time. Maybe we should have come back here sooner.

We use the next few minutes to catch up. They've all been staying in Olympus. Apparently, the gods have been arguing for days about the winner, and the champions still aren't sure who it will be. Though, like me, they all assume it will be Diego. I'm tempted to ask Jackie if she ever saw that weird net-like veil over Zeus' face, thanks to her ability to see through enchantments. But now's not the time to solve that mystery.

"Champions." Zeles and Nike enter the room. "It's time to join your patrons."

Each of us is led off through a different walkway. I'm last, as always, and find myself in a small room with Hades. One with massive double doors.

"When they open those," Hades says as he tucks my hand around his arm, "we'll go out onto a stage. There will be a dais. Zeles will present us, and then we'll sit."

"Okay."

I can hear cheering and the muffled sound of Zeles' voice on the other side. It doesn't take too long before Nike appears suddenly and shoots me raised eyebrows. Her version of a smile. I smile back. Those days in jail with the Daemones netted me a few more friends, I think.

A chorus of trumpets sounds from outside.

Nike swings the doors open wide.

We step out into a roar of crowds. All the Olympic gods, demigods, and non-homicidal creatures are gathered in an amphitheater that extends into the skies, like a stairway to the clouds. We make our way to the center of the floor, as we were instructed to do. But before we can turn to take our seats on the dais, Zeles' voice rings out. "Before we begin, I have been asked to announce the winner of this century's Crucible."

I look over my shoulder and search for my friends' faces among those seated on the dais behind us.

Zeles waits for the buzz from the crowd to settle. "The winner is... Lyra Keres, the only Survival virtue in the Crucible, champion of Hades, god of death!"

I stumble, and only the fact that Hades goes still as a stone, pinning my hand in the crook of his arm, keeps me from falling flat on my face.

Wait.

I won the Crucible?

I look around wildly.

I won.

"Fuck me." The words just pop out unbidden.

The crowds in the seats, already murmuring in shock, chuckle, but I'm not paying any attention to them. I turn stunned eyes to Hades.

Zeles raises his voice over the din. "The Daemones unanimously voted that Lyra was still mortal when she crossed the finish line, was killed by something unrelated to the Labor, and, as the winner of the challenge, was also allowed to be healed, even to the point of bringing her back from death. With Zeus' addition of three wins added to her earlier win of Apollo's Labor, Lyra has the most points. Congratulations!"

"Like you said, my star," Hades murmurs. Then smiles in a way that lights up his eyes and flashes his dimples. "Fuck me."

Then he shocks even me, taking my face in his hands and kissing me in front of everyone.

He lifts his head and laughs. "And your virtue isn't Survival, my star. It's Loyalty."

Hades kisses me again, and the vague sound of the crowd's gasps disappears under the feel of his lips against mine.

Not fast and hard. Not soft and swift. He takes his time. He kisses me over and over until I sigh under his touch, until I forget the entire world exists as I lean into him. And he still doesn't stop. Not until he's damned good and ready.

By then, I'm wrapped in his arms.

He slows our kisses, sipping at my lips in softer and softer caresses until he reluctantly lifts his head, smiling down into my dazed eyes. "We can fix it all now," he whispers.

No convincing the other gods. No negotiating. No subterfuge or deals.

I blink. "Boone?" Then frown. "You'd have to give up a crown to make him a god, and you don't hold both crowns anymore."

His eyes twinkle at me. "But as winner of the Crucible, you get a boon. And you can ask for him to be made a god."

My heart swells, then ebbs a little. "Persephone?"

He shakes his head. "Even your prize can't reach her in Tartarus. But now that I'll be king, I have a way."

Sheer happiness bubbles in my veins.

Everything fixed. Boone. Persephone. And, if I have my way, which I know he'll let me, we're going to do away with the fucking Crucible forever.

A new ruler is just what Olympus needs.

He rights me and, as if none of that just happened with all of the immortal world watching with bated breath, takes me by the arm and leads me to stand before the empty throne, where Zeles waits.

Who might as well be tapping a foot in impatience.

I look stonily past the mostly dour-faced Olympian gods and goddesses seated around the throne in their own chairs in a semicircle, dressed to the nines. Their champions, my friends, are at their sides.

They cheer for me.

Not the gods, though, who are both furious and, though they hide it, scared shitless by this turn of events. I think the only thing keeping them from losing their shit and descending into another war here and now is the fact that *I* am Queen of the Underworld, so at least Hades won't hold both titles.

What happens next is full of pomp and circumstance and bullshit that I will myself to get through.

I hold Hades' hand through the golden laurel leaf crown of the winning champion being placed on my head by Zeles. Not Zeus. He's not here, thank the gods.

Which I guess now means I'm thanking myself.

That'll take some getting used to.

Hades has to let me go when the power to rule Olympus is granted to him. All that is required is that he sit on the throne. One by one, the Olympian gods and goddesses drop to a knee, bowing their heads. And when they do, a rainbow arcs from them to Hades.

"You too, young goddess," Zeles murmurs beside me. "Acknowledge him as your king in your heart. Your magic will do the rest."

And I, too, bow.

When the rainbow of light pours from me, it feels like the purest warmth wrapping around me even as it also feels like a part of me is drawn out of my body and floats across the colors to Hades.

It feels...right.

The Daemones are next. And then all the crowds of immortals stand, kneel, and bow, and the entire sky is filled with rainbows.

Our lights strike Hades in the chest, flowing into him until he glows with unearthly brightness.

When the rainbows dissipate and everyone rises, the glow around Hades fades and a crown manifests on his head.

Not golden laurel leaves.

Not golden at all.

He wears a dark crown made of black gold, obsidian chips, and smoke. He catches the way I'm buttoning my lips around a laugh and winks. Then smoke swirls around my own head, and I reach up, touching the pointed spikes of a matching crown.

I think the entire world might hold its breath as power crackles across Hades' body, absorbing into eyes gone dark, swirling gray.

"My first act as king," he announces in a voice as dark as his crown, "will be to keep a promise and grant the winner's prize."

He looks at me, and I say clearly, "I ask for Boone Runar to be made a god."

Hades snaps his fingers.

Boone appears on the dais. He has faded a bit more since I saw him last. He blinks, then looks around, visibly confused until his gaze lands on mine. Then his eyes widen before his mouth lifts into that cocky grin.

"About damn time," he says in an echoey voice.

"What's this about, Hades?" Poseidon demands.

Before anyone else can so much as move, Hades holds up his hands, and power goes out of him. It's not black like I'm sure the world expects but a brilliant, sparkling blue—the color of the River Styx.

Boone's ghostly form absorbs the light, then slowly turns from translucent to opaque and then to radiant, incredible health. Suddenly, a beam of that same blue light shoots from Boone straight to Hermes where he, like the other gods, is on his feet.

"No!" Hermes throws his hands up to ward off what's coming, but it's too late.

Boone has already taken what he needs, and the glow around him dissipates, that cocky grin widening. "Looks like there's a new god of thieves in town," he says.

The way Hermes stares at him, Boone had better watch his back.

Boone dismisses the messenger god without another glance, turning instead to offer me a bow. Me, not Hades.

I grin back before facing Hades, my smile changing to one of gratitude. "Thank you," I whisper.

He would never admit it out loud, but he knows what Boone once meant to me, and with my curse gone, he knows it's possible for Boone to love me back. Making my friend a god might be the most selfless thing Hades could have done.

"And to the champions," he announces next. "I made you promises as well."

Hades turns to Zai, his expression softening. "First to Zai. For giving Lyra what she has always wanted, a best friend, you may choose a boon. And I swear on the River Styx no harm will ever come to you again, so choose for *yourself*." Then he shoots a look to Zai's father that sets the man to trembling—and my heart swells.

Zai stands taller and holds Hades' gaze. "May I take some time to consider? For now, I want to remain by Lyra's side"—he tosses me a cheeky grin—"and see what she does with the Underworld."

Hades' eyes narrow, but he gives a brief nod, then turns to the rest of the champions. "Every champion shall receive the same blessings as the winner of the Crucible—abundance for your families as well as your homelands—and one boon each. Both those here *and* those champions in the Underworld."

Every one of my friends stares at Hades in slack-jawed shock.

"You can't fucking do that!" Poseidon yells, jumping to his feet.

Hades silences him with a single look. He doesn't even have to speak before his brother sits back down, visibly shaken. The other gods and goddesses are all exchanging worried glances.

Because they know for sure now.

Hades is about to change everything.

They *should* be afraid.

He looks at me, and only me, and his smile is everything the god of death's should be.

I can't help but smile right back at him. Ready for whatever comes next as long as it's with him.

"A dark king and queen, ruling Olympus and the Underworld side by side," Aphrodite murmurs behind us, an odd lilt of trepidation in her voice. "This could be interesting."

Hades ignores his sister and turns to Zeles, then commands, "As my rightful boon as ruler of Olympus and King of the Olympian Gods, I demand Pandora's Box."

The room erupts in chaos as an ornate, wooden container suddenly appears at Hades' feet.

The box rumored to have the power to unleash all evils on the mortal world. I swallow back my own panic at the one secret Hades still managed to keep from me.

He gives me a look swirling with guilt. "I'm sorry, Lyra."

EPILOGUE
EVEN GODS MAKE MISTAKES

I stand on the balcony of Hades' penthouse, looking out over my city at night. The lights of San Francisco might be even more beautiful now that I see them through different eyes.

It's all in the perspective.

Lightning flashes over Zeus' temple in the distance, and I'm considering knocking that thing down and making this our patron city instead when strong arms steal around me. Hades drops his forehead to the back of my head, and I hear him breathe me in.

"You're sure you want to do this?" he asks.

It's only been a day since he was crowned. After a whole lot of explaining on Hades' part all last night and today, I now know *everything*. We have something important to do. And we have only one shot.

It all comes down to saving Persephone.

I already knew she wasn't dead, that she'd been trapped in Tartarus somehow. Pandora's Box is how we get her out. *That* is why Hades needed to be King of the Gods all along. So he could get the box as his boon.

Pandora's Box—the container that appeared actually held something more like a jar, which he informed me was very large when it was fired but has been shrunk for easier carrying—is, apparently, a back door to Tartarus. A magical portal that will work for a single person to enter or exit. Persephone somehow already knows to be waiting on the other side of the gate at the appointed time.

But Pandora's Box can only be used once. And it's dangerous.

It's not the evils of the world Pandora's Box could release. Like a lot of the myths and legends of this pantheon, mortals got that wrong, too. It has the power to unleash something much, much worse. The Titans.

But Hades says there is no other way, and I believe him. He's tried everything else he can think of since she disappeared. Plus, he'd been informed ahead of time that I could win the Crucible. Come to think of it, who informed him is still vague. I'll have to ask him after we're done freeing Persephone.

Which of course we're going to do.

After everything he put me through to get that damned box, Hades is giving *me* the final choice.

I lay my arms over his and squeeze, leaning into him. "I'm sure. Stop asking."

He's been uncharacteristically unsure of himself since explaining. Or maybe feeling guilty.

He takes another breath. "It's time, then."

In a swirl of smoke, Hades ferries us down into the Underworld. It takes three teleports, because of the wards and the depth.

The second we arrive, we're hit with Charon's snarled, "For the record, Phi, I don't like this."

He's already waiting for us outside the gates of Tartarus with Demeter, Boone, and Cerberus.

Hades scowls. "You've been more than clear for the records."

I put a hand on Charon's arm. "If you were trapped in there, you'd want us to try," I argue.

Charon shakes his head. "Not if it was too dangerous."

"This *is* a foolish gambit," Demeter agrees slowly. "But…my daughter doesn't deserve to be in there with…them."

She bites her trembling lip, her red-rimmed eyes welling with more tears. I insisted last night that Hades tell her what really happened to her daughter. As her mother, Demeter had the right to know, to be part of the decision, and now to be here to help.

"We've already been through this," Hades says. "We agreed."

Charon looks away, then gives a jerking nod. He may hate it, but he's backing his best friend anyway.

We all do foolish things for the people we love. And sometimes we win. Either way, we have to try.

The Crucible taught me that.

In heavy silence, we make our way over the narrow bridge that spans an unending pit that is a moat around Tartarus. Hades has already warned the Cyclopes and the Hecatonchires who live in the abyss below, guarding the gates from the outside since they were released from that same prison. They won't attack us tonight.

Standing in front of the massive, metal doors carved in scrollwork that makes me think of thorny vines, Hades takes a deep breath, then slips the container into a hidden lock of the same shape and size that only the seven gods and goddesses who created the gates of Tartarus can see. Just before he pushes it all the way in, he pauses, then turns his head to meet my gaze.

He searches my face, and like he's laying his soul bare, I can suddenly see our future—secure, strong, trusting, loving—right there for the taking. When I smile, utter satisfaction burns in the molten silver of his eyes.

Then he faces the door and presses Pandora's Box into place with a *click* that sets off a series of clanks as each of the magical wards is altered.

I don't know what I expected to happen.

I think I pictured her just appearing before us. That or for the Titans to burst free and start a murderous rampage. Which is why the others are here, too. Backup should this go sideways.

What I didn't expect was for the door to open at all, but it does. Just a crack.

I'm not sure what he sees from where he stands, but Boone suddenly shouts, "No!" and grabs my arm. In that instant, we all go dead still. Not scared still. I mean frozen, as if time itself has stopped.

Then, together with Boone, I am sucked past Hades inside, and the door to the prison closes behind us with an ominous *clang* followed by a series of clicks—the wards locking back down. The finality of the last *click* jars me out of my shock.

Or maybe time resumes?

Because I'm standing on the wrong side of the prison door of Tartarus, staring into the face of a man who looks so much like a slightly older version of Hades that I gasp. There is only one Titan this could possibly be. The worst conceivable option.

Cronos.

"Lyra!" The shout is so faint, I can barely make it out.

I spin around, my hands flat on the doors. *Oh gods. Hades.*

My chest squeezes tight as the pounding on the door gets louder and louder, the shouts more frantic as he tries to get to me. And he will. I know he will.

Hades will stop at nothing to save me.

A sob breaks free as two thoughts strike in rapid succession. First... he'll blame himself for this. I know it in my bones, in my soul.

And second...I should have paid more attention to Rima's prophecy during the Crucible—one I honestly thought we'd stopped from happening.

A vision of Hades burning down the world.

We are so fucked.

ACKNOWLEDGMENTS

Dear Reader,

I hope you loved the first book in Lyra and Hades' story! What a ride it's been. The second those two appeared on the page together, the words just flew out of me. I love writing these characters and this world so much and can't wait to bring you more!

I thank God every single day for a life where I get to live my dream of being a writer, and I try to soak up every single step of this journey with gratitude and joy. Writing and publishing a book don't happen without the support and help from a host of incredible people.

To my wonderful readers... Thank you from the bottom of my heart for going on these journeys with me, for your kindness, your support, and generally being awesome. I love to connect, so I hope you'll drop a line and say "Howdy" on any of my social media! Also, if you have a free moment, please think about leaving a review.

To my agent, Evan Marshall...thank you for your faith in me from the very beginning!

To my editor and publisher, Liz Pelletier...your brilliance knows no bounds. I am so grateful for your friendship, for hours-long chats, and getting the opportunity to work together with you. Thank you so much for everything!

To my editing team, Mary, Hannah, and Rae, as well as all the internal readers, copy editors, proofreaders, and my mom...thank you for helping make this book the best it could be.

To my publishing family at Red Tower / Entangled...you are a dream to work with, and your support and friendship (and patience) make a world of difference and a very fun journey.

To my publishers all over the world who are bringing this book to even more readers...thank you. Seeing your responses to it has been a dream come true.

To my cover and interior art team...Bree Archer, LJ Anderson, and Elizabeth Turner Stokes, you all make me gasp with your artwork every single time.

To my endpaper artist, Kateryna Vitkovska…thank you for bringing Olympus to such exquisite life.

To Tracy Wolff, Alyssa Day, and Devney Perry, for reading an early copy at the drop of a hat and saying such lovely words.

To Heather Howland…this journey started with you, and I learned a thousand ways to be a better writer working with you.

To my assistants, Izzy, Pam, and Amy…thank you for keeping me together and even more for keeping me company.

To all my author friends and writing community…you are my found family.

To Michelle, Nicole, Kait, Avery, Chrissy, Cate, Tracy, and Steph… thank you for listening to me talk about this book ad nauseum for a while now, for your advice, and especially for your friendship.

To my team of sprinting partners, beta readers, critique partners, TXRW, Cathy's writers group, and awesome writing retreaters…your discussions, feedback, support, and friendships make me a better writer and a better person.

To all my friends, both near and far…you are and will always be lights in my life, and I hope I am in yours, too.

To all my family…thank you for your love and for teaching me to look at the world through eyes of love, hope, joy, faith, bravery, empathy, and adventure!

Finally, to my husband and kids…I love you with every part of my heart and soul.

Xoxo, Abigail Owen
abigailowen.com

P.S. To T-Bone, our furbaby and my writing buddy for almost all of my published author journey…unconditional love is how you burrowed so deeply into our hearts. Every day without you will be just a little bit harder. Wait on the other side of the rainbow bridge for us, little dog.

They take what they want. They kill who they want. Now she's going to end them all...starting with her own family.

From *New York Times* bestselling author Sara Wolf comes a pure adrenaline shot of a read— about retribution, catastrophic attraction, and becoming the fury *within* the machine.

Available now everywhere books are sold!

CONNECT WITH US ONLINE

@redtowerbooks

@RedTowerBooks

@redtowerbooks

RED TOWER
BOOKS™